JUST BEFORE DAWN

Copyright 2023 by Mark Allen

No portion of this book may be copied, reproduced, lifted, sampled, or otherwise used or exploited, except for short excepts used for reviews and critique purposes, without the express written consent of the copyright holder.

Please respect my copyright. As an artist, it's the only protection I have.

DISCLAIMER

This novel is a work of fiction. It is the product of a sick, twisted imagination and a fevered, over-caffeinated mind. Vampires aren't real. Unfortunately, serial killers ARE. The characters within these pages are fictional and any resemblance between them and any real person, living, dead, or undead is completely unintentional and purely coincidental.

Certain public locations described in the novel are real places. Others are completely made up. All have been fictionalized, except for LeStat's Coffeehouse, the management of which gave me permission to use their proper business name in the book.

My mom was right back when I was a kid – you'd be amazed at what you can get if you ask nicely.

Thanks, Mom!

"To live is to suffer. To survive is to find meaning in the suffering." – Friederich Nietzche

"Jesus said to her, "I am the resurrection and the life. He who believes in me, even though he may die, so shall he live again." – John 11:25

"Whoever fights monsters should see to it that he does not become one." – Friederich Nietzche

"And behold, I saw a pale horse. And the name of him who sat upon that horse was Death, and all hell followed with him." – Revelations 6:8

"Everything you love, you will eventually lose, but in the end, Love will return in a different form." – Franz Kafka

AUTHOR'S NOTE AND ACKNOWLEGEMENTS

I had never planned on writing a sequel to NOCTURNAL. I had naively thought the first book was a stand-alone, self-contained story and not the beginning on an ongoing series.

You, the readers, felt otherwise. I kept getting asked in reviews, interviews, podcasts, and at personal appearances "What happened to them next?" or "You should write a sequel!". So, I eventually got a clue, took the hint, and plunged back into the world of chilly foggy nights, vampires, cops dedicated to public safety, the eternal struggle both with outside forces and within ourselves between good and evil, and things that go bump in the night. This is the world of heroes and villains, antiheros and moral ambiguity, a world of life, death, what happens in between, and what might come next.

You asked for it, and now I give you what I hope will be a satisfying answer. The fate of this novel now rests in the hands of the reader. I and my team of supporters have done all we can.

They say writing is the loneliest art form. While that has some truth to it since writers spend quite a bit of their time alone in front of their laptops immersed in the fantasy worlds they create, they do NOT work alone. It takes a village to raise a child, and it takes a village to produce a book: consultants, subject matter experts, friends and colleagues, beta readers, editors, proofers, agents (if you're traditionally published), and of course, the publishers themselves. This where I say THANK YOU to the following:

My mother, Dale McCorkle, for always being my cheerleader.

My brother, Sergeant Clark Allen, Dallas Police Department (retired) for our conversations about real serial killers. Having dealt with psychopaths in real life, his insight proved invaluable.

My Beta Readers Kris Wahl, Kelly Styles, and Fiona Young. You are all strong, smart women who keep me artistically honest and force me to become a better writer.

The Public Affairs office of the San Diego Police Department for their help in precinct organization and deployment.

LeStat's Coffee House, for allowing me to use their name and location in this novel. I wrote NOCTURNAL at the LeStat's in Normal Heights on the corner of Adamas Ave. and Felton. If you're ever in San Diego, a visit to LeStat's is a must.

Amazon, whose KDP (Kindle Direct Publishing) allows me to reach my audience.

And most of all, I thank YOU, dear reader, for without you I am just another unpublished writer with a bunch of manuscripts collecting dust. I owe you EVERYTHING because without you, I am nothing.

Mark Allen
Port Orchard, Washington
August 2023

For Fiona. Always

JUST BEFORE DAWN

Journal entry, February 01

My night began the way they all do, with my reanimation. This rebirth is jolting.

Painful.

In over 110 years, the agony of this Rebirth to Darkness never diminishes. One would think that I would have grown accustomed to it.

That would be incorrect.

People aspire to immortality. They dream, fantasize about it. They create books, plays, movies, and TV about it. They pine for it, lust after it, pursue it. People are afraid of death.

As a mortal, so was I.

Immortality is a fool's errand. Reality does not live up to the hype. Mortals do not understand the nature of immortality, or the terrible price one must pay to attain it.

My excruciating rebirth is not the only payment rendered. Mornings are no better. I do not slip blissfully into unconsciousness or blessed hibernation before the dawn like in the movies. If only it were that simple.

Each dawn, I die. Again, and again.

Every. Single. Sunrise.

I feel every bit of torment, every inch of suffering, every second of anguish. Perhaps I feel all the pain I would have endured over the course of a natural lifespan compressed into minutes as opposed to several decades. All part of the price I paid that rainy night in Hoboken.

My nightly awakening feels no better. The pain recedes over several minutes while I stagger through the apartment pursued by a mental fog, lumbering on stiff legs that grind bone-on-bone, joints haphazardly held together by rubber band tendons.

Since vampires are vulnerable in those minutes, I have always lived alone. A solitary hunter, I only venture out when needed. I hunt live prey when warmed Blood Bank blood bought under the table no longer curbs my craving. Then that ancient need to hunt overwhelms me.

I have rules. Stalk before I kill. Make sure my victim deserves the death I bring.

I hunt scum: criminals, drug dealers, sexual sadists, rapists, pedophiles. No one cares when they go missing. Good people are made safer.

I provide a service to society.

My rules help ensure my survival and anonymity. The last thing I need is for some teenager's cell phone video of me feeding to go viral on social media. There would be no place on Earth to hide. People would hunt me down and kill me. And while I do not fear the Final Death as some of my kind call it, I do not wish to embrace it yet.

Rules are important.

Of course, there was some excitement a few years back when I assisted my great, great grandson in taking down that drug cartel. That was fun. I reconnected with my descendants, even bought my favorite granddaughter a house. She lives right down the street from me here in Kensington, just north of Adams Avenue. I have not seen her in a couple of weeks. I really need to stop by for a visit.

I spoke with Reginald a few nights ago. He has been quite busy since his promotion to Lead Detective for his precinct. He reports directly to the newly minted Lieutenant Nick Castle, who replaced Captain Morris Horn upon the latter's retirement. Not only is Reginald responsible for building his own cases, but he also supervises all the junior detectives in the squad room.

Both still work out of the same precinct, east of downtown on 25th Street, just a stone's throw from the trolley station. Reginald moved to the East Village, near the precinct. From what I understand, he walks to and from work most days, so his commute time practically nonexistent.

I am still a licensed stockbroker and still cover the Asian markets. I put in less time, functioning as a consultant and mentor now. I spend most of my time calming down panicky junior brokers.

Tedious.

There is a peace of mind that comes from sitting atop a diversified fortune valued at over sixty million dollars, especially when you know how to keep the cash machine flowing with minimal effort. Fact is, I could retire and not have to work for about one hundred fifty years.

Earlier this evening, I was speaking Cantonese to a protege in Macao. The markets are jittery, spooked by increased volatility here in the U.S., along with rising in inflation and interest rates. Anyone who fails to acknowledge what is coming will lose their shirts, and it will be their own fault.

I understand people make mistakes. What I cannot condone is making the same mistake over and over, ignoring the lessons of history. Then, it is no longer a mistake. It is a pattern of behavior, a conscious choice. A character flaw.

Those who refuse to learn the lessons of history are doomed to repeat its mistakes.

I got caught unawares with the crash of 1929. I lost over fifty percent of my money. But I learned from my mistake, got back in the market in 1933. I have made money ever since. Pullbacks, corrections, bear markets, and recessions come and go. But one can make money in a down market if positioned properly. Since 1933, I have only lost money on the year six times. The rest have been profitable.

But I digress.

Something happened tonight that spurred me to write this entry. As I spoke to my protégé, a powerful sensation hit me.

Unpleasant, unfamiliar.

Gob smacked and unable to concentrate. I inadvertently switched to English. When she asked me what I was saying, I apologized in Cantonese, told her she was doing fine. I impressed the importance of remaining calm when everyone else panicked.

I ended the call, then ripped the headset off my face. I sat back on the sofa, rubbed the bridge of my nose between my thumb and forefinger.

What was this? A headache? Seriously? I had been a walking corpse for over a century, and now suddenly, I was going to suffer a migraine?

No. This had to be something else.

My apartment remained silent as the grave, as dark as a tomb. My vampire eyes saw everything in full detail and perfect clarity. Being a creature of the night, my pupils open wide, encompassing the entire surface area of my eye. Even the tiniest scrap of light gets in. Like other nocturnal creatures, I see quite well even in what humans would perceive as total darkness.

Despite the tranquility of my apartment, this disquiet seeped inside me. It festered in my mind until it metastasized and spread like cancer down my spine and throughout my body, burrowing deeper into my being.

Something bad is coming.

The question is, how do I respond? What level of threat will it be? Yes, I used the word "threat", because somehow, I know that is precisely what this is. How will I meet the threat? Will I prevail, or will I fail? Will I live, or will I die?

Because this time, I sense that death would be forever.

CHAPTER ONE

Friday night in San Diego.
Again.
Everyone wanted to party, have fun. Drink, eat, laugh. Boomerang like so many coiled springs; put the frustrations of the workweek behind them even if only for a few hours. Some of them might get lucky: hook up and get laid.

The Goth community was no different from other demographics, and Splinter was the busiest Goth fetish club in town. The thirty-dollar cover charge didn't faze the club's clientele. Thirty bucks a pop not only kept the lights on; it functioned as customer quality control: it helped deter the riffraff.

Clubbers in dark attire approached the painted steel door guarded by a scowling blonde bouncer roughly the size of a silverback gorilla. He looked mean enough to eat rusty nails. Over six feet tall with a linebacker's physique. Hair cropped short to stubble. Square jaw. Hard hazel eyes that missed nothing.

Big for his age since he was ten, he had been nicknamed Kong after the ape in that movie. It had bothered him then, but the name stuck. In fact, the more upset or angry he got about it, the more he wanted to fight over it, the worse the other kids teased him. He eventually learned to keep his mouth shut, and things calmed back down. This taught him an important life lesson. Oftentimes, no matter who you were, you had to take shit to get by in this world.

He learned to take it, get used to it, accept it.
He never learned to like it.
Tonight, he surveyed the line, running a mental checklist: were they dressed appropriately for a rather unique nightlife experience? Had they been here before, and if so, had they ever

caused trouble? Not the kind of trouble everyone came here to find, but *real* trouble. The kind that got someone banished.

Banishments were forever here. One strike and you're out. The club owners said so. No second chances.

Kong wasn't emotionally invested in any of that; he simply enforced policy. If you met the age requirement and dress code, didn't cause trouble, and passed personal muster with Kong, you were allowed the privilege of coughing up thirty bucks to get inside.

Ah, inside.

Throngs of beautiful young people, along with some not so young or as beautiful, wore leather, satin, and velvet. Corsets, stiletto heels. Pushup bras, tight pants, buffed and blacked combat boots. Black lipstick and eyeliner contrasted against pale, powdered faces. Some lounged at tables. A mob crushed at the bar. Others undulated on the dance floor.

If you were into dark clothes, dark eyes and pale skin, fake fangs, contact lenses, watered-down drinks, sex of an infinite variety, and off-key death metal played at ear-splitting volume, Splinter was the place to be.

Outside, Charlie Simpkins approached Kong. Charlie didn't look like a serial killer. He looked nowhere near the stereotypical large, hulking, soul-tortured outcast; the misanthropic loser type seen in movies and TV. Charlie Simpkins was rather attractive, a smooth-faced handsome young man.

But Charlie's dark, slimy soul slithered deep within him; a roiling snake twisting and turning, feasting upon itself. He epitomized all that was evil in the world. Under thirty with a slight build, his appearance belied lean muscle rippling beneath oversized clothes that allowed more freedom of movement and created a less-than-accurate memory of him in other peoples' minds if they remembered him at all.

Anonymity.

His secret weapon against getting caught. He was not afraid of prison and certainly not concerned about the death penalty. This was California, where no one had been executed since 2006. To Charlie's mind, Death Row was Solitary Confinement with more privacy.

More time to read, perhaps.

The reason Charlie wished to evade capture was more fundamental. If he went to prison, it would put a serious crimp in his freewheeling psychopathic lifestyle. For Charlie Simpkins was a serial killer who wanted to keep on killing. And killing.

And killing.

For a long, long time.

His work was nowhere near complete, oh no. In fact, he had barely gotten started. His mission might take the rest of his life to complete. He might never fully complete it, but that came with the territory. Time would tell.

Tonight, Charlie was decked out. Boots, black skinny jeans, black T-shirt, and black leather jacket with metal rivets. Pale white makeup accentuated with black eyes, lips, and fingernails. Silver earrings danced on his earlobes. His natural straw-colored hair hid beneath a jet-black wig. Iridescent amber snake-slit contact lenses completed the look.

The fog was not too thick tonight yet. Kong saw him coming. When the club shut down at two, it would be pea soup out here. And colder.

Kong had an excellent memory. This pipsqueak had been coming since opening weekend. Something creepy about this kid, something the big bouncer couldn't quite determine. Whatever it was, it even made him uneasy. And no one made Kong uneasy.

Well. *Almost* no one.

"Good evening," Charlie said.

His voice made Kong's skin crawl. "Hey." Noncommittal.

They stared at each other a moment, silent. The Killer's eyes did not bat away. He just kept stared unblinkingly into Kong's lined face. Like a snake or something.

"May I enter?"

"Thirty dollars."

Charlie handed Kong cash, moved past him, descended the staircase inside. Kong shook his head. What the hell was it about that fucker's eyes? It wasn't the contacts. Kong saw that here so often it didn't faze him. No, it was like he was a Goddamned hypnotist or something.

As the twit disappeared from view, Kong exhaled, whooshing air out of his body. That this short-stack frightened Kong disturbed him even more. He had been a bouncer or a bodyguard most of his adult life. He could read people, could tell within seconds who posed a threat and who was harmless.

Kong had seen the real deal, had gone up against the real deal. Hand to hand, up close and personal. And Charlie was trouble with a capital T. If he and Kong ever got into it, that little bastard wouldn't back down. Not an inch. He would not hesitate. Unlike most people, he was not afraid of Kong.

So few truly fearless people walked the Earth. Not the brave, people who felt fear and rose to overcome it, but the truly fearless. People who felt no fear at all. About *anything*. Those who either discounted or ignored physical pain. Those who truly did not worry about injury or death.

Kong thanked God those people were few and far between.

Those few were the most dangerous people on Earth. Why? Because if they felt no fear, they likely did not feel much of anything else within the range of normal human emotion. They tended to not feel empathy towards others or have any close family relationships. They tended to have difficulty creating and maintain social relationships of any kind: friendships, business acquaintances, lovers.

Psychopaths.

They scared Kong because they were capable of anything. There was no limit to the impulses they fed. The dark, the twisted, the downright evil. And they can do this because they live their lives under the assumption that since they have nothing to fear, they probably have nothing to lose.

The scariest part of that is, they are probably right.

Ramsland Domingo sat alone at a bistro table in a dark corner downstairs. Ramsey to her friends and family, she sipped vodka that tasted like had been made by Monsanto instead of Grey Goose. She watched the masses of young humanity ebb and flow like waves on a beach. All genders, shapes, and sizes. She felt no connection to them.

Ramsey huffed a sigh. She had come here on business to meet someone but had been stood up. She had arrived fifteen minutes early, had found the table, and had turned down several offers to dance. Despite her corset that acted like a push-up bra, black skinny jeans to show off her firm ass and powerful thighs, and leather heels that practically forced her calf muscles into spasms, Ramsey was here to work.

She watched as everyone around her pursued their versions of fun. Some of it creeped her out. In another corner, a girl carefully cut her male companion's inside arm with a razor blade just above the wrist. Not deep enough to sever tendons or arteries. Just deep enough to draw blood.

Morbidly enthralled, Ramsey watched the young man lean back and close his eyes. The girl stroked his chest, ran her hand down his belly, then gently cupped his crotch. She repositioned herself, her head inches of his belt buckle.

The girl's tongue extended out of her mouth, all glistening pink muscle. It curled around a drop of blood just as her mouth latched onto the arm. Then she moved up to the incision itself, sucking as much blood as she could.

The young man ground his hips into her hand. He grabbed the back of her head and pushed her harder onto his arm.

Ramsey turned away. Some people here were into horrifying kinks. Blood and bondage was not her thing. Her research into the vampire goth subculture had shown just how dangerous some of these acts could truly be. If someone, either by accident or by design, cut too deeply, things could turn terminal in a heartbeat. And there was always the danger of bloodborne diseases.

Ramsey decided to leave. Time wasted, money blown on getting in and watered-down drink. She wondered if she could submit a voucher to her publisher for reimbursement.

Doubtful.

Ramsey huffed another sigh. Unreliable flakes. Some of the people had a tenuous relationship with the truth. Hell, some people had a tenuous relationship with reality. Some of these people pretended they really were vampires.

Vampires?

Where does that get fun?

From the darkened VIP lounge set above the main floor against a wall directly underneath the city street above – The Grotto, they called it – unblinking black eyes scoured the scene below. The female vampire had already fed earlier in the Ladies' Room from a willing partner. She embraced many sins, but gluttony was not one of them. She swayed to the music, enjoyed the energy of the amusingly dressed revelers below.

All of them sheep, she judged.

They watch a few movies, read a couple of books, and think they're experts on vampires and the nature of death. They convince themselves they've stared into the abysmal blackness of it all.

Utter fools, the lot of them.

She remembered her earlier feeding. The woman had approached her first, told her how beautiful she was, how she seemed different from everyone else.

The female vampire had agreed. She was, indeed, quite different.

They had begun kissing near the bar. After making out a bit and getting whoops of encouragement to keep it going, she had taken her partner's intoxicatingly warm hand and had led her to the bathroom where they kissed and groped each other, passions rising. Sexually aroused, her living victim felt like a human blast furnace against her own eternally cool skin.

She had told her victim she wanted to bite her. The willowy auburn-haired woman in her arms said yes, closed her eyes and practically swooned. *Swooned,* like in one of those black and white vampire movies! She had pushed her unwitting prey into a toilet stall, kicking the door shut behind her.

Rather than going for the jugular, the Female Vampire had bitten elsewhere. Swept up in the passion of the moment, the Female Vampire had run her tongue down the woman's chest, stomach, and to points South.

Her lover had sighed, spread her legs for easier access. The human thought she knew what this strangely hypnotic woman wanted to do, and she was more than amenable.

The female vampire had bitten on the inside of the thigh. She had avoided the femoral artery for the same reason she had avoided the jugular. Her lover gasped in astonishment, then sighed as an unexpected orgasm washed over her. The female vampire supped enough to satisfy her immediate need and leave her victim weak and woozy, but alive.

The nameless woman fainted from ecstasy. The female vampire had supported her arms to keep her from falling. She had lowered her partner onto the toilet and balanced her so she would not fall over. The human looked asleep. The wound had already stopped bleeding, coagulating from dark red to almost black.

Then, the female vampire slipped out, closed the door behind her.

Now she sat alone in The Grotto. She had accomplished what she had come here to do. She had fed, had left her mark. She could go home and reading, or perhaps watch a movie before sunrise.

The band, a testosterone-filled quartet called Borgo Pass, thrashed around the tiny stage, putting on what passed for a show. Music blared red and raw, as jagged as shards of glass. The lead singer's voice sounded like he gargled with road gravel. When he hit his high notes - sustained screeches would be more accurate - she could imagine his vocal cords bleeding.

Borgo Pass wasn't any good, but they gave it their all.

The female vampire sensed something different. She frowned, scouring the crowd with all-seeing eyes, listening with acute ears. Her head turned towards the staircase to her right.

She zeroed in on a short, thin man descending the stairs wearing ridiculous clothes and even more ridiculous hair, laughable contact lenses. Something about this guy, though. Something interesting.

Evil.

Did a wolf now prowl amongst the sheep?

She watched him turn his head left as he descended slowly, deliberately, one foot on each concrete step, one hand steady on the handrail. Cautious. Thoughtful.

Methodical.

Compelled? Yes. Compelled. This human had a compulsion to feed unlike anything these other mortals felt. He had a ritual to follow, a goal to achieve.

Her lips spread into a cunning smile.

On the stairs, Charlie scanned his environment. A creature of habit, he always took notice of any change, no matter how small. New chairs. Different tables. A change in décor. Nothing escaped his attention.

Predatory eyes behind those amber contacts looked over men, women, guests, employees. Anyone was fair game.

Everyone was fair game.

He liked killing women best, but he'd do a guy if all else failed. He had killed a couple in the past. They made a fight of it, fear and adrenaline driving them into Fight or Flight.

Both were dead now.

Ramsey crossed her long legs at the knee, pushed her naturally dark brown hair away from her pretty face. Her smooth olive complexion and dark eyes were a gift of her Hispanic heritage. She crossed her arms across her breasts, eyed the remnants of her drink. She'd already been there for over an hour and all she wanted to do was go home.

She had been warned prior to coming here to insert some of those small foam ear plugs that people use at shooting ranges. Foamies, people called them. She had taken that sage advice, yet her ears rang from the atrocious band that sounded like suicidal pot-clanging amateurs.

At the bar, Charlie paid for his drink. He stepped away, began another visual sweep. His OCD dictated he start upper left, then scan downwards, then back up, each scan moving incrementally from left to right until he had scanned and noted everything and everyone present.

His eyes settled on a beautiful Hispanic woman sitting in a dark corner. She was pissed about something. It emanated off her in waves, like smokey tendrils wafting upwards. He took a sip of his drink, waited. No girlfriends joined her from the dance floor. No beefy boyfriend came back from the bathroom.

A woman alone.

How interesting.

Charlie glided towards her with ease and grace. Even in the crowded club, he managed to avoid bumping into anyone and spilling his drink.

Ramsey tossed her head back and slammed the last of her drink down her throat. She closed her eyes, feeling that characteristic burn as the vodka slid down her gullet and the vapors rose into her nose. Then came the biting aftertaste.

She opened her eyes.

A man stood across the table from her. He had not been there just a moment before. His expression appeared to be one of curiosity.

"Good evening," he said. He motioned towards the empty chair. "May I?"

"Sure. I was just leaving."

He sat. "Please don't."

"Why not?"

"I saw you from the bar. I wanted to come talk to you."

"And why is that?"

"You're distinctive," he replied.

She rolled her eyes. "Seriously?" She grinned. "Does that line actually work?"

He sipped his drink, undisturbed.

"An observation. Nothing more."

Now she appeared more interested than before.

"You don't belong here," he stated. "All this," he gestured widely with both hands, "isn't your scene."

"It's that obvious?"

"From a mile away."

The conversation lulled. Ramsey looked back at the stranger in front of her. He stared back, directly in the eyes. Even though her corset accentuated her curves and revealed cleavage, he was not trying to peak down her front. A tad surprising, perhaps even a bit odd.

Maybe he was gay?

His eyes, though. Hypnotic. Like looking into a pool and seeing the bottom. Maybe it was those contact lenses.

He looked like a snake that had grown limbs. That was it.

He looked *reptilian.*

"So. Some dweeb obviously stood you up," Charlie said. "Was he your boyfriend?"

"I was doing an interview for a book I'm writing."

"A writer?" He watched her nod. "What do you write?"

"Nonfiction. I've had a few articles and short stories published in magazines."

"How exciting."

She grinned. Pearly white teeth, perfect alignment. She probably had braces when she was a kid.

"It's not like in the movies," she said. "It's tedious. Boring research, hard work. Pounding keys on a laptop when you'd rather be doing something else."

"Nothing is ever like the movies," Charlie said. "I knew a Hollywood screenwriter once. She's dead now."

"I'm sorry."

"She told me once the first rule of screenwriting is, 'Never let the truth get in the way of a good story'."

Ramset laughed. Those white teeth again. Alluring.

"So, what's your next step?"

"Find someone else to interview."

"What's the book about?"

Ramsey threw her arms wide. "All this. The vampire Goth community. What draws people to it, what they get out of it. Why some stay and others leave."

"Sounds cerebral."

She grinned. "I hope so."

"What is it that you want to know?"

"Everything. The allure, the benefits, the pitfalls, the dangers."

This got his attention.

"Dangerous people?"

"The scene might attract a certain type."

"Well then," Charlie smiled, "you've come to the right place."

"You'd be willing to tell me about the scene?"

"How about I show you?"

She looked at him, wary. "Show me what?"

"Everything you need to know," he said. "*And then some.*"

From her darkened perch in The Grotto, the female vampire sighed in satisfaction. The little man was a true predator. The stench of Death hung cloaked around his shoulders, following him everywhere like the swirling wake of a passing ship.

She felt no moral imperative to intervene. After all, humans were her *food*. But sometimes they provided a temporarily amusing diversion from the dull sameness of a life lived of interminable nights measured not in years, but in *centuries*.

She watched the two make their way towards the staircase. The woman stopped and started, bobbed and weaved to avoid bumping into people. The man moved fluidly through the crowd, like the serpent his contact lenses suggested.

He got to the bottom of the stairs first. She arrived several seconds later.

Shiny black eyes followed as they ascended, then disappeared just as the door opened. A silvery knife blade of light stabbed down the staircase. In that instant, she could smell exhaust fumes from outside.

The two were swallowed up as the door closed.

The next time anyone would ever see Ramsey Domingo again, she would be dressed only in blood.

CHAPTER TWO

Father Justin Ng hobbled through the all-night liquor store. Harsh lights overhead bathed everything in a chill blue. He pitched a can of soup and a box of saltines into his hand basket. His last meal had been oatmeal with blueberries earlier that morning.

He wanted to go to sit down diner for a proper meal. But he needed the money to purchase another item, so soup and crackers tonight. He rounded the far end of the aisle, started looking for what he had really come in here to buy.

He browsed, even though he knew precisely what he was going to get. He just liked taking the time. Just a few seconds, but it calmed him. His hand snaked out; fingers wrapped around the neck of a bottle. He lifted the cheap blended Scotch off the bottom shelf, placed it in the hand basket. This stuff was so cheap, it tasted like it might be to degrease engine parts.

Soup, crackers, Scotch.

Breakfast of champions.

The store's clerk, Jackson Clements, Jack to his friends, sat on a stool behind the cash register. Top-shelf booze, lottery tickets, and tobacco products sat behind security barriers behind him. Over sixty and wearing a threadbare shirt, he had last shaved four days ago with a dull razor and cold water. He had finger-combed his uncut hair earlier, so there was that.

Jack looked up as Father Ng approached.

"Hey, Father. How's the God business these days?"

"I wouldn't know. I'm retired five years."

"You still live there, right?"

"In a converted storage room," Ng said. "I rarely see the priests who actually run things."

Jack rang the Father's purchases up. "I had an uncle who was a cop."

Ng handed Jack cash.

"Thirty years," Jack continued. "He retired. That steely glare, what I call 'cop's eyes' never left him. Ever."

The register beeped and the drawer slid out. Jack placed the bills inside, pulled out change.

"It's not a job. It's a lifestyle."

"Neither occupation comes with nine-to-five hours," Ng admitted.

He handed Ng his change, bagged up his purchases. "You'll always be a priest."

"I will always be a child of God." He grabbed his groceries. "See you, Padre."

Ng pushed through the front door, stepped out into the street. The door had swung shut, and Jack went back to reading.

The humid night enveloped Father Ng, darkness swirling around him. He glanced inside his bag, then walked off dangling it from a couple of curled fingers.

The Vampire's nightly financial consultations had concluded quickly. He delegated several tasks to two of his more capable junior brokers in Macao. He would check on their work when he returned to the safety of his apartment and blackout curtains.

He had wanted to visit his granddaughter, Lottie, but it was late and she turned in early these days. His Lot-Lot was well into her seventies, overweight, and suffered from diabetes, high blood pressure, and congestive heart failure. Her eyesight was getting worse, and the last time he had visited, he had smelled the faint decay of advancing kidney disease. As she neared the end of her life, her body was slowing down, her organs inching towards failure. Death was inevitable. It was simply a question of which organ system would fail first.

Which left him infinitely sad.

He loved all his descendants, of course. How could he not since he had loved their great, great grandmother, Danae so completely? Yet his little Lot-Lot had always held a special place in his heart. She was one of the purest souls he had ever encountered. The Vampire understood better than most the natural order of things – people were born; they grew up, grew old, then died.

It did not mean he had to like it.

His own existence served as a constant reminder that sometimes, the natural order of things got disrupted. He also served as a walking, talking case study of the terrible long-term repercussions such a disruption could unleash.

In need of distraction, the Vampire slipped out of his apartment, then slid like a low cloud to the alley in back. His Lexus squatted in its assigned space, quiet and gleaming in the low light. He got in and started the engine.

The Lexus crept southward through the alley, paused at the end, then turned right on Adams Avenue. He drove across the bridge spanning Interstate 15 and left Kensington in his rearview mirror. Normal Heights was quiet at this hour, practically deserted. Uncannily quiet. If he had been human, the Vampire might have found it disturbing.

A police cruiser approached out of the gloom, then passed him by. He glanced in his side mirror, saw the cruiser take the Southbound onramp for the Interstate.

The Vampire drifted past darkened homes, silent café's, antique stores. He turned left at the intersection of Adams and Felton. He parked along the curb just south of the fire station.

LeStat's was a San Diego institution. A hangout catering to locals far removed from the tourist traps downtown, its reputation was common knowledge. LeStat's had enjoyed so much success over the years that a couple of other outlets had recently opened. But the Vampire preferred this, their first location occupying the Southwest corner of Adams and Felton. He rounded the corner into streetlights. Even with sunglasses on, light pierced his eyes. He watched his feet as he walked. His pale, skinny hand snaked out, grabbed the handle on the screen door.

The subdued light inside comforted him. The building was a century old with a ceiling close to twenty feet high. Perhaps it had originally been a warehouse or stable. He did not know. He had not lived here then. No one from that era was around to ask. He just knew he dug the place.

Tables and chairs, settees and ottomans lay scattered about. Haphazard. Clashing.

Eclectic.

Eccentric.

Nothing matched. Different fabrics, colors, textures, patterns. Original art for sale by local artists adorned the walls. Classic rock drifted from speakers above.

Few people inside this time of night. He noticed a couple on a date. The Vampire could smell their pheromones. They would wind up in bed together within the hour.

Ah, to be young and in love again. He had been there, of course.

Once, long ago.

With Danae.

The past is gone forever, he told himself. Live in the present.

Easier said than done. The past had a nasty habit of coming back around into one's face.

Danae!

A woman in nurse's scrubs coming off shift wandered in. Dull sunken eyes, mouth turned down at the corners, and slumped shoulders screamed exhaustion. Her aura told the vampire she was a dedicated professional. She did not see nursing as a job; it was her calling.

Even if he were starving, he would never coerce a drop of blood from anyone like her.

The Vampire found an empty red velvet wingback chair, the velvet starting to disintegrate at the tufts and corners. The previous day's newspaper lay in sections strewn across the scarred side table. He found the front page. He tried to read but could not concentrate. He was still preoccupied by Lottie's physical deterioration.

Antsy, he tossed the paper aside. This had been a mistake. Usually he enjoyed hanging here, reading a paper or magazine, sipping hot tea or black coffee.

What books, movies, and TV got wrong about vampires was that while blood was their main source of sustenance, real vampires could and indeed did take in other fluids, primarily water. He could not add sugar and cream to coffee; he would become violently ill. But plain coffee, unsweetened tea, or water were as essential to him as to a human.

He found himself back on the street. A soft breeze fluffed the lank hair that hung from his scalp. Before he realized, he was in his car again, motoring through the dark streets.

Perhaps a *darker* distraction was in order.

Making his way through North Park, he headed south into Golden Hills. A few maneuvers later, he turned right on Broadway, moved down the hill towards Downtown. The East Village and the Gaslamp Quarter lay to his left, with Banker's Hill to his right.

He turned right on 5th, drove into Banker's Hill. The grade changed from level to a gentle incline after B Street. He pulled over near an all-night convenience store, killed the engine.

He sat there thinking. He was near Laurel Street, which ran straight into Balboa Park just a block and a half to his right. A hunt in the park might be just the thing to cheer him up.

He was, after all, a child of the night.

The Vampire sensed movement, saw an Asian man slouched with age shuffle out of the convenience store. He carried a bag dangling from one hand. The Vampire read him instantly. An aged insomniac tottering home.

Harmless.

No threat to the Vampire. No threat to anyone.

Then the Vampire watched as three Asian youths materialized from behind the store where they had hidden. They advanced up the side of the brick building, keeping to the shadows. They paused near the storefront, watching the old man hobble across the street, haul himself up over the curb, then continue tottering down the sidewalk.

The Vampire frowned, repulsed. Shimmers of evil intent emanated from them.

He slid out, pushed the door shut with one long finger. He crept towards the store, his unblinking eyes on his prey. If they saw him, he would move quickly. The hunt would devolve into slaughter.

Ahead, the youths momentarily disappeared. They moved fluidly, not wanting to spook their prey. The old man was long gone, probably down close to the next intersection.

The Vampire stepped off the curb at the southeast corner. He trotted diagonally, towards the northwest corner. His movements were quick, precise. No wasted energy. Completely silent. His targets had no idea that something else was out here tonight. Something far more dangerous and deadly than any of them could ever be.

The hunters had become the hunted.

Charlie Simpkins sat in the all-night greasy spoon diner. Ramsey sat across from him. Ordinarily he would never lower himself to eat in a joint like this. But Ramsey was hungry, and the diner was open. She did not share his disdain for their surroundings.

They occupied a booth in the back corner. That had been Ramsey's idea. He had thought it odd that a single woman would want to spend time in a diner with someone she did not know. She exuded confidence. Perhaps she was overly confident in her abilities to fight off unwanted advances. Perhaps at barely five foot five inches and barely one hundred forty pounds, she assumed he posed no serious threat.

Boy, was she ever seriously fucking wrong about *that*.

She sat across from him, eating bacon and scrambled eggs. He drank coffee. Even with sweetener and creamer, it still tasted like it had been brewed with used dishwater and battery acid. She kept droning on with some pretentious bullshit about how all writers, even nonfiction writers considered themselves artists.

About how took what they did seriously, wanted to have their voices heard and communicate with the world.

Jesus Christ, he groaned inwardly. She sounded like those grungy documentary filmmakers he had seen online when they win some trophy at whatever film festival, talking about bringing their truth to the world.

Their truth?

Seriously? What in the Sam Hell holy fuckwad was that, anyway?

There can only be one truth, and that is *THE* truth. Anything other than *THE* truth was just opinion or spin.

In other words, bullshit.

"You feel strongly about this," he blurted.

"Yes, I do," she said, biting into a piece of sourdough toast. "Are you ready to be interviewed?"

"Yes."

"She activated an audio recorder app on her phone. "I need to record this," she announced, "so I get my facts straight later."

He nodded.

"Okay. Let's start with the basics. What's your name?"

"Call me Ace." No way he was going to give her anything close to his real name. Even though he was going to kill her soon, he adhered to his own self-imposed rules of engagement.

Rules were important.

"How long have you been into the Goth scene?"

"A few years."

"What can you tell me about the vampire goth subculture?"

"It not only lives," he said, "it thrives."

"I remember reading about the whole goth thing being a popular counterculture movement in the late nineties and early two thousands."

"It started the eighties in the United Kingdom, coming out of the post-punk scene."

"That's what my research indicated, too."

"It enjoyed a brief time in the sun – no pun intended -- but was nothing more than a flavor of the month for most people. The movement went back underground and did so happily."

"Why 'happily'?"

"The scene's all about individualism," he replied. "Goths enjoy living on the so-called fringes of society. If you're not living on the edge, you're taking up too much space. The last thing a Goth wants is to become mainstream."

"There's so much death symbolism involved," she continued. "What draws people to that? Are they in love with some romantic notion about death being cool?"

He sighed, irritated with her. Was she trying to be combative, or was she just stupid? He pushed his coffee mug away.

"You've missed the point. Completely." His irritation ratcheted up a notch. "It's not about the beauty of death," he growled. "It's about the beauty of life."

"Yet they gather in darkness, surrounded by images and symbols of death, listening to death metal, leading a hedonistic, nihilistic, and ultimately fatalistic lifestyle."

Charlie almost killed her right there.

He looked away, across the diner. A waitress behind the counter wiped down surfaces with a dingy towel. Behind her, a short order cook working diligently at the grill, rising steam obscuring his sweaty face.

"Ever heard of Reinhold Messner?"

"Who?"

"Italian mountaineer," he replied. "He climbed Everest –"

"Was he the first?" she interrupted.

He blinked his eyes, struggling with his self-control. Okay. Not only was she stupid, but she was also rude.

"No," he said slowly, reigning in his temper. "That was Edmund Hillary. English fellow in 1953. Messner was Italian. He was the first to climb Everest without supplemental oxygen."

"Did he have a death wish or something?" she asked.

Charlie smiled. "When he came back down, an interviewer asked him, 'Why did you go up there to die?' and Messner said, 'I didn't go up there to die. I went up there to live.'"

Ramsey remained silent, taking this in.

"Goths don't want to die any more than anyone else. They're simply living their lives. This is how they express themselves."

"As part of the general, overarching Goth movement, I can buy that. But some hardcore vampire Goths are into some... dark things."

He grew weary of this dance. "Some are." He moved to stand up.

"Come with me. I've got something to show you."

He grabbed the check and stood up. She stared at him, not at all sure what was happening or where this was going. Red flags rose in the back of her mind. The guy seemed harmless enough. Plus, she had pepper spray in her purse. He could provide valuable insight for her book.

But still...

He held his hands out at his sides. "I'm paying the bill and leaving," he stated evenly. "You can come along, or you can sit here and drink coffee until the sun comes up." He shrugged. "Your choice."

Charlie walked towards the front register. He did not look back to see if Ramsey would follow. Either she would or she wouldn't. In either case, she had only minutes left to live. No matter what, he would end her.

He stood in front of the register. The waitress, tired, overweight, about sixty years old and looking every day of it, shuffled over on sore legs and aching feet.

"How was it?" she asked. Purely perfunctory. Not like she really cared.

"Fine," he lied. He handed her the bill and two twenties. She rang him up, counted out the change. She handed it back to him.

He dropped a five on the counter between them. "For you."

About that time, he smelled Ramsey's perfume.

He smiled to himself. He had figured her curiosity would override common sense. He held the door for her.

She stepped outside into the chilly air. He followed. She shivered, clutched her jacket closer around her.

"This way," he motioned.

They walked together a few feet apart. The crossed the diner's dimly lit parking lot. She did not see him reach into his pocket.

"Where are we going?"

"Over there," he answered as he pointed to a rusted-out cargo van at the edge of the parking lot. It looked like it might have been blue once, maybe a hundred years ago.

"Wait a minute, hang on." She stopped, put her hands up in front of her.

With practiced fingers, he took the syringe in his pocket, used his thumb to flick the cap loose from the hypodermic needle. He pulled his hand out, cupping the syringe to conceal it from her.

"You expect me to climb into the back of a van with you?"

He kept his voice even and, he hoped, non-threatening. "Don't be afraid, Ramsey," he soothed. "You're seeking truth, and I have all the truth you could ever want."

He spun without warning, arm swinging wide, gathering speed. The needle went into her neck so fast she did not have time to react. She gasped a bit as his thumb pushed on the plunger. She tried to scream, but the Ketamine was already going to work.

She passed out, slumping. He caught her, surprisingly strong for such a small man. He didn't want her to crack her head open on the concrete. Death from a skull fracture was not part of his plan.

He dragged her to the van's rear door. He propped her flaccid weight against him. It never ceased to amaze him how heavy humans were once they went completely limp. He understood where the term "dead weight" came from.

He opened the door. The upper half of her body dropped into the van. He bent her knees, lifted her legs at the ankles and swung her inside. He climbed up into the rear and closed the door behind him.

Outside, the parking lot was quiet. Peaceful. Tranquil.

As if an act of supreme inhuman evil had not just transpired.

CHAPTER THREE

Father Ng walked west along Grape Street. He crossed Fourth, approaching Third. That sinking feeling in his gut kept getting worse. The hair on the back of his neck stood up.

Shoes scuffled on the pavement behind him. A chuckle here or there.

He sensed danger.

Having grown up in rural Vietnam and having seen both the French and the Americans come and go during decades of slaughter and suffering, he understood the feeling well, and never ignored it.

He turned left, began heading south down the hill. He knew better than to bolt; it would only spur them on.

The young men followed him down the hill.

So did an evil presence he had detected a few minutes ago. It floated down the hill behind them all like a black cloud, oily smoke nearly choking the old clergy. How could the young lads not sense it too?

"Hey!" One of the youths shouted. "Old man!".

No mistaking that. He was the only old man out on this street this time of early morning. He stopped, turned around to face them.

"Yes, my son?" He stood up straight. There was no mistaking the priestly collar around his throat. The white center piece practically glowed in the dim light.

One stepped closer, obviously the leader of their tiny tribe. Ng had worked the streets as a young priest and was no stranger to street gang hierarchy.

"What, you're a priest?" the leader said. The other two spread out, now each of them at forty-five-degree angles to Ng.

"How may I help you, my son?"

He looked left and right, grinning at his colleagues. "Well, Padre, since you asked so politely, let's start with what you've got in the bag."

"Just some personal items."

That black oily cloud it slithered closer with every beat of Ng's heart.

"Better let us inspect it," he said, "make sure that clerk didn't rip you off."

"He didn't," Sweat popped out on Ng's forehead even though it was barely fifty degrees.

The leader's face darkened. "Old man, we're cutting you some slack because you're a priest. You know, trying to be polite."

"What part of thievery is polite, my son?"

"What?"

"The Eighth Commandment," Father Ng replied. "And the Lord God said unto Moses, 'Thou Shall Not Steal'."

"Sorry, Padre," he answered, as if giving a confession. "Truth is, I'm not Catholic. I never even went to Sunday School."

"That matters not, my son."

"Hand over the fucking bag." The edge in his voice sliced like a knife. "Now."

That oily blackness threatened to envelop them all. Ng could hardly breathe. How could these three morons not sense the presence of true Evil?

"Please," he said, tears at the corners of his eyes. "You are in extreme danger –"

The three doomed young men cackled with laughter, even as that black cloud of death inched closer behind them, then expanded.

"You're the one in danger, old man."

The black cloud was everywhere now. Behind them. In front of them. All around them.

No hope of escape. Not for Ng.

Not for them.

A switchblade appeared in the leader's hand, clicked open, locked into place.

Then the leader got yanked violently backwards by an unseen force, his head bobbing forward to the immense backward thrust. He disintegrated into the night. It happened so quickly no one had time to react.

Ng blinked as the other two turned in the direction of their friend. Total darkness, complete silence. They glanced at each other, then peered into swirling blackness.

The silence lasted forever.

Then…

A bloodcurdling scream, the kind of scream Ng had heard more times than he cared to remember. The sound of a man for whom there is no hope of rescue.

Then came a roar. More than animal, but not quite human. A brief silence followed, then a sound like wet sackcloth being ripped asunder.

Something roughly the size and shape of a soccer ball bounced wetly towards them out of the inky shadows. But soccer balls didn't have hair and they didn't leave blood-slimed slug trails.

The two remaining youths looked down at the disembodied head of their leader. Mouths fell open in mute shock. Ng did not have to look down to know what it was.

A light, taunting laughter rippled over them from the darkness.

"We've got weapons!" one of them yelled.

"Please," Ng pleaded. "Just leave."

The one who had spoken spun around on Ng, eyes filled with anger and a fear that bordered on panic. He brandished his knife inches from Ng's face.

"Shut the fuck uuuuup—". He never finished his sentence. In that instant, *something* burst forth from the shadows at incredible speed. Nothing more than a muddy blur. But in that brief instant, the blur scooped up the second youth and flung him backwards into the shadows, all flailing arms and scissoring legs.

The second youth landed somewhere in the darkness, on concrete. They knew he landed by the wet smashing sound, like a pumpkin dropped from a great height.

And he would never make another sound again.

Ever.

Terrified beyond rational thought, the remaining youth looked wildly around, a trapped animal looking for escape. He had forgotten the priest. He just wanted to get out alive.

"I've got a gun!" he yelled.

Taunting laughter echoed off the surrounding buildings.

The youth pulled out a 9mm semiautomatic pistol. He flicked the safety off with one thumb, the tiny red dot now visible on the side of the black metal.

The black swirling cloud enveloped them both once again, but different this time. It swept around and around, not seen but sensed as movement at an amazing speed. Something so fast the human eye cold not follow.

The sole remaining youth moved his eyes, trying to catch a glimpse at what was circling them. Then, without warning, a ghostly face and thin black body appeared less than a foot away. Long, narrow face. Pointed chin. Forehead broad and pasty, cheekbones prominent, almost sharp.

Black wraparound sunglasses.

The gangster brought the gun up quickly and fired blindly.

The Vampire had anticipated the clumsy moves in advance, of course. He grinned, showing his teeth as the kid's finger went white at the knuckle around the trigger. The Vampire simply tilted his head to one side. The pistol fired, loud near his ear. The bullet whizzed harmlessly past him.

Time to end this.

The Vampire's arms shot out simultaneously. One hand gripped the kid's gun hand at the wrist while the other hand crimped off his esophagus. The kid's eyes bulged when the monster holding him applied a viselike pressure on his gun hand.

The pain was blinding. Phalanges and metacarpals compressed, then ground into powder. The Vampire twisted the hand outwards.

Bones and tendons snapped audibly; rubber bands stretched beyond their limits. The wrist bent over one hundred eighty degrees. Both the radius and ulna snapped off at the distal necks. Jagged fractures erupted through the tissue. Arterial blood gushed scarlet red, a gruesome geyser. The gun clattered harmlessly to the ground.

Filled with revulsion for this pathetic piece of human garbage, the Vampire snarled, opened his mouth, making sure his victim saw his fangs.

The kid saw them, all right. Bloodshot eyes popped wide; his face become ashen. His bowels moved involuntarily, exploding a foul-smelling diarrhea inside his trousers.

Offended by the stench, the Vampire lifted upwards, hoisting the condemned kid off his feet. He raised him higher and higher into the air until the Vampire stood there, his arm straightened at the elbow. The kid's feet dangled inches off the pavement. Liquid stool dribbled down his legs and dripped off his shoes.

The Vampire exhaled in disgust. More of a snort than anything else, like an angry bull. He moved his arm one way then whipped back the opposite direction. The kid swung up and out, sailing in a silent arc away from the sidewalk and across one lane of quiet street before landing with a thud in the middle of the road.

He bounced once, then came back down. He did not move again. Thick black blood pooled out from his ravaged head and slid greasily down the incline.

The Vampire cleared his throat and adjusted the sleeves on his leather jacket, giving each a terse tug at the wrist. He heard the priest's heart beating like a triphammer.

"Fear not, Father," he said. "I mean you no harm."

"W-who are you?" he asked.

"I have gone by many names."

Ng gasped in shock. The Vampire immediately realized his blunder.

"Fear not, good priest" he reiterated. "I am not Satan, nor am I a demon from Hell." The old priest did not look convinced. "If you wish, you may call me Eddie."

Ng nodded, still wary. What manner of man was this standing in front of him speaking in such gentle, soothing tones? His eyes swept the carnage spewed around him.

"Perhaps the question should be, what are you? And why did you save me?"

"I saved you because you are a good man," the Vampire said. "This scum would have hurt you even if you had handed over your liquor without protestation."

Without protestation?

Who talked like that nowadays?

"As far as what I am," the Vampire grinned with his lips together, "we can discuss that as I escort you home."

"I'll be fine."

"It was not you I was after, Father," the Vampire said, reading his thoughts.

"Why them?"

"They were criminals," the vampire spat. "Young men who had been bestowed all the blessings of life, the privilege of being born in this country, the potential for bright futures as contributing members of society." He shook his head in anger. "They could have been anything. Astronauts, artists, engineers, scientists. Yet they chose to walk the Dark Path."

"Satanism?"

"Evil in the generic sense of the word."

"What does that make you?"

"Something else entirely."

The Vampire gestured again, put a protective arm around the old man's shoulder. They began walking down the incline, away from the slaughter behind them.

Ng tried to process what he had seen. He had witnessed terrible atrocities as a child during the war. He had never witnessed destruction of a human body carried out so swiftly, so effortlessly, so glibly by one man until tonight.

Was this really a man, though?

He looked like a man, walked like a man, spoke like a man. But his actions were not those of a man. He had ripped a human head off its body with his bare hands. And he had thrown a person forty feet across a city street. And he himself had admitted he was something other than human.

Something else entirely.

Ng's mind raced ahead, drawing conclusions that were impossible, conclusions too horrifying to contemplate. Father Ng's mind reeled at the possibilities.

And at the implications.

The Vampire walked beside his charge, living in the moment, enjoying the tranquility of the night. He heard tires hiss on pavement blocks away on Broadway. That street never slept. Here, serenity reigned. No cars passed on the street. Dark buildings lined both sides of the road.

The ground was only the gentlest of slopes now. They crossed one more vacant street and there it stood, looming towards them out of the darkness.

St Thomas Catholic church.

They slowed as they approached. The priest stole a glance at his nocturnal companion.

"I live here. On the church grounds."

"That is wonderful, Father."

"Can you…" the old priest hesitated, then, "is it dangerous for you to set foot on holy ground?"

The Vampire stifled his laughter. "You have watched too many old movies."

They mounted the steps towards the main cathedral. A gate stationed on the left provided entrance to the courtyard. Ng lifted the gate's latch and went through first. The Vampire followed.

The courtyard was mostly dark. One security light shone bright as the sun where the administrative offices connected to the main cathedral. The orange light bathed everything close by. They were nowhere close, and Ng was not headed that way.

The Vampire noticed rose gardens planted in raised planters constructed of red brick and mortar. They were not in bloom right now but would begin to bud in a few weeks. He could smell the soil, deep, moist, nutrient rich. The flowers would be something to behold. Perhaps he would come back to admire their beauty, wonder at the artwork of nature.

They neared a small alcove, all plaster and mortar. A heavy, darkly stained door waited in a recess.

"This is me."

"Well then," the Vampire said. "I have completed my mission."

"What are you?" the old man asked.

"A creature of the night, Father," the Vampire answered. "I was born, I lived, violently. Then I died. *Violently*. Then, I was reborn into Darkness."

"I don't know what that means."

The Vampire pursed his lips. "I believe you do." He took a step backwards. "And now, good Father, I must bid you farewell."

"Really?"

"Time is a factor for me, Father," the creature explained. "I must be somewhere prior to dawn."

The old man thought for a moment, then it the lightbulb snapped on. His eyes popped wide. His mouth fell open.

"Ah", the Vampire grinned. "Now you understand." He took another step backwards. "I think I should enjoy visiting you in the future," he announced. "Oh, the conversations we might have."

Ng stood there, dumbfounded. Realizing he was standing in the presence of a vampire, an immortal creature that he had been taught all his life did not exist, he forgot that he needed to pee.

"May I call on you, Father?"

Ng did not even realize he had nodded his answer.

"Very well then. Until we meet again." The Vampire faded back into the shadows and was gone.

Ramsey Domingo only regained consciousness once.

Floating in a black ocean, slick with sludge. A starless sky above her. But that couldn't be right. She felt the sensation of movement, the ebb and flow as something warm and liquid engulfed her. Other than the pesky fact that she did not know where she was, the sensation was not fear-inducing; indeed, it was rather pleasant.

Ascending out of the ether, she thought she opened her eyes. Then she realized she had not, yet she could see a pale-yellow orb, a tiny moon that seemed abnormally far away. The dim light did not glint on the fluid in which she floated.

Ramsey's eyes fluttered, then opened. For real this time. The pale moon that shone down revealed itself to be a cheap light adhered to the interior roof of the van by a glue strip.

A shadow loomed over her.

"Ah. Sleeping Beauty awakes." A soothing voice laced with sadistic undercurrents.

Charlie Simpkins noticed her flesh raise goosebumps. Her bare nipples contracted, drained of color as her body shunted her remaining blood away from her extremities and to keep the vital organs going. A primitive, autonomic survival mechanism.

Hypovolemic shock did that to you.

"The process is nearly complete."

"P-process?"

"Shhhh," Charlie soothed. He checked his custom made, twin-pronged 16- gauge hypodermic needle he had inserted into her jugular below her left ear. He would have preferred the right side, but this would do. He knew the cops would try to build a profile. By varying his ritual slightly each time, he hoped to stay ahead of them for as long as possible.

So much important work to do!

He pressed gently on the needle, right at the soldering point where he had connected the needle heads onto a Y-joint that connected to the rubber IV tubing that snaked into the large hard-shell case that held the hand pump that "sucked" the blood out. The tubing then deposited the blood into two large clear plastic bladders.

Each held two quarts.

The bladders contained an anticoagulant. The blood would not clot. That was crucial to his work, to his personal journey. After all, that's what this was all about.

His journey.

His quest.

His search for truth and enlightenment.

The female herself was unimportant to him, other than she provided what he needed for his quest. He could have targeted a man, but she had presented herself at the club he knew she was the one.

To Charlie, she wasn't a real person. Not even human.

None of them were.

They were not like him. They were not worth his sympathy, empathy, or remorse. He had never felt those emotions anyway.

He was okay with that, never gave it any thought. As far back as he could remember, even as a kid, he had never felt emotions the way others did. Not even towards his own mother and father.

He had never been one to make friends. He never saw the advantage. Team sports? Nah. Hard pass, no pun intended. Being a loner suited him. The fact that other kids avoided him was a nonissue.

He had always been highly intelligent, a keen observer, a quick learner, and a clever mimic. He could outwardly fake emotion, albeit briefly, when he had to.

Now, squatting inside the van, he gazed down at Ramsey's naked body. Firm arms and shoulders, the perky breasts, flat stomach. She looked like an athlete with her powerful thighs and sculpted calves. That was part of why he had targeted her. Not being part of "the scene", her blood had not been irreparably tainted by years of cheap booze and bad drugs.

Charlie didn't do drugs. He drank only in moderation. He ate only organic foods.

His body was a temple through which his holy quest could be carried out.

Her body was a meat sack. A bag of bones, muscle, and sinew. Like all the others.

Worthless.

He had cut her clothing away and had put the shreds into a plastic bag. He would burn them later in the incinerator at work. The evidence would go up in smoke – literally! – and leave nothing behind that could keep him from his work.

Ramsey's eyes rolled in her sockets. She tried to get her mind to function, but it was like trying to start a car with no gas in the tank. She tried to move her arms and legs, but her extremities had become clumsy stumps.

She whispered something. He leaned down close her face.

"What did you say?" He placed his ear two inches from her lips.

She spoke again.

He sat back up. "Cold?"

She nodded. It looked like a Herculean task for her.

"Never fear," he assured her. "That won't be a problem soon."

She believed him, of course. Why wouldn't she? In this muted twilight in which she found herself, his was the only voice. A soothing presence. Like the voice of God Himself, and God would never lie to one of His children, would He?

She relaxed, smiling only in her mind. He had been correct. She no longer felt cold.

She no longer felt anything.

Just a strange sense of tranquility, an acceptance that this was where she was supposed to be right now in this moment.

Fair enough, she thought. I think I'll just lie here a minute.

Catch my breath. Yeah, that's it.

I'll just rest here for a while longer.

CHAPTER FOUR

Senior Detective Reginald Downing was a heavy sleeper. Grandma Lottie used to say he could sleep through a nuclear blast. He never understood why he slept so soundly, or why it took an alarm like a bazooka to rouse him.

Just one of life's mysteries.

He believed it was part of the marvelous differences amongst humans. At best, it made for a rich and textured human experience. But at worst, differences triggered a darkness that slithered through in the human heart. And once awakened, that darkness manifested as fear, hatred, misunderstanding. Some of the worst atrocities ever perpetrated happened because one person was different from another.

Different hair; different gender. Different skin color. Different sexual orientation or gender identity. That was a big one. Then there was the ultimate difference: a different God. Or perhaps even worse, no God.

The best that humans could be often got stymied by the worst that humans are.

Reggie lay sprawled across his bed. Legs splayed open behind him; one arm stuffed underneath his pillows. Burrowed comfortably under a quilted comforter, mouth open, he drooled onto the fitted sheet beneath him.

The bedside alarm clock snapped to 6:00am. A trumpet blasted a military Reveille at earsplitting levels. The air itself cringed. Reveille kept blowing repeatedly with only a brief respite in between.

Brown bloodshot eyes opened. He finally focused on the alarm clock. Already 6:02am. He reached out, slapped the SNOOZE button. Reveille ended instantly but would pierce the peace once more in five minutes.

He rolled over onto his back, rested a forearm across his forehead. This time right now, these few moments between sleep and awake were Reggie's favorite of the day.

Quiet.

Peaceful.

Perfection.

Reggie's cell phone rang, destroying the mood. Instantly awake, he threw the comforter off, sat up at the edge of the bed. He grabbed his phone, looked at the caller I.D.

SDPD.

Figures.

Reggie hit the SPEAK button, placed it to his ear.

"Yeah?" He listened. "No, I was up." He listened again. "I'll be there in thirty." He listened again as someone spoke on the other end. Reggie rolled his eyes and heaved a great sigh. The caller heard it, but he did not care. "She's dead, right? It's not like she's going anywhere." It was too early in the morning to be exasperated already. "Fine, fine," he acquiesced. "I'll be there in twenty."

He hit the END button, then staggered to the bathroom. He flicked the light on, winced as brightness stabbed like a stiletto through the eye sockets. He needed lower wattage bulbs in here.

He peed, flushed, brushed his teeth. No time to shave. He splashed cold water on his face, ran his hands over his head.

One last look in the mirror.

Mid-tone caramel skin glistened. A tired face, peppered with black stubble stared back. His eyes wandered across strong shoulders, bulging biceps, tight chest, flat stomach. All that gym time still paid off. He noticed the early beginnings of love handles at the waist near his back, but hey, what could he do? He was in his late thirties now.

In Reggie's profession, being in shape could be the difference between living and dying. Running down a suspect in hot pursuit was as much a part of the job as negotiating the combat course at the range.

That level of dedication had saved his ass more than once.

He stumbled into his kitchenette. It had been the only thing that had given him pause about signing the lease. But he needed new digs after what had happened at his old place. Firefights with mercenaries got you evicted whether you were a cop or not.

The coffeemaker waited for him like an old friend. He ground some whole bean coffee, poured the grinds into the basket, added water, hit BREW. The coffeemaker sighed, sputtered to life.

Back in his bedroom, Reggie gathered clothes from the floor. He had worked late last night and was running on four hours' sleep. But they had locked down a case involving a string of armed robberies and the pistol whipping of a store clerk.

Said suspect currently sat in Lockup awaiting arraignment. The D.A. would put the scumbag away for a long time. Surveillance tapes captured a clear shot of the guy's ugly mug as he pistol whipped the clerk. Video is forever, and DNA at the scene put the final nail in the coffin.

Game over, asshole.

Reggie wriggled into crumpled clothes, shoved his feet inside weather-beaten boots. He shrugged into his shoulder holster, drew his pistol. He depressed the magazine's release button. The magazine fell into his waiting hand. He saw a full magazine of fourteen .45ACP rounds staring back up at him. Plus, the one in the chamber, he reminded himself.

He slapped the magazine back in, doublechecked the safety before holstering his weapon. He checked the other two magazines he carried in leather magazine holders attached to the shoulder harness. Both fully loaded with fifteen rounds each.

Reassured, he reached for his bomber-style leather jacket. It would be cold outside. Probably damp, too. It was that time of year. Plus, an amazing number of civilians got triggered, fearful, intimidated seeing someone walking around with a loaded firearm.

He strode from his bedroom into the kitchen. The coffee was almost ready, and it smelled heavenly. He opened a cabinet, pulled out two travel mugs, grabbed the carafe, poured coffee into both. He replaced the carafe, and the coffeemaker resumed brewing.

He added raw sugar, then half and half. He stirred each with a spoon, put the lids on. He grabbed both and headed for the door. The coffeemaker would finish brewing, sit there undisturbed for four hours, then automatically shut off. If he happened to swing by later, he could nuke some in the microwave, refill an empty mug, and keep going. Worst case scenario, he could reheat it tomorrow.

Reggie grabbed his keys off the hook by the entrance. He put his mugs on the console near the door, then opened it. The heavy metal security door opened reluctantly under his strength. All the apartments in the building had them. They could only be opened at the knob from inside.

Reggie held the door open with one foot, grabbed the mugs, then slipped out before the door closed and trapped him against the jamb. He moved down the deserted hallway. Most of his neighbors were still asleep. At the elevator he pressed the call button with an elbow.

The doors yawned open. He stepped inside, poked the button for the ground floor with one extended finger. He soon stepped out on the ground floor, exited the building, and turned south.

The precinct was twelve blocks from his building's front door. He threw back a slug of coffee, delighted by the warmth tracing its way through the core of his body.

If only he could feel this good all day.

Reggie breezed his way through the precinct doors at 25th and C eighteen minutes after he had received the call. Two minutes early, he told himself. Punctuality was a trait his new lieutenant valued. Well, that and solving crimes. Building cases that got convictions.

Personally, Reggie was not convinced that lengthy prison sentences were always the best measure of true justice. Every case was different. Sometimes a lengthy sentence, even LNP - Life No Parole – was warranted. Murderers, rapists, or habitually violent felony offenders going down for the third time got whatever they got.

Justice served.

But in cases where poverty, hunger, or chronic unemployment predicated the crime – say, someone shoplifting food to feed hungry children at home -- while Reggie didn't condone it, he understood it.

Desperate people do desperate things.

He walked through the precinct lobby, threw a nod towards the Desk Sergeant. She nodded back, then went back to her duties. He zigzagged through the sea of desks. His desk sat closest to the lieutenant's office.

The lieutenant was already in, as always. The first one there and the last to leave. Sometimes Reggie wondered if Lieutenant Nick Castle didn't secretly live here.

Nick looked up through the glass partition that separated his office from the main room. Reggie nodded in his direction. The lieutenant stood, tall and lean, and grabbed his coat off the back of his chair. There was an old-fashioned wooden coatrack in the corner nearest the entrance. It had been in the precinct for years, sort of an institution by itself. But unlike his predecessor Captain Morris Horn, Nick Castle never used it himself.

Nick stepped into the main precinct room, the keys to an unmarked squad car in his hand.

"Ready?" he asked.

"Born ready, Lieutenant."

Nick grinned, impossibly white teeth glowing against his handsome Latino face. He strode towards the rear parking lot door. He did not have to look back to know Reggie had fallen into step behind him. He ran a hand through thick, graying hair, pushed through the back entrance and into brisk morning air. Reggie squeezed through a second or two after.

They walked towards the car. Nick pushed the button on the key fob. The alarm chirped, the lights blinked on and off. The doors unlocked with a soft metallic thump.

Reggie slid into the front passenger seat and shoved his travel mug into the cup holder in the center console. Nick slid into the driver's seat and jammed the key into the ignition. The engine roared to life. Nick threw the car into gear and maneuvered towards the exit.

"So. What do we have, Lieutenant?"

"Another killing."

His tone of voice made Reggie turn his head. "Like the others?"

Nick nodded.

"Jesus Christ," Reggie muttered under his breath.

"Jesus has nothing to do with this," Nick said. "Although I wouldn't mind His help."

"What does this make now? Three?"

Nick maneuvered through the early morning traffic easily. It wasn't even seven yet; the streets were mostly empty. He turned right and they started climbing the hill heading east into Golden Hill. The coastal plain of downtown San Diego fell away behind them. Reggie took another slug of coffee.

"How's Grandpa Eddie?"

"He's not involved in this."

"I never said he was," Nick said tightly. "Just wondering how he's doing, that's all."

"I haven't seen him in a while."

"Why's that?"

"Been busy," Reggie said. "This job we do. You know?"

"So how was he the last you heard?"

"Okay," Reggie answered. "He's pulled back from the active brokering." Reggie answered. "He wants to spend more time with Grandma Lottie."

"Sweet lady," Nick said. "I like her." He put his blinker on. "How's she doing?"

Reggie sighed. "That Goddamned diabetes. Her eyesight's failing, circulation in her legs and feet is shot to hell." He paused, then, "And high blood pressure fucks with her kidneys."

"Sorry, man." Nick cranked the wheel, turning left. "You think she'll need a nursing home?"

"No," Reggie said, shaking his head. "Grandpa Eddie will see to things." Nick looked at him. "Not that way," Reggie assured him. "He'll make sure she gets home health care."

"Home care's expensive."

"Grandpa's loaded," Reggie said. "Anything over and above whatever Medicare doesn't cover, he'll take care of."

They merged onto Normal Avenue, headed north. They turned right at the head of El Cajon Boulevard. A large art deco sign, which glowed neon at night, announced, "THE BOULEVARD". In the old days, before the construction of Interstates in the 1950s, El Cajon Blvd had been a state highway that connected San Diego to the smaller towns of La Mesa, and El Cajon. Now a city street, it remained a major artery connecting the city to what was now called "East County".

Nick maneuvered into the left lane. Reggie saw red and blue flashing lights ahead on the left, behind an all-night diner that proudly proclaimed, "Open Continuously since 1949!" on their side wall. His heart sank.

"Something wrong?" Nick asked.

"This is where Grandpa Eddie told me who and what he really was."

They parked on the street near the parking lot. Technicians dressed in white fiber overalls, latex gloves, and blue masks scurried about. Taking notes, conferring with one another. Bagging evidence. Uniformed cops, which Reggie referred to as "unis", stood at the police barrier tape, keeping curious onlookers at bay.

Nick and Reggie got out, showed their badges, ducked underneath the tape, assessed the scene in its entirety. Get a first impression, see the big picture. Then concentrate on the details.

The main activity buzzed around an enormous industrial-grade dumpster. Forest green metal sides dinged up. Paint peeled away showing rusted metal underneath. Heavy black rubber lids attached both thrown back wide and resting against the wall of the restaurant.

Something bad awaited them there. Something horrific.

The aftermath of evil.

The technicians stepped back as the two detectives got closer. The detectives stopped and looked in.

The naked body of a young, beautiful Latina stared up at them with dull, lusterless eyes that would never see anything again. Her slack mouth hung agape, jaw muscles relaxed at the point of death. Her pallid skin was covered in a thin sheen of clotted blood. Like she had been painted in it. Reggie leaned closer, looking for something specific.

There it was.

Two puncture wounds about two inches apart on the left side of her neck, under her ear.

A Coroner's Assistant walked up to the dumpster. "Detective."

Nick, his mind racing, did not hear her.

"Detective." Firmer. More insistent.

Coming out of his fog, Nick turned and looked at Sarah Ombaye, a veteran of the coroner's office. She immigrated from Uganda as a child and grew into an incredibly competent technician. Her work had helped them nail more than one case. As the senior forensics person present, she considered this "her" crime scene.

"Sorry." He stepped back, unsteady on his feet.

Reggie looked at him, concerned. "Lieutenant. You okay?"

"Fine."

Nick did not look fine. He staggered back, a look of overwhelming shock on his face.

Reggie stepped forward. He placed a hand on Nick's elbow in case his friend's knees buckled.

"What's wrong, L.T.?"

Sweat poured down Nick's forehead.

"I just need to catch my breath." He turned away, bent halfway over, and placed his hands on his knees.

Sara Ombaye stepped onto a small ladder and leaned inside the dumpster. She held a thermometer affixed to the end of a narrow shaft that ended in a sharp point. Sara put the shaft gingerly over the victim's skin right over her liver. She applied slight pressure until the pale skin pinched inward. Then she shoved hard, impaling the victim's body, sending the point through the tissue and into the liver itself.

Once she confirmed proper placement, she pushed off the dumpster's lip and stepped down onto the pavement.

"So, what do you think?" Reggie asked.

"Two puncture marks on the neck, just like the others," Sarah stated. "Rigor is just now setting in. I'll need to get the liver temp to be sure, but I think she's only been here a couple of hours."

"Anything else?"

"She's lost a lot of blood."

"Her body is covered in it."

Sara shook her head. "No, I mean she's lost a *lot* of blood."

Reggie looked at her, not understanding what she was implying.

"This is different from the others," she explained. "Yeah, she's been painted with blood that's most likely her own. Problem is, there's not that much blood here. A couple hundred cc's at most. There's almost none in the dumpster itself. And my guess is, she's close to four quarts low."

"A gallon?" Nick croaked as he tried to recover from his shock. "That's new."

"He's refining his technique," Reggie said. He looked to Sarah. "So, where's the blood?"

"Maybe he drained her in a bathtub or something," Sarah speculated. "I'll let you know as soon as we get anything," She headed towards the coroner's van where another technician waited. They huddled together in conference.

Both Nick and Reggie leaned over the dumpster again, their eyes moving slowly over her body, taking in every detail, no matter how small.

"I got a bad feeling about this," Reggie muttered.

"So do I," Nick agreed.

"You know her?"

"I haven't seen her since she was a kid. But yeah, I know who this is."

"Who is it?"

Nick shook his head. "I don't want to say. Just in case I'm wrong." His eyes narrowed. "God, please. Let me be wrong."

Reggie noticed a rather rotund middle-aged man standing at the back door of the restaurant, watching the proceedings. Balding head of black hair, deep set eyes. Red shirt, iron gray Gabardine slacks, black shoes. He did not look happy.

Reggie approached him. "Excuse me, sir."

The man stayed where he was as Reggie neared.

"Do you work here?"

He nodded. "I'm the manager." He replied. "How long will my parking lot be tied off?"

"This is a murder investigation," Reggie said. "These things take time."

"How much time?"

Reggie dropped the pleasant façade. "As long as it takes."

The manager noted the change in attitude. He gulped, realizing he did not want to be on this cop's bad side.

"I am Ahmed Ben-Ami," he said, changing his tune. He put his hand out. Reggie shook it as Nick walked up.

"This is Ahmed, the manager," Reggie said to Nick. "Were you here in the early morning hours?"

"I got here around five thirty. I had paperwork before shift change at six."

"Who discovered the body?" Nick asked.

"I did."

"You don't seem too shaken up about it."

"I'm from Iraq," Ahmed said. "I've seen dead bodies all my life. I've seen worse than this."

Reggie and Nick both figured that was true.

"We need to talk to every employee on duty between midnight and six," Reggie instructed, taking the lead.

"They are not here now."

"Call them in."

"Don't you need a warrant?"

"Nope," Reggie replied, shaking his head. "But I can call a judge and get one. Of course, we'll have to keep your parking lot cordoned off for the duration." He looked to Nick. "Lieutenant, how long will it take to get a warrant?"

"Could be days," Nick replied.

Ahmed's eyes widened.

"Maybe longer."

Ahmed looked at the two policemen. They had him over a barrel. He knew it.

"Come with me," he said. Reggie stepped inside while Nick walked towards the dumpster.

Ahmed stalked through the kitchen, past two line cooks and a dish washer. He led Reggie through swinging metal doors to behind the counter. Several seats were empty, but people seemed to be enjoying their food. They rounded the far corner, near the overflow area where his great, great grandfather had revealed his true self five years ago. The overflow seating was currently closed, the overhead lighting turned off.

Ahmed turned left into a tiny alcove that served as his office. Someone had wedged a metal desk in there. A rickety stool with no back support and a Naugahyde seat awaited. A metal plate nailed to the wall denoted the space's function: MANAGER.

Ahmed sat down. The stool groaned under his weight. Reggie stood behind and to the side so he could always see the manager's hands. Every cop knew hands were dangerous. Always keep an eye on them.

Ahmed typed something into the ancient desktop in front of him. He leaned in, squinted at the screen.

"Sorry," he mumbled. "I forgot my reading glasses at home."

"Just magnify the screen."

"Huh?" He looked at Reggie as if he was from another planet. "You can do that?"

"Certainly." He pointed. "May I?"

The luddite manager pushed off, the wheeled stool careening away from the desk. Reggie showed him how to do it. He pressed two buttons, showed Ahmed show to get to "View" and then magnify the page, making the print larger. He took a step back and the astounded manager rolled himself back in front of the screen.

"There were four people on last night," he announced, squinting at the screen. "They're probably asleep."

"Wake them up," Reggie ordered. "I need to talk to them while last night is still fresh in their minds. Or have you forgotten the naked dead woman in your dumpster?"

Ahmed's entire body sagged. Reggie had seen that response before. It was when people understood what they were being asked to do was going to be a major-league pain in the ass. But compliance was nothing compared to the hassle that inevitably came when they told the cops to go fuck themselves.

Ahmed picked up his cell phone.

Reggie said, "I'll be back in a minute."

He retraced his footsteps. He stalked through the kitchen walking towards the back door. The cook and dishwasher seemed nervous. He discounted them. People were always nervous around cops.

He stepped outside into a gray, dreary morning. He saw Nick talking to Sarah at the far corner of the parking lot. Sarah wore a grave expression. Nick looked like someone had punched him in the gut.

"We've I.D.'d the body," Nick announced.

"Who is it?"

"Who I was afraid it was."

"Who?"

"Ramsland Domingo."

Reggie frowned. The name sounded familiar. Nick looked at him, to Sarah, and then back to him.

"You don't get it?"

"Not really," Reggie admitted.

"Ramsey Domingo is a true crime writer. She's also the only child of multi-gazillionaire Alejandro Domingo."

"Oh shit." Reggie's eyebrows popped upwards.

"Yeah," Nick confirmed. "Active in local politics, involved in the Amnesty movement for illegal immigrants. The guy's juiced both in Sacramento and in D.C., and he's one of the richest men in the country."

"Oh of course," Reggie said as if this was nothing at all. "That Alejandro Domingo. Why didn't you say so?"

They watched as two technicians hoisted Ramsey's remains out of the dumpster, put her into a black body bag on the ground, then zipped it from her feet to over her head. The techs bent at the knees, kept their backs straight. They grabbed the handles at each end of the bag and lifted. Then they marched over to a Coroner's van and placed the body inside through the open rear doors.

"I'm glad you're Lieutenant and not me," Reggie said. "The politics on this are going to be awful."

"You'll make Lieutenant, Reg," Nick assured him. "Sooner rather than later."

Reggie jerked a thumb over his shoulder. "I've got the manager calling the night shift back in."

"You think Ramsey was inside last night?"

"We'll never know unless we ask."

"See?" Nick asked Sarah. "He's gonna make a great Lieutenant."

Reggie felt his cheeks flush with heat. Nick clapped him on the shoulder. They walked towards the restaurant's open rear door.

Ahmed was ending a call just as they came around the corner to his cubicle. He looked up at them.

"It will be some time before they can get here," he explained. "One of them is in class at City College. I left her a message."

"No problem," Nick said. "We have an errand to run. We'll be back in a couple of hours."

"A couple of hours!" the manager echoed.

Reggie put his game face on. "You got a problem with that?"

"What if they get here before you get back?"

"Tell them to wait."

"What if they can't?"

"Tell them they better not make me come looking for them."

Ahmed just sat there in wrinkled clothes on an overtaxed stool and nodded his head.

Nick and Reggie crossed the lot to their car. Nick turned to the small laptop mounted on the center console. He typed something in, hit a button.

"I've got the address," he said.

"I hate this part of the job," Reggie muttered.

Nick turned the keys. The engine grumbled under the hood. He shifted gears and pulled away from the curb.

Father Ng had brought a wooden chair and a TV tray outside his room to set up a sitting area for himself. He now sat, sipping coffee and reading the newspaper. The fog was finally lifting. Patches of blue sky peeked through from above.

Ng knew those gangsters would have hurt him last night. He still felt disquieted by his mysterious protector. There was something... wrong with that guy.

Very wrong.

Ng did not believe in vampires. But he believed in good and evil. He had seen people struggle between the two all his life. God knew, he had heard enough confessions over the course of his career.

And yet, there were questions for which Ng had no answers. Things seen that he could not explain. This mystery man had killed three people in under two minutes. He had thrown one guy forty feet. He had decapitated another with no evidence of weapons and had somehow managed to not get drenched in blood.

Ng wasn't certain he wanted to see him again.

He looked up from his paper, took a sip of coffee. The church doors were pushed back. Mass wouldn't be for some time yet, but the church was open for early confession. Not many people taking advantage of it this morning.

A young priest with reddish hair and a square jaw exited the door and walked out onto the courtyard. He seemed disturbed by something. Deep furrows ran across his forehead. Lips tightened into a grim line.

The priest noticed Ng, waved. Ng waved back, and the younger priest approached.

"Father Ng. How are you this morning?"

"I'm fine, Father Nagin," Ng said. "You look preoccupied."

Nagin pointed at the paper in Ng's gnarled hands. "Did you read the headlines this morning? Three people murdered last night," he recited. "Just a few blocks from here." He shook his head. "Practically on our own doorstep."

"You seem rattled. Don't be," Ng advised. "Violence is part of living in a major city like this. You just arrived from rural Georgia, correct?"

"Yes, but why –"

"And why did you request a transfer to Southern California?"

"Boredom."

"Welcome to Southern California," Ng quipped. "People do all kinds of horrible things for all kinds of horrible reasons here," Ng said. "We can't stop it."

"We can try. Youth outreach programs and –"

"Yes, yes," Ng nodded. "All necessary, and beneficial. But the truth is, all we can ever hope to do is stem the flow. We'll never close the tap."

"Then what are we doing here?"

"The best that we can."

Nagin looked depressed now.

Ng continued. "We're throwing starfish back into the ocean."

Now Nagin was confused. "What?"

"You never heard the story of the starfish after the storm?"
Nagin shook his head.

"There's a beach the morning after a huge storm at sea," the old priest began, "and there's hundreds, maybe thousands of starfish washed up on shore. There's little girl maybe nine, ten years old walking on the beach, and she's picking up starfishes and she's throwing them back into the water." Ng paused, then, "There's a guy also on the beach, and sees what she's doing. He says to her, 'Little girl, what are you doing? There's thousands of starfish here. You can't possibly throw them all back'. The girl says, 'I know'. And the man says, 'Then why do it when you know you won't make a difference?'. The little girl bends down, picks one up, and heaves it back into the ocean. Then she looks at the man and says, 'I made a difference to that one'."

Dumbfounded, Nagin simply stared at him.

"The moral of the story is," Ng said, "save one life, and you save the entire world."

Nagin frowned, thinking about this.

"And as for why men do the evil that men do," Ng continued, "If you ever figure that one out, be sure and tell me."

Nagin grinned. "Thank you, Father."

"Please," Ng said, "I'm Justin."

"Thanks, Justin." Nagin stepped back.

"You're welcome, James."

Nagin turned and walked back towards the front of the church. His back seemed straighter, his head a bit higher. He bounced with a spring in his step that had been missing a few minutes earlier.

CHAPTER FIVE

Nestled between La Jolla to the south and Solana beach to the north, Del Mar, California rested approximately twenty miles north of San Diego itself. Considered a suburb now, Del Mar had first been formed in 1885 and incorporated as a city in 1954. Since the early twentieth century, Del Mar had become a vacation hotspot for Hollywood stars, professional athletes, titans of industry, and of course, politicians. Some liked it so much they bought homes there. Some even retired there or relocated to live and work from there year-round.

It took Nick and Reggie about twenty minutes powering up the 5 to exit onto Del Mar Heights Road. Then took a left and headed west towards the ocean. The car clock indicated barely 8 a.m. when they turned right onto Camino Del Mar.

"Where does this guy live?" Reggie asked.

"The beach."

"Jealous?"

"Maybe a little."

Reggie thought about this briefly as they drove, got into a left turn lane, came to stop. They turned, approached a massive metal gate, complete with a guard shack and a rent-a-cop sitting on a stool. The guard stood as they crept forward, came to a stop in front of the shack.

The guard, an elderly man with gray hair, gray eyes, and wrinkled skin nodded to Nick as the Lieutenant rolled his window down.

Nick flashed his badge. "Alejandro Domingo."

The guard pointed as he spoke. "Down to the end, turn right. Go all the way down, last house on the left."

"Last house on the left, huh? I saw that movie."

"I saw the first one. In theaters. 1972."

"How's this job?"

"It sucks."

"Do you live here?"

"Not hardly," the guard said. The smile had left his face. "I live in a single-wide in that mobile home park up in Solana Beach. Bought in the seventies when a regular guy could still afford a home."

The guard leaned in, hit the button. An electric motor whined. The gate began inching back like a mouth set sideways.

"Why don't you retire?" Reggie asked.

"I did," the guard said. "Social Security, Medicare, Medicaid, EBT, all of it ain't enough to cover the bills. So here I am."

Nick shook his head, genuinely sorry for they guy. "That ain't right."

"That's Southern California."

Nick could think of nothing else to say. He hit a button inside the car. The window rolled back up. They inched forward through the yawning gate.

"You think that'll be us when we retire?"

"Depends," Nick answered. They approached the end of the road. A right turn loomed ahead.

"On what?"

"How well we manage our money when we're young and working, and whether or not we stay here when we retire."

The car pulled into the driveway of the last house on the left. A relatively small place, two stories, roughly three thousand square feet, Reggie estimated. California modern.

Nick noticed the garage door up, a Bentley parked inside. Reggie noticed him grimace. They walked towards what appeared to be the main door. Up three steps, and they stood in front of the impressive entry.

Trained professionals, their eyes never stopped moving, scanning their surroundings, eternally alert for danger. They noticed things in those first few seconds: the potted plants on each side of the steps were fake. The façade of the house was burnished wood, stained a medium honey tone. But the house was no log cabin by any stretch of the imagination. Two CCTV cameras gazed down on them from above, one on each side of the alcove in which they stood.

Nick pressed the doorbell button sitting chest high to the left.

Seconds later, a Hispanic man, around sixty, thin with a balding head and silver hair, pulled the door open. Black shoes, slacks, and vest. Immaculate white shirt. Black bow tie.

"Can I help you?"

Both Nick and Reggie showed their badges.

"Lieutenant Nick Castle and Detective Reginald Downing for Alejandro Domingo," Nick announced.

The butler stared at Nick for a very long time. Recognition flashed in the old man's eyes, and Reggie saw it.

What the hell was going on here? he wondered.

Finally, the butler said, "And what may I say this is regarding?"

"A matter of great urgency, of which Mr. Domingo needs to be informed directly."

The butler opened the door wider. "This way, please."

He strode ahead of them, leading them deeper into the house. Formal living room to the left. Enormous fireplace at the far end looking like it had never been used. Hallway extended, presumably to bedrooms and bathrooms. High vaulted ceilings and a series of skylights stretched down its length. Ambient light steamed in from outside.

The butler walked straight back, then veered slightly right. Nick and Reggie followed. The house suddenly opened into an open-living Great Space. A spacious kitchen, complete with a chef's stove and stainless-steel appliances to their right as they entered. A long narrow dinner table ran perpendicular to them, surrounded by eight chairs. The far wall looking west was tempered glass from floor to twelve-foot ceiling, boasting spectacular views of the beach below, the frothing surf, and the blue ocean beyond.

Breathtaking.

At the far end of the table, near where the glass wall connected to the north wall of the house, Alejandro Domingo sat finishing his breakfast. He chewed bacon while checking something on his tablet. A coffee mug sat near an empty plate. A French Press carafe looked within easy reach.

Middle aged, early to mid-fifties, Reggie guessed. Still trim, a full head of hair. Just starting to gray at the temples. Clean-shaven and broad shouldered, he looked younger than he was. Dressed casually. Loafers with no socks, faded olive green jeans, grey hooded T shirt stretched across a muscular chest.

Alejandro looked up as the tiny knot of people approached across polished hardwood floors. He lay his tablet down, stood up.

"Pepe," he said, addressing the butler, "Breakfast guests?"

Both Nick and Reggie showed their badges once more. Domingo stiffened a bit. Neither Nick nor Reggie read anything into that. They saw it all the time from practically everyone they met in a professional capacity.

"Lieutenant Nick Castle, San Diego Police Department," Nick said stiffly, like he was reading from a script. Reggie saw that same, now familiar hint of recognition in Domingo's eyes.

What the hell? Was he the only one who didn't know what was going on?

"This is Detective Reginald Downing," Nick added.

Domingo invited them to sit. "Pepe, please get our guests some coffee."

"No, thank you," Nick countered. "We're fine."

Finally, Domingo glanced to Pepe. "Thank you, Pepe. That will be all for now."

Pepe looked sourly at the two cops, then threw Nick a particularly poisonous glare. He turned without a word and walked away, his footfalls making almost no sound at all.

"Please forgive Pepe," Domingo said to them. "He means well; he's just very protective of me." Nick and Reggie glanced at each other. Domingo could not tell what that meant. "So.

Detectives." He emphasized that last word. What an odd thing to do. "What can I do for you?"

"For the record, you are Alejandro Domingo?" Nick asked.

"Yes."

"Again, and for the record, you are the father of one Ramsland Domingo?"

Domingo stiffened. "Is Ramsey in trouble again?"

Reggie frowned. "Again, sir?"

"I paid a fortune for her drug rehab. She's been clean for three years."

This was new information to Nick and Reggie.

"Look, what's going on here?" Domingo demanded. "Did she get arrested or something?"

"No sir," Reggie responded. "Nothing like that."

"Mr. Domingo, I'm afraid we have some bad news," Nick said as diplomatically as he could. He did not say anything else. Neither did Reggie.

Dread coursed throughout Domingo's body. His eyes widened. Pupils dilated. Nostrils flared. Color drained from his face.

"Is she... hurt?"

"Sir, she's... she *passed away* early this morning," Nick said.

There it was. The terrible truth. Delivered as softly as something this devastating could be. Reggie's heart went out to Domingo in that instant.

Alejandro exhaled, sat back in his chair. Eyes bulged; jaw dropped open. The initial shock. Then he frowned, as if someone had just spoken a foreign language to him.

Confusion.

Disbelief.

Denial.

The first of the five stages of grief.

Nick and Reggie had seen this response thousands of times before, too. News like this coming out of the blue was often such a complete and overwhelming shock, it simply did not compute at first. It took time to sink in.

Domingo finally found his words. "What... *how*?"

"It appears she... fell victim to murder, sir," Reggie said when it was obvious Nick wasn't answering.

"*Murder!*" Domingo shouted in disbelief. His eyes darted back and forth between them, searching for more. His shock widened, deepened with their silence. Grief would not be far behind.

Nick and Reggie watched as Domingo, now looking *very* old, leaned forward, propped elbows on the table, sunk his head into his open hands. He sat there quietly.

"Mr. Domingo, we're very sorry."

Domingo stayed still, quiet. He did not acknowledge the condolences. Nick and Reggie watched him, knowing this was not over yet. After what seemed like a very long time, Domingo mumbled something unintelligible from beneath his hands.

"Excuse me?" Reggie asked.

Domingo raised his head out of his hands, looked at them. Tears streamed down his face.

"This must be a mistake."

"There's no mistake, sir."

"You're certain it's her?" Eyes darting between them again, searching for a glimmer of hope that would never come.

Ever.

His head fell back into his hands. "This is a nightmare," he said. "A Goddamned nightmare." He raised his head again, eyes filled with rage. "Who did this?"

"We're haven't made an arrest yet, sir," Reggie stated.

"Why not?"

"We just found her a couple of hours ago." Nick again, this time with an air of formality. "Evidence is being collected as we speak. Detective Downing and I came here to notify you personally as soon as possible."

Domingo thought about this, then squeezed his eyes shut, nodded. "Of course," he wheezed. "Forgive me." He looked directly at Nick. "Thank you for coming here yourself."

"Think nothing of it, sir," Reggie said when Nick did not respond. What was going on with Nick? It seemed like he was almost enjoying this man's pain. He had known the Lieutenant for a long time and had never seen him act this way with any next of kin when they were given this kind of news. Usually, he was the poster boy of sympathy and compassion.

Not today.

Nick rose from his chair. Reggie followed suit.

"Sir, we must be going," Nick said. "We have a lot of work to do."

Dazed, Domingo nodded. He rose on wobbly knees, leaned on the table for support. He gulped, swallowed, blinked his eyes like he had just been gut punched. And in a very real way, he had.

"Thank you again for telling me yourself, Nicolas," Domingo said sincerely, using the Spanish pronunciation of the name. "This couldn't have been easy for you."

Nicolas?

Aw shit, Reggie thought. They know each other!

"On the behalf of the entire department, let me say we are all very sorry for this terrible loss," Nick said with an air of detached formality.

Domingo stared at him a moment, completely lost. Then he nodded, called out for Pepe, who had been standing on the other side of the room the entire time. He had heard everything. He came forward, obviously shaken by the news.

"Please shows these gentlemen to the door."

Pepe nodded solemnly.

"Oh, detectives," Domingo said, a new thought crossing his mind. "You will keep me informed, yes?"

"We'll be in touch," Nick assured him.

He nodded. Then Pepe lead the detectives back to the front door. He opened it for them. He had tears in his eyes.

"Please, Nicolas," Pepe said, and Reggie wondered for the second time in as many minutes just what the actual hell was going on here? "I cannot imagine how difficult this must be for you," he continued.

Now Nick just looked irritated.

"I've known Ramsey since the day she was born. Please, please find whoever did this."

"Finding murderers is what I do, Pepe,"

Pepe studied his face a moment, then nodded. A moment later the door closed. Nick turned and saw Reggie staring at him.

"What?"

"Nothing."

"Let's get the fuck out of here."

The sun rose higher, reached its zenith, then began a long slow slide down the western sky.

The Vampire's apartment was dark as Death, quiet as the grave. Heavy curtains hung closed and tied over the windows. No outside light got in.

Sunlight on a vampire, even when inanimate, meant Final Death. It didn't happen like in the movies, of course. Hollywood never got it bright. They didn't burst into flames like some sort of spontaneous combustion.

But the reality was just as bad. And just as painful.

Their white skin would redden like sunburn immediately. Blisters would form within fifteen seconds. The mottled skin would peel away like layers of an onion. Deep red third degree burns on all exposed surfaces within forty-five seconds. Skin flaked away like embers born on the wind. Muscle and subcutaneous tissue atrophied and burned black. Within one minute, all that remained would be a charred corpse.

The longest one minute of their unnaturally long lives.

The Vampire's desiccated corpse lay on the queen bed beneath heavy blankets, covered from head to toe. Between blackout curtains and burying himself underneath multiple blankets, sunlight never touched him.

Safety first.

Outside, the sun finally disappeared below its watery vanishing point. Inside the Vampire's bedroom, a dark miracle occurred. Just as it did every evening the instant the sun disappeared, a creature of the night was reborn.

Skin regrew across exposed boney protuberances. Claw-like fingers curled. Nails lengthened, grew to points. Sunken eyes refilled with vitreous humor. The chest heaved, inflating flat lungs, burning like the fires of hell.

Eyes popped open. Violent coughing forced all the air in his lungs out at over one hundred miles per hour. The croupy coughing left him lightheaded. His chest squeezed as intercostal muscles painfully contracted.

Panting like he had just run five miles, the vampire realized he was alive yet again. Another night. Another night in one long, endless procession of nights. As it had been for him for over one hundred years.

He pushed the blankets off as he swept his arm wide. They settled onto the middle of the bed. He hated this part -- slow, plodding, as weak as a kitten.

Vulnerable.

Not a condition a predator such as himself enjoyed. Like all predators, he understood how quickly tables could be turned to make that short journey from predator to prey. He was grateful for a life lived quietly, under the radar.

There had been that nasty business a few years back with that drug cartel. He had exposed himself back then to the possibility of being discovered for what he really was. But his great, great grandson had been in imminent danger. And his great, great grandson was a good and honorable man. There was no way the Vampire could sit idly by while a bunch of lowlife hoodlums murdered him.

He sat there, listening. Cars outside, the hiss of tires on pavement. The downstairs neighbor's TV as she watched *Jeopardy!* No human would have noticed the hushed tones as the host spoke to the contestants. The couple immediately below him making love. They had fought the night before.

They must have made up.

The only sound inside the apartment was the hum of his refrigerator. His pupils dilated wide, covering the entire front surface of the eyeball. Nothing seemed out of place.

He placed his bare feet flat on the hardwood floor. He stood up, knees threatening to buckle. He shuffled to the window, peeked through the curtains.

His street was bathed in the coming darkness. Cars drove with headlights on. A blue glow to the west from behind nearby buildings. Too bad the only way he could see a sunrise or a sunset anymore was on TV or in a movie.

He had not given spectacular sights such as sunrises and sunsets much thought when he had been a living, breathing person back in Hoboken. But he had thought about them quite a bit in the long dark years since.

Human nature, he supposed.

People treasured what they had after it had been ripped away from them.

The Vampire turned away. The curtain fell into place like a chunk of lead. He moved through the shadowy apartment, not bothering to turn on lights.

He didn't need them.

He reeled into the kitchen, opened a cupboard, and pulled out a mug. He shielded his eyes as he reached inside the fridge and grabbed the half empty blood bag from the top shelf. O Positive. Not the most exotic, but it would do. He pulled out the plastic plug and upended it, squeezing it between both hands. Syrupy red dribbled into the cup.

This was his last bag. But he would need to either visit the Blood Bank or go hunting soon.

He opened the microwave door, placed the mug in the center of the rotating glass tray. He closed the door, pushed a couple of buttons, hit START. He needed to take the chill off, get it close to body temp without overheating it. He had made that mistake before. Blood cells, if cooked too warm, would lyse. The red blood cells exploded, releasing all their hemoglobin, and the continued cooking left an inedible chocolate-colored gelatinous sludge.

The microwave went, *DING!* The Vampire pulled his mug out, wrapped cold dead hands around it. The warmth reminded him of what it felt like to be alive. To be human.

To be a man.

Being the weekend, the Asian markets were closed. He shuffled into the living room, plopped down on the sofa. He put his mug down on the coffee table, pushed a button on his laptop.

He read through his emails, typed terse responses. The Vampire finished quickly. He grabbed his mug, sipped the rapidly cooling blood.

What to do tonight?

He should go see Lottie. She was not doing well, and he knew what that meant. He wanted to spend as much time with her while he could. He considered calling Reggie, perhaps leave a message. Lottie's house was right down the street from the Vampire's apartment.

Still, he felt antsy, unable to focus. There was nothing overtly out of place in his life, yet this vague, nebulous sense of dread clung to him like a shroud.

He trudged back into the kitchen, rinsed out his mug. Placed it upside down on a dish towel. His brain fog clearing, he headed to his bedroom to dress. He chose underwear, of course. Socks. Slate gray pinstriped slacks, his favorite Italian leather shoes, a black silk T shirt.

The Vampire did love his clothes. Wearing unique, quality clothing was one of the few human pleasures he could still appreciate. After having been dead for over a century, he took his pleasure wherever he could.

He grabbed his heavy black leather bomber's jacket, threw it on. Being a walking corpse, the Vampire felt cold all the time.

His body did not generate any heat. Layering helped keep the cold out.

He strode out the front door, locked up. He lived in a high-income, low-crime neighborhood. But the Vampire knew that crime could happen anywhere, infest any neighborhood, then metastasize like cancer. The Vampire knew all this because a long time ago, he had been a criminal himself. Not just some street punk, either. By the time he was nineteen, he wore silk ties, tailored pinstripe suits, wingtip shoes, and enjoyed his status as an established member of the mob back in Hoboken.

His career choice had led him to be shot three times in the chest on a rainy night in a filthy alley by a traitorous member of his own crew. It had also led to a rash decision made by a dying and desperate young man, an impossible choice offered by she who became his Vampire Mother.

The Vampire stood as proof positive that a life of crime and violence did not end well. Sooner or later, you wound up in prison or dead. In his case, worse than dead.

Live by the sword; die by the sword.

It had been that way for thousands of years. It was still that way now, though many in modern society did not want to admit that, either for social or political reasons. But facts were facts, and facts did not care about time, place, politics, or societal norms because those things were fleeting, ephemeral, everchanging.

Facts were like the laws of nature. They simply *were.* Human behavior, with both its potential and pitfalls, was eternal.

Times change. People do not.

The Vampire silently made his way down stucco stairs flanked by twisted iron handrails. A red brick walkway at the bottom led to the concrete sidewalk. He turned left and headed north, moving deeper into the serene neighborhood.

He inhaled, breathing in the evening air. Part vampire instinct and part learned behavior, the night now carried new meaning with every sight, sound, smell, taste. Stimuli a human would have missed flooded his brain.

Someone in an Audi cruised by, yellow pools from its headlights reaching out for yards in front of it. A Rolling Stones song played on the sound system.

At least they had good taste in music.

The Vampire ducked between cars parallel parked at the curb, looked both ways. Though immortal, he was not impervious to injury and pain. He had no desire to get run over. Then he skipped into the street, skirted to the other side, hopped the curb.

Panicked rustling in the bushes at the corner of a nearby house. The Vampire's head swung that way, his vision penetrating the gloom and muddy shadow. A skunk scampered off down the side of the house and away from him, its tail fluffed and high in the air.

Another block and a half, he turned onto a walkway leading to Lottie's red brick home with hints of both Tudor and craftsman architecture. A strange blend of influences when one thought about it. The Vampire had bought the place for her with cash. It was the least he could do. After all, he had been partly responsible for what had happened at her old house when drug dealers had broken in, held her hostage, put a gun to her head.

Things had not ended well for them.

Nobody threatened his Lot-Lot and lived.

An LED motion sensor security light above the door snapped on. Lottie has assumed Kensington was so safe she did not need security. Both Reggie and the Vampire had convinced her that some low-key security measures were prudent. An elderly lady living alone could be an easy target for home invasion, even if her grandfather, an immortal creature of the night, lived only a couple of blocks away.

He stepped onto the stoop, rapped loudly. Lottie's hearing wasn't what it used to be. He waited, heard no immediate movement in response from inside. Seconds ticked by. He frowned behind his sunglasses. He rapped again, louder this time. Longer. More insistent.

More seconds ticked past. He had offered to arrange for a repairman to repair the broken doorbell. Lottie had waived him off, assuring him that there were some things she could do for herself, thank you very much.

That had been over three months ago.

He heard footfalls coming from the back of the house. Shuffling closer, getting louder. She must have been in the kitchen, which made sense. It was dinner time for her. He should have gone to the back in the first place.

He heard the floorboards creak, heard her heartbeat through the door. The lock twisted. The bolt slid back. The doorknob turned. The door swung wide.

And then Lottie filled in the doorway, childlike glee on her face. "Grandpa!"

The Vampire grinned and embraced her, squeezed her tight. "Oh, my little Lot-Lot," he whispered. He had known her since she was three. He had loved her since the day she was born.

"Come on inside," she smiled. She stepped back, allowing him room to enter. She shut the door behind him.

"Did I catch you at a bad time?" he asked.

"Not at all." She gave him a wave, then waddled deeper into the house. He followed.

The short hallway opened into a spacious kitchen, which had been remodeled in 1997. He had offered to pay for another remodel, but Lottie wouldn't have it. The kitchen functioned perfectly well the way it was. The stove worked, the refrigerator worked, the freezer worked. The dishwasher worked, too. That was her pride and joy. To finally live in a home with an automatic dishwasher was a dream come true.

"Make yourself at home," she said happily. She eased her bulk into a chair at the kitchen table. A half-eaten plate of food waited for her return.

The Vampire sat down.

"Can I get you anything?" she asked.

He smiled. "No, thank you." He noticed her hair. Almost completely silver now. Her clothes seemed tighter around her than before. Her lower legs, ankles, and tops of her feet were swollen, her dark African skin mottled with black rings. That was not a good sign. She wore open-toed sandals. Her toes were almost coal black.

Circulatory insufficiency in the lower limbs. A hallmark of the ravages of advanced, long-term diabetes.

"So, what brings you by?" she asked. She resumed eating a plate of chicken breast, potatoes, and sweet peas.

"I wanted to see how you were doing."

"Oh, I'm fine," she shrugged between mouthfuls.

"You are taking your medications?"

"Yes, Grandpa," The grin fell from her face. "Look, I'd never say this to Reggie, but I think I can talk to you."

"You can talk to me about anything."

"I'm dying" she stated flatly. "We both know I don't have much time left."

The Vampire simply nodded in agreement.

"I'm not afraid of it, but at the same time, I'm not in any hurry, either."

The Vampire grinned. He understood that.

"So, I take my meds and keep my doctor appointments."

"And how do you like your new doctor?"

"The endocrinologist?" she asked. "He's lovely. Wonderful bedside manner." She paused, then, "And he's certainly a handsome fellow. That doesn't hurt."

They both chuckled.

"How about you?"

"One night is pretty much like the next."

"Doesn't that ever get boring? The never-ending sameness of it all?"

The Vampire sat back in his chair, giving the question serious consideration. He removed his sunglasses, ran a hand down his pale face.

"Sometimes," he admitted.

"What do you do about it?"

"I seek diversion."

"Don't we all?"

The Vampire chuckled.

"Have you heard from Reggie?"

"Not lately," the Vampire answered. "He has been quite busy since his recent promotion."

Lottie nodded. "More money, more headaches, less time."

"Precisely."

Lottie pushed her finished plate away from her.

"So. What do you have planned for this evening?" the Vampire asked.

She heaved a great sigh. "Oh, I'm going to turn in early." She paused then, "What about you?"

"I seek… diversion."

CHAPTER SIX

Back in the chill night air, the Vampire walked home. His mind heaved and twisted with rapid-fire thoughts. He shoved bony hands into jacket pockets, drove fists down deep until they hit the bottom.

Lottie was unwell, had been unwell for months. Everyone knew it. But she had deteriorated since the last time he had seen her. He could smell the progression of her various medical conditions.

The Vampire's granddaughter, Lottie, his little Lot-Lot, was not long for this Earth.

Lottie was not interested in becoming a vampire. He had broached the subject tactfully when he realized how advanced her ailments were. She had been resolute in her desire to live out a normal life span, then "shrug off this mortal coil". Not only was this the natural and necessary course of human events, but Lottie believed in Heaven and was curious to see it.

And so, the Vampire's hands were effectively tied.

He had vowed to never force vampirism on anyone, especially her. In fact, he had never Turned anyone. Becoming a vampire had been his choice, and he would never think of Turning someone without their consent. Who was he to impose his lifestyle upon someone else?

Who was he to force his lifestyle choices on *anyone* else?

There it was again. That pesky moral compass raising its ugly head, forcing him to keep his nose out of things not his business.

He was still stewing when he got back to his building. He took a narrow brick path around the side, gliding like a specter through a metal gate and into the back alley.

His vampire eyes scanned the area, alert for danger. He checked the blind corners, all possible angles of attack.

Satisfied no danger lurked, he pressed a button on his key fob. The lights on his Lexus flashed once. A dull thump as the doors unlocked. He opened the driver's door, slid in as smooth as a wisp of smoke.

He slid the key into the ignition. One quick twist and the engine purred to life. Headlights snapped on automatically. He maneuvered out of his parking spot, inched down the alleyway towards Adams Avenue and the city beyond.

Reggie leaned back in his uncomfortable chair. At over thirty years old and no lumbar support, the chair had seen better says. It been manufactured via Government contract by the lowest bidder. It didn't belong in the squad room; it belonged in the bottom of a deep hole.

Night had fallen. The day shift was long gone. And here he was, obsessing over a new murder case.

Ramsey's case files lay open on the computer screen in front of him. There wasn't much to them yet. The autopsy was not yet completed. Nick had called the morgue and pulled some strings to expedite things.

Reggie poured over the crime scene photos. Ramsey had been a beautiful woman in life. In the photos, though, she was just a blood-streaked, pale slab of lifeless meat.

Empty eyes. Slack jaw. Limbs limp.

Ramsey Domingo had lost more than just her life. Her inner core, her being, her soul, call it what you wanted. Whatever it was within her that made Ramsey Domingo a unique, whole, and complete human being with sentience, vibrance, and feelings, with all her hopes and dreams for the future, had been stolen from her, just as she had been stolen from her family. Deliberately stolen by someone whose own soul was black and cruel and twisted and evil.

It made Reggie angry.

No. It made him fucking furious.

This was the kind of thing that had inspired him to join the force in the first place. Growing up poor in a low-income, high-crime neighborhood and living mostly hand-to-mouth, he had seen so many crimes go unsolved and unpunished because the cops were either incompetent or uncaring. By the time Reggie was in his mid-teens, he had decided he would never be incompetent or uncaring. Everyone – man, woman, black, white, rich, poor, straight, gay, transgender, it did not matter. They deserved equal protection and equal justice under the law. Not because they were rich or powerful or influential.

They deserved equal justice because they were *human beings*.

Reggie didn't care that Ramsey came from a rich family. He didn't care that Daddy had money and political connections going from the Mayor and City Council on up to the State legislature and the United States Congress.

Detective Reginald Downing didn't give a tinker's damn or two bat-craps about any of that.

This young woman had been murdered in a sadistic, ghoulish fashion by some animal completely devoid of empathy or compassion, and her spirit, her very *blood* cried out for justice.

Reggie heard mumbling coming from Nick's office. The door was closed so he couldn't hear the words, but he understood the tone. Someone was reading the lieutenant the riot act. Nick sat at his desk, phone to his ear, other hand pressed against his forehead above tightly shut eyes, mouth puckered into a thin line.

Then came the only sentence in the whole conversation Reggie could understand.

"Don't you fucking tell me how to do my Goddamn job, asshole!"

Nick slammed the phone down, pushed his chair away from the desk. Fuming, he struggled to regain control. When he finally calmed down, he heaved a great sigh, then rubbed his face in his hands.

He picked up the coffee mug resting on his desk. He downed a slug of low-quality police precinct coffee, with all the flavor and aroma of sulfuric acid. Disgusted, he slammed the cold cup back down on the desk.

Reggie watched as Nick stormed to the door, swung it open. He stepped out into the precinct squad room, breathed deeply like he was breathing fresh air for the first time in ages.

"Everything all right?" Reggie asked.

"I just interfaced with the Mayor's office," he explained as he got to Reggie's desk.

"It sounded like you told them to go fuck themselves."

He shrugged. "Yeah, I guess I did, didn't I?" A sly grin of satisfaction spread across his mouth.

"Yeah, but right now they're calling the Chief of Police," Reggie said, thinking tactically. "They'll be demanding your head on a plate."

"Fuck 'em," Nick responded.

"What will you tell the Chief?"

"Same thing I told them. The Mayor's office has no Goddamned business telling me how to investigate a case."

"They could fire you for insubordination."

"They could," Nick admitted quietly. "But they can't tell me what to do."

Reggie grinned. "See, this is why I like you. You don't take shit from anybody."

"I'm a forty-year-old gay Hispanic man who also happens to be a cop," Nick said. "When it comes to taking shit, I've already hit my lifetime quota."

Both men's attention drifted back to the case in front of them. Their eyes crawled over the crime scene photos again, even though they had scrutinized them a dozen times already. They would scrutinize them at least a hundred times more before the case was finished.

"What are you still doing here?"

The question caught Reggie off guard.

"Go home," Nick said. "Get some food, Get some sleep. You're going to need it."

Reggie nodded. He knew Nick was right. He stood up, stretched.

Nick's face brightened as if a new thought had come to him. "Oh, and by the way."

Reggie hated it when he said that.

"We've got a newly minted detective assigned here beginning tomorrow morning. She's working on this as her first assignment."

Reggie looked at Nick askance. "That's throwing him into the deep end of the pool, don't you think, Lieutenant?"

"*She* will do just fine," Nick responded, emphasizing her gender. "She practically aced her Detective Exam. Bring her up to speed."

Reggie felt like he had been poleaxed. "Lieutenant, I'm in the middle of one of the highest profile cases of my career."

"You've handled high-profile cases before," Nick said, referring to that drug cartel Reggie had almost singlehandedly taken down.

"I don't have time to train some snot-nosed, wet-behind-the-ear baby detective who probably thinks they're Dirty Harry."

"Supposedly she's a real firecracker, an up-and-comer. She's already impressed the higher ups."

"How'd she do that?"

"Graduated top of her Academy class, made several collars as a uni that resulted in felony convictions, youngest female to take the Detective Exam, and like I said, she scored higher than anyone in the history of the department."

"Okay," Reggie admitted, "so she sounds impressive on paper." His eyes bored into Nick's. "But can she handle herself under pressure? Has she ever been in a firefight? When the chips are down, can I trust her to cover my ass when we kick in a door?"

"You'll have to gauge that for yourself."

"I don't want her."

"Well, you got her, Detective," the lieutenant said. "Deal with it." He walked towards his office. "Get out of here," he shouted over his shoulder. "Go home. Get laid. That's an order."

The graveyard shift. How apropos.

The last place Charlie Simpkins wanted to be was at his J. O. B. Someone had once told him that the word "job" was an acronym – J.O.B. meant Just Over Broke. Charlie found truth and dark humor in that. He had bills to pay just like everybody else. His frustration arose from the fact that his J.O.B. interfered with his work.

His job at Center City Blood Bank should have been intellectually challenging. For anyone else, it probably would be. But the technical aspects of the work were the same, day in and day out. Or rather, night in and night out. The only time a practice or procedure changed was when they got a new piece of equipment or technology advanced significantly. Otherwise, the job became a colossal, repetitive bore.

Though not new to Blood Banking, he was new here. It was important work, something that saved people's lives. Not that he gave a rat's ass about that. But his technical skills were impeccable. Everyone knew that, even the people who didn't like him.

Like his boss, who was a TFB – Total Fucking Bitch.

The coworkers here seemed impressed because his results were accurate and turnaround times were fast. Everyone here who preferred the night shift often walked to the beat of a different drummer. So, his brand of crazy fit in. He was a freak who tried to act "normal", whatever that was.

Charlie had recognized Ramsey right away in the club. He had seen her photo plastered inside the window of his local bookstore. He knew she was a nonfiction writer of some weight with an agent, a publisher, an attorney, a publicist, all that stuff.

Charlie detested nonfiction, especially that "True Crime" stuff. He had read several, and he had never found any of them to be "true". Details always got altered, tweaked, reworked, edited, or smoothed out, covered over, watered down, or deleted entirely to make the book "more commercial" for public consumption.

Never let the truth get in the way of a good story.

Money-grubbing vultures.

If one were forced to change the truth into narrative nonfiction so it read like a novel, then why not just write a fucking novel? What was the point of true crime if it wasn't true?

Charlie huffed a sigh. He needed to keep it together here at work. He needed to appear at least close to normal. No sense alarming his co-workers.

Not yet.

His true nature would surface eventually. It always did. He had been fired so many times, his resume looked shabby. He was trouble and hiring managers knew it. They could smell it on him. But the City Center Blood Bank was critically short-staffed and desperate for qualified, licensed help.

Lucky break for him.

He had been out of work for months and had exhausted his savings. Disowned by his family at eighteen for his escalating antisocial behavior (he had beaten a kid unconscious in high school and had bitten his ear off), he had never asked them for anything since. He had never called, never sent a card on holidays or birthdays. In turn they ignored his very existence, which suited Charlie just fine.

They still lived in the same house. Still had the same landline phone number. They had no idea where he was or what his nocturnal pursuits had grown into. No idea of what he was searching for.

This probably ate away at his mom. Good. Served her right. He had never felt close to her. Despite her best efforts, she had never been able to connect with him even as a child. And she never defended him with his father. His father, an aloof and emotionally distant man, probably couldn't care less. Probably never mentioned his son's name, never really thought about it.

"Nothin' to talk about," he could hear his father bark out if his mom brought it up.

That was the Old Man.

As far as Charlie was concerned, they were already dead. Both retired, both aged and sickly. One foot in the grave. It wouldn't really be murder if he went home and killed them both. He would be helping them, doing them a favor.

Nah, fuck that.

He didn't owe them any favors.

The cruelest thing to do was to do nothing. To take no action *is* an action. Let them grow older, sicker, inching ever closer towards death never knowing what became of their only son.

They deserved no better.

Charlie proceeded through his work efficiently, quietly. Give him a task, pile on the work, then leave him alone. He would complete the work to meet or exceed all Government regulations and Federal laws.

Label test tubes; put them in a rack. Drops of blood added. Chemical reagents added. A timed reaction observed and quantified. The work was not particularly creative. But the technique, repeated over and over, became ritualistic.

Charlie had always gravitated towards ritualistic behavior, even as a child. Repetition brought proficiency. Proficiency eliminated errors. Once proficiency was achieved, the task could be accurately performed practically through muscle memory.

If you had to think about it, you were doing something wrong.

The Vampire parked at the corner of 6th and G. He got out, stretched, locked his Lexus, and glided away. He did not bother to look back as the lights flashed and the activated alarm chirped its warning. He walked towards 4th Avenue.
Barely ten thirty. Still early, especially for a weekend night.
The crowds were getting thicker as people poured out of restaurants and bars. Some were headed to the nearby movie theater to catch a late screening. Some headed to other bars and clubs. Others were simply heading home. Their auras emanated off them, some dim and muted, some in flashes of garish color only he could see.
Most of them were decent people or at least harmless. A good number thought they were badass but were not. Some truly were. And then some, very few, were evil. True predators, wolves amongst the sheep.
They all paled in comparison to the immortal monster moving unnoticed amongst them.
The Vampire had not come for them. He was not a capricious creature. He never succumbed to whims or flights of fancy. He had a reason behind everything he did, motivation behind every act either performed or not performed.
That continuing sense of unease and dread that had never left and had become intolerable. He had attempted to push it. Mentor his protégés. Visit Lot-Lot. With those responsibilities fulfilled, he could investigate this preternatural sense of doom.
He had followed it here into the Gaslamp District, a hound following a scent. The feeling was stronger here. He moved west. The feeling grew stronger still.
Hyperalert and tense, the Vampire's impulse for high-order violence pulled tight, a taut spring wanting more than anything to be sprung.
Downtown revelers swelled and surged around him, parting in front of him as he moved, then closing behind him like the

wake of a ship at sea. None of them had any idea of what moved among them, otherwise they would have run for their lives.

With a few notable exceptions, the Vampire still considered most humans as food. The sidewalk looked like a walking buffet to him. Ordinarily, he would choose someone with a particularly evil or criminal aura, find an excuse to touch or bump into them. Once his bare skin touched theirs, he would see their soul, their past, their dirty secrets. Then he would track them, close in for the kill.

The Vampire's kills tended to get... *messy*.

That sense of impending doom hung over him like the Sword of Damocles. The blade was descending, inching closer towards his neck. He stood at 4th and G beneath the large streetlight.

Something was terribly wrong. The delicate balance of living death in the Vampire's world had been upset. Tilted. This led to one simple, inescapable conclusion.

The Vampire was in mortal danger.

His eyes settled on a neon sign above the heavy metal door across the street and up the block. Pale blue letters glowed against rusty red bricks, spelled out S-P-L-I-N-T-E-R.

A predatory anger arose. He could see malevolence wafting out from around the edges of the door. No one else could, of course. Human senses were dull and limited compared to his.

But through a revulsion that threatened to overwhelm him, malevolence shimmered like an illusion in the desert. It called to him, a siren's song. His jaw clenched. His eyes narrowed behind his shades. His chest heaved.

There was another vampire here. In this club. In his town.

In his territory!

He would defend his territory, his hunting grounds, to the death if need be. San Diego was *his* town, and he would stop at nothing to drive the intruder out.

It was the Vampire Way.

Pure predator now, he stepped to the curb, swiveled his head left and right, from side to side, waiting. The traffic light changed. Southbound cars and trucks stopped. The white WALK indicator appeared. He stalked forward, crossing the street.

Kong stood by the door, waiting for the bartender downstairs to talk into his earpiece and let him know when to let more people in. He had worked here several years now, all the way back to when the club was called FETISH, not SPLINTER. Maybe he was getting old, but he was growing weary of this line of work. It was certainly not what he thought he would do when he was a kid. It certainly was not what he wanted to be doing now. It paid the bills, but that was it.

About twenty-five people waited to get in dressed in leather, corsets, combat boots, stiletto heels and heavy makeup. He recognized the regulars by sight. Most of them were simply attractive strangers. Over time, their faces melded together.

Yet some rare individuals made such an impression that even after just one meeting, Kong remembered them vividly.

Movement at the corner of his eye. Someone striding forward out of the fog, ignoring the line. Short, slight, dark lank hair that clung to a pasty forehead like seaweed. Thin mouth. Pointed chin.

And those Goddamned sunglasses.

Oh my God.

Fear spread throughout his enormous body. Sweat popped on his forehead and upper lip. Stains formed on his shirt at the armpits. It was all he could do to keep from pissing himself right there.

People in the line protested as the Vampire stormed forward past them, telling the Vampire where the line was. They did not even exist to him. He remembered this club when it went by a different name. He remembered the bouncer. This poor shlub had actually tried to interfere with the Vampire's activities one night.

The consequences had been dire for him.

Kong towered over the Vampire but gave thought to running away. The Vampire stopped in front of him less than three feet away.

Kong instinctively massaged the wrist this deceptively powerful man had snapped like a twig.

The vampire said. "It seems I made a lasting impression."

"What do you want?" Kong finally managed to croak out.

"To enter."

The Vampire smelled Kong's fear rise.

"I, uh, I can't do that." Fear. Nearly panic.

The Vampire took one step forward.

Kong took a step back, put his hands up in front of him. "Please. I can't."

"Which wrist shall I break tonight?" the Vampire growled.

Kong waved the undead thing in front of him towards the door. He looked past the Vampire. The unruly crowd rushed the velvet rope, threatening to become a mob.

The Vampire pulled the door open and slipped inside. He descended the concrete stairs slowly, one hand absently wrapped around the iron safety railing. Canned music blaring over speakers. A band setting up onstage in the far end. The bar at the bottom of the stairs, a dancefloor between the bar and the stage. Tables to the left. Booths further back, extending into a specially constructed Grotto. Everything bathed in blue light. Bright enough for humans to see, but also dark enough to project a certain ambience.

The Vampire saw everyone's aura's wafting off their bodies. Nothing too extraordinary. Even for humans dressed like vampires, they were surprisingly sedate under the skin.

He remembered the last time he was here. He had slaughtered two people out back who wanted to play dangerous gay BDSM games with him. But he had not killed them because they were gay. The undead carried no bias about gay, straight, or any combination thereof. Nor was it because they were into kinky sex. Other than an occasional intellectual curiosity, he just did not care one way or the other.

No, the Vampire had killed them because he had been hungry, and with evil emanations floating off their bodies like the stink off decayed carrion, they had tried to set him up as their victim.

That mistake had proven fatal for them.

He prowled forward, away from the concrete staircase and the bar where two bartenders poured watered-down drinks for thirsty clientele.

His head swiveled to the right, towards a hallway that resembled a tunnel. He could make out the metal door at the end that opened onto the loading bay. He knew the two doors on the righthand side were bathrooms.

No vampire lurking in that direction.

He swiveled back to front, scanned the room. All human, here for the music, booze, good times, and sex. He noticed two separate males who were into some deviant kinks. Ordinarily, he would have picked one, isolated him from the herd, then killed him.

Eddie.

The Vampire recoiled in shock. What was that? Someone calling his name. He had not heard it with his supernaturally sensitive hearing. It had simply materialized inside his consciousness.

He scanned the room with a renewed intensity. Humans milled about, passing him on all sides. Some to the bar, some to the bathroom, some heading back to tables and darkened booths. His attention zeroed in on the booths against the wall, then drifted along, moving from the main floor up to the VIP section.

The Grotto.

Steeling himself, the Vampire glided gracefully across the main floor. He moved like a river winding and turning, seeking the path of least resistance as he flowed towards his destination. He could feel eyes burning through him. They had seen him first.

This put him at a disadvantage.

The Vampire climbed the steps slowly. Deliberately. Made it to the top. He moved forward one pace, looked around.

There she was, sitting alone in the back booth. Black eyes, silver hair, ebony bloodless skin. Death black dress, flowing over small breasts and waifish body to feet sheathed in stiletto heels.

An otherworldly beauty.

Compelling.

Their eyes locked. She smiled. No hint of aggression. She ticked her head, made a closing motion with her fingers, inviting him to join her.

His Vampire Mother.

CHAPTER SEVEN

"Why are you here?"

The Vampire's maker smiled. Not affectionate.

"Hello to you, too," she responded.

The Vampire grimaced, outwardly calm while dealing with conflicting emotions. They were in public. If not, this would go a lot differently. Both knew that.

The Vampire slid into the booth across from her uninvited.

"You did not answer my question."

"Is this your territory?" A question, a challenge.

The Vampire removed his sunglasses, leaned forward.

"For over sixty years."

"Look at you," she breathed, beaming with pride. "Over a century and still thriving."

The Vampire's unblinking eyes burned into her.

"I am simply here by chance," she stated at last.

"You have entered my territory without my consent. You know the Vampire Way. "You should have made yourself known to me at once."

"I did not know this was your territory, she repeated. "And as far as my making myself known," she spread her arms, "here I am."

The Vampire wanted to twist her head off her body.

"Because you are my Vampire Mother, I shall show you this courtesy," he said. "I shall say this only once."

"I'm breathless with anticipation."

"The Vampire knew right then. He refused to take her bait. "You came here without permission, and you flaunt the Vampire rules, and you mock me. I should kill you right now."

The smile faded from her face. "Why don't you?"

The Vampire knew better than to lose his temper in public. When one loses one's temper, he reminded himself, one loses control of the situation.

But did he have control of this situation?

The Vampire pushed himself sideways, sliding out of the booth. He stood, grabbed his sunglasses.

"You are not welcome here." His voice was glass shards and gravel. "Leave my territory. Do you understand?"

"Yes."

"By the way," he said, "what is your name?"

After a moment, she said, "Maya."

"Maya," the Vampire repeated softly. "Maya, I guarantee you safe passage out of my city."

"What if I decide to stay?"

The Vampire's mouth tightened. "Then we have a problem."

"You're telling me an area of over three million people isn't big enough for the both of us?"

"You heard me."

There.

The line had been drawn.

The Vampire walked away, found himself moving through the human masses. He turned right at the bar, ascended the concrete stairs. Then he was at the top, flinging the door open so hard it swung around and crashed into the wall. Tiny pieces of brick and mortar chipped off the façade and drifted like pale silt to the sidewalk.

The people outside gave a collective gasp as the Vampire emerged. Even Kong took a step back, giving him a wide berth.

The Vampire ignored them all. He had darker things on his mind. Bigger fish to fry. He moved through the crosswalk as his mind raced ahead considering different contingencies and their consequences.

On the other side, the Vampire stopped as if suddenly frozen into place. He turned back towards the way he came. His saw on the neon sign, then bis eyes drifted upwards to the roof. His tongue flicked across sharp fangs.

Maya gazed down from the roof, looking directly at him. She attempted a disarming smile. The Vampire showed his teeth. Maya's smile faded.

The Vampire stalked off. Maya watched him go until he was swallowed up by fog and darkness.

The new day dawned gray and overcast. Fog clung to the coastline. East County cities woke to sunshine. But the Gaslamp and downtown were shrouded in mist. Condensation beaded on every exposed surface.

Reggie woke up early, his mind already on the case. He went through his morning routine. He dressed, checked his firearm and extra ammo, shrugged into his shoulder holster, threw on a jacket. Poured his coffee, rode the elevator down alone.

He stepped outside, checked his watch then walked briskly. He was three minutes behind schedule and had not eaten. Normally, he would have stopped for a breakfast burrito.

Not this morning.

He rubbed his hand across his forehead, gulped coffee from one of his mugs. With a furrowed brow and a heavy heart, he walked on. Senseless murder could dampen anyone's mood.

He passed improvised lean-tos at the sides of buildings, undulating oceans of low blue tents in vacant lots. The most unfortunate slept exposed or curled up in doorway recesses.

Private organizations and various churches banded together to do what they could, and certain Government agencies like Social Security and HHS were mandated to help, but the result was as depressing as it was inevitable.

With crime, drug use, and mental illness rampant among the homeless, there simply were not enough resources to solve the problem. Some individuals got off the streets, but they were few and far between.

Politicians, man.

He hopped across the trolley tracks to the other side of the street, turned a corner. By the time he made it to the precinct, his mind was back in the game. Reggie Downing had a murderer to catch.

The first thing he noticed as he walked inside was that Nick was not at his desk. The office was empty, the door closed, the lights off.

The second thing he noticed was a woman.

An incredibly attractive one at that. Red wavy hair, intelligent green eyes, plump lips, alabaster skin. Obviously a cop, with her firearm strapped to her right hip. He gauged her to be around five foot two, around a hundred and fifteen, maybe a hundred and twenty pounds.

She looked vaguely familiar. He had seen her before but couldn't remember when or where.

He detested breaking in newbies. He had done it before, and he found it about as pleasant as drinking warm rhino piss.

As Lead Detective, though, training newbies was a collateral duty whether he liked it or not. He did not want a new detective getting killed the first day on the job or doing something stupid/illegal that allowed some guilty as hell scumbag to walk on a technicality. That embarrassed the department, stymied careers, and made for months of bad PR.

He glanced towards the newbie as he set both mugs down, peeled his jacket off. She sat on a bench against the wall, alert. Those keen eyes of hers took everything in. Nothing would pass her by unnoticed. And her eyes trained on Reggie, following every move as he hung his jacket across the back of his chair.

He sat down, stared directly at her from across the room. Taking this as a sign, she rose and walked towards him, back straight, shoulders squared.

"Detective Downing?"

"That's the rumor."

"I'm Detective Valerie Wahl."

He stood to his feet, put his hand out. They shook. She had a firm grip. He liked that.

"Pleased to meet you, Detective."

"We've met once before. About five years ago. I was a rookie."

"What case?"

"A massacre at your old apartment."

Now Reggie remembered. He, Nick, his great, great Grandfather, and Captain Horn had engaged in a firefight against world-class mercenaries working for a drug cartel. Of course, Grandpa Eddie had not used a gun during the melee.

Grandpa Eddie had no need for one.

Things had ended badly for the mercs.

"You stood guard outside the apartment."

She nodded.

Reggie realized she was still standing.

"Call me Reggie. Let's get you settled in."

"Reggie," she repeated. "I like that. And please, call me Val."

The ice was now officially broken.

"Okay, Val." Reggie pointed to an empty desk right beside his. "Park yourself there."

Valerie inspected her new digs. "Nice," she said. "Was this place decorated by the lowest bidder?"

Reggie grinned. "Probably."

He was liking her more and more.

She sat down in her chair, placed her hands flat on the level desk surface in front of her. He watched her inhale, hold it, then exhale. A satisfied smile crossed her lips, and she was radiant.

Reggie knew that feeling, that sense of accomplishment, that sense that one had *arrived*. That sublime satisfaction one feels when a long-sought goal finally becomes achieved after months or years of hard work.

Reggie remembered one of those motivational quotes he had read once.

Do the things that others are not willing to do, and you will achieve the things that other people never achieve.

Making detective was a career milestone, something not every cop achieved. He had felt the same sublime satisfaction himself.

"Enjoy it," he said. "You earned it. But I must warn you, we're dropping you into the meat grinder right off the bat."

"Wouldn't want it any other way."

Reggie wondered if she would still feel that way tomorrow.

The rear precinct door opened. Nick entered, looking like he had not slept. Reggie did not envy him the Lieutenant's chair. Not only was he under the normal pressure to solve crimes and make arrests that resulted in convictions, now he oversaw every officer in the precinct. What they did and how they did it now became a reflection of his fitness to lead.

Nick was now held to a higher standard for the success or failures of anyone under his supervision. If an officer failed to close a case, made a procedural gaffe, or – God forbid! – did something illegal, it was Nick's head on the chopping block right alongside the offending officer.

Such was the nature of leadership.

"Boss Man just arrived."

Valerie turned her head, saw Nick lumber inside his office. She continued watching as he removed his coat, rub his face with both hands, then sit down and fire up his computer.

"Looks like he's already having a bad day."

Nick looked their way, motioned to them. They headed his way.

"Close the door, please," Nick said to Reggie as he and Valerie entered. Reggie closed the door. Nick stood.

"Lieutenant Nick Castle."

"Valerie Wahl," she replied, shaking his hand. "Pleased to meet you."

"Actually, she was telling me you two have already met," Reggie said.

"Oh really?" Nick seemed genuinely surprised.

"About five years ago. That shootout at Detective Downing's old apartment."

"Ah. Big case," he reminisced. "A career maker. It led to promotions for both of us."

"What happened to the big guy? Captain Horn?"

"Morris Horn. He retired. He's a private detective now."

Valerie nodded, taking all this new information on board.

"You ready to get your hands dirty?" Nick asked.

"Sure thing."

Nick's face was dead serious. "I hope so," he said. "Because we've got a doozy, and I don't have the manpower to cover for you if you're don't bring your A-game."

She looked Lieutenant Castle dead in the eye. "I *always* bring my A-game, sir."

Nick grinned knowingly. "I heard that about you."

She looked confused.

"I talked with every Watch Commander, every Sergeant, and every Field Training Officer you ever had," he stated. "I even talked to your Academy instructors." He paused, then, "You know what they all told me?"

She shook her head, raised her hands palms upwards.

"They all said you were smart and capable. Your marksmanship is spot on, you know how to go through a door, and you know how to deescalate."

She made no reply.

"They also said your admin skills are spot on," he continued. "That's good because everything here is detail oriented. The smallest detail might be the thing that leads to a conviction. Work your cases, pay attention, and follow all protocols and procedures to the letter. I don't want some scumbag getting off because we cut a corner or missed something." He paused for effect. "Nothing in this job is trivial."

She nodded solemnly. "Yes sir."

"Any questions before we start?"

She shook her head.

"Let's get to work."

Moments later, the three of them stood before a large pin-up board approximately four feet high by seven feet across. The portable wall stood high on two wooden legs adorned with wheels. Several gruesome photos hung on the wall, all the victims grayish from blood loss. No bruising where blood had settled in the back or front of their bodies. There had simply not been enough blood left to pool.

"Okay," Nick opened. "Reggie. What do we know so far?"

Reggie stepped closer to the board, began pointing to various photos as he spoke. "We have three victims who were last seen in or near the Goth club SPLINTER."

"Vampire Goth," Valerie said.

Reggie looked perplexed. "What?"

"Vampire Goth," she reiterated. "Splinter caters to a special subculture within the larger Goth community."

Silence in the room.

"Go ahead, Val," Nick said. "You're among friends. Speak freely."

"Most Goths are disenfranchised teens and young adults who dress up in black Edwardian clothing and spiked heels, get together to feel a connection, a sense of community they don't feel anywhere else. They listen to Death Metal and get drunk, get high, get laid."

"So, it's a phase they're going through?" Nick asked.

"Mostly," she said. "But some get deep in it, move to a really dark place."

"You sound like you speak from experience," Reggie observed.

"I dabbled when I was a kid," she admitted. "Never got high. I was always afraid of doing drugs."

"And the other stuff?"

"Oh sure," she replied. "Lasted about eighteen months for me. Then I found direction and moved on."

Reggie rubbed a finger in the space between his nose and upper lip. Nick simply appeared to be deep in thought. Valerie looked back and forth between the two of them.

"What?" she asked.

"Have you ever worn a wire? Gone undercover?" Nick asked.

"Not yet."

"Depending on how this thing plays out, we might send you in."

"Whatever it takes," she stated.

Both Reggie and Nick were impressed. Valerie had the makings of a fine detective.

Nick opened the folder in front of him. More photos, police reports. He looked through the reports for Ramsey.

"No toxicology on Ramsey Domingo?"

"Not yet," Reggie said. "But they are fast-tracking."

Nick shuffled reports, came up with the autopsy reports on the other two. "What do we know about these other two?"

Reggie pointed again. "First victim. Robert Saget. White male, twenty-four years old. Worked in the back warehouse at an auto parts store filling online orders. His manager said he was a quiet guy, didn't talk much."

"Any friends at work?"

Reggie shook his head. "He gave off a weird vibe. They never warmed up to him."

"Personality disorder?" Nick suggested.

"No history of mental illness," Reggie countered.

"So, he was weird," Valerie chimed in. "Sort of antisocial." She shrugged. "He fits the profile."

"What profile?"

"The kind of person who gravitates to the Goth scene." She paused, then, "Did he ever act aggressively at work? Ever arrested for assault?"

Reggie grinned knowingly. "You're good," he said. "The answer is yes. He had trouble with the law starting in high school. He got arrested when he was a senior. He beat someone so bad he gave the poor kid a concussion. The judge gave him anger management classes and community service."

"Didn't do any good?"

"He bounced around, worked dead-end, minimum wage jobs. Kept getting into trouble. Low-level stuff. He didn't deserve this." Reggie pointed to the photo of Robert Saget's pale bloodless corpse with those dark, dull glassy eyes staring off into eternity.

"Next," Reggie pointed to the next victim, "is Althea Robinson." The main photo showed a partly nude young Black woman, probably younger than Valerie, staring upwards with the same two puncture wounds on her neck.

"Althea was a Political Science major at SDSU," Reggie said, referring to San Diego State University. "Nothing indicates she was hardcore Goth. Academic overachiever. Graduated high school Valedictorian and was carrying a 3.98 grade point average in college. She had a bright future ahead of her."

"Anything connecting these two, other than their deaths?"

Reggie shook his head. "No evidence they ever even met."

"Toxicology?" Valerie asked.

"Saget had a laundry list of illegal substances in his blood," Reggie answered her. "Althea Robinson had traces of alcohol, but not over the legal limit. No other drugs."

He scanned to the bottom of the page, frowned. Nick noticed. Reggie put his finger on a line near the bottom, flipped the page to see the next, then let the page to fall back into place.

"What is it? Nick asked.

"It says here Saget had traces of Ketamine in his blood."

"That's one of the date rape drugs, isn't it?"

"Ketamine is a powerful sedative and anesthetic." Valerie paused, seeing both men were listening. "It induces a trancelike state that often includes a dissociative episode that the victim may not even remember later on."

"So how does the killer administer it? Slip it into their drink at the club?"

"Too risky. Someone at the next table could see him." She shook her head. "No, he's doing something else."

"Like what?"

"Were there any other puncture found anywhere on the bodies?"

Reggie flipped through the pages. Then he looked up, surprised. "Yeah. Both had single tiny punctures on the backs of their left shoulders."

"Tiny like a hypodermic needle?" Nick asked.

"Could be."

"That's how he's doing it," Valerie said. "He's stabbing them in the back – literally – with a syringe full of Ketamine.

"How long would it take for the drug to take effect?"

"Injected like this? Seconds," she replied.

"Okay," Nick said to Reggie. "Continue."

"And now we have Ramsey Domingo," Reggie said.

Valerie felt the atmosphere in the room get heavier.

"What?" she asked.

Nick sighed heavily. "I have a moral and ethical obligation to make a disclosure here," he said. He pointed to Reggie. "I think you already suspect." He swallowed, sighed again. "I know the Domingo family."

"How close are you?"

"It's complicated," Nick parried. "The important thing is, Ramsey's death brings attention."

Valerie grunted softly, stared hard at the photos. She rubbed her chin.

"This looks like the work of a serial killer who has found his sweet spot."

Nick looked at her. "Meaning?"

"These aren't his first kills. There may be previous homicides with slightly different M.O.'s by the same killer."

A birdlike chirp rang from Reggie's computer. He walked over, opened an email.

"Toxicology on Ramsland Domingo," Reggie reported. "Alcohol, not much over the legal limit. Oh, and… ketamine," Reggie answered.

"Any needle punctures other than the neck?" Valerie asked.

"Jesus Christ," Reggie muttered. "Posterior aspect of the left shoulder."

"All right then," Nick said. "We know there's a serial killer, we know where he's hunting, and how he's killing." He pursed his lips. "We also know he is left-handed."

"We do?" Valerie asked.

"Turn around." She did. He inched forward, curled his left hand into a fist. "Imagine I'm holding a syringe in my hand." He brought the fist forward and down, replicating an arc. He lightly touched the back of her left shoulder. "If he had his thumb on the plunger, he would already be injecting the ketamine into his victims before they even felt the needle."

Both Valerie and Reggie thought this over. It made sense.

"All right," Nick said, fully in command again. "Valerie, run your hunch down. Find out when and where our killer got started."

"Got it." She turned and headed for her desk.

"Reggie. My office."

They walked inside. Nick closed the door. Then he rounded his desk, sat down in his high-backed chair.

"Someone is out there playing vampire."

"This isn't Grandpa Eddie."

"I know. But he might be able to provide perspective."

"You want him brought in on this?"

"He might see things we don't."

"Can't argue with that."

"I'm thinking about calling in another outside consultant."

This surprised Reggie. "Who?"

"Morris Horn."

Reggie grinned. "Getting the band back together?"

"This is the biggest and the most dangerous challenge we've faced since the drug cartel."

The phone rang just then. Nick leaned over, read the Caller I.D. he closed his eyes and shook his head. "Chief of Police," Nick breathed.

"I'll leave you to it."

"Gee. Thanks."

Reggie moved to the door, opened it. Just as he stepped through, Nick picked up the receiver and punched a button.

Just before the door closed behind him, Reggie heard, "Good morning, Chief. What can I do for you?"

Journal entry, February 03

MAYA.

My Vampire Mother. She Who Made Me.

I had never known her name until last night. And I do not know if that is her given name, an ongoing alias, or something she made up specifically for me. I suppose it does not really matter. At least I have something to call her.

Her motives are not altruistic. She knew I was here and intruding on my territory was not accidental. She was not surprised by my presence.

She knew I was here.

She will not move on. She whisked into my town to establish her own territory, her claims to the contrary be damned. And while it is true that there is, in theory, plenty of room for two vampires, she incensed me with her haughty manner.

I despise arrogant, entitled people, either living or dead.

She must leave my territory. If not of her own volition, then by whatever force is necessary. Even deadly force if need be.

Maya is my Vampire Mother. That is supposed to mean something, I know. But she never took time with own Vampire Son. She only stayed one night, taught me the barest of minimums -- to feed and avoid the sun. Then she abandoned me to my wits, never to darken my door again until this night.

She thinks that because she is my Vampire Mother, I owe her. But when all is said and done, when I take everything she has done (and NOT done) into account, she burned her bridges with me long ago.

I owe her nothing.

CHAPTER EIGHT

Alejandro Domingo sat in his beach house gazing west through the immense, immaculately clean window. He watched the sun slide down the sky. Spectacular colors exploded across the horizon. Pinks morphed into purples; oranges deepened to reds. Blues sunk into iron gray and then black. The shoreline below splashed its eternal froth. The azure waters of day slid towards the inky blue-black of night.

He saw all of it.

He appreciated none of it.

His clothes cost more than most people made in a month. Hell, his shoes cost more than most people made in a week.

So what?

The house cost more than most people made in a lifetime. Alejandro was worth more than most of the so-called "one percent".

For all the good that did him now.

He had inherited his father's business, which his father had inherited from his own father. Agricultural land, initially. They were a long line of farmers and farm workers. His father had bought more land over time in both in the Imperial and San Joaquin valleys, expanding the empire.

The family had prospered.

The problem with that business model was that in years with poor crop yields, the business lost money. In a few bad years, the business had "taken a bath", as his father would say. So, they could be up one year and down the next, always one bad season away from bankruptcy.

Born with a head for numbers and a business acumen far beyond what his father and grandfather possessed, Alejandro had always known his future: high school, college with a degree in business with a minor in Economics, then expand the family business. It was after a few years working in the business when he had first suggested to his father that a change in the business model might be in order.

Intrigued, his father had asked for a presentation. Alejandro had prepared a PowerPoint presentation he projected onto a blank wall from his laptop. He gave a detailed SWOT analysis (Strengths, Weaknesses, Opportunities, and Threats) for both the current business model, and the one Alejandro proposed.

His father told him he would consider it, then never said another word about it.

Alejandro was the only son that his father claimed. There had been women over the years who had claimed to be mothers to illegitimate children. Alejandro knew his father had engaged in trysts both before and after his mother died. But without DNA or any other kind of admissible evidence, he simply denied all. If one of them pushed the issue, he reminded them of his money, his power, his lawyers.

That, along with a surreptitious envelope stuffed with cash, usually shut them up. But Alejandro was the only son born of his father's wife.

The Old Man had been old-school about that.

As CEO, Alejandro had wasted no time embarking on his plan for the company. With those years when the crops sucked, or commodities prices fell… well, there *HAD* to be a better way to make money in agriculture.

Alejandro found it. A company based in Argentina owned vast tracts of land throughout South America and leased it to farmers and ranchers. The farmers and ranchers took the risk. By owning the land and charging a rental or lease, the company got paid no matter how much or how little the farmers or ranchers profited.

Alejandro had called a meeting with his executives. One of them had attempted to argue with him, Alejandro had told him to get on board or shut up. When the executive had become insubordinate, Alejandro fired him on the spot.

All the other execs were aghast. Alejandro calmly explained he would not allow his authority to be challenged. Ever. If anyone had a concern, they should approach him in private to air their grievances. But make no mistake about it: now that he was in charge, the old way of doing things was *over*.

From now on, it was Alejandro's way or the highway.

Three executives, old men loyal to his father, quit immediately. Four more resigned, retired, or got fired by the end of the week. Then Alejandro had set about bringing in new blood, young smart executives on an upward trajectory in their careers.

Exactly the kind of people Alejandro wanted. Push the Old Guard aside if they couldn't keep up. Evolve, or go extinct.

In the years since, Alejandro's vision had flourished beyond his wildest dreams. The company had grown by leaps and bounds. Switching over to leasing the land they already owned had been simple enough. Buying tracts of land had not been much harder. Finding tenants had not been difficult as Alejandro had secretly feared. Money flowed in steadily month after month, year after year.

The company bought a couple of bankrupt wineries in the Napa Valley, then turned right around and leased the wineries right back to the very people who had gone bankrupt. It was his idea to build guest accommodations so people could visit the wineries and stay overnight, over a weekend. The longer they stayed, the more wine they drank, the more food they ate, the more money they spent, and all that added to the company's bottom line.

The last great expansion had come during the Great Recession in 2009.

By that time, Alejandro already owned vast tracts of land in California, Oregon, and Washington. All of farmland and vineyards. When the real estate market collapsed, even his business contracted. But instead of retreating to a defensive position as his CFO had counselled, Alejandro bought vast tracts of prime ranchland in Texas, Colorado, and Wyoming. Lessees were a bit more difficult to come by as money, but demand for food never waned. People had to eat in both good times and bad.

But right now, none of that meant anything to him.

Like his father before him, Alejandro's wife, Rachael – whom he had always affectionately called "Raquel" -- had died young. Unlike his mother, Rachael had died in a head-on collision with a drunk driver.

The marriage had largely been one of convenience and had cemented two of California's most powerful and influential Hispanic families. Both families amassed more wealth and power through the pairing.

Alejandro and Rachael had liked each other well enough and had always gotten along, but the relationship had been largely platonic. Neither loved the other in the way a man and woman were supposed to. Both had engaged in affairs. As long as it was kept discreet and out of the media, neither cared much what the other did.

Ramsey's conception had been due to pressure heaped upon them by both families. Coming from a devoted Roman Catholic background, it had been strongly felt that Alejandro and Rachael (Raquel!) needed to have a child to consider the marriage truly blessed.

What Alejandro never could have known at the time, was the absolute joy he felt upon becoming a father. He adored his daughter from the moment he held her in his arms and those little eyes had opened to briefly look at him before closing again.

His love for Ramsey grew as she got older. And much to his own surprise, he found himself becoming a doting father. Rachael sometimes scolded him about spoiling her, but he did not care.

Ramsey always had her own room, the best clothes, the finest toys. She attended the best schools. No low-education public schools surrounded by apathetic students, defeated teachers, clueless administrators, crumbling buildings, and antiquated infrastructure for his little girl, oh no. She attended the finest private academy in San Diego, a Catholic all-girls academy located just down the road in La Jolla. Most days, he drove her to school himself. Rachael picked her up in the afternoons. The arrangement had worked well through high school graduation. Then she took off for college at SDSU.

He had been dismayed by her choice of majors. No business degree, no real estate, no Economics major, nothing that would prepare her to run the family business one day. Her argument had been that she had grown up in the family business, knew enough basic business principles from growing up in his house and working at the offices during summer vacations since she was sixteen. She had promised to work there during summer semesters at college. Her final argument was that she would not run the company by herself. She would have an entire suite of C-level executives and attorneys to advise and counsel her.

So, he had acquiesced to her Journalism degree. She burned to write articles and books to impact peoples' lives and raise awareness. And when he had asked "raise what awareness?", she had responded, whatever she was writing about.

How could he argue with that? He had always wanted to make money and be rich. And he had done that. His little girl wanted to change the world, make it a better place. Who was he to stand in her way?

And now, just like that, she was dead.

What the hell am I supposed to do now? he wondered, sitting in his chair in his expensive shoes, expensive clothes, in a hollow, empty expensive house, none of which meant a damn thing to him anymore.

It wasn't right. It wasn't *fair!* No parent should ever have to bury their child. It went against the natural order of things.

The sun outside dropped below the horizon, until even the arced glow dissolved into black sky and twinkling stars.

The beauty of nature's spectacular show was lost on him. Just a vast darkness now, the perfect metaphor for the darkness into which he had sunk and the emptiness from which he feared he might never escape.

He did not hear Pepe creep up to him around seven and ask if he wanted anything for dinner. He likewise did not respond when Pepe approached him again around eight to announce that unless Mr. Domingo needed anything else, he, Pepe was retiring for the evening. He did not see the pain and concern in Pepe's eyes, never heard him walk away.

That night, Alejandro Domingo was just a sad, lonely, angry, grieving father.

It was well past eight when the Vampire's doorbell unexpectedly rang.

As he entered the short hallway, he heard two heartbeats, soft and steady, outside the door. Then he got a whiff of a rather unfortunate aftershave.

Lieutenant Nick Castle, a man of impressive dress, coiffed hair, impeccable tastes, and an affinity for exotic foods. The Vampire genuinely liked him. The one failing the Vampire had ever noticed was a lack of intelligent choice in cologne.

And as for Castle's companion, the Vampire had no doubt. He hastened to the door, turning lights on as he went. Not for him, but for them.

After all, they were only human.

He twisted the deadbolt back, flipped the lock open, grabbed the handle, pulled. Nic and Reggie stood outside just on the other side of sea grass welcome mat.

"Reginald! Nicholas! Please come in." He took a step back, made a sweeping gesture with one arm.

Reggie went through first, gave the Vampire a big hug. "Grandpa." Then he moved into the room.

Nick came through the door next, shook hands with him. Nick tried to hide his instinctive unease. The Vampire was a predator against which humans had few defenses. His glassy black eyes, deathly pallor, lank lifeless hair, cold bloodless hand, and lethal pointed fangs reminded Nick that in this creature's eyes, man was not the top of the food chain.

The Vampire closed the door, twisted the deadbolt back into place.

"Please sit," he said after he had turned around to face them. They did. "Can I offer either one of you some coffee? Or tea, perhaps?"

"No thank you," Nick replied too quickly. "We're fine."

"Reginald?"

"No thanks."

The Vampire eased himself down into his favorite creaky leather chair. He crossed his legs at the knee.

"Gentlemen. To what do I owe this pleasure?"

"Have you been keeping up with the local news?" Nick asked.

"Not closely."

"Are you aware of some rather unusual murders?" Reggie now asked.

"Vaguely," the Vampire replied, his mind remembering something he had overheard on the eleven o'clock news.

"What did you make of it?"

"I hardly paid any attention," the Vampire said truthfully.

"They look to be connected," Nick revealed.

"And it's landed on our desks," Reggie added.

"Most of the details have been withheld from the press," Nick said, taking the lead once more.

The Vampire waited. There was more coming. They were working in tandem, trying to lead him to a preestablished endpoint. While impressed by their smoothness and skill, he did not relish where this was going.

"See, Grandpa, the details are so outlandish that divulging them could lead to either a public panic or a media circus." Reggie said. "Or both."

Smooth, the Vampire thought. Appeal to my emotions because you don't think the facts will be compelling enough to guarantee my involvement. Smart.

Or desperate.

"As you've no doubt already surmised, we're wondering if you might... consult with us," Nick chimed in. "Much like you did before."

"If memory serves, I did more than merely consult."

"True enough, sir."

"And I never did get reimbursed for that imported Scotland wool sweater that got shot full of holes."

"And I'm really sorry that requisition came back disapproved," Nick responded. "That decision was made by people above my paygrade."

"I really loved that sweater."

"I don't blame you. It was beautiful."

"Grandpa Eddie," Reggie interjected, gaining the Vampire's attention. "This case is, shall we say, unique."

"As you both know, I generally avoid involving myself in the affairs of man," the Vampire finally said.

"You involved yourself when Reggie's life was on the line," Nick challenged.

"Indeed," the walking corpse said, ceding the point. "I interceded because he was, and is, a good and honorable man. If not, I would have left Reginald to his fate."

"You mean that you would have let your own great, great Grandson be gunned down aboard that ship?" Nick asked.

"If he had been a gangster like I had been when I was alive, yes. That is precisely my meaning," the Vampire said with finality. "It was my own misguided life of crime that led directly and inevitably to my own death." The Vampire smiled, showing his fangs. "Of course, I managed to seize upon a last-minute reprieve, the results of which have proven... *mixed*."

Memories of Danae, his long-lost love returned in sharp relief out of the ether. That look of horror on her face when he had presented himself to her after his Rebirth into Darkness. She had understood immediately what he was, what he had become. African culture was filled with tales of vampire-like creatures.

He could still hear her shrieking at him to get out of her sight and never return. Even after all the years, the decades, these memories squeezed his heart like a vice.

"This case is different, Grandpa."

"The crimes of one mortal against another mean little to me."

"Because you still hunt us for food?" Nick countered.

"Indelicately put," the Vampire replied, keeping his own temper carefully in check, "but essentially correct. Might I remind you, Lieutenant, that I feed only on criminals of, those whom you label scumbags. Murderers, rapists, drug dealers, pedophiles."

"Who still have rights under the law," Nick pointed out.

"As do their victims," the Vampire replied darkly.

"Grandpa," Reggie interjected, "there's somebody out there killing people and making it look like vampire attacks."

It is not easy to shock a dead man.

But the Vampire's mouth fell open. Absolute silence permeated the room. His black eyes darted back and forth between them. Tense detectives waited for his response.

Finally, the Vampire growled, "Gentlemen, you now have my undivided attention."

Charlie Simpkins crept through his cramped studio apartment, listed online as an "enormous 350 square feet".

Enormous my ass, he thought.

One room with a kitchenette and two-burner stove in the far corner, a bathroom so tiny he had to stand against the wall to close the door. When swinging shut or open, the bathroom door missed the toilet seat by less than an inch. There wasn't a proper tub, only a shower stall. What was listed as a full bath was only a three-quarter bath.

Charlie didn't need a tub. He hadn't taken a sit-down bath since he was nine. But that wasn't the point.

Truth in advertising was the point. If he was only going to have a three-quarter bath, then fine. The ad needed to say that. And three hundred fifty square feet was NOT enormous. Less than a month after moving in, the walls were pressing in on him.

Maybe that was why he had murdered his landlady one Thursday morning a few years back. She didn't own the property, but she had been the one to write and publish the deceptive ad.

The deed itself had gone off without a hitch, quick and quiet. A strong hand clasped over her mouth from behind at the back end of the outside walkway, away from passing traffic and prying eyes. He thrust a knife between her ribs and into her left lung, collapsing it.

One quick shove and over the railing she went, careening ass over teakettle into the arroyo below. Thanks to careful calculations and a stealthy approach, the blood spray had been mostly outward and away. He didn't get any blood on himself, and precious little on the concrete walkway.

She never even had a chance to scream.

And now, he was preparing for another hunt. He had to work tonight, but that was fine. He still had time. And the mysterious stranger he had been told about was due to show up later, sometime in the wee hours.

Charlie did not know the stranger's name or what he looked like. He was told, "When you see him, you'll know".

Whoever this weirdo was, if he wanted to buy a few bags of expired blood under the table, who was Charlie to tell him no? If the money was right and paid in cash, he didn't care.

Good business was where you found it.

He opened his scarred briefcase. At one time it had been a general use case suitable for many professional purposes. Charlie had since customized the interior.

IV needles, transfusion tubing, clamps, and hand pumps rested strapped into place. Two large clear plastic bags and a several fresh rolls of tape. The interior lining was stained with long-dried blood from leakage, most of which had occurred on his first two kills. He refined his technique became adept at securing the tubing into interchangeable bags with a leakproof seal.

He looked everything over one last time, ticking items off in his head. He did not want to hunt down prey, then discover he lacked something essential to completing his ritual. This is why he used a squeeze bulb to hand pump the blood from his victims. He had considered rigging up something battery-operated, then decided against it. Hand pumps were more reliable.

Needles and tubing were easy. He worked in a Blood Bank. He simply pilfered supplies when no one was looking. And no one ever looked because they were understaffed and overworked.

He had originally used blood donor bags. But they did not hold enough to bleed out his prey. So, he had adapted equipment and custom-rigged what wouldn't work any other way. It had taken some trial and error, a few sleepless nights, and a couple of killer headaches. But he had finally gotten things smoothed out.

Smoothed out? Yeah. That was it.

Smooth, baby, smooth.

Charlie Simpkins, Serial Killer Extraordinaire, liked it smooth.

Morris Horn sat slumped in his overburdened desk chair at his cramped office. Wedged into a strip mall between a bail bondsman and a laundromat, this was not prime real estate. But the rent was cheap, and the office provided a professional façade.

He had opened his agency the day after he retired. A cheap desk from Goodwill, a comfortable chair, a laptop and Wi-Fi, a coatrack, and a chair for potential clients. Plus, a box of business cards and some fliers his son had made up for him.

Something about computers. The kid was an absolute genius with that shit. He never ceased to amaze his old man. What was rudimentary and fundamental to his son was uncomprehendingly complex and inexplicably technical to him.

Most of his cases proved pedantic and tedious. Cheating husbands, cheating wives, runaway kids. Meh, but it paid the bills. He gathered evidence, ran down leads, then turned his findings over to the interested party, or to his/her attorney. It all depended on who paid the invoice.

After that, he got put on retainer with a divorce practice. That lasted a couple of years while he got the biz running and adjusted to not being a cop anymore. But he had refused a third retainer. The work had simply become boring professionally and depressing personally.

Didn't anyone keep their vows anymore?

In the interim, he took one-offs with criminal defense attorneys around town.

That was weird.

Here were all these criminal defense lawyers who had berated him in court, questioned his methods, his tactics, his chain of evidence, and had cast aspersions regarding his ethics for years who now welcomed him with open arms, congratulated him on his retirement from a stellar career and fell all over themselves trying to send work his way.

He took enough of their work to keep the business afloat. He didn't want to turn them down too often because then they'd just quit calling. But he tried to be selective. He insisted on looking over the case first, read the police reports, autopsy reports.

If he thought the case conclusively proved the accused was guilty and there was no evidence of police entrapment or prosecutorial malfeasance, he refused the work. But if the evidence was weak, or if a confession had been illegally obtained or coerced, if there was enough there to make him think the accused might be innocent, Horn would snatch it up in a New York minute.

Now that he was no longer a cop, his concerns were not within the narrow parameters of legal and illegal. He now had the freedom to consider broader, more esoteric concepts.

Guilt or innocence.

Morality.

Right and wrong.

Back in his cop days, Morris Horn had not been in the "right or wrong" business. He had been in the "legal or illegal" business. It had always been collect evidence, follow the evidence, build a case. Hand it over, preferably with a suspect, to the D.A.'s Office. Let *them* navigate the labyrinthine court system. Let *them* prove guilt or innocence. Everything black and white, a binary choice.

But life wasn't always black and white. Most of life came painted in varying shades of gray. Private investigation was all about the gray. Oftentimes, suggestion and innuendo were enough to rule the day and shove a paycheck into his hand.

Now that he had time to think about such things, he realized that he could have done his old job with more empathy. Following the evidence without regard to its consequences had torn families apart, ended marriages, divebombed reputations, destroyed lives.

Over the course of his career, Morris had not always been right. In his headlong, bull in a China shop pursuit of "justice", he had committed injustices himself. He had hurt *innocent* people. Torn *innocent* families apart. Ended *innocent* marriages. Divebombed *innocent* reputations. Destroyed *innocent* lives.

Three people proven innocent at trial – not just acquitted but proven innocent! – had committed suicide after losing spouses, children, friends, reputations, livelihoods. A couple of others had wound up homeless eating out of garbage cans. Because even after being proven innocent, they were never really trusted again. Why would they have been accused if they weren't doing something shady, dirty, unethical, or underhanded? The stigma of an arrest and a trial, regardless of the outcome tended to cling to a person like stink on shit for the rest of their days.

The Internet was forever.

These things weighed on him now. More than he would have admitted to anyone other than himself.

But the real paradox was, he genuinely missed being a cop, missed it every single day. He understood he was done; he could never go back to it. And he believed he had been a good cop. But he wished he had been a better cop. A better human being.

A better man.

The night outside seemed deep as ocean water, and just as black. He had nowhere to go except to his single-bedroom apartment that he had leased ever since he and his wife had split up. Truth was, he preferred his office. Here, he could fool himself into thinking his life was more than a steaming pile of neon dogshit.

Maybe he should move out of San Diego, out of California, he thought for about the ten thousandth time. But his kids were here, so that was that.

Morris was currently between cases. Nothing new over the transom in close to three weeks. He had finished his last case and had simply not gotten anything new. It happened sometimes. Feast or famine.

His cell phone chirped. An incoming call? At this hour? His mind immediately went to his children. God, he hoped nothing was wrong. He picked the phone up off his desk, hit the green button.

"Morris Horn Investigations."

"Hey, Captain. How's it going?"

"Nick! Hey, how you doing, man?" He recognized the voice immediately. They had not spoken lately.

"Can't complain," Nick replied.

"What are you calling me about this time of night?"

"Something's come up," Nick said.

"Talk to me, Stringbean," Morris joked, referring to Nick's perennially slender build.

"I'd like you to consult on a case we're working," Nick said. "Paid, of course," he added.

"Of course," Morris said, as if money had ever been an issue.

"Can you come down to the precinct?"

"When?"
"Now."
"Am I on the clock now?"
"Yes."
"On my way."

CHAPTER NINE

Eleven p.m., and Morris Horn pushed his grizzly bear physique through the precinct front door. His heart leapt into his throat. Déjà vu washed over him: the sights, the sounds, the smells. Cheap wood polish and bad coffee.

Goddamn, he missed this more than he had thought.

The lighting was subdued, as it always was during the night shift. It saved electricity, sure, but it also evoked a different mood, a different ambience.

Most of the detectives were new. Busy with their respective workloads, they ignored him as he cruised by. He didn't recognize any of them. But he did note their youth with a pang of nostalgia.

Jesus, he thought. Was I ever that young?

Motion at the edge of his periphery. Nick near his office, waving him forward. Several others milling about nearby.

No. It couldn't be.

Morris moved his massive bulk on powerful legs, gaining momentum. He swerved around desk corners, avoided toppling over a uniformed cop carrying coffee, veering ever closer.

Familiar faces turned towards him. Nick, or rather Lieutenant Castle. Lead Detective Reggie Downing, and... the Vampire, pale and thin. The word "cadaverous" came to mind. The Vampire grinned at him from behind those ubiquitous wraparound sunglasses.

"Morris," Nick held out his hand. "Glad you could make it."

The two friends hugged. "It's been too long," Nick said.

"Good to see you, too," the big man said, releasing him.

Reggie and Morris shook hands, embraced. Then it was time for the undead thing called...

"Eddie Marx." He thrust out his ham-sized hand. The vampire smiled, shook it with a narrow, bony, perpetually cold hand of his own.

"Morris Horn," the Vampire said. "Lovely to see you again." Neither of them made a move to embrace.

"We're waiting on one more," Nick announced. "Our newest detective. Still on probation." Nick chose his words carefully. Now everyone understood the power dynamics.

"Her voice was foggy when she answered," Reggie said. "Sounded like she was asleep," he added.

"Where does she live?" Morris asked.

"University Heights."

"Shouldn't take long."

"What's up, guys?" Everyone turned. Detective Valerie Wahl stood before them. A frantic look on her face, red frizzy hair, dark circles under her eyes, mismatched clothes hastily thrown on. Panting with exertion, the men eyed her heaving chest despite themselves. The Vampire, however, listened to her heart pounding, watched the carotid artery pulsate at the side of her neck.

"Detective Wahl," Nick said. "Sorry about having to turn you around so quickly."

"No problem, sir," she wheezed. "I'm all about the job. What did I miss?" Her eyes drifted to the Big Guy. Dark skin, even for a Black man. Built like a brick wall, all bulk and muscle. Like a six-foot-tall fire plug.

She remembered him. A man to be reckoned with. If she had to venture down a dark alley or burst through a door, this was the man you wanted coming with you.

Her eyes moved to the stranger. Pale and thin. Useless hair. Long narrow face. Pointed chin. Almost no lips to speak of. Mouth a thin gash beneath a narrow, hawkish nose. Pasty forehead. Eyes hidden behind opaque wraparounds. Who the hell wore sunglasses at night inside a police precinct?

Something different about this man. Something beneath the surface, hidden in the subtext. Barely five foot seven, probably around one forty dripping wet. At first glance, he didn't look like he could whip a ten-year-old in a schoolyard fight.

But she felt something unsettling about him. Unnatural. Wahl had been around warfighters, dangerous men back during her Army days in Afghanistan. She could tell by what they said, what they didn't say, how they acted, how they moved. The air around them was unmistakable.

Valerie Wahl knew dangerous men when she saw them.

And she knew, as sure as she was standing there, this guy was more than dangerous; this guy operated on a whole other level of high-order violence.

Evil? Perhaps. Something coiling under his skin. Primordial. Serpentine.

Reptilian.

Despite his unassuming posture, Detective Valerie Wahl understood right away that in a world of dangerous men and women, this man was in a class by himself. The kind of man that made warfighters, even assassins flee in terror.

A cold blooded, amoral killer. And he frightened her to her very core.

Nick led the group to where the mobile corkboard waited. Timeline scribbled along the top; grisly autopsy photos attached below, according to their deaths in the timeline.

A cursory glance brought a furrow to Morris Horn's brow. "Jesus Christ," he muttered.

"Everybody grab a seat," Nick said. Everyone but the Vampire sat. He stood in the back, arms folded across his chest.

"This will be old hat to you two," he motioned to Reggie and Wahl, "but let's bring our consultants up to speed."

"Excuse me, Lieutenant," Wahl interrupted, "I'm a bit confused.

"About what?"

"Bringing in civilian specialists I understand," she started. "I understand asking him for help," she motioned to the former Captain with one hand, "but who is this?" she jerked a thumb over her shoulder towards the Vampire.

"He's helped us before," Reggie answered. "The firefight at my old apartment."

She turned in her chair, looked directly at the walking corpse. "I don't remember you. Just who exactly are you?"

The Vampire had been listening not only to her words, but also her vocal inflection. Her outward animosity was a thin veil to conceal her fear. And while he knew she was a good person by the wavy aura arising off her, he was in no mood to be particularly magnanimous. Other pressing matters required his attention.

"I am the creature you were never meant to see."

Creature?

Huh?

"And what do you bring to the table?" she demanded, instantly suspicious.

"Me."

"Detective." There was a warning tone in Nick's voice. She recognized it, snapped her head back towards the front. "Let's bring our consultants up to date, shall we?"

Nick spoke, breaking only to pass police reports or autopsy reports or toxicology results around the room. A couple of times, he turned the floor over to Reggie, who spoke assertively. It was the first time the Vampire had seen Reggie working since his promotion. But the way Reggie handled himself, he could not have been prouder of his great, great grandson.

But what he saw before him shocked him. He knew a serial killer was imitating vampirism to cover their tracks, but this went beyond the pale. A growing anger welled up within him.

His mind raced to the end. The news media would glom onto this, dig down into this sick person's twisted mind, explore the lurid details, then conclude the killer was sick twisted, delusional, paranoid, psychotic.

As usual, they would be wrong. This killer was neither delusional nor psychotic. Delusions and psychosis indicated a mental break, a separation from reality often punctuated by audiovisual hallucinations. The afflicted had no idea what was real, what was imagination, what was right, what was wrong.

The legal definition of insane.

Not this guy.

His method was too deliberate, his planning too detailed, his execution too careful. His was not the method of a psychotic. This was psychopathic, which contrary to popular opinion of those who did not know what they were talking about, had nothing to do with psychosis.

Psychopaths knew the difference between reality and fantasy. They knew the difference between right and wrong.

They just didn't care.

This pissant had deliberately chosen to copy bad western pop culture literature, having no idea vampires did exist. He drained wayward innocents whose only crime was questionable taste in clothes and music.

Before, the Vampire was going to help because his great, great grandson had asked him. But now, he understood the totality of what was really going on.

And it made him seethe.

"Okay," Nick wrapped things up. "That's it. Anything to add, Detective Downing?"

Reggie shook his head.

"Detective Wahl?"

Stunned at hearing her name and title pronounced formally, Valerie likewise shook her head. Then she smiled to herself. Even though she was the greenhorn around here, the Lieutenant had shown her respect in public and in front of peers by asking for her opinion. She would not forget that.

"Consultants. Any questions?"

Neither consultant had any.

"Very well. Meeting's adjourned. I realize it is the weekend, but I need to see you here again tomorrow." Nick looked at the Vampire. "I understand you won't available until evening."

The Vampire nodded. Everyone in the room seemed to understand this. Wahl noticed. There was something running under the surface, and she was being kept in the dark. Having an ingrained curiosity since childhood, Valerie Wahl detested being kept in the dark about *anything*.

Reggie headed for his desk. Morris and Nick huddled in the office doorway. Wahl turned towards the creepy stranger behind her, deliberately stepped close into his personal space. If he was taken aback by this, it did not show.

"May I be of assistance, Detective?"

"I want to know who you really are."

"My name is Eddie Marx. I have been asked to consult on this case."

"That doesn't answer my question."

"I value my privacy," he stated. "If anything else regarding my existence becomes germane, I shall divulge it."

"You talk weird."

"Do I?"

"Yeah. You do."

"How so?"

"Word choices. Sentence formation. It's like you learned how to talk a hundred years ago."

"Indeed?" One eyebrow arched high above his sunglasses. "I had never noticed anything amiss with my vocabulary."

"You speak quite formally," she observed.

"A show of respect," the Vampire explained. "Surely that does not arouse suspicion?"

"Everything about you arouses suspicion."

One eyebrow cocked above the sunglasses again. "Indeed?" Though the word was the same, it carried a different inflection. A warning? His stance had shifted subtly. He no longer smiled.

She didn't care. "Why can't you help us during the day?" she challenged. "You didn't help on the drug case during the day either, did you?"

"You will find that I am superbly adept at hunting my prey at night."

Wahl's green eyes widened. "Hunting your prey?" She stared at him a moment, appraising him. "Are you some kind of Special Forces guy, some super soldier?"

"I never had the privilege of serving my country in the Armed Forces."

"Why not?"

"Regrettable life choices from a woefully misspent youth."

"Then what the hell are you? CIA? NSA? You're some kind of operative, aren't you?"

The Vampire was genuinely surprised. He looked away from her for the first time they had begun this conversation. He turned the term over in his mind, then looked back at her and smiled, careful to not show his fangs.

"Feel free to refer to me in that fashion if you wish. I promise to take no umbrage."

More of that formal, outdated speech pattern! She inhaled to say something else, but the Vampire was already moving past her, away from her.

"Reginald," the Vampire called.

Reggie looked in his direction.

"I have pressing matters which demand attention."

Reggie waved. The Vampire waved back, headed towards the entrance.

Wahl looked at her watch. What kind of pressing engagements could this guy possibly have at this time of night?

Charlie Simpkins was bored out of his skull. Life seemed like one interminably long never-ending cycle. Get up, eat, go to work. Work; go home. Pay rent. Pay bills. Wash. Rinse. Repeat. If this is what adult life was, then why was it everyone he knew when he was a kid was so desperate to grow up and join their ranks?

The allure of forbidden fruit, he supposed. People wanted what they could not have. Kids wanted to do adult things. They wanted to drive cars, drink alcohol, have sex, all the things adults seemed to do with impunity. And yet most adults wanted only one thing: to be kids again.

Charlie had figured out by age seven there was something different about him. Not wrong, just different. He did not feel emotions like other children. They all exhibited fear, surprise, anger, exultation. He did not feel much emotion at all.

He watched other children with cold, calculating eyes. He found their lives like an alien landscape in a science fiction movie. The few emotions he did encounter seemed muted, desaturated, like faded clothing.

Small for his age, he had not made friends easily, which was fine. He enjoyed reading, watching TV. Anything to avoid interaction with others. But instead of cartoons or kid shows, Charlie watched videos about serial killers, read books about Manson, Dahmer, Gacy, and Gein.

His parents had worried themselves sick. They knew something was wrong and began to get an inkling of what. They took him to several child psychiatrists. By the time he was twelve, he had memorized all the proper buzzwords. He gave the shrinks what they wanted to hear so he could get the fuck out as quickly as possible. If they saw the real him, the game would be over.

So, he had successfully evaded classification as a psychopath with antisocial personality disorder. Of course, it was difficult for a mental health professional to diagnose, especially in a child without ongoing psychotherapy and extensive testing. Charlie did not stay with any one therapist long enough for anything to get accomplished.

Frankly, Charlie had never understood his parents' concern. They seemed hyperbolic and hysterical about the slightest little thing. So, he had killed his pet rat. Big deal. Some of the neighborhood dogs and cats "went missing". So what? Nobody had seen him do anything, and his attitude was always "pics or it didn't happen".

As far as he was concerned, he was fine. His fascination with death was a thing, sure, but neither a good thing nor a bad thing.

It just simply… *was*.

And here he was now, educated, graduated, certified, and licensed as a Medical Technologist, processing blood donor units, running types and matches, types and crosses, performing antibody testing, looking for bloodborne pathogens like hepatitis,

HIV, among others. He was considering testing for his national certification as a Blood Bank Specialist. It was highly technical work that required organization and attention to detail.

That suited Charlie.

He had just completed some work and was going to take a break. It was past two in the morning. He was irritated when Monique Rivers, his immediate supervisor, approached him. She had never warmed up to him and the feeling was mutual. In fact, he was considering applying some of his more esoteric skills to her. Not only would he be able to scratch his particular itch, but he would also have the rare pleasure of killing someone he genuinely disliked.

Middle aged and thick through the middle. Café colored skin with the dark eyes, close cropped hair, a broad flat nose. Full lips. He knew she had a family, college-aged children, but like the others, she rarely spoke about anything personal at work.

Monique approached Charlie guardedly. She couldn't put her finger on it, but there was something about this scrawny little guy that gave her the creeps. Every time she interacted with him, she always felt like she needed a shower.

She stopped about six feet away from him. "Charlie."

He laid his hands palm down on the counter on either side of several bags of blood. "Yes?"

"You have a visitor," she said. "Out back on the loading dock."

He scooped up the bags of freshly typed and labeled blood bags. "I'll put these in the reefer and go see who it is."

"Don't take too long."

"I won't." He turned and walked carefully towards an enormous industrial-sized refrigeration unit near the back of his workspace.

She turned and muttered, "You're welcome" under her breath as she moved away.

He hooked the reefer's latch handle with two fingers, pulled. The door's rubber gasket pulled away from the frame with a slight tearing sound. The door swung open. He heaved all the bags onto the top metal shelf, which was reserved for O Positive blood. From there he distributed the O Negatives and the A Positives to their proper places on the lower shelves. Then the lone A Negative and a lone B Positive got squared away.

He closed the reefer door, looked around to see if anyone was looking his way. Confidant he would not be seen, he reached into a different reefer, pulled out four bags of blood that had been designated "expired". These bags had been dutifully removed from the working stock and tossed here, to be incinerated by the tomorrow's Day Crew.

No one would miss a few bags.

He shoved two units into each of his lab coat's waist-level pockets, kept his hands there, and strode through the main Blood Bank. A windowless corridor led to a single heavy door. Long metal bar attached at waist level. He pushed it with one hand and then he was outside on the loading dock.

The dock itself was nothing special. Charlie figured most loading docks were pretty much the same the world over. Thick slab of poured concrete about four feet high. This one was level at first, then a gentle slope down to the concrete lane where the Blood Bank vehicles backed in, to either be loaded or unloaded. A single large, powerful lamp bolted into the red brick wall bathed the area in yellow. It reminded Charlie of movies he had seen about Soviet Russia, the searchlights in the gulags. Angled downward, it lit the area nearest the door in garish brightness.

Charlie squinted, shielding his eyes. He put his back to the light and cautiously made his way down the ramp into the gathering gloom. At first, he did not see anyone.

Then a dark figure materialized out of the clammy night, coming together, coalescing, solidifying, until Charlie could clearly see a human figure standing beside a sealed barrel, dressed in black clothing and adorned with dark hair facing away from him in the dim light.

Charlie stopped on the other side of the barrel. The dark figure did not turn towards him.

"You are Sadie's replacement?" the dark figure asked, referring to Charlie's predecessor.

"Yes."

"Are you aware of our arrangement?"

"Yes,"

"Are you content to continue under the same terms?"

"Yes."

The stranger turned to face him with a grace that flummoxed Charlie. He had never seen such a simple movement executed with such fluidity.

Charlie was taken aback. Short in stature like him. Thin of build, dark hair hanging like seaweed off an alabaster forehead. Prominent cheekbones, hawkish nose, pointed chin. Impossibly pale skin contrasted against dark clothes and the black wraparound sunglasses.

How was this guy able to see anything?

The Vampire had picked up Charlie's exhalations, his heartbeat before he had pushed through the door. He had not turned around on purpose. He was dealing for the first time with someone he did not know and had no reason to trust.

His senses had snapped on full alert as the human emerged from inside. Every warning signal, every internal bell, flashing red light, every siren fired off in his head. This newcomer was not merely a corrupt technician looking to score extra cash every few weeks. This human was different. Malignant.

This human had the smell of death, the stench of murder on him.

He absolutely *reeked* of it.

When the Vampire turned around, it was all he could do to keep from rending this piece of human garbage asunder and bathing in his blood.

"Please stand right where you are, and please do not turn around."

Charlie remained frozen in place. "Why?"

"Because by standing exactly, precisely where you are, and my standing exactly, precisely where I am, separated by this barrel," he pointed to the 55-gallon drum between them, "neither of our faces are detectable by the surveillance camera attached to the Blood Bank wall above that rather dreadful spotlight."

"Smart," Charlie reasoned.

"I assume you have the product," the Vampire said.

"I assume you have cash."

He pulled his hand out of his pocket, several folded bills between his fingers.

Charlie pulled the blood bags out of his pocket, laid them out on the barrel top, like a poker player laying out his cards at the end of a hand.

The Vampire glanced down. Four bags. Yes, this would do. He extended his arm, intending to lay the money flat. But the vile mortal creature in front of him reached out to take it from his hand. The Vampire snatched his hand back.

"Let me put it down," the Vampire instructed. "We must not touch."

Charlie retracted his hand and waited. He was not angry or surprised. His heart rate never changed. If it had, the Vampire would have heard it.

The Vampire laid the bills out, the fronts facing up. Four bills, all with Ben Franklin gazing upwards. The Vampire pulled his hand back. Charlie reached out and took the bills. Only when he was stuffing his hands back in his pockets did the Vampire take possession of his purchase.

"That's it?" Charlie asked.

"That, as they say, is it."

"Not quite."

Behind his sunglasses, one eyebrow arche upwards. "Oh?"

"Next time, instead of four of these bills, I'll require six."

"I shall procure product somewhere else." The Vampire took a step backwards, never taking his keen eyes off this creature before him.

"Wait."

The Vampire froze.

"One more bill."

"Why?"

"Inflation."

The Vampire sighed irritably. It was not the amount of money. It was the haggling he loathed.

Finally, he snarled, "Very well. One more."

The Vampire took another step backwards.

"You never mentioned your name."

"I did not," the Vampire replied. "And I have no desire to know yours."

And then, the stranger was gone, melting into the darkness.

"What if something comes up?" Charlie asked, but it was already too late. Business was concluded, and the Spooky Stranger was not much for small talk.

His buyer was not a normal person. A new thought hit Charlie's brain.

Perhaps his buyer was just like him.

The Vampire dashed out of the Blood Bank alleyway and onto the street. He turned into the wind. The fresh air helped wash the putrid wickedness he had smelled pouring off that despicable human.

It was after three a.m. now; no one on the streets. All the bars and nightclubs had closed at 2 a.m. Splinter was closed. He could not check to see if a miracle had occurred, and Maya had heeded his warning.

But ever since he had emerged from the loading dock, that same feeling of dread had returned. He took his sunglasses off. His black bottomless eyes scanned the shadows at ground level. He saw rats, food wrappers, used syringes, bent needles, human feces. But not what he has looking for.

"Maya".

The word emanated from parted lips as a grating whisper. Ragged, all balled up, as if it had difficulty working its way up over his vocal cords and out his mouth.

He knew she was there. He also knew she could hear his softly spoken words. But try as he might, he could not discern her location. His lip pulled up in a snarl, exposing one fang.

"Remember what I told you."

And with that, he turned away. He had neither the time nor the inclination to play hide-and-seek. Blood bags pressed close to him underneath his leather jacket, the Vampire approached his Lexus. He pressed the key fob. Lights blinked; the alarm chirped. Doors unlocked. Those sounds, distinct and separate, and yet somehow combined and blended, made him feel better.

At least *something* was happening the way he had anticipated.

He slid into his car, dumped the blood bags into the passenger seat, buckled up. He started the engine, knowing that soon the blackness of the eastern skies would lighten to gray, then to a blue glow before the actual dawn. This time of year, that process would begin in approximately one hour. The dawn itself would occur in approximately two.

Still feeling the disturbing sensation he knew to be Maya, he looked through the windows. He saw nothing suspicious. Nothing out of place.

But still…

He huffed air out through his nose. He shifted his car into gear.

Time to get the hell out of there.

Journal entry, 08 February

I have not found time to write lately, so I shall attempt to set everything down and catch up. I am bewildered by unexpected events.

Yet again, I find myself assisting the Police Department, this time with a murder case. A serial killer, no less, whose technique is draining blood from two puncture wounds to the neck, simulating vampirism.

This savage cretin's method emulates what he assumes is a mythical creature. Why? I believe this is calculated to inspire fear and cover his tracks. Mission accomplished. But a deeper question remains unanswered:

Why does this particular killer do what he does? What is he looking for? What compels him? What does killing people accomplish for him? And how will this killer deal with his continued and mounting frustration? Will he turn inward and commit suicide, or will he explode outward in some kind of public bloodbath?

We have all seen lone gunmen walk outside one day and open fire on total and complete strangers, and then attempt to shoot their way out of a confrontation with the police. That usually does not work out well for the gunman. Sometimes, death is part of the plan – suicide by cop, I believe they call it.

One thing I know. Nothing on this Earth is more irritating than an itch one cannot scratch.

There is also the matter of Maya, my Vampire Mother. What am I to do? Despite words and deeds to the contrary, I hold onto a gossamer thin hope that she will move on to new feeding grounds. That is the Vampire Way.

She has never been one to follow the traditions of our kind. A direct confrontation lies on the horizon. Conflicting emotions course through me, none of them good. Anger, rage, indignity at my wishes as Territorial Vampire being disregarded; me being disrespected.

I still harbor resentment towards her. Why did she abandon me all those years ago? Why did she not care enough to train me properly for life as a vampire? Was there something wrong with me? What did I do as a newborn vampire to drive her away?

Direct confrontation would certainly be a way to express my anger, my resentment, as only those like us can.

My mood tonight is dark, melancholy. Time grows short. I try to get as much done before I die each dawn much like humans try to accomplish all they can in their short time on Earth. Like them, time remains my enemy. I feel it now. The coming dawn and the ultraviolet light that would destroy me.

I must finish this entry quickly. I shall journal more completely tomorrow. My earlier epiphany has come back to haunt me as I realize I have something in common with this serial killer we must find.

Nothing on this earth is more irritating than an itch one cannot scratch.

CHAPTER TEN

The Vampire completed his journal entry, hit SAVE. He closed his laptop, got up and stretched.

He ran through his security precautions. He checked the front door, secured the deadbolt. He checked the window locks. Satisfied, he walked into the kitchen. He checked the back door, secured the deadbolt.

He padded into his bedroom, closed the steel-reinforced door behind him, shoved the deadbolt home. He repeated the action with a second deadbolt at knee-level.

The final fatigue made thought difficult. He peeled his clothes off, folded the shirt, hung his pants on a hanger. Shoes went onto a shoe rack. He shut the closet door, clambered towards his bed.

Vertigo crashed over him. He wobbled a bit, placed his hand on the nightstand to steady himself. He had to act quickly, otherwise he would die on the floor.

Joints locking up, the dying Vampire flopped into bed, pulled the heavy quilt up to his chin. It weighed a ton.

His timing was impeccable.

His last breath escaped his body, a weak, barely audible gasp. Skin dried, flaked, then desiccated and mummified. A fine dust of loose skin cells peppered his forehead. Lips disappeared, pulled back to reveal elongated teeth and gray gums. Tissue atrophied; muscles disappeared. Arms and legs reduced to nothing more than skin-covered twigs. Three bullet holes appeared over the left upper chest near where his heart should have been.

The Vampire was dead now. Just as he had died every morning for the past century since that rainy night in a Hoboken alleyway.

During the day, a vampire was completely vulnerable. This was why historically; vampires had slept in coffins or crypts safely ensconced in cemeteries. Few people ventured there even who during the day. People were less literate then, uneducated, superstitious. They needed little prodding to believe vampires were demonic creatures bent on the destruction of mankind.

Nowadays, most people didn't believe in God or Satan or Heaven or Hell, as real entities and places. Most saw them as parables and metaphors at best, or propagandic superstitious dogma meant to control the minds of the gullible unwashed masses at worst. People now turned to "science" as their religion. Anything they could not see, touch, hear, or smell; anything not already explained with a mountain of empirical evidence admissible in court, then it didn't exist. If it was real, then science would have proven it already, right?

That logic was inherently, hilariously, and tragically flawed. Relying so heavily on scientific evidence (but only evidence cherry-picked to support a preexisting belief or forgone conclusion), people substituted one psychological crutch for another. It gave them peace of mind without having to expend any effort to obtain it.

Ignorance is bliss, sayeth the Lord?

But this voluntary myopia also allowed the creatures that lived in the dark recesses of this world, that lived alongside man since the beginning of time to survive and flourish under their very noses. And since "science" currently provided no evidence of these beings' existence, then they obviously could not be real.

The greatest trick the Devil ever pulled was convincing the world he did not exist.

The morning came gray and dull. Fog blanketed the coast. Moisture coated everything outside; condensation dripped from cars and metal railings. Vehicles drove with their headlights even though the sun had been up for over an hour.

Alejandro Domingo had been sitting in the same chair all night. Swirling grays outside reflected the void he felt inside. He had sunk into a dreamless sleep after midnight. He awoke just before five a.m., achy and disoriented.

Then he remembered.

Ramsey.

Gone.

Just like her mother.

Then guilt punched him in the face like a prizefighter.

What kind of father, what kind of husband, what kind of man was he? He couldn't protect either of them! The wife dies from a cancer that all the money in the world can't cure, and now his daughter gets murdered by some psycho the police can't catch.

And Nick Castle was running the case! Of all the cops in all the cities in all the world, why did it have to be him? What cruelty had Alejandro inflicted that the Gods saw fit to torment him so?

True, his family had done some things, had not been generous with Nick's family back in the day. But those decisions had been his father's, not Alejandro's. But those things had happened long ago. Years.

Decades.

So why were the sins of the father being heaped upon the son? He didn't deserve this! And Ramsey had nothing to do with any of it, had never even known about it. She was a complete innocent!

And why was he going by Nick Castle instead of his real name, the name his mother had given him? What the fuck was that about?

Madre de dios!

His mood grew darker by the minute. Mixed with his overwhelming grief, another emotion coalesced in the back of his soul. This was different, something to spur him to action.

But what kind of action? That of a grieving father? A desperate parent? An angry citizen?

An avenging angel?

"Sir?" Pepe. Standing behind him. "Were you here all night?"

"Si."

"Did you sleep?

"Poquito," He held one hand up, thumb and forefinger held an inch apart.

"Would you like some breakfast?"

"I'd just throw it back up," Alejandro said in English.

"Coffee, sir?"

"Si."

"And sir? Might I suggest you shower and shave," Pepe said diplomatically. "You will feel better."

As Alejandro watched Pepe shuffle off, regret tugged the corner of his mouth down. He knew he should say something to Pepe, something compassionate; something to bring him some level of comfort. Unfortunately, Alejandro could not do that yet. His own pain raged raw, red, still bleeding.

Alejandro staggered through his bedroom, to his walk-in closet. He stripped, threw his clothes into the laundry hamper. He lumbered through the far doorway and into his cavernous bathroom.

Hot shower water stung like thousands of tiny hornets. He cranked the temperature up until it scalded him. He needed this pain, the sensory diversion. He placed his hands on the tile in front of him, plunged his head under the stream of liquid fire.

He stood there, the swirling steam reminding him of the fog outside.

Alejandro Domingo knew what he wanted to do. He wanted to track down whoever did this to his little girl. He wanted to mete out his own justice – a painful death by slow torture, augmented with pliers and a hacksaw, a blowtorch to the testicles.

He also knew a man in his position could not go off the rails and turn vigilante. That only worked in the movies, not real life. He was a public figure. But money buys results, doesn't it?

Para la familia.

Such an outdated paradigm. But Alejandro, for all his education and intellect and success as a thoroughly modern man could not disregard the traditional values instilled in him. Never allow injury or insult to your family go unanswered.

He toweled off, staggered back to the closet, threw on mismatched clothes.

He had figured out the first step in his plan.

Pepe poured fresh French pressed coffee as Alejandro entered the kitchen. He gratefully accepted the offered mug, added sweetener and cream.

As Alejandro made a phone call, Pepe slid a warm plate containing a butter croissant stuffed with ham and cheese.

"You need to eat something, sir," Pepe stated.

Alejandro looked at his butler. Well, he was more than merely a butler, wasn't he? Ex-military, ex-*Federale*, still deadly with a gun. Pepe stood there, implacable, unyielding.

"Gracias, Pepe."

Alejandro dug into the croissant between slurps of coffee. He had not realized how hungry he was. He devoured the croissant, drained his mug.

"Will you be going in today, sir?"

"I'll work remotely today." Some dark and dangerous behind his eyes.

Pepe smiled, nodded imperceptibly, almost to himself. His whippet chest swelled with pride. He had seen that look in Alejandro's eyes before. Alejandro was not thinking about business.

Today, the only thing occupying Alejandro Domingo's mind was revenge.

Detective Valerie Wahl was already working when Reggie cruised in, his customary two travel mugs in hand. She looked up, nodded towards him.

"What's with the two mugs?"

He explained it to her, how he drank one on his walk to work, and the second was sipped throughout the morning.

"Don't you worry about all that caffeine?"

"Nope," he said. He sat. His chair squeaked loudly enough to be heard throughout the squad room.

"Downing in the house!" someone shouted. A wave of chuckling followed, then died back down.

"Why don't you oil your chair?" she asked.

"And take away their only source of levity? Never."

Reggie sipped his coffee while his system booted up. His security screen, a blue field emblazoned with the official SDPD shield and emblematic lettering, faded in. He typed in his username and password. The screen darkened, then opened to his home page. He immediately opened the files on the victims.

For what seemed to be the hundredth time, Reggie poured over the crime scene photos, police reports, evidence lists, forensics results, autopsy reports. Nothing new jumped out at him. There had to be more here, something he was missing, something that connected the victims.

Why these particular people? They had little in common. Most serial killers hunted in a particular area, somewhere they felt safe. They tended to be white, male, between 30 and 50. They tended to kill within their own ethnicity, or within a certain ethnic or gender demographic: women with a certain hair or eye color. A certain age range. A certain occupation, like prostitutes. Victimology usually provided a link, though this was not always the case.

What did this killer seek? How did his victims serve his purpose? Was he killing randomly, or was he deliberately random, trying to throw them off the scent?

If so, it was working.

Something about these murders bothered Valerie. Something in the recesses of her mind. She had heard about or had seen something about similar murders. She just couldn't quite put her finger on it. She dug deeper, expanded her search to outside her jurisdiction. Then she hit SEARCH.

Bingo.

Encouraged, she pulled her cell phone out of her pocket. She got up, hit something on speed dial, walked away from her desk with her phone to her ear.

She headed for the coffeemaker. The carafe was half full, left over from the night shift. The heating element was still hot underneath. She grabbed a mug while her call went through.

She poured and doctored her coffee while wedging her phone between her lifted shoulder and her cheek. The other line picked up, a sleepy voice on the other end.

"Roger? Hi. It's Val."

A moment later, she ended the call, dropped the phone back into her pocket. She grabbed her mug and turned around. Reggie was still at his desk. Morris Horn, the human grizzly bear, sauntered in and headed straight for them. She looked to her right. Lieutenant Castle was not in yet. Well, RHIP, right? Rank Has Its Privileges. After all, it was a Sunday morning.

By the time she got back to her desk, Reggie and Horn were exchanging pleasantries. They turned towards her.

"I see they're still serving the same shit coffee," Morris observed.

"Tastes stale," she admitted.

"That stuff was canned sometime around Desert Storm."

They all chuckled.

"She looks like the cat that swallowed the canary," Morris added. "What gives?"

"I'm waiting for the Lieutenant and that other guy, Eddie, to get here."

She noticed Reggie and Horn glance at each other, their smiles frozen on their faces. She made a mental note but said nothing.

"Lieutenant should be here any minute," Reggie said. "Eddie will join us this evening."

A veil seemed to cover Valerie's face. "This other guy. Eddie. He gets a lot of leeway. So, what. The. Fuck?"

"What do you mean?"

Valerie's patience grew thin. "Look, I may be new here, but I'm not stupid." Neither man said anything. "There's something about that Eddie guy. He's wrong."

"Wrong?"

"He's *wrong*. As in, there's something about him that's *not right*. He gives me the fucking creeps."

Both men simply stared at her.

"Why does he only work at night? And what's with the goddamned sunglasses?"

"Good morning, all," Nick Castle said a bit too loudly as he approached.

Everyone turned in his direction.

"I was inquiring about our mystery consultant," Wahl said.

"So I heard," Nick replied. "What do you want to know?"

"Why can't he work during the day?"

"He's… allergic to sunlight."

"Allergic?"

"Solar urticaria," Reggie chimed in.

"What does that mean?"

"Sunlight does bad things to him," Nick said. "Like anaphylactic shock." He paused, then, "Exposure to ultraviolet rays would most likely kill him."

Valerie could tell he was not joking. She looked to Nick and Morris, who simply stood there, stone serious. "Wow. I didn't know."

Nick shrugged as if the matter was settled. "How could you?" He looked to the other two. "Anything new since last night?"

Wahl motioned for them to gather around her desk. She sat down, started working her keyboard as they crowded around behind her to see the computer screen.

She clicked something with her mouse. Crime scene photos of a dead young woman popped up. She was dressed in the black clothing, gauze, and combat boots. Her eyes stared blankly upwards, mouth open and slack. Her carotid artery had been cut. Blood was everywhere.

"Let's go back two years ago in Oceanside," she said. She pointed at the screen. "Charlene Dayton. Twenty-two years old, part time cashier, found dumped in a garbage can in an alley off Hill Street."

"Looks like a traditional lateral cut," Morris observed.

"Notice though, the killer did not cut fully across the throat. He went straight for the carotid."

"He knew where it was," Reggie said.

"Someone with a medical background?" Nick posed, thinking out loud.

"Or a military background," Morris countered. "You got the biggest Marine base on the west coast just north of Oceanside.

"What kind of weapon?" Reggie asked, squinting. "This was no Kaybar," he said, referring to the standard combat knife issued to Marines.

"Autopsy report suggested it was most likely a straight razor or a scalpel," Valerie said.

"There's the medical aspect again," Morris said.

"This was messy," Nick observed. "This might have been his first. A clumsy cut instead of the puncture wounds."

Wahl nodded, clicked again with her mouse. Another crime scene photo popped up. A young man, frosted blonde hair, pale skin, black fingernails and lipstick. Same vacant, unseeing eyes. Same slack jaw, head turned to the side. Similar black clothing. Thin as a rail.

"Darren Willoughby," she announced. "He was killed four months later, found six blocks from a North County Goth hangout. Only this was not a club. It was a rave. Anybody sensing a pattern here?"

Reggie pointed. "The killer's refining his technique," he said, noting the tiny vertical incision on the kid's neck over the carotid.

"We're looking at the maturation of a serial killer," Wahl said.

"What did Oceanside PD have?" Nick asked.

"No murder weapon, no prints, no DNA, no witnesses, no video surveillance, nothing."

"If this is the same guy," Morris said, "and if he has a medical background, he might know enough about forensics to avoid leaving clues behind."

"That's a scary thought," Nick commented.

"But wait. There's more." She clicked again. Another photo popped open. A young Hispanic woman, thin and lithe, dressed in similar clothes, lying in an alley, arms and legs splayed out. Same vacant eyes, open mouth. "Victoria Mora," Wahl recited, "age twenty-one. And look here." She pointed to Victoria's neck. Two puncture wounds, neat and tidy, showed evident over her carotid.

"Not nearly as much blood on the ground here," Morris observed.

"Refining his technique," Wahl said.

"Where did this happen?" Nick again.

"Nine months ago. El Cajon."

"Sweet Jesus," Nick groaned.

"Was this in chronological order?" Reggie asked, referring to her presentation.

"Yes."

Reggie pointed. "So, two years ago, fifteen months, and nine months, right?"

"Does that fit our timeline?" Nick asked.

"It fits *him*," Reggie said, now on the scent. "This guy doesn't have just one club, one city that's his hunting ground. For him, the entire county is his hunting ground."

"His de-escalation period between kills is becoming shorter." Wahl added.

"And he'll keep killing until we stop him," Nick said.

Alejandro had spent the last hour pouring over his electronic phone book on his tablet. He still sat at the dining table, sipping coffee. Pepe had already cleared away the breakfast dishes. He found the number he was looking for and called out.

Pepe walked in from another part of the house.

"Yes sir?"

"Who runs the United Farm and Ranch Workers union? Collins, right?"

"The new man is Perkins."

"Did I have anything to do with him being instated?"

"Yes sir, you did."

"Please get Mr. Perkins on the phone."

Pepe nodded, then left the great room. Alejandro leaned back, gazed out the window. He felt better knowing that he was doing something rather than just sitting around wringing his hands.

Moments later, Pepe reappeared, walking towards him with a cordless landline phone. He handed it to Alejandro, who put his hand over the mouthpiece.

"What's his first name?"

"Robert, sir."

Alejandro took his hand away from the mouthpiece, placed the phone to his ear.

"Hey, Bob. Alejandro Domingo. Sorry to call you so early on a Sunday."

"No problem, Mr. Domingo," Robert said on the other end. "And might I say how sorry I am about your daughter."

"Thank you." A pause. Then, "Bob, I need your help."

"Happy to help those who have helped me in the past."

Good, Alejandro thought. He knows which side his bread is buttered on.

"What do you need?" Perkins asked.

Alejandro smiled. "Something you are uniquely qualified to provide."

Reggie and Valerie called Splinter, found out when the owners would be there. On a hunch, Reggie had asked who was working the door over the weekend. KONG? Yeah, Reggie wanted to talk to him.

They took a squad car over, parked directly in front of the heavy metal door and the dark sign. They got out, walked to the door. Reggie grabbed the handle, held it open. His mother had taught him chivalry, and it was a lesson he had never forgotten. Valerie went in first, descended the concrete staircase with Reggie following not far behind.

Reggie looked around as they descended the stairs and stepped onto the main floor. The place had been called FETISH the last time he had been here, a kinky BDSM club. The décor was different now, but the booths, tables, and chairs were the same.

Valerie turned around when she noticed he had stopped. She watched him looking around. Those intensely green eyes of his, she thought. Against his coffee-colored brown skin, his eyes just drew her in. For the briefest instant, she was no longer a cop on the job. She was a woman appraising an incredibly handsome man.

"You must be the cops."

The voice came from behind them, too loud for the room. The booming voice echoed off the plaster walls and cement floor.

Valerie and Reggie turned in unison. Kong stood at the end of the bar, wearing jeans and a black T shirt that stretched across his muscled torso, arms bulging out of inadequate sleeves.

He did not look happy to see them.

They both flashed their badges.

Kong sniffed dismissively. "This way."

He walked behind the bar and down a short hallway. Reggie and Valerie followed. Kong led them into a surprisingly large room, probably a storage room originally, now converted into a modern office. Two desks with laptops, two chairs pushed under the desks. A widescreen TV mounted on the wall. The screen displayed four different views from video surveillance cameras mounted strategically around the club.

Two men, one middle-aged and one about thirty, stood waiting for them, both dressed casually. The older wore a shirt of some shiny material open enough to show chest fur. Thinning hair with a ridiculous combover, two gold chains surrounding his chubby neck.

The younger had olive skin and thick dark hair. Nervous, twitchy. Hostile. Blue dress shirt, black slacks, oxford shoes.

"Good day," the older man greeted. He spoke with a thick accent. "I am Achmed Asif, and this is my son Zaid."

They flashed their badges again. "I'm Detective Downing. This is Detective Wahl."

"What's so important you call us in on a Sunday?" Zaid said, taking a seat. He did not speak with an accent.

Achmed smiled. "Please excuse my son's lack of manners. Have a seat."

Valerie and Reggie sat down. They would have anyway, whether they had been invited to or not. Just to prove a point.

"Can we get you anything?" Achmed asked.

"We're fine, thanks," Reggie responded. "We just have a few questions."

"What about?" Zaid growled.

"Murder." Reggie had taken an instant dislike to Zaid.

"Murder!" Achmed shouted. Sweat immediately popped out on his face.

"My father grew up where the police are feared," Zaid stated.

"But not you," Valerie ventured.

"No."

Reggie noted the challenge in Zaid's voice. "Do you have a problem with the police?"

"I see the news," Zaid said. "I see cops killing black people, brown people."

Valerie rolled her eyes. Jesus. Here we go.

"I see them doing nothing when innocent minorities are attacked and assaulted," Zaid continued, his eyes blazing. "And I see how whites are treated with kid gloves when they get arrested. You mind explaining that to me?"

"The only thing I'll explain that we're looking for a killer who is hunting people in your club," Reggie said, refusing to take Zaid's bait.

Zaid started to say something else, then thought better of it.

Achmed cleared his throat. "How can we help you?"

"We'd like to see your video surveillance footage for the last few weekends."

"Of course," Achmed said. "Kong, could you—"

"Do you have a warrant?" Zaid interrupted.

"Zaid –" Achmed began.

Reggie held up a calming hand. "It's all right, sir." He looked to Zaid. "No, sir. We do not have a warrant."

"Then we don't have to show you shit," Zaid spat.

"Zaid!"

"You're right. You don't have to show us anything," Reggie said in a soothing voice. "We're simply asking politely. Out of respect."

Zaid grinned, and it was ugly. "Well, then I am politely telling you that without a warrant, you can both go fuck yourselves. You know, out of respect."

Achmed was too horrified to speak.

"Well, then I'll go get one," Reggie replied amiably.

Zaid grinned triumphantly.

"That will take me hours," Reggie continued. "Detective Wahl will have to stay here with you until I get back. Finding a judge on a Sunday, well, I probably won't be back until tonight."

Dead silence in the room. Zaid's infuriating grin had fled his face.

"And once we've served the warrant, we'll just take everything," he continued. "Not only the surveillance footage, but your laptops, hard drives, office files."

"We'll need to get a forensics team in here, too," Valerie added. "Check the place from top to bottom."

"What for?" Zaid demanded.

"Fingerprints, chemical residue, DNA. We'll examine every square inch of this place. Every plate, every glass, every bottle,"

Valerie said. "You do have proper receipts for all the booze in this place, right? Because we'll need to check receipts against your inventory."

Achmed was sweating again. Dark stains at the armpits.

Zaid knew they were being squeezed.

"And how long would this 'investigation' take?"

"After going to the trouble of getting a warrant on a Sunday? Oh, I don't know." Reggie looked at Valerie. "Days?"

"More like weeks," Valerie nodded.

"Weeks!"

"Oh yeah," Reggie confirmed. "Three or four, at least. And you'd have to stay closed for the duration, of course."

Zaid seethed with impotent rage.

"It's too bad," Reggie said, feigning compassion and regret. "Weekends are probably when you make most of your money."

"And there's a three-day weekend coming up," Valerie added.

"Now listen –"

"Zaid!" Achmed shouted in a tone that shut Zaid down immediately. "Give them the hard drives."

"But Pops –"

"Give it to them." The steely look in Achmed's eyes told Zaid everything he needed to know. Achmed was still his father, and he was still in charge.

Zaid grimaced, spun around in his chair. He opened a cabinet, leaned in. He disconnected come cords, came back out holding an external hard drive in his hand. He spun back around in his chair, extended it across the desk.

Valerie reached out, took it. "Thank you."

"Shove it up your ass."

"Do you kiss your mother with that mouth?" Valerie refused to show anger. She refused to give the little prick the satisfaction.

"My mother's dead."

"I apologize," Achmed said. "I really have taught him better."

"No apologies necessary, sir," Valerie said.

Achmed nodded gratefully.

Reggie and Valerie stood. "Thank you for your cooperation," he said.

"Ernest," Achmed said to Kong, "would you please show our guests out?"

"Certainly, Mr. Asif."

Kong led Reggie and Valerie out the way they had come in. When they were beside the bar in the main room, they stopped.

"What's your name?" Valerie asked.

"Everybody calls me Kong."

"I mean your real name."

Kong looked embarrassed. "Ernest." He paused, then, "Hemingway."

"Ernest Hemingway?" Reggie echoed. "You expect us to believe that?"

"Kong pulled out his wallet, produced his driver's license, showed it to them. His name was indeed Ernest T. Hemingway.

"What does the T stand for?"

Kong looked embarrassed again. "Tiberius. It was my great grandfather's name."

"Well. There you go," Valerie said. "A fine family name."

"You work the door, right?" Reggie asked. "You must see every person who comes in."

"Nobody gets in without getting past me."

"Exactly," Reggie said. "I want you to think back. Anyone who came in that you remember? Somebody who stood out. Left an impression."

Kong thought for a moment. "Yeah," he said at last. It was like a lightbulb had just come on over his head. "Two. Both give me the creeps."

Paydirt.

"Tell us about them," Reggie said, all business.

"One's young. Thin, short. Kind of scrawny," Kong reported.

"Ethnicity?"

"White."

"Hair color? Eyes?" Valerie asked.

Kong thought for moment. "Light color," he said at last. "Blonde, maybe? Light brown?"

"Which is it?"

"Can't remember. He wears a wig. A lot of them do."

"Eye color?"

"Can't be sure."

Reggie and Valerie shifted their weight in impatience. Valerie crossed her arms over ample breasts.

"Look, guys," Kong pleaded, "They wear contact lenses a lot. He does, I know that much." He looked from one to the other. "Come here on a weekend," he said. "It's like Rocky Horror cosplay up in there. Everyone's in costume."

"Okay, fine," Reggie said, putting his hands up. "Tell us about the other guy."

Kong's face fell just then, eyes filling with dread at the thought. "Oh, God. This guy," Kong shook his head. "He's an entirely different animal."

"Explain."

Kong got serious. "You're a cop. You come across all kinds of people. You learn to read them."

They both nodded in acknowledgement.

"My job's kind of the same," he stated. "Most people are harmless, you know. Sure, you get the loudmouths and the braggarts who talk a good show, but they can't back it up." He paused, then, "Every once in a while, you come across a genuine tough guy. Someone who can back it up. Someone who has training and real-world experience. Ex-military types, cops, people like that. But true real bad asses are few and far between."

"Thank God for that," Valerie interjected.

Kong agreed. "But there's a few that are like something from another planet. You don't know what they're capable of, but you never want to find out." A pause. "That's this guy."

"You got a name?"

"No one gives names here," Kong replied. "Not real ones."

"Describe him," Valerie instructed.

"Short, thin, maybe five seven, a hundred and forty, a hundred and fifty pounds."

"Go on."

"Pale skin. Pure white, almost translucent like you can see through it to the blood vessels underneath. He ain't wearing makeup the way the rest of 'em do. It's real. If he wasn't walking around, I'd think he was dead."

Reggie was now interested.

"He dresses in black, but not like them," Kong continued. "It's just the way he dresses. Expensive. Upscale. But he ain't trying to impress anybody."

"Hair?"

"Dark brown. Limp. Just hangs there."

"Eyes?"

"He wears these Goddamned wraparound sunglasses all the time, even at night, even when he's down in the club. Who the hell does that?"

"You say he's dangerous," Reggie said, wanting to reestablish control over the conversation.

"He's beyond dangerous." Kong confirmed.

"Like how?"

"Like he could kill me as easily as you drink water," Kong answered. "And then he could rip off my head, shit down my throat, and then go home and sleep like the dead."

Reggie thought, you don't know how right you are.

"What makes you think a pipsqueak like him could do all that?" Valerie asked.

Kong rubbed his wrist without thinking as he spoke. "I tangled with him. *Once.* I'll damn sure never do it again." Dread dripped from his words.

"Why's that?"

"He broke my wrist," Kong confessed. "Didn't even break a sweat. Nobody's bested me in a fight since I was like, twelve."

"Did he use a weapon?"

"Just one hand."

Valerie frowned. "He used karate? Jiujitsu?"

"Nope. Just grabbed and twisted. I was in a cast for eight weeks."

Valerie looked at Reggie and caught him for an instant before he realized she was looking at him. What was that she saw behind his eyes?

"Well," she said to Kong, "thank you for your time."

The afternoon sun had already crossed the top of the sky and was sinking towards its resting place in the west. Though it was still hours before sunset, the shadows of the tall buildings threw the narrow street into a twilight gloom.

The metal door swung open, pushed by Reggie as he exited onto the street. Valerie followed close behind. The door swung back and clanged shut behind her. She followed Reggie, stalking towards the car.

He unlocked the doors. They slid into their seats. He buckled up, looked over at her, and everything came to a screeching stop.

Valerie was red-faced with rage, eyes burning, lips tight and blanched white.

"What?"

"Kong just described one of our consultants." She stated. "Why did you and the Lieutenant call in outside help so early in the investigation? And now that we know we're hunting a serial killer, why have we not called the FBI's Behavioral Unit?"

"Who to call and when to call them is the lieutenant's decision, not mine." He looked at her sharply. "And *not yours*."

She grimaced in anger.

"There's the way things get taught at the Academy, and there's how we do it in the real world," he instructed.

She stared at him a moment, choosing her next words carefully. "I may be a new detective, but I'm not that scared rookie you met. Don't make the mistake of thinking I am."

"Okay," he acquiesced. "Cheap shot. Sorry."

"Kong's description still sounds like our consultant."

"That description could fit anybody."

"Not me," she said evenly. "Not you."

Reggie swallowed in discomfort. "Let's get back to the precinct."

Journal entry, 09 February

I have not written about my new friend, Father Justin Ng. Such a peasant fellow. I have visited him a few times now, in the early morning before heading home.

He sleeps poorly and is up all hours of the night. He naps for a while, then is awake and cannot fall back asleep, even when he wants to.

I researched insomnia in the elderly. There may be several reasons why a person may have difficulty sleeping. In Father Ng's case, it appears to be two-fold. He has arthritic joints, and the pain increases in cold or wet weather. I suggested moving to a warmer, drier clime, but he likes San Diego. I have since left the subject alone.

Also, as humans age, their natural production of melatonin decreases. The older one gets, the more marked the decrease.

Imagine my surprise when I discovered one can walk into a store and purchase melatonin in tablet or capsule form. Such amazing and modern times in which to live!

I purchased some and gave it to him one night as a gift. He was most appreciative.

We have wide-ranging conversations. Naturally, we have spoken of God extensively. While I believe that God (for lack of a better word to name the concept) exists, I do not believe Him to be an aged, bearded benevolent Father figure in flowing white robes sitting atop a throne of gold. Father Ng, much to my astonishment, agreed. He believes that "God" lives inside each one of us and manifests Himself in our ability to exercise compassion, mercy, empathy, and love. Likewise, he tells me, the Devil (again, for lack of a better term to identify the concept) also lives within all of us and manifests himself through our ability to exercise cruelty, coldness, and indifference; our propensity to heap hatred, sadism, high-order violence, and gruesome death upon others.

As to which one governs us, he tells me, all boils down to which entity we serve. I told him I am a child of both fathers.

Father Ng said, "As are we all, Eddie. But we each choose which father to follow".

I have told him about my life of a vampire, how I adapted to this nocturnal existence. He knows about my life before. My misspent youth; my life of crime. My attempt to escape it and venture to a foreign land with Danae and build a life for ourselves. He knows how those plans got disrupted on a cold rainy night in Hoboken. I told him about being shot and left for dead, then given an impossible choice by my Vampire Mother.

Fascinated, he asked me the one inevitable question: What was it like to die? Where did I go? What did I see?

I told him the truth: I did not go anywhere. I saw nothing. No sense of time or space, simply darkness. Complete nothingness.

He seemed deeply disturbed by this. He had given Last Rites to many people. Most of them simply passed. Others were resuscitated by doctors and their medical teams. Those that had come back spoke of leaving their bodies, floating above themselves, feeling completely at peace. They spoke of a long tunnel, a light at the end of it, and of seeing family and friends, long since dead, waiting to greet them.

If only that had been my experience.

Father Ng proposed a hypothesis. The people who had died and come back told a story of their soul leaving their mortal bodies to journey on to the Next Place.

Father Ng believes that based on my UNIQUE circumstances, perhaps my soul never left my body. Perhaps because Maya mingled her blood with mine and made me what I am.

If Father Ng is correct, then perhaps if I ever experience the Final Death, whatever is left of my tattered soul will likewise shed this mortal realm. And if that happens, then I perhaps can leave all this strife and pain and blood and death behind and be welcomed by family and friends.

Perhaps I will see Danae again.

Even a dead man can dare to hope.

CHAPTER ELEVEN

The ride back to the precinct was short, silent, sullen. Valerie glared out the window all the way. She decided to speak to Lieutenant Castle directly.

They parked the car in the back lot, approached a metal door secured with a keypad entry system. Valerie punched in a six-digit code. The door buzzed unlocked. She pushed through without giving her partner a second glance.

She stormed down the hallway and into the main squad bay. The Lieutenant was in his office, reading a report. She headed straight for him; entered his open door without knocking.

"Lieutenant, I've had it," she blurted.

Nick's head did not move, but his eyes drifted upwards to look at her.

"There's something fishy going on here," she said.

Nick lay the report down on his desk. "Close the door."

She complied.

"Have a seat."

"I prefer to stand sir."

"Very well." He sat back, folded his hands in his lap. "Proceed."

She drew in her breath, ready to unleash a tirade, then paused. "Request permission to speak freely?"

"Always, Detective."

From his desk across the squad room, Reggie heard Valerie's angry voice. He looked up from his report where he had been documenting their interview with Achmed and Zaid. He couldn't make out words, but tone and body language were unmistakable.

When she finished, Nick shifted his gaze off her, locked eyes with Reggie. He waved for him to join them.

This was awkward.

Reggie understood how she had made Detective so quickly. She was smart, intuitive, she made cases that resulted in convictions, and she knew the law. She had a mind like a steel trap and missed nothing. And she took no shit from anyone.

That made her a formidable police officer.

As he trudged towards the closed door, Reggie realized with great mortification just how incredibly *hot* she was.

That made her dangerous.

Reggie felt like the coyote in a Road Runner cartoon.

He opened the door and stepped through. "You wanted to see me, Lieutenant?"

Nick motioned for Reggie to close the door. Reggie did so.

"Valerie has... *suspicions* about one of our consultants."," Nick said.

"Why would Eddie be hanging around Splinter, Detective?" Valerie asked.

So now it was "Detective" again.

"I can't say," Reggie dodged.

"The guy creeps me out," she said. "And when I pressed him yesterday, I didn't get any answers," she said.

"Look, can't you just work with the guy?" Nick asked. "He genuinely wants to help."

"How?" she countered. "And why? What's his skin in the game?" she demanded. "And by the way, what is it with his skin? He's not an albino. I looked it up online. And the UV light allergy? It doesn't really work with real patients the way you explained it to me." She paused, waited for them to say something.

They didn't.

"You've both been lying to me from the start."

"We haven't lied," Reggie said.

"We just haven't told you everything," Nick stated.

"A lie of omission is still a lie," she countered. "What does he have on you two? Why are you protecting him?"

"We're not protecting him," Nicked answered. "We're protecting you."

She looked incredulous.

"There are things in this world that you don't know," Reggie said, "things that believe me, you don't want to know."

"Why not?"

"Because knowledge comes the burden of truth."

"Since when is the truth a burden?"

"When the truth is so ugly and weighs so heavily that it rocks your very foundation, makes you question your perception of reality, question your own sanity."

"See, this is what I'm talking about," she looked back and forth between them. "You make like he's a vampire or something."

She had meant it as a derisive joke; it failed spectacularly. She noted the alarm behind Reggie's eyes. Nick simply sat, stoic and serious.

Nick checked his watch. "He'll be awake soon," he said.

A vampire? Seriously? How could someone convince the men in front of her that vampires were real, and that he was one of them?

Movement caught Nick's attention. He looked out across the squad room, saw Morris coming in.

"That's enough for now" he announced. "Reggie."

"Yes, lieutenant?"

"Make this right," he ordered. He pointed to Valerie. "We need her on the team."

"Yes sir."

Nick stood. "I need the room."

They opened the door and filed out just as Morris barreled in like the force of nature he was. He sat, and Nick brought him up to speed. Morris glanced out at Reggie.

"Tough spot," he observed. He looked back to Nick. "I'm glad it's not me."

"He's got it easy," Nick said. "I've already been ass-reamed by the Chief of Police, the Mayor, and one State Senator, and we've only been on this case for less than seventy-two hours."

Morris shook his head in sympathy. "I'm glad I'm not you."

"I don't know if this is just posturing by a man accustomed to getting his way, or if he's thinking I'm dragging my feet on purpose."

"I can understand why he might think that."

"This isn't personal, Morris."

"How can it not be?" Morris challenged.

"I would never allow anything personal to get in the way of solving a case."

"I know that, and you know that," Morris assured him. "But Alejandro doesn't know that."

Nick shook his head, at a loss. He sighed, placed one palm over his eye, as if he had suddenly come down with a migraine.

"He thinks it's personal for you because it's personal for him," Morris stated. "Not only is his daughter dead, which is bad enough, but he also knows about how his family fucked over your family. He also knows that between himself and his old man, you personally have been fucked over all your life."

Nick's lips winced into a thin line, blanched themselves white. "I don't want to talk about it."

"Not an option, my friend. You're in charge of finding his daughter's killer."

"I said I don't want to talk about it," he snapped.

"You'll have to talk to somebody about it sometime," Morris stated. "Make sure you talk to someone who can actually do something about it."

And in that instant, Nick experienced an epiphany, a moment of absolute clarity where all suddenly became clear. He knew what he needed to do.

What he had always needed to do.

"Let's grab coffee," Nick said as he stood.

"The coffee here sucks."

"Not here."

"Who's buying?"

"Me."

"Let's go."

They walked out of the office, left the door open behind them. Nick saw Reggie and Valerie at their desks, each logging their reports on their computers. The air was icy between them.

Jesus, Nick thought.

Then he thought about the decision Reggie had to make regarding Valerie and the Vampire. That led him to think about the decision he had to make regarding Alejandro Domingo, and he shook his head to himself.

He picked up the phone, dialed a number. Someone on the other end picked up.

"Pepe? It's Nicolas. Tell Alejandro I'm coming to see him."

"Now would not be a good time, sir."

"I'm not asking," Nick barked.

Nick hung up before Pepe could respond.

Nick took a raincheck on coffee with Morris. He drove directly to Alejandro's beach mansion, parked, got out. Conflicting emotions swirled inside him, like waves in a pool. He had to keep himself in check, maintain a level of self-control no matter what Alejandro might do or say.

He stopped on the stoop, looked up at the surveillance camera, waved. Then he rang the doorbell. The door opened within seconds. Pepe had stationed himself near the door in anticipation of Nick's arrival.

"Nicolas," Pepe said, using the Spanish pronunciation.

Nick crossed the threshold without responding or being invited in. An intentional breach of protocol. Pepe swallowed his displeasure and closed the door.

Nick marched forward into the main living area with the beautiful kitchen and the breathtaking views. He headed straight for Alejandro.

Alejandro stood up from his chair. He faced Nick, put his hand out.

Nick slapped the outstretched hand away.

"Fuck you, dipshit" he spat. "I ain't fucking shaking hands with you."

Alejandro's mouth dropped open. Then anger flashed in his eyes.

"Who the fuck do you think—" he began.

"Shut your motherfucking mouth and *listen* for once in your Goddamned ultra-privileged, one-percenter's life." Nick noted that both Alejandro and Pepe were shocked silent and still as his own anger and pain boiled over.

"I am sick and Goddamned tired of getting calls from Mayors, Governors, and assorted politicians you have in your pocket demanding updates, action, and generally trying to micromanage me and my detectives."

"Then my daughter's killer," Alejandro countered.

"You don't fucking dictate how I do my job."

"Then do your fucking job," Alejandro shot back. "Why haven't you arrested someone?"

"Because we don't have enough evidence," Nick said.

"And why not?"

"Because he's smart," Nick answered. "This guy targets different genders, different ages, different ethnicities. He even hunts in different cities. He bounces around so that by the time the local cops know something's wrong, he's already gone." He drew a breath, knowing that technically, he should not be saying all this to a family member of a victim. Then he continued. "This guy behaves the exact opposite of how a traditional serial killer behaves."

Alejandro took this in. "Why would be do that? How would he know to do that?"

"There some very accurate police procedurals on TV," Nick answered. "He's probably watched some TV, some documentaries, read a few true crime books, took notes. Then behaved accordingly."

"Why haven't you called in the FBI?"

"I have," Nick said, surprising Alejandro back into silence. "We're waiting to hear back from their profilers. In the meantime, my team and I are working a profile of our own. We will catch this guy."

"Wait a minute," Alejandro said, looking confused. "If you called the FBI, why haven't they sent in their Behavioral Unit like on that one TV show?"

Nick sighed. "Real police work isn't a TV show," he said. "We don't solve cases inside of an hour with time for commercials. It takes days. Weeks. Months. Sometimes years."

"Are you saying this will take years?"

"It takes however long it takes," Nick responded. "But the more you fuck with me, the slower everything goes. Get it?"

"So. You're slow walking this?"

"The more time I spend dealing with your shit, the less time I spend working your daughter's case, numb nuts."

Alejandro sighed, all the anger leaving him to be replaced by his sorrow and grief. His legs folded. He collapsed. Pepe rushed forward to catch him but was too late. Alejandro sunk into the chair.

Pepe turned his angered face towards Nick. "Satisfied?"

"Stay out of this," Nick warned.

"I can't."

"You'd fucking better."

Pepe gulped. He was not documented, and he knew Nick knew it. And although local police were currently barred from dropping a dime on illegals to ICE, he also knew an anonymous tip from a payphone or a burner could never be traced.

"I'm sorry," Alejandro muttered. He rubbed his face with his hand. "You don't know what it's like."

"You're not the first family member I've had to console."

"You call this consolation?"

"This is tough love."

"Anything else?"

"You think I'm slow walking the investigation to get back at you for what your family did to mine.

"We're the same family."

"I don't see it that way."

Alejandro sat forward in his chair. "If you want to get technical about it, we're half-brothers."

"I'm not here to get technical," Nick said. Ice in his voice. "I'm here to tell you if you want to help me catch Ramey's killer, then stay the fuck out of my way."

Alejandro closed his eyes, remorse playing across his face.

"Just so there's no misunderstanding between us," Nick said. "Your father tried to pay my mother to abort me. He ignored my mother after she gave birth to me. He continued to ignore her until the day she died. Your entire family ignored my very existence. I've never been recognized in the Domingo family tree. We never got anything, financially or otherwise. But none of that, and I do mean *none of it*, means that I'm gonna ignore what happened to Ramsey. Got it?"

Alejandro did not answer immediately. He rubbed his eye, his body sagged with the weight of the world upon him. Nick threw a challenging glare at Pepe, who simply stepped back and stared at the floor.

Alejandro spoke. "I'm sorry, Nicolas."

"Then leave me and my detectives the motherfuck alone. Let us do our fucking jobs."

"You don't need to use that kind of language," Pepe said.

"Shut the motherfuck up, Pepe," Nick barked. "This is between me and him."

Pepe said no more. He snaked his tongue between his teeth and his cheeks.

"Are we clear?" Nick said to his half-brother.

Alejandro nodded.

"I'll see myself out."

Nick turned and stormed back the way he had come. He did not look back. Pepe trailed after him. When Nick got to the door, Pepe touched his arm. Nick turned around.

"You were pretty hard on him, Nicolas" the older man said.

"He deserves worse."

"He's sick with grief."

"He's always known where I was," Nick countered. "He's had decades to reach out."

"It's not his fault your father never did the right thing."

"True," Nick allowed. "But he never did anything to make it right. So, don't ask me to take it easy on him."

"Nicolas—"

"Cancer took her," Nick said sharply, cutting him off. "I was twelve. I was the only one there. All alone. No one offered to help pay for her care, no one visited her in hospice, no one attended the funeral, no one sent flowers, not even a Goddamned sympathy card."

Pepe said nothing.

"I got the message loud and clear. We meant *nothing* to these people." He paused. "But that door swings both ways. I put the Domingo family in my rearview mirror." He grinned a bit. "I graduated high school, graduated college, joined the Force, built a life and a career for myself completely separate from all... *this.*" He gestured around. "I've worked my ass off to get where I am. My success is mine and mine alone." The hard glare to his eyes reappeared, as did his sharp tone. "So, don't call me Nicolas Castillo ever again. The man you see is not the boy you remember. I'm Lieutenant Nick Castle, San Diego Police department. Got it?"

"Yes, *Lieutenant.*"

Nick stormed out. As he slipped into the driver's seat of the car, his mind recounted everything that had transpired.

Score one for me, he thought.

Pepe watched through the window, still as a statue. Only when the lieutenant had left did Pepe turn away. He found Alejandro still in the living area.

"Did he leave?" Alejandro asked.

"Yes, sir," Pepe answered.

"I just want him motivated to find Ramsey's killer."

"Nicolas Castillo has grown up to be a right and honorable man."

Alejandro thought for a moment. Pepe had a rare gift for seeing right into a person's heart and judging their intentions. And he was never wrong about people, good or bad.

"It's just the injustice of it, you know?"

"Injustice demands justice, sir," Pepe said. "Any slight, no matter how small or how deeply buried in the past, demands an accounting. A reckoning. A balancing of the cosmic scales."

"What do you mean by that?"

By then, Pepe was walking out of the great room and into another part of the house.

The Vampire was awake, shaking off the brain fog. He had thrown some clothes on and had sat down in front of his laptop. As the computer booted up, he microwaved his second mug of blood.

His laptop was up and running by the time he got back. Sunday night here, but already Monday in Tokyo, Hong Kong, Shanghai, Macao.

He punched a few keys, frowned. Lots of red across the screen. All the Asian indexes were down. They had been up on Friday. But rising interest rates and a nagging, non-transitory inflation threatened to stall the markets. This did not bode well for tomorrow when the American markets opened.

An awareness distracted him. A snarl rippled across his face.

Maya.

She was not far away. Not downtown. The sense was stronger, sharper. Like a knife's cutting edge. She called out to him, a vampiric siren's song, drawing him to her.

To his own destruction.

He pushed back with his own consciousness. *Do not anger me.*

I am your Mother.

A mother teaches her young, nurtures them. You are simply She Who Made Me.

I am your Mother.

You deliberately violated my territory. You refuse to leave. You are trampling on every vampire rule of peaceful coexistence amongst our kind.

I wish to see you.

Begone.

I will not.

Then face Final Death.

He deliberately broke the psychic connection before she could respond. It was impolite, even rude. That was intentional.

He heard three heartbeats approaching. Two he recognized, one seemed vaguely familiar. He moved around the living room, turning on lights for his guests. He put his sunglasses on, opened the door.

Reggie, Nick, and Valerie all stood outside his door, grouped closely together. Reggie stood there, one hand raised, knuckles ready to rap on the wood. He seemed startled when the door swung open.

"I hate it when you do that," Reggie muttered.

"Reginald. Nick. Detective Wahl. What a pleasant surprise." The Vampire stepped back, gestured. "Enter freely, and of your own will." He smiled to himself. Quoting that line from *Dracula* always amused him. At his age, he took his amusement wherever he found it.

The three detectives entered. The Vampire closed the door, bade them to sit and be comfortable. He sat where he had been previously.

The Vampire closed the laptop. "To what do I owe this pleasant surprise??"

"We have a problem," Reggie stated.

"And what, pray tell, is that?"

"You," Valerie said sharply.

The Vampire's eyebrows arched behind his sunglasses. "Indeed?"

"You're wrong," she spat. "And these two won't talk."

"I see."

"Here's the bottom line. Either come clean with me, or I go straight to Internal Affairs."

"What is it you think is 'off' about me?"

"Do you have a criminal past?"

"Oh," he smiled, "you have no idea."

"That's what I thought," she said. "I tried checking you out. You know what I found?"

"No."

"Nothing. No name, no aliases, no birth certificate, no social security number. No fingerprints. No DNA. No social media. It's like you don't exist."

"By your own admission, I am a covert operative," he said. "A ghost. Someone who does not exist."

Anger flashed in her eyes. She bolted out of her seat.

"We'll let Internal Affairs figure this out." She made for the door.

Suddenly, the Vampire was in front of her, barring her path. He was no longer smiling. Appalled, she wondered, *how the hell did he get in front of me so fast?*

"Please do not leave."

"Get out of my way."

"You seek answers?"

"Detective," Nick said.

Valerie paused.

"Our backs are against the wall on this one, Grandpa," Reggie said.

Valerie frowned. What was that?

Grandpa?

"She won't stop until she knows," Nick said. "Best get it over with."

The Vampire considered this, ran the possibilities in his head. Even if she knew, who could she tell? Who would believe her?

"Detective Wahl, please take a seat. I shall reveal all."

Unsure, Valerie looked to Reggie and Nick. Nick shrugged in a "what are you going to do?" manner. Reggie merely nodded his head, indicating everything would be fine. Her curiosity overrode her uncertainty, and she moved back to the sofa and sat in the middle between Reggie and Nick.

"Okay," she said. "Reveal all."

The Vampire stood in front of them. "What I am about to reveal may be difficult to accept."

"Everything about you is difficult to accept," she countered.

"The creature you see before you, this thing that I am, is flesh and blood," he intoned. "But I am no man."

"What?"

"I am not human," he continued. "I died over one hundred years ago."

Valerie read the room. Both her partner and her superior officer sat there like this was common knowledge. So, what was going on here? Some kind of hypnotism, mesmerism, or perhaps a mass hysteria.

"Okay," she said evenly. "I'll play along." She noticed the pale man's face change subtly. Was she getting under his creepy skin? Maybe.

Good.

"So how did you die?"

"I was shot. Three times." He lifted his shirt, exposing his washed-out torso. Three circular scars shone on his chest under the light. He dropped his shirt back down.

Valerie frowned. The scars were real enough. And any one of them would have been a kill shot. But three of them grouped so tightly together?

"As I lay in a rainswept alley bleeding out, the inevitable result of my misspent youth, a strange woman appeared from the shadows and made me an offer." His bony fingers wrapped around one side of his sunglasses.

"It was, as they say, an offer I could not refuse." He pulled his glasses off in one swift motion, exposing his black, bottomless pit eyes.

Valerie gasped instinctively.

The Vampire smiled, this time baring his fangs.

She recoiled back into the sofa's cushions. "Jesus Christ!"

"No," the Vampire responded, "not even close."

The initial shock wearing off, Valerie croaked, "What are you?"

"I. Am... *Vampyr*," he said, using the ancient word.

"*Vampyr?*" She ran the word through her head. "Vampire?" She watched him nod. "You mean, coffins, crosses, blood, all that?"

"I spend my daylight hours in bed, thank you very much," he said. "And I am rather fond of looking at crosses. I have a deep abiding respect for the ideals they represent."

"And blood?"

"Food."

"So, you run around biting people on the neck?"

"Not when I can help it."

Valerie bolted off the sofa, spun around to her colleagues. "How the fuck can you two idiots be involved with this clown?" She whirled back around to face the Vampire, her face flushed with rage. "And I don't know what the fuck you're trying to pull but take those contact lenses out and take those fangs out of your mouth."

The Vampire stood there. He did not move or speak. He simply stared at Valerie.

"Motherfucker, I carry a gun."

"Use it."

She could not believe her ears.

"What?"

"You heard me."

Valerie pulled her handgun out, allowed it to dangle in her hand at her side. The Vampire knew she would not actually draw down on him and fire unless provoked.

This was going to be interesting.

She stood in front of him, about eight feet away. He bared his fangs and hissed, like in a bad movie. He raised his arms over his head, fingers curled into claws. He moved forward menacingly.

Valerie took one step back, raised her firearm, aimed at center or mass, and fired. The shot rang loud in the apartment. The man in front of her grunted and spun around, his arms flashing across his body. He fell to the floor.

Valerie stood there, eyes wide as saucers. What had she just done?

"Oh my God!"

"Don't worry," Reggie said.

"I just shot him!"

"He's fine," Nick said.

"Happens all the time," Reggie added.

She shoved her handgun back into its holster and moved to check out the damage. He was probably dead by now. As she squatted beside him, she heard a gentle chuckle. It was coming from the body beside her. The chuckle extended out, grew in volume and mirth, becoming uproarious laughter as the Vampire rolled over on the rug and gazed up at her.

"Is that the best you can do, Young One?"

Her jaw dropped. Her mouth fell open as the Vampire propped himself on one elbow, casually. As if he had not just been shot. Where was the blood? It should have been gushing out of him like Old Faithful.

Then her eyes focused on his hand, the one he held out between them, clenched in a fist. She watched as he slowly uncurled his fingers, opened his hand.

In his palm lay the bullet she had fired. A red trail of ripped skin traced the line of the bullet's path where it had dug a furrow as the hand had clenched around it when it was traveling at sixteen hundred feet per second.

"A souvenir?" he asked casually.

He moved to stand up. Startled, Valerie jumped up, swung her firearm up again.

What happened next happened so fast Valerie did not see it coming. The Vampire was on her in a millisecond. He wrenched the handgun out of her grasp quickly, efficiently, careful to not break any bones. He tossed it aside with one hand as he simultaneously grabbed her by the throat and hoisted her high above the floor.

Dangling there, she grabbed his arm and pushed to take the pressure of her body weight off her neck. Choking, gasping for breath, she stared down at the undead creature, and yes, he was truly an *undead creature*, standing below her. Black lifeless eyes like in those nature shows about Great White Sharks. He snarled, baring his fangs.

They were real, she realized.

He was real.

Detective Valerie Wahl tapped out then, patting his forearm with one hand. The Vampire lowered her with great care until her feet touched the floor once more. He released his viselike grip, let his arm drop as one of her hands flew up to embrace her throat. She coughed, gulping in great amounts of air.

Finally, she managed to croak out, "Both of you knew about this?"

They nodded.

"He's my great, great grandfather," Reggie answered.

Valerie frowned, jerked a thumb over her shoulder towards the Vampire. "But he's…", then she pointed at Reggie. "And you're…"

"I understand your confusion," the Vampire said. "Just know that true love does not know skin color – even back in my time. I loved Danae, his great, great grandmother with all my heart. With every fiber of my being, I loved her. I love her to this day."

She noticed the strain, recognized the emotion in his voice. Even after all this time? What kind of burden did he still carry?

"I loved her so much I was willing come back from my own death to flee the country of my birth so that we go to France live in peace."

"Wait. Why France?"

"France was the only country at the time that had legalized interracial marriage," Reggie explained.

"I was giving up my criminal life," the Vampire said. "But my criminal life was not content to let me go. I loved Danae so much I became… *this* in my gambit to not lose her."

"You lost her, anyway, didn't you?"

"When I revealed my new self to her, she recoiled from the sight of me," the Vampire whispered, remembering it as if it had occurred yesterday. "She cast me out."

She began to understand the enormity of his perpetual pain. "I'm sorry."

"As am I, Young One."

"Why are you calling me 'Young One'?"

"It suits you."

Both Nick and Reggie rose from their seats.

"Now that we've gotten this resolved," Nick said, "we still have a serial killer to apprehend."

"How do we know this isn't the killer?" Valerie asked.

"Do you remember the drug cartel case?" the Vampire queried.

"Sure."

"You saw the bodies from the apartment?"

"Sure."

"The damage inflicted?"

"Yes."

"Then you are familiar with how I feed," he concluded. "Criminals only, and in such a way they cannot become like me." He shrugged. "Do any of your victims look anything like those from the cartel?"

"No," she allowed.

"And the clock is ticking," Reggie added. "Morris should be at the precinct by now."

The Vampire still felt Maya's pull. "I must first attend to another matter," the walking corpse said.

The three humans gawked at him.

"I shall meet you there later."

The detectives moved towards the door. The Vampire smiled, opened the door for them. They filed out, Valerie taking one more look at him, both fear and fascination dancing in her eyes. He closed the door behind them.

Maya's mental tug had become more insistent. San Diego had been his ever since he had arrived. He liked being the only vampire in town. His occasional live feedings went largely unnoticed. Just another criminal who met a violent end as far as the cops were concerned. Maya had put all that in jeopardy.

And the Vampire simply could not, *would not,* allow that.

This was his home.

He had roots here. Family here.

And the Vampire would fight to protect what was his, to the death if need be. Win or lose, live or die. He was fine with either outcome.

He would face Final Death without compromise and leave this world without regret.

CHAPTER TWELVE

The white Lexus crept south through the alley, turned right onto Adams Avenue, and prowled across the bridge over Interstate 15.

The Vampire drove within the speed limit as approached Normal Heights. If pulled over, he might lose control and eat someone. He was in danger of falling into the Vampiric Abyss.

A vampiric "no man's land", the Vampiric Abyss pushed a vampire towards devolving into a mindless killing machine that could only be satiated by devouring every living thing in sight.

The Vampire had been there, remembered it clearly. That night five years back, in that sagging hovel that at the time served as Lottie's abode. It had taken every ounce of self-discipline he possessed to keep his rage for revenge to completely engulf him, drown him.

Destroy him.

The man's name had been Rick Oakley. He had been the boss of the cartel the Vampire and his human allies dismantled, one gruesome piece at a time. And Mr. Oakley had gotten his comeuppance worst of all.

He had put a loaded firearm to Lot-Lot's head.

A fatal error.

The Vampire had torn Oakley's chest open with his bare hands, ripped out his heart, and had begun *eating* it before Oakley had a chance to die. The last image Oakley's brain registered on this Earth before descending into whatever hell awaited him was the Vampire dining on the still-beating organ. And then the Vampire had ripped the head off the still warm corpse, upended the ragged remains over his open mouth, and bathed in his enemy's blood.

Nobody put a gun to his Lot-Lot's head and lived.

The pull grew stronger. At the intersection of Adamas and Felton, he knew. She was inside Le Stat's.

Waiting.

He stopped at the red light. Rumbling inside, trembling with rage outside. Hands tightly gripping the steering wheel. Powerful emotions, threatening to explode.

Taut springs, waiting to be sprung.

The light turned green. He turned, pulled to the curb just south of the Fire Station. He locked the doors, looked at the rear entrance and small back patio.

Maya had further violated his territory.

Careful, he told himself. Losing your temper is what she wants.

The Vampire concentrated on the sounds around him: firefighters in the station lifting weights. Night owl coffee drinkers lounging on the back patio, conversations about sex and drugs and how much they hated their low-pay, dead end jobs. The smell of coffee and quiche, hot teas and ham sandwiches, the oily stench of road grime and automobile drippings.

He shrugged his shoulders, rolled his head on the end of his neck. Resolute, he stepped forward, rounded the short red brick wall that established the patio's perimeter. Small bistro tables and chairs scattered about. People drinking, eating, vaping. All dressed similarly yet distinctly, tattoos and piercings visible on some, others not so much. A few kept to themselves, absorbed with their tablets or phones, scrolling through text from friends and lovers.

The Vampire focused, closed his mind. A sort of vampire stealth mode. He opened the screen door and slipped through.

The clatter of mugs, and plates assailed him. Humidity from coffeemakers, heating elements, and the deep sink scullery peppered his face. The coffee smelled heavenly, but he knew he should not drink it. He could sip black coffee now and then, but he disliked the bitter taste. If he added sweetener or creamer, he would become violently ill.

He had learned that the hard way.

He had learned everything about vampire survival the hard way.

He emerged from the back-kitchen, moved around the glass pastry case near the cash register. A young woman, Hispanic and curvy, ordered a coffee and pointed at a slice of breakfast quiche. The barista, tall and thin with a whippet chest and a shock of dark wavy hair, smiled as he took her order. The Vampire could smell their pheromones as they experienced mutual attraction.

The seating area ahead of him sat immediately inside the front entrance on Adams. To his right, through a short hallway sat the main room, a cavernous area with a twenty-foot ceiling and decorated with assorted mismatched pieces – tables and chairs, sofas, settees. All different colors, different patterns, different fabrics. Different styles from different eras.

He entered the huge room. He paused, scanning systematically.

There she was.

Sitting primly on a gray settee near the back, a scarred coffee table crouching low in front of her. More cushioned chairs surrounded the table. She sat with her back to the wall. She could see everyone in the room, their comings and goings.

Maya had sensed him arriving, approaching, then slipping inside like a wraith. How proud she was of him! What a marvelous monster, what a wonderous vampire he had become! But she could not allow that to derail her agenda.

The Vampire snarled slightly. She saw the nose crease, one side of his lip raise, showing one white fang underneath. Then the thin lip dropped back down, the fang disappearing behind waxy flesh. When he moved, it was smooth. Deliberate. Exuding confidence.

Dominance.

He winded his way around tables and chairs, passing humans who sat blissfully unaware of the terrible creatures, God's and nature's abnormal apex predators, two immortal monsters for whom humans were their food. He ignored them, ignored their heartbeats, the warmth of the blood gushing through their arteries…

Focus, he chided himself. He slid sideways around the scarred, stained coffee table and sat in a soft wingback chair ninety degrees to Maya's left. Like her, his back was against a wall.

"I see the resentment wafting off you," she said.

The Vampire said nothing.

"You think I abandoned you?" She seemed genuinely surprised. "I allowed you to spread your wings and fly."

The Vampire was shocked.

"And look at how you've succeeded!" She clasped her hands. "Look at what you've become!"

"And I am supposed to thank you for that?"

"You've succeeded wildly on your own," she answered. "No one can take that away from you."

"True," he conceded. "No can take it away from me." He leaned in. "Not even you."

Maya flashed a fang, then sat back.

"That night in the alley. Why did you Turn me?"

"Is that important?"

"I am aware of circumstances surrounding your tragic human death," he revealed. "I am aware of the… *assault* you suffered at the hands of white men."

"White *boys*," she corrected. "Real men would never commit such an atrocity."

"Agreed," he said.

"And as far as my assailants," she smiled, "they died. Violently."

"The question remains. Why me, a white man, after what happened?"

Maya sat there a long time, barely breathing. The Vampire sensed her turmoil at bringing up past acts of sadistic cruelty.

"You were different," she said at last. "You truly loved her."

"Danae."

"Your love for her was complete and overwhelming. You weren't using her; you were building a life with her. You deserved a second chance."

"A second chance you knew would fail miserably," the Vampire added. "You told me so at the time."

Maya nodded. "I could have been wrong."

The Vampire grimaced.

"Look at you," she marveled. "You love her still. You grieve her passing." She smiled. "You are one of the finest men I've ever met."

The conversation lulled. Neither vampire opened themselves up for the other to read.

"Why are you here?"

"I go where I want. And don't blame me that things didn't work out with Danae."

"I do not."

"Then show me some respect."

He leaned father forward, intense. "If you were not my Vampire Mother, I would have already bathed in your blood."

She grinned, a jungle cat licking its lips.

"Leave my territory by dawn tomorrow," he ordered. "Do not return."

"And if I don't?"

"Then prepare for Final Death."

"And if I kill you instead?"

"Then all of San Diego is yours – if you can keep it."

The Vampire rose slowly from his chair, never taking his eyes off her. She watched him, waiting for any false move, any feint, any hint he might attack right here and now.

He backed away several paces, finally turned around and stomped towards the hallway through which he had come. He had conducted himself better than she had hoped, better than many would have in his position.

Maya needed new hunting grounds. She had hoped her progeny would accept her, give her sanctuary. She had already fled two thousand miles from New Orleans to escape a marauding gang of vampires. It would take decades to recover from her humiliation. They had overpowered her, bound her to a chair and placed her in a room under a skylight.

And then threatened to leave her there.

She knew they were serious. They would indeed leave her there. The ultraviolet rays would char her, fry her like chicken. She would never reanimate again.

Final Death.

She had watched the black sky slowly replaced by the dull gray of the coming dawn. She had cried blood. She had begged for mercy, had screamed aloud that she would leave New Orleans, now and forever, if they would let her go.

A door at the far end had opened. A vampire she had never seen before stepped inside, introduced herself as Lilly. Black hair, sallow skin, petite body. She had been Asian in her human life. Maya felt her power immediately.

Lily cordially repeated the terms of Maya's release. Leave New Orleans. Never return. She then slit through the duct tape bindings with one flick of her wrist.

Maya had fallen out of her chair, weak from shock and relief. She had crawled towards the door and had fled for the safety of her bed. The very same night she reanimated, she fled.

The stench of her shame still clung to her.

Maya would not run again, even if that meant killing her own Vampire Son.

The Vampire drove through the city streets. Fingers gripped the steering wheel so tightly his dead, inelastic skin threatened to rip at the knuckles. He huffed and grimaced as glaring lights and blaring horns made him angrier. He needed to calm down before he got to the station. Driving surface streets added minutes to the commute.

He knew that Maya would not leave on her own. He cruised south, Balboa Park to his right and the old Navy Hospital administration building to his left. The decision came to him just before Park Avenue became 12th Street.

He had to kill Maya.

Father Justin Ng had just finished a long day. Though retired, the Church was still his life. Service to God was in his blood. He simply did not know what to do with himself otherwise.

He had sought an audience with the archbishop. He had pitched his idea for a scholarly tome that could be particularly beneficial to young priests as they endured the pull of earthly pleasures.

The archbishop had been enthusiastic. Times were tough for the church, especially with all the bad press in recent years. Recruiting young people to become priests was at an all-time low. Retaining them had become a bigger problem than anyone in the established hierarchy had anticipated. Anything that could help was welcome.

He now sat on the simple wooden folding chair outside his room. He smoked a cheap cigar he had bought from the convenience store on Grape Street. But he had splurged on a small bottle of a more expensive whiskey. Between the cigar and the whiskey, he felt a sublime satisfaction. He would start tomorrow.

"Father Ng?"

The female voice coming out of the darkness startled him. He had neither seen nor heard anyone approaching. He peered into the darkness.

"Yes," he responded.

A shape materialized out of the muddy shadows. Backlit from a security light attached to the chapel wall, he could see her form, but not her face.

"Come closer," he beckoned. "Don't be afraid, my child."

She stepped a bit closer, then repeated, "My child?" Then she moved close enough for him to see her.

Ng's eyes widened at what he saw. Black hair frosted silver, long and flowing. Lifeless eyes. Pallid, bloodless skin. And when she smiled, the fangs of a vampire.

"It's been a long time since anyone has called me that," Maya said. "A very long time indeed."

The Vampire had calmed down considerably by the time he walked into the precinct. He saw Nick, Reggie, Valerie, and Morris already in Nick's glass-walled office. He glided towards them.

He regretted committing himself to this. He would have declined anyone other than Reginald. A serial killer operating in a large city in America? How incredibly... *prosaic*.

Yet the methodology was anything but.

The Vampire knew that most serial killers did not stop on their own. Whatever need they satisfied with their kills was elusive, and quickly dissipated. Like a drug addict, no matter how good one hit was, the killer was forever searching for that next fix. This killer would not disappear anytime soon.

He was just getting started.

Inside the office, Nick stood behind his desk speaking to the others. He stopped, eyes drifting over towards the approaching creature. Everyone else's collective gaze followed his.

The Vampire opened the door and strode in.

"Greetings," the Vampire said.

"Did you get that other matter resolved?" Reggie asked.

"The other party is proving to be obstinate."

"Please find a way to deal with it simultaneously," Castle said. "We need your *unique perspectives* on this."

"Of course."

"Now," Nick said, "there's nothing you don't already know. We're still waiting on DNA. That takes days, sometimes weeks."

"Do we have a new strategy to ensnare our quarry?"

"An interesting way to phrase it," Castle said. "Yes. We're going to stake out Splinter again, see who comes and goes. See what patterns we can detect."

"Splendid," the Vampire said. This could serve dual purposes.

"I'm going undercover," Valerie replied. "Reggie is my backup."

"I'd like you in there too," Castle said.

"Of course," the Vampire replied.

"Let them do the heavy lifting," Castle said to the Vampire, pointing to Valerie and Reggie. "Hang back. Anything goes sideways, you swoop in. Don't let them get killed."

The Vampire nodded his understanding.

"Morris and I will be in the surveillance van outside," Castle continued. "Once we identify a suspect, we'll all swarm him, cut off his escape, and arrest him."

"And if he doesn't want to come quietly?" Reggie asked.

"Fuck him up until he comes around to your way of thinking," Castle said.

"And if that is not enough?" the Vampire queried.

"If their lives are in danger, do what you do." Castle paused, then, "Eddie, I'd prefer him alive, but I'll settle for dead."

A slow grin spread across the lower half of the Vampire's face. Thin lips parted, exposing sharp fangs.

"We'll have backup units on standby," Castle concluded. "Let's catch this fucker before he kills someone else's son or daughter." He paused, checked his watch. "We'll meet here tomorrow after sundown. We head out around nine thirty. I want the three of you inside and blending in by ten. Questions?"

"Are the owners aware?"

"They know and have promised to stay out of our way. Something about their business license, a tax issue or two, and it seems there may be some question about immigration status."

"I wish we didn't have to squeeze people like that," Valerie said.

"You're serving a greater good," the Vampire said.

"Still doesn't make it right."

"This isn't something we can fix," Castle said. "Now get out of here. Get some sleep."

The Lieutenant's tone told them all he was in no mood for either political or philosophical discussions. Reggie, Valerie, and Morris stood as the Vampire reached for the doorknob behind him.

Outside, the Vampire pulled Reggie aside. "When was the last time you visited your grandmother?"

Reggie immediately sagged. "Too long," he said.

"Rectify that."

The Vampire turned and breezed towards the exit. Valerie watched him go, turned to her partner.

"Family issues?" she jibed.

"Shut up," he said good-naturedly.

She grinned in response, then glanced at the clock. "The bars are open a couple more hours. I thought I'd go knock one back."

"You want company?"

Outside, the Vampire buttoned his wool Navy blue peacoat up to his chin, popped the collar up to protect his neck and cheeks. Cold and dampness still seeped in. Being devoid of inner warmth, the Vampire felt cold all the time.

In death as in life, it was often the small things one noticed the most. Things taken for granted when one has them are often greatly missed once gone.

Like being an endotherm.

The Vampire unlocked his car, slid in. The engine started; he pulled away from the curb. He cruised the empty streets, heading home. Minutes later, he parked in the alley behind his apartment building.

He rounded the building, then came to a sudden stop. He snarled.

Maya.

He removed his sunglasses, looked around. Seeing nothing, he stepped away from the bottom of the stairs. The Vampire glided to the front sidewalk, sniffed the air. The scent, only half-remembered, beckoned him north. He crept up the sidewalk, testing the air with his nose and tongue.

He slipped between parked cars, crossed the dark street to the other side. His feet eventually left the sidewalk. Eyes down as he sniffed the dank ground, picking up a scent. Her footsteps. The scent became stronger. Then overpowering.

She had stopped here, spent quite a bit of time here. But where exactly was here?

He lifted his head, focused on the structure in front of him.

He gasped audibly.

His first emotion was fear, replaced a deep, visceral anger, a rumbling rage.

The Vampire stood where She Who Made Him had stood. He stood now where NO vampire, save for himself, should EVER stand.

He stood in the back yard of his Lot-Lot's house, with a clear view of the kitchen and dining room windows.

Eddie Marx's fury knew no bounds.

"Pick your poison," Valerie said as they sat down at a table.

Reggie scanned the area behind the bartender's head. The place was upscale and well stocked.

"Aberlour," he responded. "On the rocks."

She turned away, headed towards the bar. From the table, his eyes drifted slowly from her shoulders to her butt.

Reggie smiled appreciatively.

He sure did love to watch her walk away.

Valerie sashayed around chairs and tables. She stopped at the bar. The bartender, a young woman with visible tattoos and a delicate gold nose ring, moved down to Valerie's end.

"What can I get for you?" the bartender asked. Her name tag said Amy.

"A double of Aberlour over real rocks, and a straight shot of Kentucky bourbon," Valerie answered.

"Any particular bourbon?"

"Whatever you have."

Amy nodded. She grabbed up two glasses, began practicing her craft.

Valerie looked behind Amy at the mirrored wall with bottles of spirits stacked there. She could see the room. Her eyes darted from one side to the other, scrutinizing everyone and everything.

Maintain situational awareness. What is around you? Who is behind you? Check your blind corners. Danger lurks everywhere.

Then her eyes slid right so she could see Reggie. He sat straight in his chair, checking something on his phone. Whatever he was doing, it was not recreational. The look on his face was serious, intense, focused.

Movement from behind her left shoulder drew her attention. Amy stopped in front of her, three feet of mahogany separating them. She placed the drinks on the rubber mat.

Valerie paid, told Amy to keep the change. Amy smiled gratefully, nodded, and moved away. Valerie grabbed the drinks, made her way back towards Reggie. Holding one glass in each hand, she negotiated the chairs and tables like she was walking through a minefield.

Reggie closed his phone and put it aside as she placed the drinks on the table and sat down. She realized she really liked him smiling at her.

"Thanks," he said.

"You're welcome."

They sipped their drinks, relished the burn sliding down their throats.

"God, I needed that," she breathed.

"Indeed," he agreed. "What are you drinking?"

"Really good Kentucky bourbon."

He grinned, leaned back in his chair. He inhaled, blew out a great sigh.

"Tired?"

He nodded. "I've been up for, oh," he quickly checked his watch, "about twenty hours now."

"Is that unusual?"

He nodded.

"Well, if you're getting your sleep, I hope that means I'll get mine."

"So, you're serious about your sleep, eh?"

She nodded, took another sip of bourbon. "I've got a question."

"Shoot."

"How do you stay in such good shape?"

Surprised, he momentarily had no response. Finally, he said, "Good genes. Men in my family tend to be muscular. We don't start gaining weight until our fifties or sixties." He paused. "Plus, I work out. There's an exercise room in the back of the station."

"What kind of equipment?"

"TRX straps, resistance bands, a couple of treadmills, an elliptical. There's a speed bag and a heavy bag but bring your own gloves and hand wraps."

"Good to know."

He looked at her muscular shoulders. "Do you box?"

"Mixed martial arts."

"I'd better watch myself around you," he joked. "You might kick my ass."

Kicking his ass was not what she had in mind.

In that moment, Reggie Downing realized just how beautiful Valerie Wahl really was. His eyes flickered down, and he noticed just how gently the fabric of her shirt caressed her breasts.

He caught himself, looked away. Took another sip of his drink.

Stop it, he admonished himself. She's a fellow officer. She's your junior partner, your subordinate. You're her immediate supervisor. Power dynamics, man. Don't get stupid and start thinking with the wrong head.

When the dick gets hard, the brain goes soft.

Valerie knew Reggie was attracted to her, and it warmed her. She had not been looked at *that way* for a long time. Occupational hazard. She knew any hanky panky was strictly *verboten*. She knew the rules existed for a reason, and ordinarily, she agreed with them.

But tonight, after having not gotten laid in over a year, the only thing she wanted was to take Reggie home and fuck his brains out.

"Last call!" Amy shouted from behind the bar.

Valerie sighed irritably. She grabbed her glass, threw her head back, downed the rest of the bourbon. It burned all the way down. She slammed the glass upside down on the table. She sat back in her chair.

Reggie asked, "What's wrong?"

"Just thinking about the job." No way Valerie was going to tell Reggie she was horny.

"It'll still be there tomorrow," he said.

He stood up, glass in his hand. He knocked back the last of his Scotch, placed the glass back on the table.

They walked towards the door. He held the door as Valerie walked through.

"I'm this way," Reggie said, pointed down the street.

"This is me," she said, pointing in another direction.

"See you tomorrow."

"Yeah. See you then."

They turned away from each other, walked away. As they gained distance from each other, they each felt a certain level of relief.

By the time he got home, all Reggie wanted was to collapse across his bed. He was so exhausted he didn't care he would be sleeping alone.

Again.

As usual.

He needed a girlfriend.

He unlocked the door, slipped inside. He closed the door, listened for the latch to catch. He turned the deadbolt, moved away from the door. He removed his coat, hung it on a coatrack.

"So, who's the hot chick?"

Reggie spun, drew his weapon, and hit a light switch that bathed the room in light as he dropped to a kneeling firing position behind a chair. He quickly found his target, aimed directly at her head. At this distance, there was no way he would miss.

"Who the fuck are you?"

She smiled, showing her fangs. "I'm Maya."

CHAPTER THIRTEEN

Maya stared with wide unblinking eyes that reminded Reggie of an insect. A praying mantis. That was it.

"Your firearm will not stop me," she said.

"A bullet to the brainpan will slow you down."

She grinned, stood up from her chair, smoothed her long skirt. The black leather corset barely held her breasts inside. She flicked her hair back over her shoulder.

"So, you know."

Reggie thought back. A comely woman, silver hair, with a habit of stepping from out of the shadows and gloom.

"Yes," she said, reading his thoughts. "I am your great, great grandfather's Vampire Mother. In a way, we're related."

"I beg to differ." He never took his firearm off her. His finger encircled the trigger. "I know time must be becoming a factor. Dawn's coming. Say whatever you came to say."

"How do you know I didn't come here to kill you?"

"Because I'd probably already be dead."

"You're probably right."

She eyed him up and down. A faint smile flitted across her mouth. He could not tell if the smile was that of a woman who liked what she saw, or a predator sizing up its prey.

"Perhaps a bit of both," she responded. "And yes. I can read your thoughts."

"Of course, you can." He said it with a slight shrug of his shoulder as if this was the most natural thing in the world. "What can I do for you, Maya?"

"I wanted to make you aware of my presence, and my proximity." Her face went cold. "I also wanted to you to know that I can reach out and touch you any time I want."

He cocked the hammer back, aimed at her forehead. "Bring it, babe. But I'll die fighting."

He meant it.

She knew it.

A smile slowly spread across her mouth. "I like you," she said at last. "You've got balls. That's rare these days." She moved towards the door. "I hope I never have to kill you."

Reggie's gun stayed on her as she moved. "I'd prefer that."

As her hand reached for the doorknob, she paused. "You should sleep with that young redhead you were with earlier."

"Well. Now that you've entered my home uninvited, threatened to kill me, and given me advice on my sex life, you would please just fucking leave?"

She opened the door and slipped out, the folds of her black dress slipping after her like smoke. Then the door closed.

Reggie stayed where he was, stock still, aiming at his door. He did not know if this was some kind of vampire trick to get him to drop his guard, or if she was already heading downstairs. But he was not taking any chances. A full minute ticked by. When she did not come back during that time, he relaxed, put the safety back on his weapon and holstered it.

He plopped down on the foot of the bed.

What the fuck had that been about?

Maya, Grandpa Eddie's Vampire Mother was projecting power, establishing dominance. Why else enter Reggie's apartment without permission? Vampires didn't usually that. It went against their code. They considered it... *rude.*

Maya was a threat.

She was a threat to Grandpa, that was for sure. But she had threatened Reggie, too. Then another thought occurred. He chilled to the bone.

If Maya knew about Reggie and had no compunction entering his apartment, then she probably knew about Grandma Lottie.

Aw, shit.

He thrust his hand into his pants pocket, fumbled around. He found his phone, pulled it out. He checked his watch, then hit #1 on his speed dial. The phone rang at the other end.

"Yes?"

"Grandpa Eddie?"

"Ah, Reginald."

"Did you drop by Grandma Lottie's house after you left the precinct?"

"I did," the Vampire answered. "Why do you ask?"

"Are you still there?"

"No. What is this about?"

"Maya."

Dead silence at the other end. Then, "I see."

"Grandpa, what's going on?"

"Maya seeks new feeding grounds."

"And that's a problem?"

"San Diego *is mine*."

"No room for compromise?"

"None whatsoever."

"Sounds like it's going to get terminal for someone."

"It is an old score. It is time to settle it."

"Is there anything I can do?"

"Check on your grandmother tomorrow," the Vampire said. "Let us speak again tomorrow evening."

The line went dead. Reggie sighed, placed his phone on the nightstand. He peeled his holster off, fell back across the bed. As he lay there, he stared out through the window at the dark night beyond. Only a couple of hours until dawn.

Maybe he would just rest a bit.

Within seconds, Reggie was asleep.

Maya could feel her energy draining away with the coming dawn. Muscle weakness, lack of motivation, intractable fatigue. Vampires felt the same death pangs as humans at the end of life. But humans only endured it once. Vampires relived it every night.

No wonder vampires were referred to as The Damned.

Yet as Maya's body faded, she smiled, fangs peeking. She had achieved much tonight. She had further turned the proverbial screws to her Vampire Son. She had killed the priest. Outside the elderly Black woman's house, Maya had decided against her.

Maya had spied Lottie at the kitchen sink through the window. Rotund frame bathed in a yellow glow from the light above, gray hair, puffy face, sad tired eyes. She knew instinctively that Lottie was sick, very sick, and not long for this earth. So, Maya had decided to allow the old biddy to live for now.

She would be dead soon enough as it was.

The foundation for Eddie Marx's destruction had been laid. Each intrusion just a bit more invasive than the last, twisting the knife, calculated to push him more off balance, overwhelm him.

And that's when she would strike, dispatching Eddie Marx to his Final Death.

Then, the circle would close in full accordance with the Vampire Way. She grinned. Was that irony, or poetic justice?

No matter, she told herself. Either way, the result was the same.

Morning came early for Valerie Wahl. The blaring squawk from her merciless alarm pulled her up from the depths, forced her towards an unwilling level of consciousness.

Bloodshot, red-rimmed eyes opened. She sighed, already angry, pulled herself to the side of the bed. She slapped out blindly at the incessant alarm clock. By pure luck, one finger hit the snooze button on the fourth or fifth attempt.

She stood on unsteady feet. Holding her hands away from her sides to maintain equilibrium, she stumbled towards the bathroom. She managed to get on the toilet without keeling over.

Life's little victories.

When she was done, she caromed out of the bathroom, bumped her shoulder on the door frame. Pain exploded through the brain fog. She jolted, immediately awake. She wasn't certain if that was a blessing or a curse.

She rifled through her bedroom closet. She had not done laundry recently and was almost out of fresh clothes. Green jeans from yesterday, fresh shirt. Fresh socks, her trusty sneakers.

She shrugged into her holster, checked her firearm. She pressed a button on the side of her weapon, dropped the magazine out. She counted the rounds, reinserted it into the firearm. Then, she gently pulled the breech open about halfway, visually checking that there was indeed a round in the chamber. She secured the safety; thrust her weapon back into its holster. She grabbed her jacket and wallet on her way out the door.

Gray clouds hung low, obscuring the sun to nothing more than a pallid yellow orb in the eastern sky. The dull morning reflected her mood.

As she drove by the precinct, she noticed several men loitering near the front entrance. A van from a local news affiliate crouched along the curb. The camera guy tended to his equipment while the reporter, whose face she recognized, talked informally with one of the men. Picket signs leaned against the steps.

She made a left at the corner, then again into the police parking lot. No way she was walking through the front door today.

Reggie was already there, filling out a requisition form on his desktop. He looked to be in a foul mood himself. Tight lips, Laser-focused eyes.

She grabbed her travel mug off her desk. "Who are those guys out front?"

"Their signs say, 'Justice for Ramsey'."

"Oh, shit. There's a news van out there."

"They probably called everybody. Just a matter of time before more show up."

"Lieutenant's gonna be pissed."

"Lieutenant's gonna go ballistic," he corrected. "I don't want to be anywhere near him when he does. Get coffee. I'm requisitioning a car."

Valerie filled her mug, doctored it up. By the time she had done that, Reggie was walking away. He motioned for her to follow. She fell in behind him as they headed for the back exit.

Outside, they saw Nick's car pull in. They watched him get out, trying to read his face. It seemed neutral. They gave him a quick rundown on what appeared to be brewing out front. His jaw dropped in surprise, then closed. His eyes narrowed. His lips pursed, blanched white. He exhaled audibly through his nose, stalked forward without another word. They watched him enter the building.

"Come on," Reggie beckoned. "We're gonna go get the best breakfast in town."

They slid into the car, buckled up. He pulled out of the lot and into the nearly deserted streets. Buildings slid silently past them, concrete ghosts in the gray morning.

"So where is the 'best breakfast in town'?" she asked.

"Kensington."

Reggie turned right at 28th, took the onramp to Highway 94 East. They accelerated, entered traffic. The traffic flowing west into downtown San Diego was already heavy. As was the case in many cities, people worked in San Diego, but could not afford to live there. They lived in places like La Mesa, El Cajon, and Spring Valley where rents were cheaper.

Reggie took an exit off the 94, turned north in a gentle arc, and then took a ramp onto Interstate 15. Moments later, they exited at Adams Avenue, turned right. They turned left at Kensington Drive.

They crept up the tree-lined street, stopped in front of a red brick home.

"Here we are," Reggie announced. He killed the engine and unbuckled.

They walked up the walkway with Reggie in the lead. They stopped on the stoop. Reggie rapped loudly on the door.

"There's a doorbell," Valerie said, pointing.

"It's out of order."

A dark round face appeared in the window of the door. Female. Silver hair pulled back into a tight bun. Eyes popping wide. The lock slid back, the door opened, and a large Black woman, appeared. Joy erupted from her face. She held her arms out wide.

"Reggie!" she exclaimed. She wrapped her arms around him and crushed him to her. He hugged her back.

"Hi, Grandma."

Now Valerie understood. The elation on Grandma's face was evident. This woman adored her grandson, and he loved her back.

Reggie extricated himself from Lottie's arms. "Grandma, this is my new partner, Valerie Wahl. Val, this is Grandma Lottie."

Valerie put her hand out, expecting to shake Grandma's hand and exchange pleasantries. Lottie grabbed Valerie by the shoulders and pulled her forward into a huge hug just as warm and affectionate as any hug Valerie had ever experienced. She smiled instinctively, hugged her back.

"It's so nice to meet you," Lottie said.

"Nice to meet you, too, ma'am."

"Come on in," Lottie invited. She turned and waddled back inside. Reggie and Valerie followed. Reggie closed the door behind them. They wiped their feet, then followed Grandma Lottie down the hallway into the kitchen.

"You two want some breakfast?" Lottie asked.

"We'd love some," Reggie piped up.

"I wouldn't want to impose," Valerie said.

"Pish posh," Lottie replied. "No imposition at all." She pulled two coffee cups out of the cabinet and grabbed the carafe of steaming hot coffee she had made just minutes before. "Y'all seat yourselves."

Reggie and Valerie sat down at the vintage dinette. Lottie placed mugs filled with coffee in front of them. A sugar-filled mason jar sat on the table. A spoon lay beside it. Lottie bustled back in with a quart carton of creamer.

Reggie began doctoring his coffee. Valerie waited her turn. Lottie pulled a package of bacon and a carton of eggs out of the refrigerator.

"Ma'am, would you like some help?" Valerie asked.

"Don't you worry about me," Lottie said as she placed bacon strips into the bottom of a cast iron skillet. "I was gonna cook anyways. And it's just as easy for me to cook for three as it is one." She placed bread slices into the toaster.

Not wanting to intrude, Valerie looked at Reggie, the question in her eyes. He saw it, smiled at her. God, could he be any more scrumptiously handsome? He was telling her everything was indeed okay.

Soon they all sat at the table, plates of steaming bacon, scrambled eggs, and buttered toast in front of them. As they ate, they talked, mostly small talk. Valerie said little, preferring to watch, listen, and learn. Reggie obviously loved his grandmother to pieces, and she loved him back just as much. It warmed her heart to see such strong bonds between family members.

The food was delicious. Better than what Valerie could order in a restaurant. The eggs were creamy, fluffy, the bacon succulent and juicy. And the coffee! Several notches above the swill she usually choked down at the precinct.

"You know, there is another reason why I dropped by," Reggie stated.

"You mean, you need more reason than to get fed by your favorite grandmother?" She leaned towards Valerie. "He doesn't eat enough, you know."

He looked sheepish. "Grandpa Eddie got after me the other night because I hadn't been by like I should."

"Aw, that's all right," she said with a wave of her hand. "You're a Lead Detective. You're busy putting criminals in jail."

"Grandpa Eddie thinks there might be a prowler in the area," he said diplomatically. "I was wondering if you have seen or heard anything unusual."

Lottie stared at her grandson.

"It's okay, Grandma," he said, nodding towards Valerie. "She knows."

"Knows what?" Lottie asked guardedly.

"Everything about Grandpa Eddie."

Lottie swiveled her head towards Valerie. "Is this true?"

Valerie nodded.

"Have you seen anything?" Reggie reiterated.

"No." Lottie shook her head.

"Look, I don't want to scare you, but Grandpa thinks this prowler might be... someone like him."

Fear froze Lottie's face.

"Like I said, I don't want to scare you, but you deserve to know."

"Why would someone like that seek me out?"

Reggie shrugged. "It has something to do with Grandpa Eddie. Some of vampire thing."

"So, I'm safe during the day?"

"Yes."

"At night, won't she be safe if she stays inside?" Valerie asked. They both looked her way. "Vampires can't enter a house without permission from the owner, right?"

"That only works in the movies," Reggie said gently. This was all so new to Val, and he understood she still needed time to catch up. Initially, he had been the same way.

"Well, I'll lock all the doors and windows anyway," Lottie stated.

"If this one wants in, she'll get in."

Tension hung in the air, heavy as lead.

Suddenly, both Reggie's and Valerie's phones started beeping, an auditory signal that the incoming message was from Police Headquarters. They both grabbed quickly at their phones, stared at their screens.

Reggie looked up. "Sorry to eat and run, Grandma. Duty calls." Both he and Valerie rose from their seats. Lottie started to stand, but Reggie put a gentle hand on her shoulder.

"It's okay, Grandma. We'll see ourselves out."

"It was wonderful meeting you, Miss Lottie," Valerie said, shaking her hand.

"Well, it was wonderful meeting you, too," the elderly woman beamed. "I hope you come back soon to visit."

Valerie grinned from ear to ear. Her heart swelled. "I'd like that very much, ma'am."

Lottie's eyebrows rose. "Ooooooooh," she said, looking at Reggie. "I like her. Somebody taught her manners."

Reggie smiled approvingly. "Yes ma'am, they did."

Lottie turned in her chair towards Valerie, spread her arms out wide. "Give me a hug before you leave."

Valerie bent at the waist and put her arms around Lottie's massive shoulders. Lottie's arms enveloped her, pulled her close into warm folds of skin. It was the purest love Valerie had felt in a long time. She fought tears back.

"Now, you two run along," Lottie said, releasing Valerie. "Go put them bad guys in jail."

"Yes ma'am," the two detectives said in unison. They turned and headed towards the front door.

Outside in the car, they buckled up. As Reggie started the car, Valerie checked her phone. A sense of dread spread down her spine.

"Where are we going again?" Reggie asked.

"The Catholic church on Second Street," she said. "They found a priest dead."

"So?"

"It wasn't natural causes."

Reggie and Valerie arrived, and the church grounds were already buzzing. Yellow police tape laced up to the left of the main entrance. Uniformed cops stood guard for crowd control, which was meager this time of morning.

The detectives brandished their badges, ducked underneath the tape. Ahead of them, CSI techs collected evidence. They saw Sarah Ombaye ahead, her dark, almost black skin and short natural hair contrasting sharply against her white jumpsuit. She was busy directing a junior technician in proper field protocol. To their right, sitting on the edge of a brick-bordered flower bed, a priest leaned forward, red hair disheveled, eyes rimmed with red, looking shellshocked. He stared into infinity, saw nothing.

Sarah turned towards them as they approached.

"Detectives."

"Hey, Sarah," Reggie returned. "Have you met Detective Wahl?"

"I don't believe so."

Reggie made the formal introductions. The two women shook hands, exchanged greetings.

"So, what do we know about the victim?" Reggie asked.

She led them over to the body, gestured to the technician there to pull the cover back. Father Ng lay on his side near his wooden chair. Had he not been so pale, he could have been asleep.

They all squatted beside the body. "At a distance, it would appear he simply passed away and fell from his chair."

"He looks peaceful," Valerie observed.

"Looks are deceiving." Sarah pointed as she spoke. "If he had died and fallen over, there'd be cuts and abrasions on his head and face." There were no marks or blood present. "If he had fallen out of the chair before death, I'd expect to see abrasions on the palms of his hands, at the knees or elbows." She pointed again. "Nothing."

Sarah laid her clipboard down reached out and grabbed Ng's corpse by the neck, lifted his head and shoulders up from the ground. Then she moved him at the neck. The head rolled around atop his neck like a disconnected pod atop a stalk.

"Jesus Christ," Valerie breathed at the ghastly sight.

Sarah looked at Reggie. "Feel this."

Reggie put his hands precisely where Sarah's had been. He palpated deeply, felt the spinal column, found what Sarah wanted him to find. Cervical vertebrae out of place, facets snapped off. He gently laid Ng's head back down.

"Feel this," he said to Valerie.

"No thanks."

"Have you ever felt a broken neck?"

"No."

"Then you need to know what this feels like."

Valerie glanced back and forth between Sarah and Reggie, then leaned forward hesitantly. She looked as if Father Ng might wake up and jump at her. Before she knew it, Sarah had gently grabbed her hands and guided them to Ng's neck. She placed them over the break.

"Here," Sarah said. "Feel deeply. Beneath the muscle and tendons. Feel that displacement?"

"Yes."

Sarah guided Valerie's hands above the fracture. "Feel that?"

"Yes."

"That's what it's supposed to feel like."

Then she guided the inexperienced hands back to the fracture. "Notice the difference?"

"Ooh. Yeah. Yeah."

"This is murder," Reggie concluded.

Sarah pointed to an area along the left side of Ng's jaw. "See that?"

Reggie looked closely. "Faint bruising." He leaned back, spoke for Valerie's benefit. "Someone grabbed him from behind, left hand behind the neck, right hand around the front, under the chin and dug into the flesh of the jaw." Reggie demonstrated with his hands positioned on his own face and neck to illustrate. "Then, kkccck!" He made a twisting motion to indicate the fatal act.

"So, the killer is right-handed?" Valerie suggested.

"That doesn't narrow it down much," Reggie muttered.

"It narrows it down by ten percent," Valerie countered. "About ninety percent of the population is right-handed," she recited. "That means we've already ruled out anyone left-handed. Including that other person we're tracking."

He smiled, liking her even more. "I stand corrected. We've narrowed the search by ten percent."

"Who would want to murder an eighty-year-old priest?" Valerie inquired.

"Outside my job description," Sarah relied.

Reggie jerked a thumb over his shoulder. "Who's that?"

"Father Nagin, the priest who found him."

Reggie and Valerie rose, walked towards him.

"Father Nagin?" Reggie asked.

Nagin's reaction was delayed. First nothing, then a startled look, followed by comprehension of the world around him. He looked up at Reggie and Valerie, seeing them for the first time.

Reggie and Valerie flashed their badges. "We need to ask you a few questions," Reggie said gently.

"Okay."

"Tell us in your own words what happened here this morning, sir," Valerie said.

Nagin still looked like his mind was completely blank. "I pray here in the rose garden at dawn," he said, gesturing around him. "It's peaceful. I came out and saw Father Ng laid out on the ground, the chair turned over. I thought he'd had a heart attack."

"What happened next?"

"I ran over to start CPR," he answered. "I'm certified, you know."

"That's good, Father," Reggie said, meaning it.

"But he wasn't just dead," Nagin continued. "He was cold and dead. And his head, turned that way at such an unnatural angle, well..." His voice trailed off.

"You dialed 911?"

"Right away." He pulled a small cell phone from within the folds of his robes, held it up to show them. "Then I stayed with him until officers arrived."

"Do you know anyone who would want to kill Father Ng?"

"I've been wracking my brain asking myself the same question," Nagin responded.

"Any problems here lately? Any break-ins, gang trouble?"

Nagin shook his head. "No. Nothing like that. Everyone loved him."

"Father Ng was retired," Valerie stated. "What was he doing here?"

Nagin's face glowed with compassion. "He had no family, very little money. He was old school; took the vows of poverty seriously. He had no place to go, so we fixed up an old storage room for him."

"Was he working on anything?" Reggie asked.

"Like what?"

"Like anything for the Church that might be, how shall I put this? Controversial? Something covert. Off the books."

"No," Nagin answered.

"What about friends?" Valerie queried. "Any visitors?"

Nagin's face brightened. It was the look when something clicked inside a witness's head and suddenly pieces started falling into place.

Nagin said, "He's had two visitors of late."

"Did they come together?"

"No. Each came by alone. But they both came late at night."

Reggie narrowed in with laser-sharp intensity. "Tell me about them."

"One was a man. He creeped me out."

"Why?" Valerie prodded.

"He just did."

"Can you describe him?"

Nagin thought a moment. "White guy. Very white. Short, maybe five six, five seven tops."

Reggie and Valerie glanced at each other as Nagin continued. "Slight build. Dark hair. Leather jacket, dark pants, looked Italian. Custom shoes." He paused, then, "He wore sunglasses. Who wears sunglasses at one in the morning?"

Reggie wanted to change the subject. "Can you describe the other one?"

Nagin chewed his lip. "She was something else."

"She?"

"Yes. And when I say, 'something else', I mean otherwordly. Almost supernatural."

"What did she look like?" Valerie asked.

"Thin, willowy. Taller than the guy. Pale skin, but she looked like if she'd had normal skin tone, she might have been Black or Puerto Rican."

"You spend a lot of time with Blacks and Puerto Ricans?" Reggie asked.

"I spent my first seven years out of Seminary in Brooklyn and the Bronx."

"That'll do it," Valerie commented to Reggie.

"I only saw her once. Last night, in fact," Nagin continued. "Black dress. Long and flowing. The thing I remember most was her hair."

"Her hair?"

Nagin nodded. "Yes. It was white. Or silver maybe. But even in the darkness, it caught what little light there was. Almost like it was glowing."

Nagin leaned forward, stared off into space. He appeared to be done talking.

Valerie handed him her business card. "If you think of anything else, call us right away."

Nagin nodded, stood up for the first time since they had arrived. He shook hands with them.

"Please. Find out whoever did this."

Reggie and Valerie stepped back, took one last look around, getting an overview of the scene. The corpse had already been zipped up in a body bag. Sarah supervised two technicians who were picking the body up by the handles at each end of the bag.

"What's our move?" Valerie asked.

"Grandpa Eddie was the male visitor, obviously. We need to talk to him tonight before we go to Splinter."

"You think he knows this other person?"

Reggie nodded. "He's having an issue with another one like him. A female."

"What kind of issue?"

"Some vampire thing."
"You think she did this to get at him?"
Reggie gestured around them. "Circumstances indicate it."
"And now?
"Back to the precinct."

CHAPTER FOURTEEN

Reggie maneuvered the car into the one-way street. Everything was one-way in this part of the city. No U-turns. The city planners had obviously thought this would aid in orderly transit. All it did was make it more difficult to get anywhere.

"What are you thinking?" he asked at her silence.

"That Eddie is somehow involved in this."

"He didn't kill the priest."

"How do you know?"

"He doesn't kill good people," Reggie shrugged. "And he never leaves a corpse looking that good."

She looked at him, remembering the carnage from five years ago.

"Who is this other vampire?"

"Maya, his Vampire Mother."

"What does she want?"

"San Diego." She looked over at him. He continued, "Vampires are solitary apex predators. They stake out a territory, and then fiercely defend it.

"So," she concluded, "this is Eddie's feeding ground, and Maya is moving in."

Reggie grunted.

"How do you know all this?"

"Maya was waiting for me in my apartment last night," he said, as if having a vampire in one's apartment was the most common thing in the world.

"What?"

"She introduced herself and then threatened my life." He turned his head towards Valerie. "And she's been stalking Grandma Lottie."

"She's made it personal."

Reggie nodded as the light turned green. "Things are about to get bloody in a way that you've never seen."

"When?"

"What time is sunset today?"

Nick Castle had been at work for the better part of an hour and had not accomplished anything. It had been a long time since he had been this deeply angry.

Damn Alejandro Domingo!

As soon as he had gotten inside the precinct, he had dropped his laptop bag on his desk. He had straightened his tie, adjusted his blazer, and had gone out the front door.

He counted about twenty people, mostly Hispanic men, hanging around. He had slipped outside so quietly that for an instant, he went unnoticed. But when they saw him standing there in the dreary morning with his badge clipped to his belt, they grabbed up their signs and quickly surrounded him.

"Justice for Ramsey! Justice for Ramsey!" they screamed in unison.

Nick made his way down the steps in a delicate dance. The demonstrators backed away, giving him just enough room to move. If they bumped into him, it could be construed as assault. For him, he was careful to not touch anyone for fear it could be exploited into shrieks of police brutality.

The female reporter and her cameraman shoved their way past the demonstrators.

"Lieutenant! Lieutenant!" Nick looked at her. She looked vaguely familiar.

"Doris Stallworth, Channel Seven news."

"Lieutenant Nick Castle, San Diego Police Department."

"What can you tell us about the Ramsey Domingo investigation, Lieutenant?"

The shouts had switched to "No Justice, No Peace!" Nick said a few words on camera but made sure to not divulge anything the Public Affairs Liaison had not already given out. He cut the interview short and headed back into the precinct amid jeers and boos, and picket signs shaken within inches from his face.

And now he sat, staring at nothing. An incessant noise finally made its way through the ether. He picked up the phone.

"Lieutenant Castle." His voice dripped with fatigue.

"Nick?" A male voice. Tentative.

"Alejandro?" Hot anger returned. "You got a lot of balls calling here!" He did not realize that he had bolted out of his chair and was standing at his desk. His voice as so loud that cops in the main area glanced his way.

"What are you --?"

"You know precisely what," Nick said, cutting him off. "Fucking picketers outside the precinct? Outside *my* precinct?"

"Oh, God," Alejandro groaned on the other end. "I completely forgot to call them off after our last talk."

"Call them off now. Right now."

"Of course. I—"

"Right. Fucking. Now."

Nick slammed the receiver down, abruptly ending the call. He stormed out of his office and headed straight for the coffee station. He poured a mug, headed back into his office, sat down. The phone rang.

Again.

"Jesus," he muttered. He picked up the phone.

"Lieutenant Castle."

"Nicolas." Alejandro again. "Please don't hang up."

"What is it?" Nick barked.

"I was wondering if there's anything new concerning Ramsey?"

"Not yet," the Lieutenant answered truthfully. "We're following up on several leads. We don't have his name, but we've deciphered his method. It's only a matter of time."

"The wheels of justice are grinding too slowly for my liking." There it was. The real reason Alejandro had called.

"They often grind slower than I'd like," Nick countered. "But I've told you, we can do it fast, or we can do it right. I don't want this guy to walk on a technicality. When we find him – and we will find him – I want the case to be airtight."

"For Ramsey?"

"For both Ramsey and the other victims. They deserve justice too."

Silence on the other end, then a disconsolate sigh. "Yes. They do. Of course, they do. I'm sure their families mourn them just as I mourn my Ramsey."

"I wish I had better news."

"Just catch this guy, Nicholas. *Por favor.*"

Nick hung up. That had gone better than he had thought it would. Maybe blowing up at the beach house and reading him the riot act now had finally gotten through Alejandro's thick, smug, overprivileged, one-percenter's skull.

He glanced over just as Valerie and Reggie appeared through the back door. They veered directly towards him.

They closed the door behind them, gave him a full report. They told him what they knew, what they suspected, and why they suspected it. Nick, who thought he had seen it all, stood visibly shaken.

"So, you think she killed the priest because he's a friend of Eddie's?"

Both Valerie and Reggie nodded.

"Why didn't she kill you last night?"

"She's holding me in reserve," Reggie answered.

"And your Grandma Lottie?"

"Same thing."

"What do you think he'll do about this?"

"I think blood is about to drip from ceilings again."

Nick facepalmed his forehead as if suddenly suffering from an acute migraine. "With everything else on our plates; now we have a territorial dispute between two vampires?"

"They'll settle it privately," Reggie offered.

Nick rubbed his eyebrow. "Stay on forensics. Lean on the lab. We're still waiting for toxicology."

Valerie and Reggie took this to mean the meeting was over. They rose from their chairs. Reggie assured the Lieutenant he'd stay on the lab like white on rice. The Lieutenant smiled briefly, then shooed them out of his office.

He glanced at his watch. Mid-morning now, past ten thirty. He needed to bounce all this off someone he could spill his guts to, and they would never breathe a word of it.

Morris Horn.

Nick entered the old building through a single door carved out of the one-hundred-year-old edifice. A laundromat on one side, a bail bondsman on the other. Living the dream, Morris, Nick thought. No lobby, a small waiting area. He noticed a closed door with "Morris Horn Investigations painted at eye height. He knocked.

"Who is it?" Morris's voice sound thin, tinny, far away.

"Nick Castle."

A buzzer sounded, followed by the unmistakable sound of a security latch unlocking. Nick pushed the door open quickly. If he did not within five seconds, the lock would latch again. He stepped into the suite.

The office was a simple square room, one window that boasted a dazzling view of the brick side of the next building. Desk in front of him, laptop, a small printer on a roller console. A couple of chairs in front of the desk. Bookcases off to one side, filled with books. He figured this was to impress clients, make the place look like an oasis of legitimacy and professionalism.

Behind the desk sat Morris Horn, human grizzly bear. Skin so dark it appeared black except in the brightest of lights. A flat nose broken too many times. Eyes that had seen too much death and destruction; too much hopelessness, suffering, and misery in one lifetime.

"Nick!" he exclaimed, genuinely happy.

"Morris." They shook hands across the desk.

"Please," Morris gestured. "Have a seat."

Nick sat. Morris sat too.

"What brings you to my end of the swamp?

"You have recording equipment installed?"

"Of course."

"Is it recording now?"

"No."

Nick shifted in his uncomfortable chair. He brought Morris up to speed on everything that had transpired since they had last seen each other, and how the separate incidents interconnected. Morris sat and listened intently, never interrupted, never asked for clarification, never said a word.

"Sounds to me like vampire shit is hitting the fan," he said when Nick had finished.

"Pretty much."

"Any more midnight calls from Congressmen or Senators?"

"Not lately."

"Maybe he's had a 'come to Jesus moment'."

"One can always hope," Nick replied. "But with Alejandro, there's always another shoe waiting to drop."

Morris sat back in his chair. "What about this other vampire? This Maya?"

"Let Eddie handle her. That's vampire shit."

"And Father Ng? Doesn't he deserve justice?"

"Whether Maya gets taken out by human or vampire, her punishment remains the same."

"But the world will never know that justice was served."

"We'll know," Nick whispered intensely. God will, too."

Morris shifted a bit, rested his face in a crook of his left hand, thumb along his jaw, index finger extending up his check and near his temple.

"So, a cosmic balancing of the scales is good enough?" He shrugged. "Works for me."

Nick looked at Morris, dumbfounded.

"Sometimes, a cosmic balancing of the scales is the closest thing to justice you ever get. As cops, we fight a losing battle against crime and corruption and evil our entire careers. So, take your victories where you can find them, Nick. Savor them. Then move on. Trust me on this. I'm telling you this now because I wish someone had told me back in the day."

"And for those times when there's no justice to be found?"

"Perfect justice does not exist," Morris said. "Sometimes, close is close enough. Always do your best, but never forget that you can only do what you can do."

"And the rest of it?"

"Out of your hands."

"I don't want out of my hands."

"It bears repeating. You can only do what you can do."

"And that's good enough?"

"It has to be. That's all there is." Morris leaned on his desk. "I believe that sooner or later, everyone, I mean *everyone*, gets held accountable for their sins, in this life or the next." He opened his hands. "A cosmic balancing of the scales."

Nick couldn't suppress his smile. "You've become quite the philosopher."

"I think more these days."

"We're running Splinter tonight."

"There'll be hardly anyone there on Monday."

"I want my undercovers get a feel for the place," Nick said. "Plus, you never know. Splinter is his killing field. He's probably a regular."

"Just keep me in the van," Morris advised. "I'd blend in there about as well as a turd in a punchbowl."

Nick laughed out loud.

Maya lay dead and mummified in the basement of the home she had commandeered. When she had ventured into town, she had already chosen this house for herself. It had a basement, a rarity in Southern California.

She had walked up to the front door and knocked. When the lady of the house opened the door, Maya had moved past her, slitting the woman's throat with her claws in the process. As the nameless woman gurgled on the floor, her husband blundered into the living room, dumbly asking who was at the door.

The poor wretch never even saw her coming. She latched onto his throat with her fangs, bit into his carotid to drink. She viced her lower jaw, crushed his windpipe.

He dropped there like a bag of bricks. She wiped her chin and wandered through the house. Photos adorned the walls in the living room, depicting a family history. The husband and wife, smiling younger versions of themselves cutting a wedding cake. More photos, young parents with infants. More pictures in the hallway, babies that grew into young adults through the progression down towards the back of the house. The final pictures showed the grown children, now adults themselves.

The kitchen was tidy, well stocked. But kitchens held no useful function for Maya. No other heartbeats from inside the house.

She sat down in the late husband's office. Once she booted up the computer, she located the legal documents regarding the house. She copied and pasted forged signatures of the couple onto a bogus Quick Claim deed. She doctored docs in the County Clerk's supposedly secure database. Now it appeared the deed and transfer of ownership had been properly filed.

Now, as far as the Hall of Records and was concerned, the house was legally hers. She just had to dispose of the bodies and clean up. No problem there; she had become quite adept at covering her tracks. She ditched the family SUV at a recycling yard owned by a scumbag that owed her a favor.

The car was stripped for parts, then crushed with the dead couple inside.

The police came out one evening about a week later. She spoke to them briefly, told them after selling the house to her, they had left. No, no forwarding address, phone number, or email. The police were skeptical. She knew by reading their thoughts.

They stated the adult children were worried, that their parents never simply took off without leaving word, and the kids absolutely did not believe their parents had sold the house. The cops had performed their due diligence; all the paperwork had been documented, notarized, signed, and filed with the County Clerk. On paper, everything looked legal, neat, tidy.

They left her a business card, along with instructions that if the couple contacted her to call them ASAP. She had assured them that she would. They assured her that if they found anything amiss, they would be back.

Maya decided that if they ever did come back, they would never leave the house alive. The same went for the slaughtered parents' family.

She'd get away with it if it weren't for those meddling kids!

Outside, a red SUV drove by, slowed, turned into the driveway. It stopped just at the entrance to the carport. The driver put the car in PARK and killed the engine.

Inside, Johnathan Slater II, son of Marilyn and Johnathan Senior, glared intensely at the house through the windshield. His eyes inched over the property, searching for anything not right.

But this entire situation was not right.

His parents had lived in this house forty years. They had made improvements, paid off the mortgage while the market value skyrocketed. A close family, they always talked over big life decisions: who to marry, who to go into business with, what house to buy, and so on.

If his parents were thinking of selling and relocating, he would have known months ago. They never mentioned a word.

Something was fishy.

The police had found nothing illegal. Weird to be sure, suspicious even, but not illegal. But they had not located his parents, either. No bank activity, no ATM use, no credit cards, no in-person withdrawals since the date before the Quick Claim deed transfer.

This new "owner" had a lot of explaining to do.

Johnathan opened the car door.

"Johnathan," his wife Miriam said, "what are you going to do?"

"Ring the doorbell."

Miriam started to protest, but Johnathan was already out and moving. He barged to the front door, rang the bell.

He heard the bells "Ding Dong" inside. Then, nothing.

He rang the bell again. Same nonresponse. He knocked on the door. When that didn't work, he pounded.

Loudly.

Now Miriam was out, standing by the passenger door. "Can't you see no one's home?"

"Can't you see I don't give a shit?" he retorted.

pulled out his keys, found what he was looking for. He took the key, tried the lock. No dice.

"Someone changed the lock."

Growing angrier by the minute, he stalked across the porch and around the carport.

Miriam asked, "Where are you going?"

He put one hand up, palm flat. Like telling a dog to stay. He disappeared from view.

Miriam ground her teeth. She was worried about her in-laws, too. But creeping around checking doors and windows was not the way to go about this. What if someone called the cops?

In the back yard, all appeared serene. Nothing out of place. Then Johnathan noticed all the windows on the back, which faced east, had either heavy curtains pulled tight, or had been blacked out by what appeared to be spray paint.

What kind of wierdo did that?

He decided not to bother knocking. He went straight to the backdoor key his father had given him a few years back.

The key no longer fit the lock.

Shaking with impotent rage, he stepped back from the door. His eyes scanned the entire back side of the house, as if the structure itself might reveal some hidden clue.

The house told him nothing.

He stormed back around the side of the house and towards the car where Miriam waited. They got in, shut their doors. Miriam stayed quiet. Johnathan's face told her everything she needed to know.

Johnathan backed out and drove away. They stopped at the end of the street, turned left, and accelerated towards town.

All remained quiet inside. Night was coming, racing from out of the future, stampeding towards the present. The centuries-old corpse lay waiting. Waiting for the Dark Miracle to trigger her nightly regeneration from the realm of the Dead.

The immortal monster known as Maya had an agenda to pursue. Plans to execute.

People to kill.

Reggie napped in the bunk room; a small space adorned with two sets of Government-issue bunk beds. Though having already seen decades of service in various Marine Corps barracks at Camp Pendleton, the frames remained sturdy. Cheap mattresses provided little comfort.

Dreams haunted him, quick-cut glimpses into his subconscious. Long teeth, sprouting from snarling mouths. Blood gushing, running in rivulets across the floor. Necks snapping. Teeth sinking into throats. Blood spraying across walls. Dripping from ceilings.

A warm hand on his shoulder. A voice, quiet and caring, called his name.

He rolled onto his back. Eyes opened, mere slits. The face of an angel hovered above him. Green eyes, alabaster skin ringed with a red halo. He grabbed the angel, brought her down to him, kissed her deeply.

Rapturous.

The angel kissed back. Lips caressing. Tongue exploring. Then the angel pulled away.

Confused, disappointed, he blinked. The smiling angel came into focus.

Valerie Wahl.

He gasped, pulled his hands back and showed her his palms.

"Oh Jesus," he breathed, "I'm sorry."

"If you kiss like that all the time, I probably won't sue."

"It wasn't intentional, I –"

"Oh, you didn't want to kiss me?"

"No. Yes. No, I—"

Valerie sat back on the edge of the bed and laughed.

"You seem more traumatized over it than me."

Reggie huffed, needing to change the subject. "What time is it?"

She stood. "Time to get up, lover boy."

He threw the blanket off him, swung his legs around and over until his stocking feet touched the floor. He sat hunched over, rubbed one hand upwards over his face, forehead, then over his scalp. Finally, he stood up.

Valerie noticed the erection visible under his jeans. She smirked again.

"Shake off the cobwebs and get your head in the game," she winked. "Time to catch bad guys." She threw him another good-humored grin, then whirled around and strode to the door. Hand on the knob, she turned her head.

"Oh, and do me a favor?"

"What?"

"Next time, kiss me when you're wide awake. I want the full-on experience."

She left without waiting for a shocked Reggie to reply.

Next time?

What had he just done? And what might the consequences be? Sure, she had handled it with good humor, even with understanding. But what if she changed her mind later and decided to file a complaint against him? That would be it for his career, that's *what if*.

Oh Jesus. He was so screwed.

Outside, Valerie sank into her chair. She understood that in his half-sleep state, Reggie had not meant the kiss in any kind of aggressive or power dominance way. If he had, she probably would have decked him.

She turned her attention to the case. She wondered if there was any connection between the serial killer and Maya. Did they know each other? Were they working in tandem?

Such a strange world. Here she was, calmly considering whether an immortal, supernatural creature that feeds on human blood might be a target in her case. Just a couple of weeks ago, she believed that vampires were the figment of a mediocre writer's overworked imagination. Now she knew these preternatural monsters were quite real, and quite deadly.

What would she know in another two weeks?

Valerie's foot brushed against the canvas duffle she had stuffed under her desk. It contained a change of clothes for later. Black leather, spandex, a corset, combat boots. It also contained black lipstick, eyeliner, and white foundation. Undercover only succeeded if you looked like you belonged.

Reggie shuffled out of the bunkroom. Yawning, he lumbered towards the coffee station. He moved stiff-legged like a zombie from those old movies she watched on late night cable.

She closed one file, opened another. All this death. Innocent people drained of life for reasons known only to the killer. Valerie wanted to take him alive. Not out of any concern for the shitbag's civil rights, but because she wanted someone to figure out what made him tick. Understanding might help catch other serial killers in the future.

Suddenly, the photos in front of her turned her stomach. She closed all the folders, shoved herself away from her desk.

Detective Valerie Wahl, seven-year veteran and one of the youngest officers to make detective, was scared. Scared to death. She was walking into the unknown.

Nothing was more frightening than that which we cannot control.

Reggie staggered to his desk, plunked down. He sloshed coffee on his desk.

"You okay?" she asked.

"Will be," he nodded, then checked his watch. "It'll be dark soon."

Valerie thought about the night ahead. Even with all her training, even with a team of experienced professionals watching her, and even with her own personal vampire guardian, she was nervous.

Being scared did not make her a coward. It made her human. Not acknowledging her fear would make her a fool.

Pushing through that fear and doing her job was what made her brave.

CHAPTER FIFTEEN

Nightfall.

Reggie had come home to raid his closet. He dug an old pair of black leather combat boots out of the back. He found some faux leather pants that he had not worn in years. He hoped he could still squeeze into them. A black T shirt with slivery reflective tape. His thick studded leather jacket would complete the ensemble.

Instead of a traditional shoulder holster, he opted for a smaller, more discrete holster that looped into his belt at the small of his back. The opening faced right, so he could reach behind and draw his weapon smoothly.

He pulled a box of bullets out of his nightstand drawer, sat at his dinette table. He methodically clicked rounds into three extra magazines.

Unlike many of his colleagues who carried nine millimeters, Reggie insisted on a .45. One hit from a .45 would punch a hole through a person with an exit wound the size of a softball and knock them six feet back. Major stopping power. If someone became such an imminent threat that Reggie had to shoot them, then by God they weren't getting back up.

With a .45, it was one and done.

He finished loading. He picked up each magazine individually and slapped the back of each into the palm of his hand to help seat the bullets. Then he stood up and considered how best to conceal them. Since his t shirt had no pocket and his pants only had one tiny slit pocket on the right front and left back (barely big enough for a credit card or a few folded bills), the roomy pockets both outside and inside the bomber jacket became his de facto armory. Since nobody would pat him down, he would be fine.

He looked at himself in the bathroom mirror. From his boots to the tight pants to the T-shirt stretched across his muscular torso to the leather jacket, he looked the part. Noting one detail, he reached into a small dish on the counter and grabbed a small hoop earring. He placed it through the hole in his left ear lobe, pushed the backing to secure it.

Okay then.

Showtime.

Lottie bustled about the kitchen cooking her dinner. A skillet sizzled as she poured a mixture of meat and vegetables into a bowl. She grabbed a wooden spoon, started stirring. She added salt, pepper, garlic, minced onions.

"Smells delightful."

Lottie gasped and spun around. She stared at a woman dressed in black leather and lace, in a style that had gone out when Lottie had still been young. The woman boasted a head of thick silver hair, curly and tumbling. African American. Broad nose. Full lips. Obsidian eyes. Ample bosom. Tight waist.

"I didn't mean to startle you," the uninvited guest said.

"Who are you?"

"I am Maya."

"I'm Lottie."

"Pleased to meet you," Maya said, smiling and flashing her fangs.

Is this how I die?

Maya smiled. "Fear not, child. I come in peace."

Lottie knew she could not believe anything this creature said.

"Oh, you can believe me," Maya said. "If I wanted you dead, you would never see me coming." Maya glanced at a chair near the rickety kitchen table. "May I sit?"

Lottie motioned for her to have a seat. Maya sat.

"Don't let your food get cold."

"So, are you a friend of my grandfather?"

Maya replied, "I am his Vampire Mother. Has he mentioned me?"

"He has," Lottie said truthfully. "He was not particularly complimentary."

"We're estranged."

Lottie took a seat and dug in without further pleasantries. This was her house, and Maya had broken in.

"I didn't break in," Maya said, wounded. "Your back door was open."

"What if the door had been locked?"

"Then I would have broken in."

Lottie took another bite, trying to remain calm. "What can I do for you, Miss Maya?"

"I am making one last attempt to prevent bloodshed. Namely, mine. And your grandfather's."

Lottie sat back in her chair. "Grandpa has spoken about something called 'The Vampire Way'. From what I gather, it's an archaic and rigid set of rules for vampire behavior."

"An accurate description."

"The penalties for transgressions can be severe."

"Another accurate description."

"So, you and Grandpa have a problem, and the only way to solve it, according to The Vampire Way, is some sort of death match?"

"That's the path your grandfather has chosen. I would rather live in peaceful coexistence."

"So, why come to me?"

'Talk to him. Convince him that San Diego is big enough for the both of us." Maya stood. "I must go now. Your grandfather will visit shortly."

"How can you be so sure?"

Maya grinned. "I like you, Lottie. The world is a nicer place with you in it." Then she was gone, like mist on the wind.

Lottie sat there completely still, save for the faint rise and fall of her chest. She finally came around, made her way to the back door. It was indeed unlocked. No signs of forced entry.

She locked the doorknob, slid the deadbolt home. She knew that would not stop Maya. She would blast through and leave the door in splinters. Yet Lottie still felt better.

A knock at the front door made her jump. She slapped her hand over her heart, spun around and peered through the hallway to the front of the house.

Another knock. Louder, harder. More urgent.

Lottie tottered through the house. She got to the door, did not bother looking through the windowpane. She turned the lock, slid back the bolt.

The Vampire immediately bolted through the door, an unaccustomed desperate look on his face. Then he hugged her close. He grabbed her by the shoulders, took a step back.

"Are you all right?" he asked.

"I'm fine, Grandpa."

He heaved a sigh, calming himself. He reached behind and pulled the door closed. He tilted his head, sniffed the air. Then he grimaced, his anger rising.

"Maya was here."

A statement; not a question. It sounded guttural, primitive. Like it had rumbled out from his chest rather than simply being air passing over vibrating vocal cords.

"Yes."

"Did she force her way inside?"

Lottie motioned him to follow her. They walked into the kitchen, sat at the table.

"You don't mind, do you?"

"Not at all, child."

Lottie returned to eating.

"She did not break in, Grandpa," Lottie said at last. "I accidentally left the back door unlocked."

The Vampire hung his head in disappointment. He removed his sunglasses, wrapping two slender fingers around one earpiece and pulling down. He ran the other hand down his face from hairline to chin. Then he looked at her with those bottomless black eyes.

"Please do not do that again."

"I don't think my lock and deadbolt would stop her, Grandpa."

"Maya is not the only danger to consider."

"I promise to be careful, Grandpa," Lottie assured him. "I'll be sure and lock up at night."

"Please make certain you do." Satisfied, he stood. "And now, I must leave."

"So soon?"

"Alas, yes. I have rather pressing obligations this evening."

After he left, Lottie scraped the last remaining remnants of dinner out of her bowl. She took the bowel and spoon to the sink, ran hot water into it, placed the spoon in the water to soak. She would wash it out properly in the morning. Her calves were starting to hurt, and her feet were killing her. She planned to get into her nightgown and watch TV until she fell asleep.

Sounds like a plan, she smiled.

The Vampire entered the police precinct. He moved quietly through the doors, slipping inside without making a sound. Stealth. He couldn't help it. He didn't even think about it. And even if he ever had thought about it, he would not alter his habits.

It was his nature as an apex predator.

Valerie was there. Her hair was brushed out and teased into a red halo around her alabaster face. Black stiletto heels. A skintight black catsuit that zipped up the front from crotch to neck, accentuating her curves. If the Vampire had still been human, he would have been... distracted, to say the least.

Reggie was certainly distracted, the Vampire realized. Though his great, great Grandson seemed to concentrate on his computer screen, the Vampire heard his jackhammer heartbeat, smelled his pheromones.

Ah, to be young and human again!

Reggie looked up. "Hey, Grandpa."

"Reginald."

Valerie turned her head his way.

"Detective Wahl," the Vampire returned, getting a whiff of her pheromones. When were these two just going to get together?

The Vampire looked past them to the Lieutenant's office. Nick sat at his desk, on the phone. His necktie hung loosened, his top shirt button unbuttoned.

"Morris Horn?" the Vampire asked.

"Meeting us on site," Valerie answered.

Reggie stood close to the Vampire. "Is everything all right?"

"Your grandmother," the undead being answered. "Her health is failing."

"I've noticed," Reggie said. He gestured in Valerie's direction. "We stopped by this morning. She insisted on making breakfast for us. It looked to me like that simple act damn near exhausted her."

Sooner or later, our bodies betray us."

"Yours didn't betray you."

"Yes, it did," the Vampire said with infinite regret.

Reggie did not know how to respond to that, so he did not respond at all.

"May I impart some wisdom that I have attained over the span of my life?"

"Sure."

"Enjoy this thing called life," the Vampire said. "Eat that slice of cake. Ask that pretty girl out. Take that vacation. Stay at the five-star hotel. Enjoy the truffles and champagne. Take chances. Live every day as if it may be your last, because one day, it will be." He paused, then placed his hand on Reggie's shoulder. "It is not about how many years you live," he concluded. "It is about how much living you do in the years you have."

From her desk, Valerie overheard the conversation. She glanced their way, saw Reggie and the Vampire embrace each other with purest affection. It struck her just how much Reggie loved his great, great grandfather, and just how much that immortal monster loved him back.

Maybe, in the end, the love we feel never really dies. And maybe that's all that matters.

Inside his glass office, Nick hung up the phone. He had been speaking with the Deputy Commissioner. The serial killer case was still Priority One, but the tone from the top had shifted from impatient and demanding to supportive and encouraging.

Greatly relieved, he checked his watch. Time to catch a killer. He stood, and his personal cell phone made its signature electronic beeping sound.

He pulled the phone out of his pocket, opened it. He did not recognize the number. He sat back down, hit ANSWER.

"San Diego Police Department. Lieutenant Castle."

"Nicolas?"

"Alejandro," Nick said, recognizing the voice.

"I've called everyone I know," Alejandro said. "You will receive no more interference."

"Thank you."

"I just... I was just so mad at what happened to Ramsey."

"I know."

"Lo siento mucho, hermano."

Hermano? Did he just call me "brother" and mean it?

"Esta bien," Nick responded.

"No, it's really not," Alejandro replied, switching back to English.

"It'll do for now."

"Anything new?"

"We're going hunting tonight."

"Donde?"

"It's better if you don't know," Nick answered.

"Well then." Alejandro sounded slightly crestfallen, as if he had not gotten out the conversation what he had wanted. "If there's anything I can do..."

"I have your number," Nick finished.

"Oh, Nick?"

"Yes?"

"We need to talk more. About *la familia.*"

Nick frowned, gathered his thoughts quickly. *La familia?* This was about to get tricky. Like walking-through-a-minefield-while-blindfolded tricky.

"Let's talk after I've caught Ramsey's killer. Okay?"

"Esta bien."

"Oh, and Alejandro?" Nick said like it was an afterthought, *"Gracias."*

"De nada."

Nick hit the END button, terminating the call. He couldn't help but wonder what that call really meant. What was Alejandro's game? Knowing the Domingo family and how they had treated him and his mother, he could not take anything they said at face value. There was always something else, something deeper, hidden.

Alejandro Domingo would have to earn Nick's trust. Until then…

He grabbed his wrinkled suit jacket off the back of his chair, threw it on. He yanked downward on the necktie, loosening the knot more. He strode into the main squad room.

The Vampire sat perched on the edge of Reggie's desk. His head moved a bit; he saw Nick approaching. He stood. The movement alerted Reggie, who turned around in his chair. Valerie followed suit.

"You all know your jobs," Nick said. "Let's catch this fucker."

The group moved *en masse* towards the back of the precinct, exited through the back door. Outside, the air was chilly and hanging heavy with the first hint of fog. It was early still. By the wee hours of the morning, it would be pea soup out here.

They approached a gray cargo van with a dent into the slide door and a crack in the windshield. Faded lettering read, "Smith's Plumbing" and even included a bogus telephone number to make things look real. The front cabin compartment held two bucket seats with a space between them, and a narrow passage through curtains into the rear area, which was stuffed to the gills with video and audio surveillance equipment.

"Impressive, the Vampire said as he gazed at the gadgets inside.

"Climb in," Nick called from the driver's seat.

"I prefer my own car."

"Suit yourself."

The vampire threw a comforting smile in Reggie and Valerie's direction. Then he slid the heavy side door closed.

"What's with him?" she asked.

Up front in the driver's seat, Nick started the engine, shifted into gear. The van inched through the parking lot.

"He has his reasons," Reggie parried. "He's not a capricious man."

"What do you mean?"

"He reasons out every choice he makes – or *doesn't* make."

The van exited the police parking lot and turned onto the city street.

"Do you understand that reasoning?" Valerie asked.

"Not always," Reggie answered. "Sometimes, I figure it's none of my business unless he tells me."

"And you're good with that?" she asked.

"He shows me the same courtesy."

Valerie gawked at him, confused.

"I'm a grown-ass man," he explained. "I live my own life, and I don't need anyone trying to babysit me."

Valerie wondered if that went for girlfriends and wives.

Reggie grinned.

"What?"

"You're thinking that's probably why I'm not married at my age," he said. "Nope. That's not it. I just haven't met the right woman yet."

In the driver's seat, Nick signaled at a light. He waited for oncoming traffic to clear, then he made a turn. In the back, the combination of inertia, acceleration, and changing directions threw Reggie and Valerie into each other. They tumbled onto the carpeted flooring.

Valerie found herself straddling him at his hips and leaned down across him, her breasts pressing into his face. Mortified, she gasped, pulled herself erect. Then she realized that she was not the only one getting erect.

She threw one leg up and got off him, like dismounting a horse. She grabbed his hand, helped him sit up. They gingerly reached for the chairs bolted to the floor in front of the monitors.

"Sorry," she murmured.

"Don't sweat it," Reggie said as he settled into his chair.

Valerie couldn't help but smile to herself. I won't, she thought.

The Vampire made his way along city streets into a paid lot on 6th. He paid at the automated kiosk, retrieved the receipt from the small tray near the bottom. He glided back to his car, placed the receipt face up on the driver's side dashboard. He locked the door again from his key fob, walked away. The alarm activated, signified by a brief *CHIRP!* from somewhere under the hood.

Shoving the keys into his jacket pocket, he moved silently towards 4th Avenue. People came and went past him. He heard heartbeats, felt blood gushing through arteries. It had been a while since he had fed directly. It was an impulse he could deny for only so long. And he was beginning to feel that ancient need again.

Stay on mission, he told himself. Maya was out there, threatening both his life and the lives of those he loved.

No way she left San Diego alive.

He crossed 5th Avenue, walked west on F. He looked up at the night sky. Heavy cloud cover. Thickening fog. He huffed through his nose. He needed a bird's eye view. He slipped into a narrow space between two buildings.

The space was barely three feet wide. Looking down the constricted tunnel, he could spy vehicles passing on the next block, winking in and out of sight. He looked upwards. The roof was four stories above him. Too high to jump without a running start.

The Vampire pressed his palms against the rough brick on either side. He pushed against the walls with his arms, lifted his legs, pressed his feet in, moved his arms, pressed palms again, lifting himself ever higher. He continued his crablike climb all the way up. He was at the roof in seconds. Pushing his feet into the walls, he twisted at the waist and grabbed the ledge with his hands, then hoisted himself up and over.

He moved diagonally towards the corner of the building. Once there, hidden in shadows and fog, he gazed down at the intersection of 4th Avenue and F Street forty feet below. He removed his sunglasses, peered downward.

He stood atop a building over one hundred years old. It had once been a rather grand hotel in the early twentieth. The structure had been reinforced, brought up to code every few decades. The ground floor was now shops and bars, with a restaurant set on the coveted corner.

The floors above were pale and frumpy, neglected rooms, tenement apartments. Each contained a bed, a nightstand, a bare lightbulb overhead, a tiny lavatory in the corner behind the door. Bathroom and shower at the end of the hall.

Standing in darkness, the Vampire detected heartbeats of depressed, defeated occupants beneath him. They were just one step above homeless, and they knew it. They had a roof over their heads for this month.

Next month maybe not.

Traffic was steady but sparse below. Monday night. People heading home after work.

The Vampire smelled something familiar, turned his head. His eyes scanned east and west below him. He zeroed in on the gray cargo van approaching. He sensed three distinct heartbeats. He recognized Reggie's, then Nick's, and finally Valerie's.

A breeze stirred. The wind shifted. The Vampire sniffed the air. Maya was nearby. He remembered how she had sensed him, found him, led him around by the nose. How she always seemed to be one step ahead of him, always seemed to know what he would do before he did it.

Two can play that game, Maya.

The Vampire slowed his breathing, calmed himself. Blocking everything else out he centered himself, concentrated. He pushed his consciousness outward in all directions as he psychically probed for her. He felt her presence to the south, down near Harbor Drive close to San Diego's famous Petco Park and the Convention Center.

He wondered what she would be doing down there. Feeding, most likely. Homeless people gathered there. No one wanted to see or hear the homeless.

And if one or two of "those people" were to die or disappear, so what? No one cared.

That made the homeless easy prey for all kinds of predators.

The van below turned left from F onto 4th, moved deliberately into the far-right lane. It pulled to a yellow-painted curb, stopped. Nick climbed out of the driver's seat, moved to the rear door. He opened it, pulled two large orange traffic cones out. He sat them up at each rear corner of the van. Then he rounded the corner to the sidewalk and disappeared from the Vampire's view.

CHAPTER SIXTEEN

Nick grabbed the handle on the van's side panel door, gave it a twist. The handle turned about thirty degrees. Placing his left hand lightly on the panel, he yanked with his right, sliding the door open.

Reggie and Valerie stared back at him. What was that impish twinkle in Valerie's eyes?

"Shit's about to get real," Nick said. "As real as it fucking gets."

"I'm ready," Valerie managed to say.

Nick's eyes shifted to Reggie. "Keep her safe."

"Understood," the veteran detective answered.

Reggie climbed out of the van and held his hand out for Valerie. A gentlemanly gesture, like his mom and grandma had taught him. She grabbed his outstretched hand and threw him a grateful smile. She clambered out in her black catsuit, leather jacket, and combat boots so highly polished they reflected the neon lights of the street.

"Where's Captain Horn?" Reggie asked, using Morris's old police rank out of habit.

"He's coming," Nick assured them.

Reggie turned away and trudged towards Splinter. Valerie followed him. Nick bit his lower lip. They'll be fine, he told himself. He looked both up and down the street, trying to see Morris approaching. He did not see him.

Nick climbed in the van and slammed the door shut.

The Vampire watched Reggie and Valerie walk towards Kong. The emanations floating off the big bouncer told the Vampire that Kong was not happy tonight.

The Vampire stepped away from the ledge, traversed to the south side. He could not get down to the west or the north; people would see him. And the east side was too narrow.

The south side it was.

Four stories below him sat an alley as big as a street lane. Industrial sized trash bins squatted against walls. No one down there.

The Vampire stepped off the roof. He deliberately stepped with his back foot, then brought both legs beneath him, feet, ankles, and knees pressed together. He flung his arms wide for balance as he plummeted towards the unforgiving surface below.

He landed with a thud and a grunt. The impact drove him down, his knees bending as his feet, legs, and hips worked together to absorb the impact. He pushed an arm out, palm flat, and steadied himself in a low squat on the cobblestone lane. He allowed himself a deep breath in and out. Then he stood up, brushed his hands off, and casually strolled towards 4th.

He stepped onto the sidewalk, all business. He kept his head on a swivel, constantly scanning back and forth, up and down, alert for danger. He saw emanations wafting off everyone around him. Most he discounted. There were a few that, under normal circumstances, he would have loved to hunt. No time tonight for hunting humans. He was being hunted by another Vampire.

Time to turn the tables.

The walk signal changed from an orange hand indicating STOP to a white outline of a person walking. The crowd on the curb moved as one into the street. The Vampire moved with them.

Look at them, he thought. Living out brief lives in fragile, decaying bodies. They have no idea the horrors that walk among them, assessing them each, picking out the weak, culling the herd. Most lived their lives sheltered the darker truths of this world.

What would happen, he wondered, if the great masses discovered that vampires are real, other "mythical" creatures are real, and that humans live in a world where they are not the top of the food chain? What would happen if they found out that there are creatures in their world, indeed within their own communities that would peel the skin from their bodies and feast on their innards if given the opportunity?

Perhaps ignorance truly is bliss.

It was not their ignorance the Vampire resented; it was their smugness. The arrogant belief that humans were the ultimate miracle of evolution. One look at the news and the Vampire saw the atrocities committed by humans against other humans. And *homo sapiens* was supposed to be the crem de la crem of God's ultimate plan?

Pfft! Please.

Kong saw his diminutive nemesis coming, saw the scowl on his pallid face. He read the approaching monster's body language, knew to not mess around with him tonight. He opened the door himself and allowed the Vampire to pass.

No words passed between them.

The door behind the Vampire shut with a loud clang. A gust of cold air from an air conditioning vent hit him square in the face. Music played on a PA system. Heavy thrash metal, of course. The stage was dark and barren. Live music only on the weekends, he supposed.

The immortal creature that feasted on the blood of men grabbed the handrail and descended the stairs.

Nick sat at his surveillance screens. He had successfully tied into every CCTV camera within four blocks. On a second monitor to his left, he had connected to the live feed from every camera inside Splinter.

A solid knock sounded on the van's side panel door. He reached over, unlocked the door. He stared into the lined face of Morris Horn.

"What did I miss?" he asked as he hauled his bulk inside. Nick situated himself in front of the CCTV screen while Morris sat in front of the Splinter live feed.

"Nothing so far," Nick answered. "They're barely inside."

The screen in front of Morris was split into eight smaller screens, each a live feed of a different camera covering a different part of the bar, the dancefloor, the club itself. The only area not covered was the Grotto tucked up high in the back of the club.

Morris pointed. "There they are."

On the black and white feed, Nick and Morris watched as Valerie and Reggie moved amongst the other patrons scattered throughout the club. Reggie walked towards the bar. The bartender slid down to meet him. Valerie shrugged out of her jacket, the black catsuit clinging to her curves.

"Is this sex kitten thing is going to work?" Morris asked.

"We gotta start somewhere."

Various cameras picked up the Vampire prowling down the stairs. His movements, head turning this way and that, the scowl reminded both men of a jungle animal pacing inside a cage.

Inside, Reggie paid for the drinks. He grabbed them and searched the murky club. He saw her at a table near the far wall. He moseyed that way, taking his time. He noticed Valerie watching him as he approached. He liked the idea of her watching him approach.

He sat at the table across from her, pushed her drink in front of her. "Anybody scoping me out?" he asked.

"Not that I could tell," she responded.

He seemed pleased by that. "I'll keep moving. We don't want anyone to think we're a couple."

Reggie took up residence at another table far enough away that he could survey the entire floorplan from the stairs and bar to his left to the grotto-like VIP booths in front of him, Valerie at her table, then the hallway to his right that led to the bathrooms and the emergency exit. He scanned the area slowly, deliberately. He saw Grandpa Eddie hanging back, clinging to the shadows, sullen and glowering.

His hand slipped surreptitiously behind him, under his jacket. His fingers ran along his firearm resting in its quickdraw holster.

The comforting caress of steel.

He sipped his drink. He focused on the small surveillance camera pointed directly at him. It was small, unobtrusive. A casual observer would have missed it entirely. The usual patron wouldn't know it was there, and probably wouldn't care. People came here for other reasons.

In the van, Nick pressed a button in front of him. "You guys in position?"

"Roger that," Reggie replied, speaking low. His earpiece acted as both a radio receiver and microphone.

"Roger," Valerie replied.

On one of the black and white screens, Nick and Morris saw the Vampire look directly into a camera and give a terse thumbs up.

"You gave him an earpiece?" Morris asked.

"He doesn't need one."

Momentarily confused, Morris finally said, "Goddamned vampire hearing." Then he saw the Vampire grin in response, then point directly at the camera.

Jesus Christ, Morris thought.

He can hear everything we're saying.

Charlie Simpkins sat alone in his crappy, cluttered apartment. Artificial light from outside filtered through flimsy curtains. No interior lights on; no television or radio on. His laptop rested dark and silent. He had called out sick tonight. He wasn't really sick; he was antsy to make another kill.

Time to do something.

True, he had a terrible headache, a blinding pressure inside his head. It was not from that Goddamned virus that was going around just now, spreading like wildfire around the world. This pain was stress-induced. The stress created when your heart says one thing, but your brain says another.

Charlie always followed his head, no matter what.

Playing cat and mouse, outsmarting the cops at every turn provided him with a certain glee. How he, just one guy, could literally get away with murder, time after time, right under their stupid noses, and then blend into the background.

Delicious.

What bothered was not what the media said, but rather what they did *not* say. Several key details had obviously been withheld. Just one missing piece overlooked, and the game would be over.

But Charlie was smarter than these dumbshit yokels. He had been killing his way across the country for a few years now, and no one had ever come close. These cops were no different. He had killed multiple people here, including a wealthy heiress, a high-profile celebrity author. And here he was, still breathing free air.

Everything came back to his compulsion to hunt. Why was he not stalking his next victim?

Something told him the time was not right. This voice inside his head had whispered to him as long as he could remember, even as a small child. It was the voice of wisdom and logic.

The voice always advised him well. Like how to not get caught when he had murdered the high school quarterback because the guy, Kent, had bullied Charlie mercilessly ever since grade school. Charlie had promised himself that someday when he was big enough, he would exact his revenge. But Kent had always been bigger than Charlie, bigger all through grade school and their teen years. Poor Charlie never caught up.

What a person puts out into the world sooner or later revisits them in kind. Revenge has an unerring way of presenting itself at the opportune time. Then it becomes a question of, is one ruthless enough to capitalize on the opportunity?

Charlie had ruthlessness down to a science.

The opportunity presented itself with Kent. And young Charlie Simpkins had capitalized on the opportunity.

Graduation night. The afterparty at the lake outside of town. Lots of alcohol, music, dancing, sex. Not that Charlie was interested in any of that nonsense.

Everyone was plastered, including Kent Musberg, All Star Quarterback and State University Prospect. More to the point, Kent was so snot-slinging drunk he never even screamed when

Charlie caught him alone on the pier contemplating the black water in front of him.

Charlie never hesitated. He plunged a knife between Kent's ribs, then slashed forward as he pulled out, collapsing the lung.

Kent never even saw Charlie until he was already dying and unable to scream. The collapsed lung strangled off his breath. Gasping Kent sunk to his knees. Charlie eased him down at the end of the pier. If anyone had seen them from a distance, Charlie was helping Kent lie down.

Kent sank like a stone when Charlie rolled him into the lake at the end of that long pier. That was a Friday night. The star quarterback was reported missing the next day. By Sunday, his parents were beside themselves. By Monday, every member of the graduating class was interviewed. Charlie handled his with aplomb. They never suspected him, never called him for a second interview.

Charlie packed up and left Podunk a week later. No fanfare. No tearful goodbyes. His parents seemed relieved to get rid of him. The feeling was mutual. He never returned or kept in contact with anyone. But he kept up with events through the online version of the local newspaper.

Kent's body was found later that fall after it had disintegrated into chunks. They theorized that the body had become entangled in some brush near the bottom. The only reason the body was found at all was because some fisherman reported finding pieces washed up onshore.

The police cordoned off the area, dragged the waters at the end of the pier and got the rest of him. They collected the chunks, tossed them into a body bag, then took off back to town. No word on if the fisherman caught anything that day.

A quick check of dental records confirmed the ID. Due to advanced decomposition, cause of death was never established. They presumed he had wandered drunk out onto the pier on Graduation Night. Boys will be boys, right? But this boy was so soused that he walked right off the pier, fell into the water, and drowned. Another life full of promise and potential needlessly snuffed out by the demon alcohol.

No one ever suspected a fledgling killer named Charlie Simpkins.

And the same inner voice at the back of his brain that had guided and advised him through that first kill along with all the others since, was speaking again. He had to listen.

Shhh. Not yet.

He bolted from the sofa to in one swift motion. He clenched and unclenched his fists at his sides, fingers digging into his palms. He beat his fists against his naked flanks, emitted a growl.

He moved to the bathroom, flipped on the light. He stepped into the bathtub, cranked open the cold-water tap. Chilly water flowed over extended fingers.

He pulled the small plunger. The water now gushed upwards to the shower head and exploded out, pelting him with thousands of frigid needles.

The sudden blast jolted him. He devoted every ounce of self-discipline to keep from screaming. His eyes stayed shut; his skin rippled with goosebumps. His nipples puckered, his penis shriveled, and his scrotum shrank as his cremaster muscles contracted, an autonomic response to the temperature change, pulling his testicles up closer to his body to maintain an even temperature.

He fumbled blindly for the faucet control, turned the water off. He grabbed a towel, stepped out of the tub. He wrapped the towel around his waist, sat down atop the toilet seat. As he shivered, he glanced upwards at the clock mounted on the wall above the light switch.

Time marched on.

Maya sat on a park bench near the Convention Center and Petco Park, feeling satiated. She had fed more than usual earlier, and now felt bloated and sluggish. She wiped the last remnants from her chin with a white handkerchief just as the alarm clock app on her phone chimed midnight.

Ah, the Witching Hour. That time when all good, sensible, God-fearing people were supposed to be home in bed; when outside, all things dark and evil went "bump in the night".

She grinned. Evil knew no timetable. Bad things happened all hours of the day and night. And as far as "things that go bump in the night", she liked "going bump" until her daily death at dawn.

Maya pulled the dark hood of her coat up and over her head. She bent her face downward, dropped her shoulders. She sat without moving for several minutes. A homeless woman pushing a shopping cart filled with her filthy belongings trudged along the sidewalk. Maya was aware of her, of course. She sensed her, heard her, heard the wheels, smelled her putrid clothing and a cancer-riddled body. This woman would be dead within a few months, maybe a few weeks. Nothing in medical science could save this human.

She turned her head slightly, listening to the sound of the cart's squeaky wheels recede as the nameless woman distanced became indistinct in the mist.

That was when Maya sensed two others, both men, approaching from the opposite direction. She heard their footfalls, their heartbeats. Blood pumping.

Juices flowing.

"Hey there," one of them, white, heavyset and in his twenties, hands shoved into front pockets of a padded coat. "What are you doing out here all by yourself?"

Maya did not answer.

The white guy waited. When it was obvious she would not respond, he looked to his companion, a Hispanic youth in his late teens. The youth merely shrugged.

The white guy looked at his companion, then stepped closer. "Maybe you didn't hear me," he said. "What are you doing out here all alone at night?"

"This is my fate, my damnation" she spoke from under her hood. Neither could see her face. "Alone in the night. Every night." She paused, then, "Night after night."

Both men were confused.

"It can be terrible," she said, more to herself than to them. "The soul sucking sameness of it all, night after night. Year after year."

"Well, I don't know anything about that," he said. "But my friend here is sick."

"He doesn't smell sick."

That threw them. Smell sick?

"Well, he is," the white guy said, trying to get back on track. "He needs an operation, but we're a bit short on cash."

"How terrible."

"We were wondering if you could make a donation?"

Maya smiled beneath her hood. "No."

"What? Bitch, I don't think you understand –"

"No," Maya said sharply. She stood, dropped her hood behind her head. "It's you who doesn't understand." She stepped close enough that they could see her face for the first time.

Eyes bulged. Jaws dropped. They stepped back as she stepped forward.

"We'll just be on our way," the Hispanic youth said.

"Too late."

Maya moved then. Really moved, with the speed, grace, and strength that only one of her kind possessed. They did not have time to turn or run before she went to work on them.

Poor bastards never had a chance.

Maya lashed out at vulnerable throats. The humans crumpled like wilted lettuce where they had stood, vocal cords severed by sharp claws.

The last thing either man saw were cold black eyes that somehow blazed from within, an open mouth with white teeth and fangs – *fangs!* – grinning down on them as they lay bleeding out on the ground.

They died quickly, eyes staring towards black heavens above, not understanding how things had gone sideways so quickly. Their final breaths left their lungs as warm blood pooled in steaming black puddles against cold concrete.

Maya glided away from the carnage. Her feet remained hidden within the folds of her coat, which reached almost to the walkway. From a distance, she resembled a ghost suspended an inch or two above the ground.

She gazed down at her fingers as she splayed them out in front of her. No blood to wash off. That was how fast she had moved.

She had not even chipped a nail on a vertebra.

Go me, she smiled.

Inside Splinter, Valerie sipped her drink, bored out of her skull. But then, that's what stakeouts always were, right? Hours, days, weeks of absolute boredom punctuated by two minutes of absolute terror.

Reggie still sat in a booth on a small riser near the back. Deeper in the shadows created by the layout and subdued lighting, he remained watchful. Alert eyes scanned everywhere, seeing everyone.

The Vampire circled slowly, moving from one table to another, sitting quietly for a few minutes, moving on.

Fidgety.

This thing with Maya combined with Lottie's poor health weighed upon him. Even Reggie had to admit that Grandma Lottie could go any day. He promised himself that from now on he would go by to see her more often, and at the very least call once a day from now on just to check in on her. With his own mom gone, Grandma Lottie was the closest kin he had, other than his great, great grandfather. Calling was the least he could do.

So far, Maya was a no-show. Reggie knew Grandpa Eddie would much rather be out hunting her down. But the Vampire had given his word. He would uphold it, regardless. Reggie hoped it would not leave him vulnerable to attack.

Reggie's senses locked onto movement. A tall skinny kid dressed in all black and metal studs approached Valerie. He had been eyeing her from the bar, waiting to see if anyone joined her. Now he made a somewhat staggering beeline towards her.

"Romeo at two o'clock," he whispered.

"Got him," she responded.

Outside in the van, Morris and Nick watched their screens intently.

"You think this is anything?" Nick mumbled.

"Probably not," Morris assessed. "My guess is, he just wants to get into her pants."

"Fat chance of that," Valerie muttered.

"Not your type?" Nick grinned.

"Not even close," she whispered.

Reggie listened, watched, said nothing. He noticed the Vampire watching, too. Good to know they both had their heads in the game.

The kid slowed as he got to the table. Valerie performed a risk assessment, and decided he was of minimum risk. He grabbed the crossbar on the back of one of the chairs across from her.

"May I?"

She nodded. He sat.

"I'm Todd," he said.

"Tonya," she replied, using the alias they had agreed upon prior.

"Can I buy you a drink?"

She raised one hand, cutting him off. "Let's save each other some time and embarrassment," she said. "I'm not going home with you."

He looked stunned, then baffled.

"W-Well, why not?"

"Just not interested."

"Oh." A new thought hit him. "You looking for girls?"

Oh, God, was this guy dense!

"Look, I'm not interested. Let's leave it at that."

The kid sat there, trying to think of something else to say. Finally, he slowly rose. He turned around and walked away without another word.

In the van, Morris gripped his hand around his mouthpiece so she could not hear him. "I think she handled that rather well, don't you?"

"Good job, Detective," Nick said.

"Thanks, Boss," came her reply.

Morris looked at his watch. It was heading towards one thirty.

"So, when do you want to call this, Lieutenant?"

Nick looked at him, a bit surprised. He had been so intent on running the op, time had gotten away from him. He squinted at the running time stamp on the screen.

"Need your spectacles?" Morris observed.

"Shut up," Nick replied good-naturedly. Morris grinned. "Okay, team," he announced. "Let's wrap it up. Call it a night."

"Roger that," came the verbal responses from Valerie and Reggie. The Vampire merely looked directly into one camera and gave a "thumbs up".

Both Morris and Nick removed their headsets.

Inside, Valerie stood up. Reggie strolled over. The Vampire moved closer.

"Good job tonight," Reggie said to them both. "Too bad Maya wasn't here."

"Maya?" Valerie asked.

"An incredibly old acquaintance of mine," the Vampire replied.

"So, your friend is… like you?"

"She is not my friend," he said flatly, his tone unmistakable.

"Well, if she's not around, what are you going to do?"

"I have a friend," the Vampire smiled. "A more recent acquaintance whose company and counsel I value. A Catholic priest. Father Justin Ng."

Both Reggie's and Valerie's faces froze. The Vampire picked up on it. Heartbeats racing, tension rising. Their auras changed colors and patterns.

"Grandpa," Reggie began, his voice thick. He chose his next words carefully. "I have some bad news."

Journal entry Feb 22

This entry shall be brief. I must prepare for bed; the dawn is only minutes away.

It is with a heavy heart I acknowledge the passing of my friend, Father Justin Ng. I have been informed he was found outside his room sprawled on the ground, his neck broken. The police believe Ng was murdered and the scene staged to appear as if he fell over in his chair and struck his head.

Maya killed him to get to me. Killed him because he was elderly, a soft target, and he was my friend. I do not have many friends, and the death of even one is a dagger into my heart.

Justin's murder will not interfere with what I must do. What I have always known I must do. From the moment I first felt her presence in my city, from the time I first heard her psychic siren's call. From the moment I first laid eyes on her at Splinter.

Maya.

I am coming for you.

Murdering my friend only strengthens my resolve. I shall not deviate from the path you yourself have forced me to walk, a path that will lead inexorably to destruction and death.

Killing another vampire is no small matter. One vampire killing another can precipitate certain ramifications within the vampire world. If she has friends among our kind in high places, her death may trigger retribution, even though I am clearly within my rights according to the Vampire Way.

Murdering an innocent person not involved in our conflict, twisting the brittle neck of a defenseless old man until the vertebrae snapped violates the Vampire Way. And it is just one more reason why you deserve the fate I have planned for you.

CHAPTER SEVENTEEN

As the Vampire died in his bedroom, Reggie shifted in fitful sleep. He had all his bedcovers yanked up under his chin. He would sleep a while like this, get too hot and start sweating. So, he would kick the covers off, stop sweating. Then he would get cold again and jealously pull the covers back up his shivering body.

When his alarm went off four hours from now, he would feel just as depleted as when he fell into bed.

A few miles north in University Heights sat a low row of white stucco one-story apartments; each one a 450 square foot studio carbon copy of the next. Built in a semicircle, the art deco-inspired eight-plex formed a small court, with each apartment having one parking space out front.

The people there were nice enough, about as nice as people ever are in a major city. Personable because they want to appear polite but not much more. Keeping a distance was how city folks protected themselves. In a city like San Diego, you never really know people. Your next-door neighbor might be a regular Joe chugging out forty hours a week to make ends meet. They may be a budding entrepreneur, developing a product or service that in a few years might revolutionize the world.

Then again, they might be a criminal. A drug dealer.

A serial killer.

A cop.

Valerie had lived there since before she went to the Academy. She had stayed there even though she could afford something bigger.

Valerie's priorities lay elsewhere. She liked the neighborhood. She could walk to a grocery store. She could walk to a new LeStat's that had opened a few years before. She was also within walking distance of bars, bistros, and a wonderful Mexican takeout place. She enjoyed the easy commute to work.

She had crashed and burned when she got home. Clothing draped over a chair, bra dangling from a bed post. Valerie in the dark apartment buried under a pink comforter. Her sleep so deep, she did not even dream.

After the stakeout, Morris Horn had dragged his dead ass home to the same barely habitable, raggedy-ass tenement he had lived in ever since his wife had thrown him out.
He stripped to his skivvies and fell across his lumpy mattress and rusted box springs. He lay there listening to a talk radio station, waiting to drift off.
The radio banter usually soothed him. But this morning his mind raced; the white noise grated. It was not the cheerful banter, the news, weather, or traffic reports.
Why did he still live here? At first, it was all he could afford. But the kids were both over eighteen and graduated, so no more child support. No alimony, either. His ex-wife made a hell of a lot more than he ever did. His attorney had campaigned for him to seek support. To not go after it was leaving money on the table.
But Morris had remained resolute. As a man, he had to have some self-respect. Old fashioned, perhaps not too smart. But he had to look at himself in the mirror in the morning.
He hated what he saw enough as it was.
Morris pushed his bulk into a sitting position. His legs, big as tree trunks, dangled over the edge, feet almost touching the floor. He straightened his arms, curled his hands into fists the size of sledgehammers and pushed himself up.
He wandered over to the kitchenette. Just a couple of countertops, storage underneath, two overhead cabinets, a single sink.
A coffeemaker sat to the side of the sink. The carafe held about half its volume in cold black coffee from the day before. He opened an overhead cabinet, grabbed one of the only three mugs he owned. He never cared which one he drank from. He

poured cold coffee, thrust the mug into the microwave. He set the timer, hit START.

The microwave hummed a tuneless song. Morris opened the fridge that should have been replaced two decades back. He pulled out some leftover ham slices and a boiled egg. He peeled the egg, tossed the ham onto a small paper plate, put a slice of bread into the toaster. The microwave dinged. He retrieved his mug, put the ham in. He doctored his coffee while he waited on the toast and ham. The toast popped. He was slathering butter when the microwave dinged again.

He hauled his breakfast over to the low, scarred coffee table that had come with the apartment. He plopped his mass down on a sofa he had purchased at the Salvation Army, used his remote to turn on his fifteen-year-old Goodwill TV.

Local news, insufferably perky hosts. How could anyone be that cheerful at this hour?

Morris ate breakfast. Sleep would not come until tonight – maybe. No matter how tired he was, he was up for the duration. Another stakeout tonight, and every night until they caught the motherfucker.

It was going to be a long day for Morris Horn, Private Eye.

Alejandro Domingo stood in his bathroom. He had showered, brushed, and flossed his teeth. The intense grief had eased somewhat. But it was like a hurricane being downgraded from a Category 5 to a Category 4. The winds were a little less, but it was still a hurricane.

He shaved for the first time in a week. God, had it been that long since his baby had been murdered? His heavy beard proved a challenge for his razor. His skin pulled and tugged under the multiblade instrument he dragged across his face. He'd probably have razor burn.

On the day of his little girl's funeral.

Nick had pulled some strings to get Ramsey's body released early. He had called the Chief Coroner and the Chief of Police directly. He had called the Mayor *at home*. Nick didn't tell

Alejandro, of course. Bragging was not Nick's style. Alejandro had been informed by certain well-placed friends what had transpired.

And now, even with a church funeral and a graveside service ahead, part of him felt like the weight of the world had been lifted off his shoulders. He had Nick Castle to thank for that.

He walked from the bathroom directly into his closet. He dressed in silence, choosing a custom-tailored dark grey suit, pale pink custom shirt, a purple silk tie and a matching silk handkerchief for his suitcoat breast pocket. He looked in the mirror as he tied the tie. He smoothed the tie down, secured it with a tie clip. This ensemble had been one of Ramsey's favorites. And since today was as much about honoring her life as it was laying her to rest, it seemed fitting.

Today was about her.

He left his bedroom, made his way down the hall, found himself at one end of the Great Room with its expansive views. No fog this morning. Breakers in the distance. People walked along the beach; dogs played. Surfers braved frigid water in black wetsuits.

Even in the face of tragedy, life went on.

Pepe stood in the kitchen at the prep table. He seemed subdued. Dressed in all black, he looked up as he poured coffee.

"Good morning, sir."

"Good morning, Pepe."

Alejandro sat at the dining table. His gaze drifted back to the window and the world beyond in the distance. He was barely aware of Pepe putting breakfast in front of him.

"Oh," Alejandro said, "Thank you, Pepe."

"You're quite welcome, sir."

"What about you?'

"Sir?" Pepe did not understand the question.

"Aren't you eating anything?"

"I have already eaten, sir," he lied. Truth was, he was too devastated about saying goodbye to a girl he had seen as a surrogate daughter.

"Am I doing the right thing, Pepe?"

"Sir?"

"With Nicolas."

"Ah. Yes sir," Pepe responded emphatically. "It is an old wrong that needs to be made right."

"People don't forget the damage done to them by family, do they?"

"No sir, they do not."

Alejandro sipped his coffee, bit into his eggs. With what he would endure today, he wasn't particularly hungry. But he knew he needed the calories, so he shoveled it down.

As difficult and as draining as today would be, Alejandro Domingo was determined to turn over a new leaf.

In Kensington, the Vampire's shrunken corpse lay beneath his heavy quilt. Brittle skin tight over gray bones. Paper thin lips pulled back in rictus. Exposed teeth created a grotesque grimace.

Heavy blackout curtains over the window kept daylight out. Reliable. Dependable. Exactly as planned.

In the living room, his laptop sat silent and dark. The only sound was the occasional hum of the refrigerator keeping his blood chilled.

Everything in order, all quiet. Do not draw attention to yourself. Fly under the radar; do not arouse suspicion. And it worked. Everything running on autopilot during the daylight hours.

Just as the Vampire had planned.

Maya had taken similar precautions. Dark. Quiet. No lights. Maya lay curled in extreme decomposition inside a great trunk in the basement.

Jonathan Slater pulled into his parents' driveway, parked the SUV. His parents' SUV was not there. He had not expected it to be.

Parents both missing. No activity on their phones, debit cards, or credit cards since before they "sold" their house. No corresponding financial windfall in either of their accounts. No listing with any agency of realtor.

Sold the house on their own and moved away without a word?

Not bloody likely.

The family lawyer had been no help. The police were either inept or uninterested. He called them several times demanding results. Did he have any idea how many people went missing in San Diego County every year? Did he have any idea how many people go missing in the United States every year and, for all intents and purposes, simply fall off the face of the earth leaving no trail to follow?

People bail on their lives all the time, one detective informed him, for all kinds of reasons. Just pull up stakes and vanish. Go somewhere else. Another town, another state, another country. Start over. New names, new identities.

No crime in that.

Miriam had suggested a private detective could look for his parents to the exclusion of all else. Maybe find something the police had missed.

Jonathan the penny pincher wanted one more "look at the house". If he still came up empty, then they could talk to a professional.

Something was terribly wrong. Something bad had happened to his parents, and Jonathan suspected foul play. This new owner, "Maya", was the last person to see his parents alive.

He flung open the car door, stepped out. Hit a button on his key fob, locking the vehicle as he walked towards the side gate. He paused there, glanced around. No one driving by; no one on the sidewalk. No one peeking over the fence or peering out a window.

Good.

Jonathan reached over the gate, flicked the latch. He slipped inside, closed the gate behind him. A few steps deeper into the back yard and he stopped, gained his bearings, noticed details.

Grass overgrown. Unkempt. So was the front lawn.

His father had always been fastidious about his lawn. "Pride of ownership", he had always said.

The lawn furniture remained. If his parents had sold the house, why had they not packed up their belongings?

This was looking worse and worse.

He crept forward, giving the house an intense once over. No motion inside. No face at the window. He stopped at the back porch. He tried the door, jiggled the knob gently.

Locked.

He pursed his lips. If he broke in, he was committing a crime.

Fuck it. I'm going in.

Alejandro arrived well before the funeral. He stood on the steps of Saint Elizabeth's, speaking in hushed tones with the archbishop, who was handling the service personally. Pepe stood beside them quietly.

People filtered up the steps towards the sanctuary doors. Alejandro shook hands with all of them, thanked them for coming. They all nodded to the archbishop, then moved inside.

Alejandro saw Nick coming down the sidewalk. His heart warmed. A brief smile fluttered across his lips, then it was gone.

Nick wore a charcoal gray suit, black shoes, buffed and shined. A plain white shirt adorned with a simple black tie held in place with a silver tie tack. Subdued clothing for a somber occasion. Nick had always known how to dress appropriately for every type of social function.

Nick alighted the steps, extended his hand. Alejandro shook it, placed his free hand on top.

"Nicolas. Thank you so much for coming."

"It's family."

Alejandro nodded.

"Look, you've probably heard this a hundred times today, but if there's anything I can do..."

Alejandro paused. "Actually, there is something I need to discuss with you."

Nick was intrigued.

"Come by the house in a couple of days. We'll talk."
"I will," Nick promised. "I need to find a seat."
"You can sit with Pepe and me."
Nick was truly surprised.
"You're family, too, Nico. You always have been." He glanced towards the archbishop then back at his half-brother. "In fact," he added, putting an arm around Nick's shoulders, "Let's go in together."

Reggie groaned, protesting his relentless alarm clock. In University Heights, Valerie silenced her own irritating alarm. She had an old wind-up alarm clock. As she was coming out of the ether, she considered hurling it against the wall.

Morris drank his fourth mug of coffee, tugged his clothes on. He buckled his pants, headed for the bathroom. He wouldn't bother shaving, but he would brush his teeth.

Nick sat with Alejandro and Pepe through the service. The archbishop's message was poignant, bittersweet. Praising Ramsey and all the good she had done in her short life, wondering of the purpose of her premature demise, what was God's plan? What larger purpose was being served by this tragic turn of events?

Not even the archbishop could answer that.

Afterwards, they accompanied the casket out of the church, watched from nearby as Ramsey was loaded into the back of the hearse. Then they followed in their cars, a solemn procession, headed for the cemetery and the Domingo family crypt.

Morning passed into afternoon. Morris sat in his threadbare office, working. Both Reggie and Valerie had wandered into the precinct. There was still much to do: autopsy reports, lab results. DNA. All the boring, mundane, yet crucially important aspects of police work. The stuff a lot of the crime shows on TV either glossed over, ignored completely, or simply got wrong. But it was the stuff that built cases. The stuff they packaged for the DA.

The stuff that put murderers behind bars so they never breathed free air again.

In North Park, Jonathan used a screwdriver to pry the backdoor open. Inside, he tried the light switch. The lights snapped on. He stood stock still, listened. He heard nothing other than the low hum of the refrigerator.

Jonathan opened the refrigerator door, looked inside. The milk had curdled inside the container. Some leftover chili had gone bad. Wilted vegetables. Fruit turning green and fuzzy.

In the freezer, the meat was turning colors from freezer burn.

His parents had not been here in a long time. Yet all their things were still here. The dining table, the decorative art on the wall, the faux vintage "Farm Fresh" signs. Silverware in the drawers. Plates, bowls, cups still in the cupboard. Even the broom and mop leaning in the corner between the refrigerator and the wall.

"Maya" had a lot to explain.

He crept into the living room as quietly as possible. Everywhere he looked, he saw his parents' furniture. Nothing had been boxed up; nothing had been moved out. Nothing replaced.

He turned on a lamp.

Dust. Everywhere.

His mother had always been a conscientious housekeeper. She took pride in mopped floors, vacuumed rugs, dusted and polished furniture. The whole house spic and span. A place for everything, and everything in its place.

He could write his name in the dust, and the lemon aftersmell of the furniture polish Mom had used for over 40 years was nowhere to be found. Usually, the place reeked of it.

In the bedroom it was more of the same. He looked inside his mother's jewelry box on the dresser; all her gold and silver jewelry was still there. So was the signet ring she had inherited from her grandmother, a couple of sapphire and ruby necklaces and an emerald brooch she had worn ever since he could remember.

He now presumed his parents were dead. Murdered. No robbery, no theft. All the furniture still here. He had checked the utility records before coming over today. The bills were still in his parents' name, on autopay, of course.

No valuables taken...

The safe!

Jonathan went to the closet, opened the door, turned on the overhead light. There it was, right where he remembered. A small safe, about eighteen inches high and wide, about sixteen inches deep. It sat directly on the carpeted floor in the shadows of the clothes hanging above it.

He dropped to his knees, which was becoming more and more difficult these days. He spun the dial, being one of only three people on the planet who knew the combination.

The tumblers clicked inside. He pushed downward on the handle, yanked the door open. He peered in.

Five thousand dollars in cash lay just inside the door. Mostly in hundreds, but a smattering of fifties and twenties. Wrapped in rubber bands with a small scrap of paper and *$5,000.00* scribbled in pen. He ducked his head, looked towards the rear.

Stacks of ten-ounce silver bars stared back at him. Also, two stacks of gold coins, each ten high. Twenty ounces of gold, total.

Jonathan grabbed a key from the inside of the safe's door, inserted it into a lock on the thin drawer located near the top of the inside vault. He pulled the drawer out. His parents' estate papers and living trust, life insurance policies naming Jonathan sole heir. Their attorney had copies of everything, plus the one of the keys to his parents' two-key, double-lock safety deposit box at the bank. The bank manager had the other.

There were no copies.

Jonathan was now convinced that identity thieves had forged a phony sale and killed his mother and father. With nothing missing except his parents and their car, no activity on their bank accounts or credit cards after the new Quick Deed claim, nothing else made sense.

What kind of identity thieves murder two harmless senior citizens, disposes of the bodies and their car, but doesn't fence everything inside and then sell the house? And why had they not plundered the jewelry? Or the safe?

None of that made sense.

His hand drifted behind him to the small of his back. His fingers traced lightly over the semiautomatic handgun he had holstered there. Maya had much explaining to do, and he was not above helping her find her motivation.

He checked his watch. Where had the time gone? He thought he had only been here a few minutes. He had arrived over two hours ago.

Jonathan walked back into the living room and found himself at a crossroads. He could simply leave the way he came, close the back door, go talk to the police again. Or he and Miriam could hire a PI.

The alternative was to stay here and wait for this "Maya" to show up. Even if it took all day.

Even if it took all night.

CHAPTER EIGHTEEN

Reggie and Valerie poured over new lab reports. The results filled in a few details on each victim, helped form a more complete picture. None it identified a suspect.

They carefully reviewed what they knew, realized they knew everything.

They could prove nothing.

Movement near the back entrance. The lieutenant came in, still dressed in the same immaculate attire from the funeral. Face scrupulously shaved; hair perfectly coiffed. Suit tailored to fit his naturally slender build. Hell, even his *shoes* looked impressive.

"Damn, Lieutenant," Valerie marveled, "you clean up well."

"Thank you," Nick smiled. He looked at their desks. "Anything new?"

"I wish," Reggie spat, his frustration showing.

Nick pursed his lips, frustrated. "Be ready for tonight." He nodded briefly, made his way towards his office. He entered, shut the door.

"What's with him?" Valerie asked.

"He attended Ramsey Domingo's funeral today," Reggie informed her.

"That's not it."

Reggie's eyes followed her gaze to the glass office. He didn't see what she was seeing.

"What do you think it is?"

"I don't know. Something." She looked at Reggie. "Maybe personal?"

Reggie considered this. "There's some connection between Nick's mother and the Domingo family."

Valerie's eyes shifted back to Lieutenant Castle. Reggie made a note of how sensitive to emotions in others she was. And how spooky accurate she was at reading people. She had certainly gotten Grandpa Eddie's number, plus his and Nick's compliance in keeping the Vampire's secret.

Reggie shuddered.

"What's wrong?" she asked.

"Just a bit chilly."

Lottie bustled about her house. Well, she didn't exactly bustle. But she was up and dressed, had made her bed, and came downstairs. Breakfast was done, dishes rinsed and in the dishwasher. She smiled to herself. An automatic dishwasher in her kitchen had long been a luxury she had assumed she would never have.

Yet here she was, living in a house that was completely hers, her name on the title, completely paid off. She did not know exactly how much the house was worth in the current market, but she lived in Kensington, one of the priciest neighborhoods in town.

But she did not calculate her riches by the house she owned or the money in the bank. Far from it. She had been married as a young woman, before gray hair and wrinkles, before aches and pains and medications and diabetes and heart disease. Before the numbness in her feet and that dull pressure that had been sitting in her chest since she woke up this morning.

She had known James, her husband since childhood. They grew up together, went to school together, and fell in love all in the same town. He had been faithful and kind. He never hit her, never played around. He died of a massive stroke at age 53.

Life has its ups and downs.

Overall, her life had been good.

She had a family that she loved, and who loved her back. True, she had lost her husband and her daughter. But she had her grandson, of whom she was proud. He had grown into a strong and moral man. And incredibly, she had her grandfather, her guardian angel, her dark avenger against drug dealers, her very own personal vampire.

How many people could claim that?

The pressure in her chest felt worse now. Tiny beads of sweat popped across her forehead and her upper lip. A wave of nausea rose.

Lottie tottered towards the living room. The numbness in her feet spread northward into her lower legs. Her numb fingers tingled. Her face went pasty gray, her skin bathed in sweat.

A massive headache kicked in from out of nowhere. Her peripheral vision dimmed. It was like looking through a paper towel tube. She could only see what was in front of her.

She made it to her favorite chair, a scuffed and scarred old leather monstrosity her husband had bought for her back in 1976. She plopped down, exhausted. Her chest pain was worse now, constricting around her ribcage. She couldn't take a deep breath.

Like an elephant sitting on her chest.

Sweat dripped from her nose and chin. She sat there, breathing hard, trying to figure out what was happening. Her brain refused to function. The more she tried to think, the less she could.

The pain encompassed her entire torso and radiated to her neck and left shoulder. Her head lolled on her shoulders, swung left. She found herself looking at a wooden TV tray that she insisted on using as a side table. On it sat an old coffee mug she had forgotten to put in the dishwasher. She could also make out the TV remote, and oh yes.

Her cell phone.

Call Reggie. He would know what to do.

In her mind, she reached out to grab it.

In reality, her arms and legs were useless tree stumps. Pale and tingly from lack of blood as her body shunted her blood supply to her vital organs. Unfeeling fingers could not grasp the cell phone. Her fumbling knocked it onto the floor, along with the remote and the empty mug.

Frustrated, she sighed, sat back. She would have to pick all that up now. But not right now. Maybe in a minute. Right now, she needed to catch her breath. That was it. She had overdone it in the kitchen earlier, and she needed to rest.

Catch her breath.

The pain worsened, ballooned up her neck, down her shoulder and into her left arm. Darkness overwhelmed her.

Fatigued in a way she had never experienced, she closed her eyes. Acceptance relaxed her. She would be okay, she told herself. All she had to do was rest.

Close her eyes.

She would feel better soon. She had been having episodes like this for weeks now. She had not bothered Reggie or her grandfather about it. She had the episodes, rested, sometimes laid down, and the episode passed, and she would feel better.

It would be like that this time, too.

Everything would be fine in a little while.

Jonathan Slater sat in his parents' gloomy living room as shadows gathered. The sofa was hard and uncomfortable, some faux midcentury modern thing. His mother had grown up in the fifties and sixties and carried a nostalgia for the time. Personally, Jonathan didn't see the attraction.

Inside her trunk, Maya's skin thickened, ligaments attached to bones, muscle fibers appeared, stretched, multiplied. Tendons appeared, attached muscle to bone. Organs regrew in much the same fashion. Finally, her lungs filled with that first agonizing breath.

The dark magic that enabled a dead body to live again pushed her towards consciousness. Bottomless black eyes opened. She pushed against the inside of the lid.

The lid opened, caught itself against the basement wall. She grabbed the rim and pulled herself up, allowing her legs to unfurl. She was not particularly tall, certainly not by today's standards. But the people of her time, especially females, had been quite a bit smaller, shorter than those of today.

Maya stood completely still, allowing her senses to drink everything in. The soft skitter of cockroaches along the baseboards. Cockroaches and rats thrived in warm, densely populated San Diego. Even the finest homes in the most exclusive neighborhoods were not immune to infestations.

Her mind became aware of the steady heartbeat of a human in the living room above. A dreamy smile spread across her lips.

She would be dining in tonight.

She stepped out of the trunk, quietly closed the lid. She brushed her hands, dust filtering towards the basement floor. She crossed the expanse to the stairs, paused at the bottom. The heartbeat was still there, slow and steady.

Upstairs, Jonathan's mind had been roaming, turning over different scenarios about how to confront whomever he encountered. One way or the other, he was going to get answers, and he was going to get them tonight!

A faint thud brought him out of his reverie. He wasn't sure where it had come from. Or even if he had truly heard anything at all. When he didn't hear anything else in the next few seconds, he chalked it up to a fatigued mind and overworked imagination.

Thud.

Jonathan sat up straight. No way he had imagined that. He peered intently into gathering darkness. He had heard it, all right. Coming from the one place in the entire house he had not thought to check.

The basement.

How could he have been so stupid?

But the only way in and out of the basement went through the kitchen. No external entry/exit. Someone had been down there all day. Had they been asleep?

So, who had stolen the house and murdered his parents? A Goddamned vampire or something?

More thuds, soft but getting louder. His hand silently snaked behind him, fingers encircling the butt of his handgun. One shot from his .45 would ruin their whole day. He smirked again, remembering one of the first lessons he had ever been taught in college by his freshman business professor.

You don't have to be the smartest person in the room. Just know something nobody else in the room knows.

Jonathan knew he was in control of this situation.

He heard the basement door squeak open, rusty hinges groaning. His father had never gotten around to oiling them. Jonathan could easily track his adversary's progress. He would know precisely where they were every step of the way.

He heard the door close, then steps across the kitchen floor. Not the heavy wide-paced steps of a man. These were light, close together. Almost delicate.

A woman?

Well, that was fine by him. He didn't care the gender. Jonathan was an equal opportunity avenger. Whoever had done this would be held to the same amount of responsibility under the law. If it ever got that far.

The steps faded. He realized she was standing at the entrance to the kitchen, her body hidden just around the corner from the living room.

"Hello."

It was a statement, not a question.

Jonathan frowned. How could she know he was here?

"I can hear you," she replied.

He gripped his gun tighter.

"You can point your weapon at me if you like," she said. "It won't do any good."

What? How could she know—

"I can smell the gun oil."

Confident that the intruder was sufficiently confused, Maya stepped into the open, stopped at the entrance into the living room. She was barely visible in the darkness. Ambient light from outside came through from the back door and illuminated her shape from behind. Jonathan could not make out her features.

"Where are my parents?" he demanded.

"Ah," she said. "You're not a thief. You're the son of the previous owners."

"Where are my parents?"

"I have no idea."

Jonathan pulled the gun, pointed at her. "What did you do with my parents?" He demanded again, louder now, his patience wearing thin.

"Oh my," she gasped. "Jonathan. It's so... BIG." She giggled.

Jonathan's fear and anger overflowed in that moment. "What the fuck did you do to my parents?"

Maya's laughter stopped. She blinked her eyes, stepped into the living room where she was visible by outside light through the front windows.

Jonathan's eyes bulged; his jaw dropped when he saw her features.

"What do you think I did?" She countered.

Stunned silence was Jonathan's only answer.

"Very well," she said with resignation. "I killed them, disposed of the bodies and the car, and performed a bit of online magic on certain housing documents so anyone looking will tell you. The house is mine."

His mouth worked before anything came out. "You killed them?"

"That never occurred to you?"

Of course, it had. Jonathan had worked hard to suppress that thought. His worst nightmares had come true.

"This is my house," she stated, her black eyes glassy and her face going cold. "And you, young man, are no longer welcome."

"Oh really?"

"You one chance to leave this house alive."

"What?"

"Leave. Now. Right now. Never return."

"I don't think so," he responded. "You just confessed to double homicide and grand larceny. You'll be leaving in handcuffs."

"I don't think so."

"I'm the one holding the gun."

She chuckled, her fangs showing for the first time. "That's cute." She shook her head at him, seemingly with pity.

Jonathan pulled his phone out of his pocket.

"Stay right where you are," he ordered. "One false move and I'll shoot."

"Sounds painful."

"It gets worse," Jonathan continued. He wagged the phone in his hand. "I have a recording app on here. I recorded your confession. I can prove you did everything you said."

She grinned again, shook her head. "Oh, Jonathan."

"I'm still pointing a loaded firearm at your chest," he replied. Then he added, "Maya."

Fangs sparkled low in the dull light. She surged forward quickly.

Jonathan fired.

The bullet slammed into Maya's chest just left of the sternum. The bullet's kinetic energy and cavitation ripped through her heart, aorta, and left lung before blowing out her back and embedding in the wall behind her. She flew backwards, arms and legs flailing ass over teakettle. She landed hard.

For a moment, the room was absolutely still. The pungent smell of gunpowder floated on the air. Maya lay unmoving. Jonathan stood where he was, eyes wide, mouth agape, arm still extended, a small waft of smoke rising from the barrel.

Oh my God. What did I just do?

He had practiced with the gun, of course. He had taken gun safety classes, went to the gun club a couple of times a month. He had never shot -- nor shot at -- another human being before.

Until now.

Holy fuck, this wasn't shooting paper targets. It wasn't like the movies. She didn't moan or give a heartfelt confession before expiring with a final gasp. She had been knocked back violently, shot through and through. The gruesome spatter on the wall was proof of that.

He swayed slightly; his vision blurred. He felt like he was going to throw up.

Holy Christ, holy Christ. What have I done?

A sound caught his attention.

Soft, coming from the body sprawled on the floor. He blinked, trying to make sense of it. Probably air escaping from the lungs or the belly.

Or the bowels.

Jonathan had read somewhere that when people died, they sometimes farted, pissed themselves, even shit themselves. It had something to do with all the involuntary muscles in the body relaxing.

But rather than turn and flee, he crept forward, inch by laborious inch. He needed to confirm the death. Then he could leave, get out of there, and ditch the gun. Because for all his bravado, he knew California's gun laws intimately. She had confessed to several felonies, but had been unarmed.

He would be arrested no matter what.

Manslaughter. Maybe even murder.

His eyes drifted up from the body to the wall. Even in the gloom, he could see where the bullet had impacted and broken apart. Ballistics would be for shit. Maybe he could wipe down all the hard surfaces he had touched and slip out the back. It might be days or even weeks before neighbors reported the smell of the decomposing body.

Maybe he could get away with this.

Feeling better about things, he stood over Maya's corpse. His gun dangled loosely from his hand. He needed to check her pulse. Leave nothing to chance. He squatted down, took his extended index and middle fingers of his free hand, felt placed them gently but firmly on the neck just to the side of the windpipe.

Wow! She was already so cold! Was that normal? Jonathan had never spent time around dead bodies, but this didn't seem right. In all those cop shows, bodies cooled over hours.

No pulse.

"Not so goddamned high and mighty now, are you?" he whispered.

Maya's head swung to look at him. She snarled with unbridled fury as he yelped and fell backwards onto his butt. He immediately forgot he still had a powerful firearm in his hand. Eyes wide, he attempted to do an awkward backwards crab crawl away as she scampered after him.

He found himself with his back against a wall, and somehow managed to stand. Maya did the same, mirroring his movements. She grinned at him, pure malevolent evil. He did not realize the warmth spreading down his legs was his own urine.

She patted the gaping hole in her chest with one hand. "That hurts!" She advanced on him. "And look what you did to my outfit!" her outage rose. "Do you have any idea how expensive this is?"

His mind reeling out of control, he formed no answer, no pithy response. Out of a sheer primal instinct for survival, Jonathan raised the handgun again.

He never got off another shot.

Maya surged forward. Black eyes, bloody dress, razorblade mouth, cruel fangs. She gripped his gun hand, raised it higher and away from her. Then she wrenched downward and twisted out. They both heard tendons snap, bones break. She pushed harder, and everything gave way. Broken bones erupted through the skin at the distal end of his forearm, sharp ends protruding. Ruptured blood vessels showered them both in warm rich blood.

The gun dropped like lead to the floor. Maya kicked it away as Jonathan inhaled through his wide-open mouth, a prelude to a scream. Her hand shot forward, grasped him in an iron grip around his esophagus. She squeezed, crimping off the air.

"Not so goddamned high and mighty now, are you… Jonathan?"

She opened her mouth, baring her fangs. She shot forward and punctured his carotid. Blood gushed into her mouth. She sucked it down as fast as she could. She had not planned to dine so early, but she needed extra blood to heal.

Maya drained him dry, then let Jonathan's corpse drop like a sack of bricks.

Maya stood there, chest heaving. She had only one functioning lung, yet the tissue inside was already mending, filling in the tunnel created by the bullet, stitching together. She would have two functioning lungs by dawn.

Just in time to die all over again.

Maya wiped her mouth on her sleeve. Now she needed to dispose of another body. She could take him to the same place as his parents, pay the owner for his patented "no questions asked" service.

Usually, this service was restricted for certain mob associates to discretely dispose of the occasional casualty. When she first approached the owner, a rather sour-smelling man who carried his excess weight poorly, had first feigned ignorance. Then he had projected anger. That was when Maya had ripped off her sunglasses, flashed her fangs, grabbed him by his fleshy throat, and hoisted him up in the air. She slammed his corpulent body into the cheap ceiling, rocking the entire manufactured building that served as his office. Maya had convinced him to extend his services to her at half the going rate. He had quickly agreed.

Wasn't that nice of him?

She looked down at Jonathan's corpse and the mess they had made. This was why she ate out.

Plus, now she needed a shower and a wardrobe change before going out.

The Vampire had already downed a mug of pre-warmed blood and had checked on his Asian protégés. Another night at Splinter lay ahead. He did not relish another night in that dreadful club watching ridiculous people who romanticized what their narrow human minds thought were vampires.

He decided to check in on Lottie. He exited the front door, twisted the key in the lock. He turned towards the night, allowing his senses to take expand. A cluster of heartbeats at the coffee house on the corner. Oils embedded in asphalt on the streets. Soft conversation from the couple on the sidewalk below. They were deciding where to go for dinner. He listened as they agreed on a place and walked off arm in arm.

He glided down the tiled stairway to the sidewalk. He crept forward, as graceful as a jungle cat. He danced lightly across the street to the other sidewalk.

Something new came to him. He stopped, turned sightly, looked back over his shoulder. What was intruding upon his serenity?

A consciousness. Not his. Someone like him. A vampire. To the south. Then somehow, he knew. North Park. Not looking for him; not searching. Under stress of her own. But he seethed just the same.

Maya.

He grimaced with anger. But family came first.

Always.

With an effort, he continued his stroll northward. He hoped seeing his Lot-Lot even briefly would brighten his mood. Because all he wanted to do right now was fight, kill, murder, bathe in his enemy's juices and drink their blood from their empty skull.

It was a vampire thing.

He concentrated on the walk ahead of him. As he drew nearer to Lottie's house, a new feeling nagged at the edge of his mind. Not Maya.

Not this time.

The Vampire bolted forward, moving more quickly than the human eye could follow. A dark blur, a smudge against the night. He covered the last two hundred yards to Lottie's front door in seconds. He stopped on the stoop, not breathing hard.

He did not hear a heartbeat inside. Lottie did not drive, and she never left her home after dark. She, more than most, understood the dangers that lurked in the shadows.

Then came the smell, so faint that even the most sensitive human nose would have missed it.

The unmistakable smell of Death.

The Vampire hung his head, squeezed his eyes shut. He knew what this meant. His Lot-Lot was gone. He pushed back down a tidal wave of grief that surged upwards from the core of his being.

He gripped the doorknob firmly, twisted to the right. Metal bent inside. The deadbolt stayed in place. He pushed, forcing the deadbolt through the jamb. Wood splintered inward.

The door swung open. Inside the dark house, the TV droned on about a feminine hygiene product.

For the first time, he stepped across the threshold of Lottie's house without first being invited. He paused, senses scanning his environs. Intellectually, he knew there was likely no danger, but with everything else going on, why take chances?

The living room sat near the front of the house. He turned his head that way, dreading what he would find.

The TV played a rerun of some 90's sitcom. With few exceptions, the Vampire had never been a big fan of sitcoms. He had given them up after I LOVE LUCY got cancelled.

Ignoring the TV, he focused on the back of Lottie's favorite chair. "This chair knows me," she had told him once. "It knows how I like to sit."

He understood. Lottie had a sentimental attachment to that leather atrocity. She had been sitting in it every night since before her husband had passed. That chair held sweet memories that wrapped her in warmth like a comforting blanket every time she sat down.

He could make out the top of her head from where he was. Silver, naturally curly, slightly disheveled. Her head slumped to the left, unmoving.

The Vampire took one tentative step forward, then another. Then another. He kept taking them until he stood beside her chair.

The Vampire's dead unbeating heart… sank.

Lottie, his beloved granddaughter, sat reclined in her chair, jaw slack, eyes lusterless and staring at nothing. Her arm rested on the arm of the chair, forearm dangling off the edge, hand limp, fingers softly curled. He waited, watched her chest for a rise and fall he knew would never come.

After several seconds, his eyes drifted down to the carpet. Her TV remote and phone lay beneath the cluttered TV tray she insisted on using as an end table. Another old habit she had brought with her and had refused to change. He surmised she had come in here, sat down, tried to reach for her phone, probably to dial 911.

And her heart had simply seized up and stopped beating.

He peeled his sunglasses off, heaved a great sigh that carried the weight of the world. He squeezed his obsidian eyes shut and sobbed. His sobs shook his entire body. Blood tears formed at the corners of his eyelids, then spilled down his cheeks, deep crimson against waxy skin.

After several minutes, he got a hold of himself. He grabbed a tissue from Lottie's box on the TV tray, blotted his eyes and cheeks. He did not want to look a bloody mess for what would come next. He replaced his sunglasses, reached into his jacket pocket. Extracted his cell phone. He pushed a button on his speed dial.

"Hey, Grandpa," Reggie answered on the other end.

"Reginald."

"Hey, we're all here waiting for you. We gonna do this thing, or what?"

The Vampire did not respond. He suddenly did not know how to break this gently.

"Grandpa? You there?"

"Yes," the Vampire croaked, answering at last.

"What's wrong?"

"Reginald," he said, his voice cracking with emotion, "I am afraid the bearer of terrible news."

CHAPTER NINETEEN

The Vampire waited silently. Reverently. He did not leave his granddaughter's side. Reggie showed up about fifteen minutes later. He was a wreck, barely holding it together. Valerie had driven.

Reggie knelt beside his grandmother, took her cool hand in his. He closed his eyes, silently mouthed a prayer. The Vampire did not hear the words. He would never have been so intrusive to eavesdrop anyway.

Reggie stood up, wiped a tear as Nick and Morris Horn walked through the open door. They hung back, respectful of the family tragedy unfolding in front of them. They had seen it many times before.

Too many times before.

While Valerie and Morris huddled with both Reggie and the Vampire, Nick stepped past them. He inspected the living room, doing what a good cop does – looking for signs of foul play.

Every death must be considered a potential homicide until proven otherwise.

He visually inspected her remains. He did not touch her. His eyes traced down her outstretched arm to her hand. He noted the remote and the cell phone on the floor beneath the wooden TV tray. She had probably been in the grips of either a cerebrovascular accident or a cardiac event, made it to the chair, and reached for the phone.

No signs of foul play.

He slipped past the knot of people and stood in the doorway. He pulled his phone out. The Vampire had called Reggie directly, not 911. Nick punched a couple of buttons, pressed the phone to his ear.

When Dispatch answered, he identified himself by name, rank, and badge number. He glanced at the numbers painted by the mailbox, rattled off the address. Dispatch assured him paramedics would arrive shortly.

He dropped his phone back into his pocket, went back inside. The air was laden with sadness and loss. The house reeked of tragedy, of how this one inevitable event that everyone knew was coming sooner rather than later, had still been a gut punch.

Even when you know death of a loved one is imminent, even if they have been in decline for years, it is still always a shock when it finally happens.

Reggie looked like a whipped puppy. The Vampire had regained his composure. His pallid, waxy face had reset itself into its default position of stoicism with an undercurrent of violence behind those sunglasses.

And yet, the Vampire was also capable of incredible compassion. He stood beside his great, great grandson, a thin bony hand resting on his shoulder, trying to give comfort.

"She is no longer in pain," the Vampire whispered. "She is free."

Reggie looked at him hopefully. "Really? I mean, you know from personal experience, right? You died."

"My death was unique," the vampire replied. "My soul never left my body. It is, shall we say, a vampire thing."

"How do you know your soul never left your body?"

"It is a working theory," the Vampire answered. "Father Ng and I had been discussing it." He paused, then added, "I shall miss our conversations. He was my friend."

"When you died the first time, you never saw…?" Valerie asked, not knowing how to finish the question.

"I saw neither heaven nor hell," the walking corpse responded. "Neither God nor Satan."

"What did you see?" Morris asked. He knew the question needed to be asked; everyone wanted to know but were afraid to ask themselves.

Perhaps they were afraid of the answer.

"All I experienced was a vast, black nothingness," the Vampire said. "An endless abyss of infinite void."

"God," Valerie breathed, "that must have been awful."

"I do not remember details."

"How long did it take you to forget?"

"When I was Reborn to Darkness, it was already fading. Think of waking up from a dreamless sleep," he explained. "You know that you were asleep, but you are not aware of the passage of time."

The ambulance arrived about seven minutes later. No lights, no sirens. The massive vehicle simply crept down the street and came to a stop in front of the house. Two EMTs swung out of the cab, dropped to the ground. One man, young, red hair, freckled face. One woman, about thirty-five, dishwater blonde hair pulled back into a prim ponytail. She held a clipboard folded in her hand, resting next to her side. They walked up the walk to the door. Nick met them there, flashed his badge.

"Nick Castle, San Diego PD."

"I'm Taylor," the woman said. "This is Jeffrey."

Nick led them through the foyer and into the living room. They walked slowly around the chair, visually inspecting Lottie's remains.

"Who is she?" Jeffrey asked.

"That's Lottie," Reggie said. "She's my grandmother."

Both EMT's nodded towards Reggie.

"I'm very sorry for your loss," Taylor said.

The Vampire watched them without making a sound. He sensed their feelings, saw their auras emanating in waves off them. They understood this was a family tragedy. The death of a matriarch. They were kind and compassionate. Respectful.

Professional.

Taylor nodded to Jeffrey. He turned and walked out of the room, through the foyer, and out of the house. Taylor pulled a pen out of her breast pocket, held the clipboard in front of her. She wrote down Lottie's name, and the street address. She noted the date and time.

She looked up. "Excuse me." They all looked at her. "Who first found Lottie?"

"Me," the Vampire said. She looked at him, then really looked at him. Her aura waves changed, turned cold.

She was scared.

"Ah," she said. The pen was trembling in her hand. "And you are?"

"Edwin Thaddeus Marx," the Vampire replied. "A friend of the family," he explained. "I came over to see how she was doing."

Taylor scribbled, trying to concentrate. "And you found her like this?"

"Yes."

"Did you touch her or move her?"

"I touched her hand," he said. "Nothing more."

She scribbled some more.

Jeffrey returned, wheeling a gurney inside. He took his time while turning the bed, careful to not scratch the walls or bump into the furniture. He wheeled past everyone and positioned the gurney as close to Lottie as he could.

Taylor put her clipboard aside. She gently took Lottie's outstretched hand, placed it across her belly. She moved Lottie's other hand to the same position, clasping one hand over the other.

"Okay, she breathed, "grab her legs."

Jeffrey did as he was told. Taylor moved one arm behind Lottie's neck, grabbed her by both shoulders.

"We're just going to slide her down out of the chair and onto the gurney," she explained. "Let gravity do the work for us."

They moved in concert, having performed this maneuver many times before, often under more arduous circumstances. They slid Lottie a bit to one side to straighten her out, then slid her down the back and seat of the chair and onto the gurney. They repositioned her, unfolded a white sheet, covered her entire body.

Taylor stood up and grabbed her clipboard. She scribbled something else while Jeffrey secured Lottie with a series of Velcro straps.

"Who is next of kin?"

"Reggie answered, "I am."

"Name?"

"Reginald Downing."

"Relation?"

"Grandson."

Taylor noted it on her form.

"Okay. That's it. We will transport her to the funeral home of your choice."

Reggie looked confused. "Ummm…"

"Parsons and Lake," the Vampire said.

Taylor nodded, noted that on her clipboard. She then helped Jeffrey lift the gurney up, the wheeled legs extending underneath it like a crab. Metallic clicks sounded as the legs locked into their extended positions.

She placed the clipboard on the gurney beside Lottie's head, grabbed her end. She and Jeffrey wheeled Lottie outside and onto level ground. From there, it was a simple push to the rear of the ambulance.

"I don't mean to be indelicate," Morris Horn opened, "but did she have a will?"

"Indeed," the Vampire responded. "A Living Trust updated less than a year ago. Everything is spelled out."

Morris thought about this a moment. "That's good," he judged. "You're going to need a level head during the days and weeks ahead."

"What do you mean?" Reggie asked.

"You're going to be grieving your grandma in addition to dealing with the job," Morris explained. "You don't need to be making decisions about Lottie's estate, too."

"Ladies and gentlemen, may I speak to Reginald alone, please?" the Vampire asked.

Valerie, Nick, and Morris all moved through the foyer and outside. The Vampire turned to face Reggie, then enveloped him in a huge hug. And in that moment, the hollow, shellshocked look on Reggie's face gave way to grief and loss. He squeezed his bloodshot eyes shut. The tears came in torrents, a flood so powerful it couldn't be kept in.

Dammit! What would the rest of them think seeing him like this?

What would Valerie think?

But the tears came anyway; then the sobbing started. He clung to his great, great grandpa to keep from collapsing. His breath came in catches, starts and stops.

The Vampire understood. How could he not? This creature of the night, this unliving and yet undying thing, this walking monster that fed on human blood, understood sorrow and loss better than just about anyone on Earth. For he had certainly endured more than most over the course of his existence.

He stood there, his own eyes closed behind his sunglasses. His lips pulled tighter, his mouth becoming a line so thin across the lower half of his face it almost disappeared. He held his great, great grandson, wishing he could do more, knowing he could not, and knowing this was not enough.

The sobs eventually subsided. The Vampire noticed that the rest of the merry band had judiciously stayed outside. None of them wanted to see Reggie like that. The sounds of his wailing were bad enough. The Vampire sensed their unease.

Reggie finally took a step back. He sniffed, rubbed tears away from underneath his eyes. The Vampire wrapped a protective arm around Reggie's shoulder. He led him out into the cool night air. Reggie's breath steamed from his nose. The night had become enshrouded in fog.

"No stakeout tonight," Nick said when they all stood facing each other.

"Lieutenant – "Reggie began to argue.

"No arguing, Detective," Nick snapped. "You're in no shape to work, and you know it."

Reggie sighed, slumped his shoulder a bit, nodded his head.

"Keep us in the loop regarding the arrangements," Nick said. The Vampire ticked his head in response. "Let's leave the family to grieve in peace."

He and Morris peeled off, headed towards the unmarked squad car. About halfway there, they realized Valerie was not with them. They turned around, saw her still with Reggie and the Vampire. She seemed to be standing extremely close to Reggie. Both experienced cops, they had seen this kind of attraction spring up within a precinct from time to time. Sometimes these things ended badly, but sometimes they ended in marriage, kids, and happily ever after.

Usually though, they ended badly.

Both men knew departmental policy, understood the wisdom behind it. Both also understood the potential legal liability it put on the department. Nick should pull her away, kicking and screaming if need be.

"Well?" Morris asked him.

"She's a big girl," Nick replied. "She knows the policy. More importantly, she knows the danger."

"That's a big risk to take, Lieutenant," Morris said, emphasizing the last word. "That's a career killer."

"My career to kill."

Maya stood under the shower's hot spray, steam clouding the mirror. Blood sluiced off her in rivulets, clouding the water swirling around her delicate feet. Gravity sent it circling the drain and down.

She turned her face upwards. The water stung, a thousand tiny needles. But she stood there all the same. A long hot shower was one of the few times when she, a vampire, felt warm. It reminded her of life before… well, *this*.

Memories came flooding back. Flashes of anger, fear, pain. Disjointed images juxtaposed, jumbled together like a quick-cut fistfight in a movie.

But what had happened to her hadn't been a movie. It had been all too real. Ugly thoughts, bad memories. And while she knew everyone had them, hers were particularly painful, even after all this time. Over a hundred years and sixty years later, and it still felt like yesterday.

Time does *not* heal all wounds.

She pushed the trauma back into the shadows. She stepped out of the shower, toweled herself dry. Now the important decision: what to wear? Her frustration rose again. She had really loved that dress with the built-in corset.

She strode out of the bathroom, crept silently through the house. She kept her clothes in a trunk down in the basement. She made her way down the stairs.

Faint light filtered in through the short wide windows that sat at ground level. This meager illumination, combined with Maya's vampire eyes, proved sufficient. She moved easily around items the previous owners had stored here. She stopped in front of an old-fashioned steamer that stood on its end. She grabbed each side and pulled. The trunk yawned open, revealing her clothing clean and pressed resting in the bottom. Her prize possessions hung on hangers suspended from a hook inside the top.

She grabbed a long skirt, frilly blouse, and a simple pair of black pumps. She pulled her clothes on, stepped into her shoes, and closed the trunk. Then up the narrow staircase she went.

She stepped into the kitchen. Jonathan's remains lay where she had left them. Blood had already soaked through the carpet and into the floorboards beneath. More blood and tissue stuck to the wall where she had been shot.

That had hurt like hell!

The pain was gone now. She was healing nicely. Jonathan's blood saw that. By sundown tomorrow, it would be like it had never happened.

Maya grabbed a large area rug from the living room. And a beautiful rug it was. Pity it would be ruined.

She lay the carpet flat, unceremoniously tossed the body atop it, rolled the carpet into something resembling a log. She opened the back door, hoisted the carpet roll onto her shoulder as if it were weightless.

Maya stomped outside. She marched to the gate, opened it quietly. She used the key fob she had lifted from her would-be executioner to open the trunk. She moved silently, like a mist on a nocturnal breeze.

She placed his corpse down gingerly, not wanting to disturb the neighbors. She looked from side to side. No lights on inside any of the surrounding houses. No cars driving, no one on the sidewalks.

She closed the trunk softly, just enough force to hear it latch. She glided around to the driver's side, opened the door, and slid in. The engine started. She inched out of the driveway aided by a rear camera that played on the dash screen. With a vehicle like this, a driver no longer had to twist in their seat and crane their neck sideways to back out.

Oh, the miracles of modern technology!

She turned right at the corner onto University, headed east. She passed the transit station that bordered the highway and turned immediately onto the onramp. Accelerating, she merged into traffic. At three in the morning, there were scant travelers.

She drove south, her mind wandering. She remembered her upbringing. Mississippi after the Civil War. Not a particularly hospitable place for freed slaves like her parents and herself. But they had made their way.

For a while, that is.

Maya turned on the radio. It was already tuned to a Blues station, belting out some early 20-century blues guitar. The music helped calm her nerves as she thought about... That Night.

The night that had changed everything.

Caught out after dark alone by some young men from town, she had been beaten within an inch of her life and then... *assaulted* by all of them, one after another.

She would have died there if it hadn't been for the Mysterious Stranger that had appeared out of the gloom as she had lay bleeding out in an open field on a muggy August night. He had knelt beside her and had explained that he could give her a chance to get revenge on the animals that had done this.

Or she could choose to die.

Maya chose revenge.

The Mysterious Stranger had bitten her, his saliva mixing with her blood. He had bitten the inside of his mouth. His blood washed into her open wound.

He drained her, of course. She had to die to be reborn, a detail The Mysterious Stranger had neglected to share. But when she awoke the next night, he had been there, smiling, welcoming her to her new Life of Darkness.

He had taught her how to hunt, how to feed, how to choose victims. He had taught her how avoid the dawn and had instructed her in the dire consequences of not being inside before sunrise. He spent several weeks training her in what she would come to understand as The Vampire Way.

Once done, he wished her well and left. He explained that as predators, they each required a territory that was theirs. He had just been passing through the night he found her anyway. So, he was moving on. This was her hunting ground now. And she knew some white boys that "needed killing".

And kill them she did. What she had done went beyond killing. She murdered them. Slaughtered them. Tortured them. And before their final blubbering, tear-soaked breaths, she had made certain they all wished they had never been born male.

Maya merged onto the 5 South, took the exit into National City. She made a couple of turns and found herself in a run-down industrial area just south of the 32nd street Naval base. Dull gray corrugated fences, razor wire unrolled across the top. She slowed as she came up to a massive iron gate on her right. A sign on the fence announced, TINY'S AUTO WRECKAGE AND SALVAGE.

She stopped inches from the gate. She lowered her window, leaned out so the security camera clearly caught her face. She looked directly at the camera and waited. She knew Tiny was here this time of night in his office. The early morning was when he cooked the books and made sure the IRS only saw debits and credits indicating a modest but reasonable profit. Just enough to avoid triggering an audit. His actual profits were enormous. But his other clandestine pursuits didn't concern her. She waited, also knowing Tiny was afraid to open the gate.

Be afraid of what I will do if you don't, she pushed with her mind.

A motor snapped on somewhere behind the fence. The gate groaned as it inched open on rusty wheels. When the gate had pulled back enough to let her through, Maya drove over the gate rails and into the dirty salvage yard.

Hulking heaps of wrinkled, torn, twisted metal stood stacked in relatively neat rows on both sides, creating a clear drive path to a small office trailer about a hundred feet inside. She stopped outside. Tiny was inside. She could hear his rapid heartbeat, feel his tension, smell his terror.

She stepped out of the car.

The trailer was bare bones. Roughly twenty-six feet long by eight feet wide, welded onto a wheeled frame with taillights and an expired license plate. Pasty white aluminum sides, a sloped green roof. A cheap set of steps with a handrail pushed up against the sole door.

The doorknob turned. The door swung open.

An enormous Hispanic man overflowed the doorway. Five foot ten, over four hundred pounds. Dark olive skin, shiny with sweat, weak chin, puffy cheeks. Small black eyes set deep in his head. Long wavy hair pulled back into a man bun. A red T shirt the size of a circus tent. Black maternity shorts stretched to their limits and a gut hanging over the exhausted elastic. Arms and legs like tree trunks. Wide flat feet shoved into flip flops.

"Tiny," Maya cooed at the bottom of the steps. "So good to see you."

Tiny stood motionless, one hand on the knob, the other on the door frame. After a beat, he simply ticked his head upwards with a jut of his chin.

"Maya."

"I need your disposal services once more."

"Of course, you do."

"Tiny!" Maya exclaimed, feigning injury. "If I didn't know better, I'd think you weren't happy to see me." She took a step forward. Tiny moved a bit in the doorway.

"I didn't say that," Tiny finally replied.

"Oh good," she cried. "Just for minute there, I thought we were cross," she continued, taking another step up, moving closer to him. "You wouldn't want us to be cross, would you?"

"No ma'am."

"Splendid." She sounded relieved. Her eyes rolled upwards. "Because we weren't friends anymore, that might be more than I could bear." She turned her face directly towards him, her obsidian eyes burning a whole right through him. "Honestly, Tiny, I just don't know what I might do if I thought we weren't friends anymore."

Tiny put his ham-sized hands up in front of him. "Now don't get upset," he said. He was being toyed with, also knew not to push back. "We're still friends."

"That is such a relief." She fanned herself with one hand.

"So, what do you need done?"

"I need this car and its contents to disappear."

"How soon?"

"Within twenty-four hours. And Tiny," she said as she began to turn away, "I was never here."

"I should be so lucky," he muttered under his breath.

"What was that?" She spun back around. "What did you say?"

"Nothing, nothing!" he shouted, clearly panicked.

Maya dropped all pretenses. Pure predator now, no trace of civility. She trudged forward, closing the distance between them.

"Oh, it was something," she growled inches from his face.

"Look, I'm sorry, all right?" Beads of sweat popped out across his forehead and upper lip. "I won't say it again. Ever."

She glared at him until he looked down and away. Perspiration trickled down his neck. Dark stains encircled his armpits. She still needed him, so she reigned in her temper.

"Just take care of business," she said dismissively. He watched as she turned away, walked down the steps and towards the car. She stopped, turned.

"Oh God, what now?"

She grinned. "If your tongue slips again – ever – I'll reach down your stinking gullet and yank it out of your Goddamned head with my bare hands."

She meant it.

He knew it.

"Have a nice evening, Tiny."

Then she was gone. She didn't walk away. She didn't run.

In the blink of an eye, she was simply… no longer there. Tiny breathed a great sigh of relief.

CHAPTER TWENTY

Maya understood Jonathan Slater's drive to find answers. He knew his parents would never simply move and leave all their belongings behind. They would never not tell their child what was happening or where they were going.

Family bonds. Stronger than chains, as strong as time itself.

Outside the salvage yard, the heavy gate hummed closed behind her. She looked both ways, crossed the street. She needed to get back home. More things to get done before the dawn.

Headlights behind her spilled bright white light along the ground, intensifying as the car approached. She inched further to the side as she walked. She heard loud music, the bass turned up, so the low notes were not heard but felt through low frequency vibrations.

She heard the heartbeats of three humans inside. And she heard them comment as they saw her, a woman walking home alone in the wee hours of the morning.

The car slowed, pulled up next to her. She stopped as the front passenger window rolled down.

A young man, Latino, around eighteen or nineteen, leaned out.

"Oy! Where you goin', Mama?"

"Home," she replied.

"You wanna ride?"

"I wouldn't want to impose," she said, grinning.

"It's no problem," he assured her. He looked to his pals. "Right?" They nodded.

"Well," she started, feigning indecision, "if you're sure."

The Latino opened the door to the classic, two-door Monte Carlo. He stepped out, pushed a small button on the side of the passenger seat, folded it forward so she could climb in the back.

"Get in."

"What is your name?"

"Roberto."

"Thank you, Roberto."

Roberto smiled as she climbed in, sat down in the back. Then he pushed his seatback erect again, got in and closed the door. The car sped off into the night, taillights receding until they were gone.

An hour later, Maya was back home. The young men in the car were all dead, and she found herself in dire need of another shower. Clean once again, she wandered the house naked. Time had flown by tonight. One of those nights where life got in the way of what she wanted to do.

And what she wanted was to kill Eddie Marx, her ungrateful and petulant Vampire Son.

He owed her. For if she had not intervened that night in Hoboken, he would be dead, decayed to dust and brittle bones by now.

He fucking *owed* her.

Tomorrow night, Eddie Marx would die.

But wait.

His granddaughter, Lottie had passed away earlier today. The family would be in mourning. She would begrudgingly show deference to it.

Damn! She thought. Me and my morals.

Well, that's all right. He still thinks San Diego is his. He's not going anywhere, and I'm not going anywhere until his lifeforce is drains out of him and he realizes San Diego is *mine.*

The sun was already up when Reggie awoke. A headache already banged behind his left eye. Great. A migraine to start out the day. Groggy, he rolled over, sat up. The covers fell away from his frame, and he realized he was naked. He did not remember taking his clothes off the night before.

He looked around. Peaceful. But the peace belied the terrible gaping hole in the middle of his chest. His grandma, his mother's mother was gone. She had lived a long life, a good life, and had died peacefully of natural causes.

That's about the best any of us can hope for, he thought. And probably better than most of us deserve.

He staggered into the bathroom, relieved himself, then stared into the mirror. Sallow skin for a black man, bloodshot, red-rimmed eyes. Curly stubble, three day's growth. He needed a haircut. But most alarming his physique. His muscles seemed smooth under the skin, Sure, the bathroom had bad lighting, but his muscles were no longer chiseled the way they had been a few years ago. Okay a few *months* ago. He had the beginnings of love handles. He was pushing forty now. He wasn't a kid anymore.

He promised himself to make time for the gym instead of making excuses. Too busy today, maybe tomorrow. Or the next day. Maybe next week. Fact was, it was getting easier and easier to come up with reasons not to go. Excuses from others like that used to frustrate him. And here he was, being one of *those* guys and doing the same thing.

The words of Grandpa Eddie reverberated through his head.

"A man will make time for whatever is important to him. So, ask yourself: what are you making time for?
What is important to you, Reginald?"

His physical health was important. Being a cop, it was a job requirement. But it was important to him as a human being. High blood pressure, high cholesterol, heart disease, kidney disease, and diabetes all ran in his family. He remembered enough Anatomy/Physiology from college to know the long-term complications from these conditions. And though he loved her dearly and would miss her terribly, he did not want to end up almost blind, barely able to walk, and practically housebound like Grandma Lottie.

Reggie promised himself then and there to take more time for self-care, and that would include workout time. Maybe some vacation time, too. And maybe find a woman, put pep in his step.

He walked out, noticed the smell of freshly brewed coffee. But he had not made coffee yet.

So, who was brewing coffee?

He had barely gotten his underwear pulled up when he heard a jiggle at the front door lock. He dove across the bed towards his pistol resting on the nightstand at the sound of a key inserting into the lock. He grabbed the pistol, pulled it from the holster and swung his arm toward the door just as it swung open.

Valerie stood there, holding a white paper bag filled with what smelled like breakfast. She froze when she saw him. A moment's surprise, then she carefully stepped over the threshold. She closed the door with her foot as Reggie relaxed, put the gun away.

"Do you always shoot people bringing you breakfast?" she asked.

Reggie dressed while she pulled white Styrofoam containers out of the bag. When she thought it was safe for her to do so, she stole a glance at Reggie. She liked what she saw. But when his head swung in her direction, she was studiously transferring eggs and hash browns onto plates. She arranged the bacon, then garnished with toast.

Fully dressed, Reggie walked over. "Smells great," he said. "I'm starved." He sat down at the bistro table that served as a dining area.

She put a plate in front of him, then one in front of her chair. "Coffee?"

"Please."

She poured both mugs, then sat down. They ate in silence for a bit. She watched him like a hawk. He busied himself by stuffing his face. He paused, seasoned his hash browns with salt and pepper, then dug in again with the enthusiasm of a puppy with a pork chop.

"Something I've been thinking about," he said between mouthfuls.

"What's that?"

"We believe the killer has a medical background, right?"

"Right."

"We need to check out the local medical laboratories, Blood Banks, places like that."

She looked at him quizzically.

"The engineering skills needed to design and construct an apparatus to drain the blood is more closely aligned at that end of the medical profession than it is with doctors and nurses."

"But wouldn't doctors and nurses know this stuff?"

"Only tangentially," he replied. "Ask yourself this: Who would come into daily contact with medical equipment, devices, or machines that extract blood through some kind of suction device or pump?"

She thought about it, then nodded.

They finished breakfast, locked up, and walked to the precinct. The Lieutenant was not in yet. Valerie texted him, explaining what they were doing. They left out the rear entrance.

Reggie had the keys to an unmarked car. Valerie walked beside him, concentrating on her phone. She held it in both hands, her thumbs moved incessantly.

"There's a bunch of them," she said as she opened her door and slipped inside the car.

"Pick the closest one," Reggie said as he buckled himself in.

She searched a few seconds more. "Eight blocks away."

They parked outside the Center City Blood Bank less than ten minutes later. Housed on the first floor of a red and brown brick building dating back to the early 1900s, it didn't look like much from the outside. Just a door and painted sign announcing its name. A single window faced the outside, a black placard with orange lettering rested on the sill announcing, "CLOSED". Venetian blinds extended from the top of the window to the bottom, shut tightly.

They got out, walked towards the door. Both Reggie and Valerie noticed a buzzer on the wall beside the door. They also noticed a CCTV camera mounted and angled downward to capture whoever stood near the entrance.

They stepped onto the thick concrete pad. Valerie hit the button. A mechanical *BUZZ!* came from inside. For a moment, nothing happened. Then a loud *SQUAWK!* blared from a speaker just below the camera.

A disembodied voice asked, "Can I help you?" The voice sounded small and distant.

They both presented their badges to the camera.

"Police," Reggie announced. "Open up."

Another *BUZZ* and a *CLICK*. Valerie grabbed the hooked door handle, pressed down. The door opened and they walked inside. The door closed behind them on its own.

Reggie grinned, motioned to his badge. "The ultimate backstage pass." He put his badge away.

A rather rotund African American woman, probably around fifty-five or sixty, appeared out of an office doorway and moved towards them. She wore burgundy scrubs and an unbuttoned white lab smock that fell to mid-thigh. She stopped in front of them.

"Can I help you?" The name embroidered on her lab smock announced her as Monique Rivers, MT, BBS.

"I'm Detective Downing, this is Detective Wahl. We're investigating a murder case. Could we speak in private, please?"

"Of course," she nodded. "Follow me."

They followed her to the same office from which she had appeared. Inside, Monique bade them to sit. Reggie and Valerie each took a chair while Monique settled behind her desk. She folded her hands on the desktop, leaned forward, her face all business.

"How can I help you?"

"We're working the so-called Vampire Killer case," Reggie informed her.

Monique's eyes widened. "A slow, low, "Ohhhhhhh," came out of her.

"You're the Night Manager?"

"Yes."

"When does the shift change?"

"In just a few minutes."

"Because of the nature of the murders," Reggie said, "we believe the killer has a medical background." He paused for effect and then added, "Specifically, a medical technology background."

"Why do you think that?"

Reggie swore Monique to secrecy, to which she agreed. He then described the two-pronged device, which they felt was part of a lightweight, portable system. He described what they believed might be an IV system powered by a small pump that siphoned blood out of the victims and into a bag, since so little blood was found at the murder scenes.

Monique thought about it for a moment. "Makes sense," she said finally. "I can see why you'd think it's one of us."

"The person we're looking for would be someone quiet. A loner."

"In this line of work, that doesn't narrow the field much," Monique returned.

"A misfit," Reggie added. "Someone who gives off a vibe."

"A vibe?"

"Strange. Weird. Someone who doesn't engage with others, except on the most superficial level."

Monique propped her elbow on the desk, covered her mouth with her hand. She was thinking. The gears were turning.

"This is someone that others wouldn't want to be around," Valerie pressed. "He would give them the willies."

"Anyone like that here?" Reggie knew Monique had something to say.

"I'm not sure I can say," she said, suddenly reluctant. "Maybe I should consult HR." A pause. "I mean, do you have a warrant or a court order?"

"No ma'am," Reggie answered. "We're just having a conversation."

"We can get one," Valerie said, sounding helpful.

"Perhaps we should –" Monique began.

"Of course," Valerie interrupted, "That will take hours, and we'll have to hold everyone here until we can get it and then serve you."

"Yep," Reggie confirmed. "No one from the night shift can go home; the day shift will also be held so we can interview them all."

"And of course, no work can be done in the interim," Valerie pointed out. "If the killer does work here, we don't want him destroying evidence."

Monique put her hands up, palms towards them. They had her in a corner and she knew it.

"Now," Reggie said, "is there anyone that fits the description we gave?"

Monique sighed, feeling defeated. "There's one guy. Works nights. Hasn't been in the past couple of nights."

"What his name?" Reggie demanded.

"I'm still not comfortable with this—"

"What's his Goddamned name?"

"Charles Simpkins."

After a few follow-up questions and swearing Monique to secrecy, Reggie and Valerie left, headed back to the precinct where they briefed the lieutenant. Castle listened without speaking. He despised being interrupted himself, so he tried to show the same respect.

"So, what do you think?" he asked eventually.

"Too soon to tell," Reggie replied. "We need to run background, talk to neighbors."

"And you?" Nick asked Valerie.

"Reggie's right," she responded.

"I know what Reggie thinks. I'm asking what *you* think, Detective."

She hesitated a moment, then, "Something about this feels right, Lieutenant."

"Okay," Nick said, satisfied. "Go prove it."

The two detectives nodded, walked out of the Lieutenant's office.

"So, what do you think?" Valerie asked as they got to their desks.

"I think he's innocent until proven guilty," Reggie answered. "Let's see which it is."

They sat down at their desks and got to work.

Across town, Charlie Simpkins stalked back and forth through his shitty apartment in a shitty building located in a shitty city. Feeling like his skin was crawling with insects, a headache pierced his skull like a metal spike. Pulsating painfully through his temples. Beating his fists against the sides of his head no longer helped. Diverting one pain with another sometimes worked.

Not tonight.

He had gone too long between kills. The police were on him. Not him personally, but they knew a serial killer was stalking the Vampire Goth scene. Maybe he should start hunting homeless people. That would confound them. It's not like anyone gave a shit about the homeless. And the homeless followed one communal rule – don't talk to cops.

Charlie could work here for years if he did that.

But the homeless didn't interest him as conquests anymore. He had killed a few in the past in other cities, and he never found even a hint of the truth he sought from their dying eyes. But these Goths, well, he knew he was getting close.

A particularly insightful news report had aired a few nights back. The cops refused to provide any additional information; the reporter had confirmed a few details through "unnamed sources".

This had proven beneficial to Charlie because the reporter tipped the police's hand. How thoughtful of her to provide him with critical intel in her desire to "warn the public" and her relentless reporter's drive for scoops, ratings, online clicks, and a bigger paycheck.

He glanced over at his ratty sofa. His briefcase lay open, exposing the twin needle device attached to the IV tubing which ran through the pump and emptied into the large clear plastic bag. He staggered over, managed to stop in front of it without falling. His eyes traced over it. Satisfied, he closed the lid, shut the latch.

He felt his way to the dark bathroom, his head heavy like concrete. The slightest sound spiked the pain. He opened the medicine cabinet, grabbed the pill bottle. One of the few things his idiot doctor had done right was to properly diagnose his migraines and prescribe medication that actually helped.

"Take two of these and lie down in a dark, quiet room," the doctor had instructed. "This will drop your blood pressure and make you drowsy."

"I'm usually tired when I'm like that anyway," Charlie had responded.

"Yeah, but this will knock your ass out so you can sleep it off."

Charlie popped the lid, shook the orange bottle. Two pills dribbled into his palm. He shoved the pills inside his mouth, took a swallow from the faucet to wash them down.

Better living through modern chemistry.

He lurched sideways, bounced off the door jamb, rambled into the main room. He flung himself onto his futon. He closed his eyes, rested one forearm across his forehead.

Vaguely, he knew there was trouble at work. He had called out sick two nights in a row, and he was about to call out again. He would get some bullshit written counseling that Monique would be only too happy to "place in his permanent record".

He didn't care. The job was a paycheck, nothing more. He had about nine month's expenses in the bank. If they fired him, fuck it. He would go on unemployment until he either found another job or moved on to new city and fresh hunting grounds. He could scrape by close to two years without a job.

Always keep your options open.

Reggie and Valerie ate lunch at their desks and worked steadily. Nick left in the early afternoon. He did not tell anyone where he was going. Reggie and Valerie hardly noticed.

They were bloodhounds, and they had picked up the scent.

Outside, Nick walked past his motorcycle. Ordinarily, he would use it for a personal errand. He always had before. But being in charge gave him more discretion in his decision-making process. And since he was going to see a murder victim's father, he could justify it to himself.

He got into the unmarked car at the end of the row. He buckled up, started the engine. The gate opened as he crawled towards it. He turned onto the street. As he drove, his phone buzzed. A new text message from the precinct. He sat at a traffic light, glanced at his phone.

Reggie and Valerie had identified a person of interest. College educated, worked at the Blood Bank. They were leaving to go knock on his door.

Nick texted his congratulations, admonished them to be careful. He knew he didn't need to tell them, but they would appreciate hearing it.

The light changed to green. He took the 163 North, driving underneath the Laurel Street bridge that connected Banker's Hill to Balboa Park. Then it was Interstate 8 West, to 5 North.

He blasted past Mission Bay, past La Jolla. He took the exit at Villa de la Valle, headed towards the Del Mar. Before he knew it, he sat outside the home of Alejandro Domingo.

He opened the door, got out. As he closed the distance to the house, the front door opened. Pepe appeared, waited patiently.

"Pepe," he said as he reached the bottom of the stairs.

"*Senor Castillo,*" Pepe replied.

This got a sidelong glance from Nick as he entered. Pepe did not speak unless spoken to. And he did not speak without choosing his words carefully. Calling Nick by his Spanish name, which Nick had previously told him not to do, carried significance.

"This way, *senor.*"

They walked into the great room, panoramic views to the left, kitchen and dining area straight ahead. Alejandro sat at the dining table, open laptop facing him. A steaming mug sat beside him.

He looked up, stood.

"Nicolas," he greeted, using Spanish pronunciation. He opened his arms affectionately, embraced the stunned Nick, gave him a huge bear hug like that of old friends or family members who have not seen each other in ages.

"Como estas, hermano?" Alejandro asked. How are you, brother?

"Bien, bien. Y tu?" Nick responded. Good, good. And you?

"Asi, asi," Alejandro said, the smile fading. So so. Then he looked to Pepe. "Pepe, can you get Nicolas something?"

"Estoy bien, gracias," Nick said. I'm fine, thanks.

Pepe bowed, moved away. Nick and Alejandro sat down across from each other at the table. Alejandro moved his mug, closed the laptop, and pushed it aside.

"Am I interrupting?" Nick asked.

"It can wait," Alejandro replied, waving his hand with the flick of a wrist. They stared at each other a beat. "Anything new on the case?"

"Yes," Nick said.

Alejandro's face brightened. "You're close to an arrest?"

"Closer than yesterday," Nick parried. "That's about all I can say."

"Let me know when he goes to trial," Alejandro said. "I want to be there. Every day. I want that *bastardo* to see my face, the face of Ramsey Domingo's father, every day."

"I will make sure." He paused. Okay. Pleasantries were over. Small talk finished. Brief update of the case. Now to the Main Event.

"So… what else is going on?" Nick asked.

"I've had an epiphany, Nico," he said, looking at him with tortured eyes. "I've treated you terribly."

"You were beside yourself," Nick said. "You were devastated by Ramsey's murder, and you lashed out. I see it all the time. I don't take it personally."

"That's not it," Alejandro said.

"Then what?"

"Me, my father, my whole family treated you and your mother terribly," he said. "I want to do something about that."

"What's there to do?" Nick responded, genuinely perplexed. "It's ancient history. I've never asked for anything."

Alejandro looked despondent. "You never should have had to."

"What are you saying?"

"You are my brother, Nico," Alejandro announced, as if reading his mind. "*Mi hermano. Mi familia,*" he continued. "It's high time you were treated as such."

"Meaning?"

"It's time to correct the sins of the past. My sins. My father's."

"That sounds great," Nick said, meaning it. "But my question remains. After all this time, what's there left to do?"

"*Una familia, Nicolas.* One family. United, and all that that implies."

"That's the thing. I have no idea what that might imply."

Alejandro smiled. "Then let us discuss it, *mi hermano,*" he said. "Would you like some coffee now?"

Journal entry, March 12

My beloved Lot-Lot is no more. I am left with a hole in my soul that may never heal. She brought nothing but love and generosity into a world that was not always loving or generous to her. And yet she never devolved into bitterness or cynicism. She was a far better person than me.

I have been going through Lottie's things the last few nights. I stumbled across her finances on her computer. She supported several charities. One for homeless veterans. Another for a children's cancer hospital. I did not know she did this. I am looking into creating a self-sustaining endowment in her name to continue funding these causes indefinitely.

She would have liked that.

I have taken a leave of absence from my job. My protégées must fend for themselves. The job has become more tedious, less entertaining. Perhaps it was time for a break.

Reginald and I arranged the services. The funeral director was ruffled when we insisted on starting after sundown. She protested about paying staff time and a half, etc. She whined so much; I considered giving her something special to whine about. Instead, I offered her three times the usual quote. The service is tomorrow night.

The night after, we have the reading of the will scheduled with an attorney, who likewise agreed to the reading at night for twice his normal fee.

Money is a powerful tool. Just like a hammer or a screwdriver. Applied properly at the appropriate time in the appropriate place with just the right pressure, one can accomplish almost anything.

Lottie and I had talked about her final wishes. After all, she knew that chances were, I would survive her. I believe the others will be quite surprised. But I will not divulge anything prematurely. That is for them to learn at the appropriate time.

As for me, I have lost another descendant, and there is something fundamentally unnatural in that. I have lost another piece of my puzzle, another connection to the human world. No wonder I find myself largely apathetic towards the affairs of Man.

I miss my Lot-Lot.

I believe I always shall.

CHAPTER TWENTY-ONE

They had an address now.

Reggie and Valerie shrugged their coats on as they strode through the precinct. They pushed through the back door into the rear parking lot. Sunshine stabbed them in the eyes. Concentrating on the ground ahead of him, Reggie trudged on. Valerie shoved sunglasses on, followed.

They got in, buckled up. Valerie entered the address into her phone's map app. It provided directions and the anticipated drive time.

"North Park," Valerie announced.

They took Broadway east. The engine revved as they sped up the steep incline into Golden Hill. The road leveled out near 25th street. They drove past an apartment complex built over an arroyo where an apartment manager had been murdered a while back.

Valerie shoved her phone into her pocket. She hung on as Reggie maneuvered into North Park. They stopped in front of a small apartment complex.

The façade facing the street was white stucco with seafoam green trim and matching street numbers. Wrought iron security gates, the black contrasting sharply with the paler shades surrounding them, guarded entry on each side.

They walked to one of the gates. A keypad waited nearby on the wall along with a cheap two-way intercom. One needed a code to enter. Reggie pushed the red intercom button.

"Can I help you?" came a tinny, distant voice.

"Police Department," Reggie responded. "Open up."

"Just a sec." The line went dead.

"How did you know it would ring in the manager's office?"

"Didn't." Reggie had his head completely in the game right now.

Valerie looked through the bars and saw a short, squat woman emerge from one of the first-floor apartments dressed in a housecoat and slippers. She waddled towards the gate, a huge set of jangling keys gripping by the ring in one hand.

"What's this about?" She inspected their badges.

"Murder investigation, ma'am. Open up."

Her dull eyes widened. Her mouth, which appeared to be permanently drooping at the corners, opened. She opened the gate.

"Charles Simpkins."

Who?" The manager looked confused.

"Apartment 219," Reggie said.

The old woman nodded. "Left side. Second floor. All the way to the back." She paused. "Follow me."

She tottered off. Reggie and Valerie followed behind and to the side, flanking her.

The two-story complex had been built in the 1960s. Forty units total; twenty identical apartments on each side, ten on each floor. The apartment sides were separated by a central court complete with desert plants and succulents, a couple of rusted barbeque grills embedded in concrete and some cheap resin furniture for dining.

The manager shook her head, thinking. "Simpkins.... Simpkins."

"There a problem?" Valerie asked.

"I'm usually good at knowing who lives here," the manager responded over her shoulder. "I don't recall the name. Can't put a face with it."

"How long you been the manager?" Reggie inquired.

"Twenty-seven years."

Reggie and Valerie exchanged glances. This was not a good sign.

They walked across the central court, headed for the back stairs. The group slowed as the manager huffed her way up the steps. By the time they reached the top, she was red-faced and wheezing. Sweat matted the hair ringing her forehead.

"You okay, ma'am?" Regie considered calling an ambulance. She pulled an inhaler out, gave herself two blasts.

"Asthma," she croaked.

"Wait here," Reggie said diplomatically. He noticed she was still holding onto the railing with one hand.

"Suits me."

Valerie and Reggie pulled their handguns. They took up positions on either side of the doorway. Reggie reached out, pounded his fist loudly on the door.

"Charles Simpkins! Open up. Police."

They waited. Nothing happened. No movement inside, no sound. Reggie pounded again, repeated his announcement. Again, nothing happened. No sound. No movement.

A door down the way opened. A young Latina cautiously poked her head out.

"What's going on?"

"Everything's fine, ma'am," Reggie said over his shoulder. "Go back inside."

She hesitated. The manager motioned for her to go inside. The young Latina finally disappeared into her apartment. A deadbolt slid into place.

Reggie looked at the manager. "Keys, please."

Still winded and diaphoretic, she tossed them over. The heavy ring fell to the concrete walkway, then slid. Reggie scooped them up. Each key had tape near the top with room numbers written with a Sharpie. He found 219.

Valerie waited impatiently while Reggie inserted the key and turned. He then took the key out, tossed the ring back to the manager.

"Now?" Valerie whispered urgently.

"Patience," Reggie admonished. Shielding himself in his position he turned the knob with one hand, pushed the door in, then yanked his hand back.

One quarter of a second later, the trip wire tied at the top of the door pulled the pin on an improvised bomb made of gunpowder and roofing nails that sat positioned on a cheap card table about five feet inside.

The shockwave and the boom came at the same time. Both Reggie and Valerie ducked for cover as wood splinters from the door and glass shards from the windows blew past them, across the walkway, filtering down to the ground floor.

Reggie felt like he had been hit in the head with a baseball bat. Dizzy and disoriented, he spilled over from his crouch, sprawled on his side across the walkway. Sounds were muffled, echoed. A terrible ringing in his ears. He did not know that he had glass embedded in his head behind his ear, or that one eardrum had been ruptured.

He saw glass glittering on the walkway in front of him. Smoke billowed out of the doorway. Valerie lay strewn across the walkway, her back to him. Her handgun lay several inches from her head.

She wasn't moving.

The manager, in shock, stood there, eyes as big as saucers.

"Dial 911," Reggie shouted. He couldn't hear himself, so he yelled louder. *"DIAL 911!"* He heard it that time, but just barely.

Valerie still wasn't moving.

Oh my God. I've gotten her fucking killed.

Somehow, Reggie managed to pull the handheld radio off his belt. He keyed the mic.

"Code 10, code 10," he repeated. "Officers down. Officers down!"

As he repeated it again, his vision dimmed. His periphery shut down. It was like he was looking down the cardboard core of a paper towel roll.

His radio dropped from numb fingers. The last thing he saw was his own hand, reaching out towards his motionless partner.

Then a swirling blackness overtook him, crashed over him, carried him away. And then Detective Reginald Downing felt nothing at all.

Charles Simpkins, Serial Killer Extraordinaire, was feeling rather good about things. In addition to being one smart and slippery eel, he was also miles ahead of those dim-witted cops. The lead story on the news was about two flatfeet who had gotten themselves blown up by a "possible IED" at an apartment complex in North Park. No word on the source of the blast, but FBI and ATF had been called in. Transported to an area hospital, the names of the officers and their conditions were being withheld.

North Park.

He rented an apartment there under his real name. He had only been there once, just long enough to rig the doorway. He paid the rent via autopay. This decoy apartment was one of three in different areas of the city. Naturally, they were rigged to blow, too. And one had an extra treat; a couple of incendiary devices that would ensure a hot time in the old town tonight if someone tried to breach the door.

This definitely raised the stakes. Chances were, though, the Feds would only work the claymore. Run forensics on shrapnel and residue, try to trace it back to its point of origin.

Good luck with that.

No one knew Charlie was the "Vampire Killer". No one was likely to find out. They were playing checkers; he was playing three-dimensional chess. These Keystone Kops weren't even in his league.

Caution tugged at the back of his brain. They had his name now. The cops were idiots, but even idiots get lucky.

He pondered again a change in locale. Someplace different. More tropical. Warmer water. More relaxed. Someplace where law enforcement was more of an entrepreneurial pursuit; where a few dollars here and there could grease just the right palms to get people to look the other way.

A couple of countries in the Southern Hemisphere sprang to mind.

Nick was already at the Emergency Room when Reggie and Valerie were wheeled inside. He had called Morris Horn, who stood by his side after having broken a dozen traffic laws and at least one land speed record to get there. Nick had left a message on the Vampire's cell phone. It would be dark soon, and he wanted the Vampire to know right away.

He and Morris waited in the hallway just inside the automatic doors when the ambulance pulled up outside, red lights flashing. They stepped aside as Reggie was rolled in on a gurney, followed by Valerie. Both were still unconscious, covered in soot and cuts. Nick flashed his badge as he and Morris followed the gurneys, a somber procession down the hallway.

The main ER ward was designed for efficient patient flow. Bed areas on either side of the room with pull curtains for the illusion of privacy lined both sides with a wide central walkway in the middle. Each area boasted a cardiac monitor, oxygen spigots built into the wall, a heart monitor with leads, and multiple drawers containing a plethora of medical supplies. There were twelve beds set up identically running down each side.

The staff had been alerted that an ambulance was enroute with two blast trauma victims, both police officers. A doctor, a resident, and two nurses had been assigned for each patient and were waiting as their gurneys rolled in.

They wasted no time getting to work.

The Vampire barged in an hour later. Those who saw him cringed. People recoiled as he stalked past them. His mouth was a thin line, his lips invisible. Even with sunglasses on, people knew this creature was on a mission, and that mission would include death. None of them wanted any part of that.

He prowled past the nurse's station. A young nurse who was less than a year out of school and all of about 22, saw him and rose from her chair.

"Excuse me, sir!" she called after him.

The Vampire heard her, realized she was addressing him. But he had more important things on his mind, so he ignored her. He meant no disrespect; he simply did not have the time to deal with her.

The young nurse, irritated by what she saw as an arrogant snub, rose from her chair and strode forcefully after him.

"Sir? Sir!"

The Vampire slapped his pallid hand against the silver button on the wall near the doors separating the ER from the waiting area. Fingers long and thin; nails extended and sharp. He was in no mood to get into an argument with someone trying to do their job.

As the doors swung open, the nurse placed her petite body directly in his path. Lavender scrubs, a hospital ID that announced her as Michelle. Dark radiant skin, traditional African American hairstyle. Red nails that resembled dripping blood.

She reminded him of Danae. He paused, took a deep breath as she spoke.

"Sir, you can't just go back there."

He did not speak. He simply stood there, glaring at her from behind his sunglasses, mouth turned slightly down at the corners.

Michelle waited a few seconds. When he did not respond, she cocked her head.

"Sir, I said you can't go back there."

The Vampire stood there, said nothing. Sometimes, silence spoke volumes. It threw people off their game.

By the look on her face, it was working.

"Sir, I –"

"Nurse." Nick had walked up, and now showed his badge. "He's with me."

Now completely confused, Michelle looked back and forth between Nick and the Vampire and back to Nick. Finally, she threw up her hands.

"Why didn't you show me your badge?"

"He's a civilian consultant," Nick answered for him.

"Next time don't ignore me. Understand?" She pointed an index finger towards the Vampire's face. It was everything he could do to keep from biting her finger clean off. The thought of her finger reduced to a bloody spurting stump calmed him.

Without waiting for a response, she stormed off, heading back towards the nursing station. The Vampire simply continued walking forward.

The sounds and smells of the ER overwhelmed his heightened senses. A gunshot patient in Bed 2. The Vampire could hear his decelerating heartbeat. He had about two minutes left. The elderly woman in Bed 6 was suffering a heart attack, what doctors and other medical types referred to as a "cardiac event".

She also suffered from diabetes, and her body was riddled with cancer. He could smell the sickness and death on her, enshrouding her with black inevitability. He heard the heart monitor beside her bed flatline, a steady, infuriating monotone.

"Code Blue, Code Blue. Emergency Room," crooned an impossibly soothing voice over a hidden intercom system. "Code Blue, Code Blue. Emergency Room," it repeated so calmly one might mistakenly think the voice was announcing the drying of paint and not a human tragedy. But it would be all for naught. The old woman's heart had simply beat its last beat.

Sooner or later, it happened to everyone. No matter how valiant or heroic the efforts to resuscitate someone and give them even just a short time more upon this earth: a few more years, a few more weeks. A few more minutes.

A few more seconds.

No matter how much time life gives us in this world, we fight for every second of it.

Nick led the Vampire to the gurney where a young female doctor, who appeared to be of Middle Eastern descent, performed a neurological exam on Reggie. The doctor worked diligently, quickly.

"How is he, Doc?" Nick asked her when the doctor had finished.

"Neurologically intact," she replied. "He's got a concussion from the blast, but I think the walls and the added wood framing around the doorway took the majority of the hit."

Nick looked at Reggie. "You were extremely lucky. An improvised claymore, that close? It should have killed you both."

"How is she?" Reggie croaked.

Nick looked at the doctor, who shrugged.

"I'll check," Nick said. He disappeared through a gap in the curtain.

The doctor glanced at the strange-looking thin man who stood there and said nothing. She left, wanting to get away from the intimidating vibe.

The Vampire stepped forward, took Reggie's hand. Reggie opened his eyes.

"Hey, Grandpa."

"Reginald."

"Got myself blown up."

"Yes," the Vampire said. "What does that tell you?"

"We're close."

"I concur." He paused a moment. "How do you feel?"

"Like I got blown up," Reggie replied, trying to smile. Then his eyes started to tear up. "I almost got my partner killed…"

"No, no you did not," the Vampire countered firmly. "Whoever built that bomb did that. From what I have gathered, your experience and adherence to procedure saved you both."

Reggie squeezed his eyes shut.

"Fret not, my dear sweet boy," the Vampire said. "I have now decided this Vampire Killer should suffer a horrific fate."

On the opposite side of the ward, Valerie lay on her own gurney, dazed but awake. An intense buzzing reverberated in her ears. The room spun. She didn't like that. Dizzy, she vomited into a bucket just as the Lieutenant poked his head inside the curtain.

Morris already in the area to keep her company, stepped back. When she finished, he helped push her back into bed and grabbed a box of tissues. She grabbed a few and wiped her mouth.

"How is she?" Nick asked.

"Concussion," Morris said. "She got her bell rung, you know?"

"She can hear you," Valerie muttered tiredly.

"Sorry," Morris said.

"How's Reggie?"

"He's okay," Nick answered. "But you both need rest, and then it's desk duty until the doctors clear you."

"But Lieutenant –"

"Don't 'but' me, young lady," Nick interrupted her. "This is nonnegotiable. Do I make myself clear?"

"Yes sir."

"Did you know, you're the first person I've ever known who can make 'yes sir' sound like 'fuck you'?"

"It's a gift, sir."

"Did you give your parents this kind of shit?"

"Goddamned right."

Nick stifled a laugh but could not keep from grinning. He rolled his eyes, then looked at Morris.

"See what I have to put up with?"

Morris and Nick walked outside the Emergency Room entrance. Nick was seething. Someone had tried to kill two of his cops. No news crews had shown up yet, but they both knew it was a matter of time.

The Lieutenant's police phone buzzed. He pulled it out of his pocket as he stepped away, leaving Morris standing there by himself for a moment.

Morris breathed in the cooling night air. A breeze had kicked up, coming in off the ocean. A chill hung over the area that would become more pronounced as the night deepened. He heard the pneumatic swish of the doors behind him. He turned, ready to step aside if a medical team was emerging. He saw the Vampire striding towards him.

"How's our boy?" Morris asked.

"They wish to keep him overnight."

Standard of care for closed head injuries," Morris said.

He saw the Vampire nod. But even with glassy and unblinking eyes hidden behind those ridiculous wraparound sunglasses, Morris saw something truly dark, violent, dreadful working on the undead corpse's face. Like snakes coiling beneath paper-thin, waxy skin.

He had seen that look before.

Morris shuddered. He remembered, all too well, what happened to people who hurt the Vampire's family. It wasn't every day you saw a vampire rip a man's chest open, splay a rib cage apart, rip a beating heart out and brandish it like a carnival prize. And then the Vampire had eaten it, right in front of Rick Oakley's fading eyes before the doomed drug dealer even had a chance to die.

"This guy better hope we find him before you do."

"Do you think that would save him from me after this?"

"You're pissed."

"Am I that transparent?"

Nick was walking towards them now. He slipped his phone into his pocket.

"I just updated the Chief and the Mayor. They're worried I've lost control of the investigation."

"Tell them to come out their ivory towers and do better," the Vampire grumbled.

"They're just covering their asses," Morris said.

"Exactly," the Vampire snapped. "The only time politicians do their jobs – serving their constituents – is when it is in their own best interests to do so."

"The Chief is a cop."

"Not anymore," the Vampire countered firmly. "He started out a cop, perhaps entertained fantasies of cleaning up the streets and helping people. But somewhere along the way, he prioritized his own upward mobility."

"So, what are you saying?" Nick asked.

"Few people achieve senior leadership within an organization like a major metropolitan police department without being a political animal," the Vampire explained. "They assure themselves that is not the case with them, that they can do better from a lofty and well-paid post. But they are lying to themselves."

"That's pretty unforgiving," Morris observed.

"We live in an unforgiving world," the Vampire returned darkly.

"You could choose to be forgiving, even if the world is not."

"Not when my family is at stake," the undead monster in front of them said. "Reginald is all I have left. If he dies, my bloodline dies with him." He paused to let that sink in. "Would either one of you preach forgiveness if the roles were reversed?"

Morris and Nick gazed at each other, looked down. Both shifted their weight from one foot to another.

Touché.

"There is another factor at play," the Vampire stated.

Both mortal men looked at him expectantly.

"Not to belabor the obvious, but I am *Vampyr*." He purposefully used the old-world pronunciation. "Forgiveness is not my nature."

"Well, I've said it before and I'll say it again," Morris piped up. "Remind me to never get on your bad side."

The Vampire's expression softened a bit. He attempted a smile but failed. The best he could accomplish was a lateral extension of his mouth. Thin lips stretched, became thinner.

"And now, gentlemen, I must bid you *adieu*," the Vampire said. He took a step away from them. "I have another matter to address."

"The killer or the other vampire?"

"I must delay Lottie's memorial until Reginald can attend."

"And if you get a whiff of these other two?"

His mouth spread slowly into a grin devoid of humor. The tips of his fangs peeked below his upper lip. The overall appearance was of a hungry predator who was all business.

"I am a hunter," he said. He opened his hands by his sides, palms towards them. "Hunters... hunt." He shrugged as if this simple truth should be self-evident. "This is my nature, gentlemen. It is what I do."

The Vampire turned away from his friends – and yes, they were his friends, he realized – and walked away from the sterile lights of the Emergency Room and into the gathering darkness.

Morris watched the Vampire become lost in the shadows.

"You afraid of him?" Nick asked.

"Goddamned right I'm afraid of him," Morris confessed. "You should be, too."

"Why?"

"Push comes to shove, we're food to him." He pursed his lips. "We're lucky he likes us."

"What about this other vampire?" Nick asked. "And what about all the other vampires out there in the world that we don't know about?"

"That scares me more than him."

A moment of thought, then Nick said, "I've been wondering about something."

"What's that?"

"If vampires are real, living and hunting among us, what else is out there? What other monsters lurk in the dark, slinking around feasting on humans?"

"I don't even want to think about that," Morris admitted. An unaccustomed chill ran up the big man's spine. "I might not get a good night's sleep ever again."

CHAPTER TWENTY-TWO

The Vampire maneuvered his Lexus through thinning traffic. He wanted to hunt his enemies, but practical matters superseded. He was low in blood, and he needed to talk to the funeral director. Then, if time allowed, he could swing by Splinter and kill Maya.

A cold rage surged through him. How close Reginald had come to being killed by this evil human! He hoped he found this degenerate before the police. Then it would simply be the two of them.

The Vampire grinned at the thought.

He turned into the parking lot for the funeral home. Black asphalt and painted white lines. A few vehicles remained. He parked well away from the others, got out. He scanned the area then trekked across the lot.

The place reminded him of some contemporary churches. A low, one-story wing stretched out on each side from a higher-roofed central area. White paint with large columns jutting upwards on each side of the front steps that deposited the bereaved at the front doors.

The Vampire grabbed the black metal lever on the door, pushed downward. He stepped inside. The pneumatic swing arm ensured the door closed quietly behind him.

"We're closing soon."

He turned his head, saw Elena Swalwell, the funeral director standing near a hallway that led to one of the wings. He had been so preoccupied that he had not heard her footfalls on the carpeted floor. He reminded himself to stay focused. If he could not hear a human walking, how could he expect to defeat another vampire?

"Ms. Swalwell."

Elena Swalwell stood about five foot seven, just a smidge taller than the Vampire. She walked towards a spot in front of the doors. As they strode towards each other, he noticed the black jacket to her very conservative pantsuit flaring in the breeze created by her movement.

"How can I help you?" She extended her hand.

He shook it. She pulled her hand back quickly.

"Your hand is freezing."

She smoothed her suddenly sweaty palms down the front of her neck-high white blouse. She suddenly felt nervous being alone with him.

"I need Lottie Tidwell's memorial service pushed back a day or two," he said.

"Excuse me?"

"Her grandson is a San Diego police officer," he explained. "He was seriously injured in the line of duty today."

"I'm sorry to hear that," she said, shaking her head. "Frankly, I'm booked solid. I can't juggle anything around."

"Are you not the Funeral Director? Do you not direct the schedule of services?"

"Well, sure, but—"

"Then you can alter the schedule of an evening service so he can attend."

"I'm afraid it's not that simple, sir."

The Vampire had anticipated this. He pulled a plain white envelope out of his leather jacket's inner pocket. It appeared to be stuffed full of something.

"What's that?"

"Ten thousand dollars. Cash," he replied. "All one-hundred-dollar bills. Nontaxable, untraceable."

"A bribe?"

"A premium for the inconvenience."

"It's not about money."

"Sooner or later," he growled, "everything is about money." He was beginning to lose his patience.

"I can't take that."

"Very well then," the Vampire said, deciding to alter tactics. "Please give me the urn containing Lottie's ashes, and I shall make other arrangements."

"I can't do that," she said, getting testy. "That is not our policy."

Here was the crux of the situation, the Vampire realized. Ms. Swalwell had made the mistake of thinking she was negotiating from a position of strength. She did not realize just how wrong she was.

Fighting back the impulse to kill her right here in her own funeral home, the Vampire cleared his throat. "Ms. Swalwell. Allow me to speak frankly. You either reschedule the service or return Miss Lottie's urn and refund my money."

Ms. Swalwell exploded. "Who the bloody hell do you think you are--!"

The Vampire's left hand shot out from his side. Bony fingers with long, sharp nails clasped around her throat and neck. The vicelike grip crimped off her esophagus. He lifted her off the floor. Eyes wide and bloodshot, her face went red and edged towards purple.

He whipped off his sunglasses, bared his fangs. She took one look and pissed her pants.

He shoved the envelop into Ms. Swalwell's inside jacket pocket. He lowered her back to the floor, let go. She dropped to her knees coughing, pulling in great gulps of air.

"I tried to be civilized," he said. She stared up at him mutely, mascara running down her face in black rivulets. He squatted down so his face was close to hers. He replaced his sunglasses.

"I care not how this may inconvenience you. Make. This. Happen."

She gawked at him in terror.

"If we have this conversation again, I will not be so... *civilized.*"

Elena Swalwell nodded. She understood his implication.

The Vampire stood. "My best wishes to your husband and your two children, Ms. Swalwell." he said darkly. The look on her face said that she understood that, too.

Outside, he slid into his car, started the engine. He glanced at his watch. Close to midnight now. Still too early for the Blood Bank. That usually happened in the wee hours of the morning.

He pulled out of the parking lot. No time for at LeStat's, either. It seemed like forever since he had hung out sipping tea and reading the newspapers and magazines always strewn about the place.

Handle your business, he told himself, or your business will handle you.

As he passed El Cajon Boulevard and its bright neon sign on his left, he thought about the choices he had made. If he had lived as a law-abiding citizen, he probably would have lived to a ripe old age and would have died surrounded by loving family. But his life choices got him shot three times in a rainswept back alley in Hoboken. Thomas, his jealous rival, had betrayed him.

Don Vincenzo had been devastated by Eddie's death. Two-Faced Thomas had tried to comfort the old man, even offered to not rest until he could hunt down whoever had done this terrible thing. He had even gone so far as to theorize that Eddie's death was the work of a rival gang, part of an opening salvo of a gang war. After all, Eddie had been a collector who had made the Don a lot of money. Taking Eddie out made sense – strangle off the Don's money supply, make him vulnerable, then strike.

Don Vincenzo had nodded through his grief and tears. He had told Thomas to do it, leave no stone unturned. He ordered Thomas to bring them to him alive. Don Vincenzo wanted to kill them personally.

Thomas understood the significance of this. Don Vincenzo had not killed anyone himself in over a decade. By killing the offenders himself, it would send a message throughout the New Jersey and New York crime families that Hoboken was Don Vincenzo's. Period. Anyone trying to muscle in would meet with severe consequences.

Of course, Thomas would never admit he was the shooter And of course, he had no idea what had happened to Eddie.

But he did find out.

Less than a week after his Rebirth to Darkness, the newly minted Vampire had begun a campaign of terror and revenge. He started with the flunkies first. One by one, they turned up dead, mutilated, torn apart, ripped asunder. He had taken his time, made certain they lived for hours and within those hours, suffered an eternity. Oh, the horror that had emanated off them mixed with pungent sweat when they recognized the immortal creature in front of them was the man, not much more than a boy, they had shot and left for dead. Once they connected the dots, they knew they were truly doomed.

And truly damned.

The Vampire eventually drained them and ripped their heads off. He did not wish for any of them to come back. He wanted them cast into the Dark Abyss for all time. They deserved an eternity in Hell.

The Vampire realized that he deserved no better.

As word of Eddie's murder spread, all of Hoboken became a powder keg waiting to be lit. Even the cops knew it. Civilians were off the streets by sundown. Even the speakeasies closed. Losing money was better than dying in a crossfire.

No other gang claimed responsibility. In fact, they made a point of telling Don Vincenzo they had nothing to do with it. He believed them. If another gang truly saw him as vulnerable, they would have told him.

This was revenge. But revenge for what? This went beyond business. This was personal.

This was hatred.

But hatred by whom? Don Vincenzo was a relatively small-time gangster who stayed in his lane, was not overly greedy, had no designs on other gangs' territory, money, or personnel. Gangland wars over turf, dames, or rackets cost money, lives, the goodwill of the people, and the indifference of the police. War was bad for business. These gruesome murders made no sense.

Of course, the Vampire had anticipated this, and paced himself accordingly. He bore no ill will towards Don Vincenzo. The guy had practically been a second father to young Eddie after his own father had died. And he had taken care of Eddie's bereaved mother financially after Eddie's "death".

That did not stop the Vampire's bloody campaign.

A couple of nights later, he had taken Thomas. He enjoyed terrorizing him, dealing pain and hopelessness after telling him who he was, who he had been. In the end, Thomas proved himself an abject coward. He had cried, wept, screamed, pissed himself. He had shouted, pled, bargained, bribed, and eventually shit himself.

Nothing cracked the Vampire's cold unbeating heart. Thomas's torture scaled new heights of pain, explored new depths of cruelty. And then with the morning sun approaching, the Vampire had announced that since Thomas had not shown mercy when he had been Eddie, the Vampire was simply repaying him in kind.

Thomas's pain was epic.

His death, legendary.

Bitter memories had put the Vampire in a mood. He tried to not dwell on the past. His past was a forest of dead trees bereft of leaves and warmth, a barren wilderness of regrets and horrors.

He encountered fog as he headed downtown. He turned left off Broadway onto 6th, drove south into a paid parking lot. He stopped, killed the engine. He paid the fee and trudged two blocks towards Splinter with his shoulders hunched, head down, fists jammed hard into front jacket pockets.

The Vampire had not felt Maya all evening. She had him running scared, and it angered him. Not just with her, but with himself. Ordinarily, he would be much quicker to act. But everything with his family – Lottie's passing, his great, great grandson getting blown up by a mine, and the whole distraction with this "Vampire Killer" wannabe had been taxing.

Maya had been conducting a psychological campaign – PSYOPS, as military types called it – against him, and she knocked him back on his heels like a punch-drunk pugilist.

No more, he promised himself.

Two can play at that game.

Relief spilled over him. His mind lifted, freed as if a great weight was suddenly gone. The Vampire spoiled for the confrontation. He was once again the ultimate apex predator, the undead creature, the savage animal who made prey of men. The monster that made hard men, mercenaries, and assassins quiver in fear.

He relished the coming carnage.

As he walked through the shadows of the tall buildings, a human stepped out in front of him, blocking the Vampire's path.

"Hey buddy," the young man addressed him. "Spare change?"

The Vampire heard his heartbeat, smelled the alcohol and drugs that permeated his diseased body. He smelled the kid's halitosis. Gingivitis was an ugly thing; of that the Vampire was certain. Then he heard the footfalls and soft breathing of the accomplice who had stepped out of the shadows and had taken up a position directly behind him.

The Vampire smiled. Now this was the kind of distraction he needed: brief and bloody.

"You need a loan, young man?"

The human relaxed a bit, pushed his hoodie back exposing blonde hair that seemed to glow in the gloom like pale butter under a black light.

"Yeah," he grunted. "I need a loan. My friend behind you does, too."

The vampire scanned over his shoulder briefly, assessing the threat risk, calculating how he would defeat them. Then he looked back at the blonde kid.

"I have about a thousand dollars on me," the Vampire taunted. "How much do you need?"

Blondie's eyes widened. "All of it."

"I can give it to you," the Vampire said, "but it comes at a terrible price. The interest rate could prove… exorbitant."

"We ain't payin' no fuckin' interest, asshole," the one behind him growled.

The Vampire shrugged. He moved to walk around Blondie. Blondie pulled out a switchblade, flicked it open. The Vampire sensed Number Two moving in from behind. Then he felt a knife at his back.

"My, my," the Vampire said, unperturbed. "And here I thought you two boys were nice people."

"Shut the fuck up," snarled Number Two.

Blondie grabbed the Vampire by the front of his jacket. "Over here," he instructed. "In the alley."

"My thoughts exactly," the Vampire grinned.

The two hooligans led the unresisting Vampire into something that was not a true alley, but rather a gap, a void between buildings. They blocked his escape route back onto the sidewalk, smug in their superior numbers and weaponry.

"Okay, dipshit," Blondie spat, "hand it over."

"Hand what over?"

"Your money, asshole. Everything you got."

"No."

"Motherfucker, I will fucking stab you."

"If you wanted to kill me, you would have already tried."

Blondie, suddenly unsure, glanced at Number Two. "Man, fuck this. Let's just go."

"Naw," Number two responded. "He gives us the money, or we fuck him up."

"You should listen to your friend," the Vampire suggested.

"Fuck you," Number Two rumbled. "I'm gonna fuck you up anyways."

The Vampire grinned, fangs glowing in the darkness. "I was hoping you would say that."

Blondie had heard enough. His heart was beating loud in the Vampire's head. His sweat smelled of fear.

"Come on, man. Let's go."

"No. I'm gonna teach this prick a lesson."

The Vampire's grin widened.

Number Two lunged forward, the knife arcing. The Vampire grabbed Number Two's arm, wrenched it back. Bones snapped audibly. He then grabbed the hapless human by the face, slammed him into the rough brick exterior of the building. He hoisted Number two up in the air, inverted him upside down, and then pile-drove Number Two headfirst onto the pavement. His skull split open like a ripe watermelon. Blood and brains everywhere.

Blondie stood frozen in shock and disbelief. Eyes the size of dinner plates gazed at what was left of Number Two. This creature they thought would be an easy mark grinned at him.

Blondie turned to run. The Vampire leapt into the air, sailed over Blondie's head, and landed on the pavement facing him. He now blocked the exit.

"Look. I'm sorry, Mister. Please –" He tried to scuttle around the undead thing in front of him. A cold, pale hand shot up from the darkness. Long, bony fingers wrapped around Blondie's throat and squeezed.

"Not so fast, my penny-ante friend." The Vampire's voice was all business now. No levity. No humor. Black and unblinking eyes cold as stones narrowed behind the sunglasses.

"Once you start the game," he instructed Blondie, "it must be played to conclusion."

Maya sat in her living room as the early morning hours progressed. She had already fed, had cleaned up the mess she had made killing Jonathan the previous night.

She understood Jonathan's pursuit of the truth. And she held a begrudging respect for his tenacity. But curiosity killed the cat, and the same could be said for him. He had sought the truth, had found it, and had died with its secrets.

She turned on the television, flipped through the channels. She settled on a local channel showing *DRACULA,* starring Bela Lugosi. Even though the movie was ninety years old, and the vampiric elements of sex and seduction were merely implied, she enjoyed this version of the classic story.

Black and white images flickered through their fictional world at twenty-four frames per second. The dated acting and stilted dialogue did not detract from the beauty of the film or the power of the story. And Bela certainly embodied the Count with a grace and style no other actor had ever surpassed.

And then came her favorite part, where Bela spoke directly into the camera, revealing the Count's true aspirations.

"To die. To be truly dead! That must be glorious!" Bela said.

"I bet it is, Bela," Maya breathed. "I bet it is."

The Vampire strode down 4th towards Splinter. He saw the dull blue glow of Splinter's sign, gauzy and indistinct in the fog. He picked up Kong's heartbeat at the door. Slow, steady. He had not seen the Vampire yet.

The Vampire paused on the northeast corner of 4th and F, looked both ways. The last thing he needed was to be dragged under a car for a city block. Between the serial killer investigation and Maya, there was just too much happening. Life had become too complicated. What might simplify matters?

Killing Maya would be a good start.

With no oncoming traffic seen or heard, he stepped off the curb, powered across the street. Kong saw him, and the big man's heart started hammering in his chest.

The Vampire slowed his approach. "Good evening, Kong."

Kong nodded, wary.

"I need one minute inside," the Vampire stated.

Kong appeared unsure.

"One minute," the Vampire repeated. "Sixty seconds. I am looking for one person. Whether she is here or not here, I will know within one minute."

"All right," Kong acquiesced.

Then the Vampire was inside descending the stairs. Almost closing time, the house lights were already on. Set high up in the ceiling, they looked like the stars in the heavens, twinkling arrows of brightness piercing a black background. The main floor was illuminated. The dance floor was empty. A waitress wiped down tables and scooted chairs underneath. A lone bartender put away glasses.

"Looking for someone?" the bartender asked.

"Yes."

She eyed him up and down. Quality clothes, not Goth garb she normally saw in here. He had come in before. Handsome in a bad-boy kind of way. Killer makeup. How did he get his skin so pale? And how could he see behind those sunglasses? He never took them off. She wondered what color his eyes were.

"Need any help, um… finding what you're looking for?"

"No." He stepped away from the bar and the disappointed bartender, glided towards the center of the room.

The waitress saw him, stood up straight. Dark hair and eyes, olive skin. Hispanic.

"No one's here."

The Vampire stared past her, peering into The Grotto.

Vacant.

He spun on his heel, made his way towards the back. The two women looked at each other. Was he mysterious, or just rude? They each went back to their work.

The bathrooms sat on the righthand side of a hallway that resembled a mine shaft. The hallway led out back to a loading dock. He pushed his way into the women's restroom.

No heartbeats.

No breathing.

No one there.

He turned and left the bathroom. He emerged from the tunnel, headed across the empty dance floor. The Hispanic waitress caught him out of the corner of her eye but kept working. She would be done in another five minutes and all she wanted to do was get home and get a few hours' sleep before her toddler woke up wanting breakfast.

The jilted bartender looked up from her work as he spirited past her and began ascending the stairs. One side of her mouth tugged with regret for what might have been. Then she went back to her closing routine.

She still had her register to count down and cash tips to pocket. Yes, she might be going home alone – again! – but at least she was going home with an extra couple hundred dollars in her purse.

CHAPTER TWENTY-THREE

The Vampire pushed the heavy metal door open and stepped into the early morning fog.

"Find her?" Kong asked.

"No," the Vampire answered as the door closed behind him. "Listen, when she comes back – and she will come back, for she is an exquisite creature of habit – it would be best to simply do whatever she says and stay out of her way."

Kong frowned in confusion.

"She is one such as I," the Vampire explained. He saw the light go on inside Kong's head.

The big man shuddered. He knew what the Vampire meant.

"Get some sleep, my friend," the walking corpse advised. "You look tired."

Kong watched the diminutive creature skip across the empty intersection. When the Vampire disappeared, swallowed up by the swirling fog, he thought once more that, given everything in his life, he really needed a different line of work.

The Vampire treaded east towards his car. Few people out. No cars. No Maya. He considered popping into LeStat's on his way home. But he wanted to stop by the hospital and check in on Reginald and Valerie.

As he passed the void between buildings where he had made his kills earlier, he smelled the sweet blood. It brought a smile to his face.

Intoxicating.

The Lexus's white enamel glowed in the pale moonlight. He pressed the button on his key fob from across the street, slid inside before he even realized he had opened the door. Key into the ignition, seat belt buckled. Engine started, lights on. Pondering the night's events, he maneuvered into the street.

His mind wandered as he drove. Somehow, he found himself pulling into underground parking for the hospital a few minutes later and wondering how he had gotten there.

He emerged from the car, slithered towards the elevator. He pushed the button on the wall. The doors whooshed open. He stepped inside and pushed another button. The doors whooshed shut.

He felt the force of added gravity as the gears above him engaged and the carriage moved within the shaft. He watched the digital readout. Red numbers advanced as he passed corresponding floors.

The doors opened quietly inside the hospital. The Vampire crept out onto the darkened hospital floor. A wall placard indicated the ward he was looking for. An arrow pointed the way.

Ahead of him, a nurse sat at the nursing station. The light from her desk provided the only light for the ward. Asian, black hair, a touch of gray near her temples. She typed in a patient's electronic chart as he approached. Sensing someone's presence, she looked up.

"Can I help you?" she asked in a muted voice.

"I am here to look in on Detective Reginald Downing, please."

She seemed unsure. "Are you family?" she asked automatically.

"Yes."

She looked at him, clearly skeptical.

"I'm sorry, sir. Visiting hours start tomorrow after ten."

The Vampire understood the nurse was just doing her job. He put his hand out, palm facing her, fingers splayed. This drew her attention.

"Sleep," he whispered. He moved his hand gently, waving fingers towards the desk. The nurse's eyes closed. Her head dropped to the desk.

He touched a single finger to her forehead.

"Forget."

He glided past her, slid like a wraith down the silent hallway to his great, great grandson's room. He pushed on the handle. The door opened silently just enough for him to enter undetected.

Reginald was sound asleep. His heart beat slow and steady within his chest. He lay on his back, a nasal canula encircling his face. The cardiac monitor affixed to the wall above his bed showed his vital signs. Pulse, blood pressure, even his oxygen saturation levels all read out as perfectly normal.

The Vampire slipped back into the hallway, crept silently towards Valerie's room. As he passed the Nurse's Station, he glanced at the slumbering nurse. She had not moved.

At the end of the hallway, he let himself into the door on his left. Inside was a setup and monitoring system much like what he had just witnessed in Reginald's room. Valerie lay in bed, sleeping. She too had a nasal cannula and a heart monitor beeping out her pulse. She had a cut above one eye. The wound was not lethal. No impediment to recovery.

He turned to go.

"Who's there?" The voice was weak, soft, almost broken.

The Vampire stepped closer. "I came by to see how you are doing."

She looked at him through veiled eyes. "How's Reggie?"

"Reginald is going to be fine."

She looked around the darkened room. "What time is it?"

The Vampire told her.

"How did you get here?"

"The elevator."

"No, I mean how did you get past the nurse?"

"I exerted my powers of persuasion."

"Oh, God. You didn't hurt her, did you?"

"Of course not."

She relaxed, closed her eyes. "Good."

"I find myself a bit offended you would even think such a thing of me."

"I'm sorry. It's just… Well, you…" She did not complete her thought. She didn't have to. He knew what she was thinking.

"I should leave."

He went to the door. As he placed his hand on the handle, she called out.

"Hey," she said. He looked at her. "I'm sorry."

He knew she was.

"I know you're looking out for us. It's just…"

"Say no more," the Vampire said. "Get some rest. Once you're better, we still have a killer to catch."

And then he was gone.

The Vampire opened his car door and slid into the seat. He closed the door, pulled out his cell phone. He pressed a button that opened his text app. He chose a phone number, then began typing with his thumbs. He had taught himself after watching a YouTube video.

Need product tonight, the message said.

He sent the message. A small check mark appeared when the message landed safely at its destination. He sniffed, shifted in his seat. He turned on the Lexus radio, tuned it to a jazz and blues station.

His phone chirped. An incoming message. He looked back to his phone. His eyebrows arched in surprise.

Unable to accommodate tonight.

He typed: *Unacceptable.*

The reply came back.

Unavoidable. My agent is not here.

His thumbs went to work. *Fill the order yourself.*

Can't, came the reply.

The Vampire's thumbs again: *On my way. Do not disappoint.*

He shoved his phone in his pocket without waiting for a response. He had an arrangement. The terms would be honored, one way or the other.

The Vampire backed the car out of his parking stall and grumbled forward looking for the nearest exit. He swung the wheel hard, throwing his weight against the car door. He grimaced, calmed himself as he drove. Traffic was light this time of night.

Finding himself on the border between the Gaslamp and the East Village, he swerved off Broadway and headed south. Closer to the water, the fog was thicker.

He parked at the curb near the Blood Bank, got out. He surveyed his surroundings, detected no danger. He glided down the shadowy sidewalk, worked his way around the corner from the main entrance. He hugged the building as he moved, silent as death itself. He disappeared down the long ramp towards the loading dock.

The halogen light above the doors blasted the area with garish brightness. Everything not directly bathed in its glow fell into muddy shadow. This suited the Vampire fine. He was a creature of the shadows, perfectly content to see and yet not be seen.

Until it was too late.

A middle-aged Black woman stood there near the dumpster. She wore a white lab smock and held several blood bags in her hands. Her aura told him she was sorely afraid. Unaccustomed to soiling her own hands, she preferred to look the other way and quietly pocket her cut.

Monique shivered, partly from the cold. Who the hell needed a steady supply of expired human blood, for Christ's sake? Witches, Satanists, maybe? She didn't want to know. Not her business. They got the blood; she got paid.

Win-win.

No one was getting hurt. Sure, this might technically be illegal, but was it really wrong? The expired blood would be autoclaved and destroyed anyway, so who cared?

A victimless crime.

The Vampire stopped at the edge of the shadows. He watched her staring into the darkness. She was not aware of his presence. Occasionally, she glanced around like she was worried someone might sneak up behind her. Little chance of that. She stood bathed in light and the only thing behind her was the loading dock and the rear door.

The Vampire cleared his throat. Monique jumped like a frightened rabbit.

"Who's there?" she demanded.

"Your customer," the Vampire whispered. "Shall we commence, madame?"

"Step into the light."

The Vampire stepped closer. His feet appeared first, then his pantlegs. The leather jacket seemed to absorb the light like a black hole in space. She could only get a glimpse of his pale face.

"Who are you?"

He pulled five one hundred dollar bills out of his pocket. "Someone prepared to pay a premium for tonight's inconvenience."

Monique seemed surprised. "Well, since I'm doing this myself, I ain't sharing with him."

"That is none of my affair," the Vampire said. He placed the money on the barrel's lid.

She took the money, handed over the blood.

"Thank you," the Vampire said. He turned to leave.

"Wait."

He stopped.

"What do you do with all that blood?"

"That, madame, is none of *your* affair."

The Vampire strode away. It was safer for her to know as little as possible. He rounded a corner, wasted no time heading towards his car.

Dawn was not far away.

His Lexus waited in the distance. Then he saw someone approach his car, pause there, and suddenly twist his body, looking around.

Checking for witnesses. Or surveillance cameras.

The Vampire was suddenly there, just a couple of yards away.

"Can I help you?"

Startled, the young man spun around to face the Vampire. His dark eyes roamed up and down the Vampire's face and body. Stupidly, he postured, his body language screamed that he did not see the Vampire as a threat.

"What are you holding?"

The Vampire looked down at the blood bags in his hands. "You did not answer my question," he said. "Can I help you with something?"

"This your car?"

"Yes."

The nameless young man and would-be car thief pulled a small revolver out of his hoodie pocket and pointed it.

"Give me the keys."

The Vampire pretended to think about it, then, "No."

"Motherfucker, I have a gun."

"And you think that makes you safe from me?"

"What?" Incredulous.

"If you want to live," the Vampire admonished, "walk away. Right now."

"And if I don't?"

"You will die."

The thief extended his arm, aimed, and fired. The Vampire had already moved. The bullet whizzed by his ear. Before the thief could get off another shot, the Vampire closed the gap, grabbed his gun hand at the wrist on the inside.

The Vampire raised his free hand back, extended his claw-like fingers with the long, sharp nails. He shoved forward with a vicious grunt, driving his talons into the thief's throat. Then the Vampire flicked his hand, slicing through muscle and blood vessels. The sliced carotid artery spewed liquid scarlet into the night.

The Vampire spun the thief away from him and pushed. The geysering blood never sprayed him, never soiled his car. He watched as the young man collapsed, his body convulsing. Dark blood pooled across the sidewalk and dribbled into the gutter. His victim gave one last feeble sigh.

At least he had the good manners to die quietly.

The Vampire hit the button on his key fob, unlocking the car door. He scooped up the blood bags he had been forced to drop. He opened the door, pitched everything onto the passenger seat. He got in, got the engine started.

Then he drove away.

The Vampire turned into his Kensington alley and pulled into his parking space. He killed the engine, scanned the area. A cat digging in a garbage can. Cockroaches skittering inside a huge green dumpster. Mr. Kittridge, the elderly man who lived in the apartment below the Vampire, snoring and gasping due to Sleep Apnea and his refusal to use a CPAP machine.

The Vampire opened the door, got out. He walked around to the other side, scooped up the bags. He pressed his key fob as he walked away. The car locked behind him. He went around the building and mounted the stairs.

Moments later he was inside, the door closed behind him. He tossed the blood inside the refrigerator. He went back into the living room and locked his front door.

He sat down, opened his laptop. His fingers hovered above the keyboard, then began flying over the keys. He checked his portfolio – stocks, bonds, real estate holdings. Though the economy was in flux, his holdings were doing well.

His mind had slowed, gone foggy. He viewed everything through a thin gossamer veil. No stranger to this, he knew what it meant.

Dawn was coming.

He reached out to close his laptop. Stiff shoulder and elbow joints groaned like rusty hinges. He got the laptop closed, sat there. He braced himself for the arduous journey from the sofa to his bedroom.

His ultimate safe space.

The Vampire briefly considered dying where he was. But if he did that, he risked an errant beam of sunlight getting through the relatively flimsy curtains. And what if the manager needed to get inside for some emergency? She would find a tiny, almost mummified body lying on the sofa. Police get called. Erstwhile first responders zip him up in a body bag, haul him out. He would wake up in a morgue and have to escape without killing anyone.

Be strong, he told himself. You are sliding into that gray land between Life and Death.

He took a deep breath. Even that hurt. He braced himself then leaned forward and used his momentum along with a push off the cushions with his fists. Suddenly his painful knees extended, locked.

Vertigo flooded in. The world in front of him slanted forty-five degrees to the left, began spinning counterclockwise. He steadied himself against the sofa. He turned carefully, gauged the distance from where he was standing to the doorway that would take him into the hallway. About ten or twelve feet, all open space. Nothing to grab if he faltered.

Then do not falter, he told himself.

He forced one foot out in front of him. Stiffening weight-bearing joints screamed at him. He planted his foot. Pain jolted from the floor up his leg and into the very core of his undead being.

He forced his other foot forward. He held his arms out away from his body for balance. He repeated his stiff-legged, gait until he made it to the hallway.

The Vampire looked at his hand. Thin skin appeared translucent now, stretched tight across bone and tendon. Bluish blood vessels traced beneath.

The Vampire's bounced off the hallway walls, staggering into his bedroom. He slammed the heavy door behind him. He pushed the lock closed, then careened towards his bed. In agony and out of breath, he glanced towards the window. What he saw that morning alarmed him greatly.

A piece of Velcro had come undone and now a tiny gap between the curtains halfway between floor and ceiling. The gap measured two or three inches high and about a half inch wide.

Big enough to be lethal.

The Vampire never made it to the bed. He dropped to his knees, pitched forward onto the floor. One arm folded beneath him. The other stretched beyond his head in a futile attempt to reach the bedcovers.

One last sigh escaped atrophying lungs. Fascia melted away. Gray skin dried, flaked, stretched across brittle bones beneath. Lank hair clung to his skull. Eyes deteriorated within their sockets.

All that remained now was an incredibly well-dressed corpse that looked like it had been dead for over a century sprawled across the hardwood floor.

Reggie felt like he had been flattened by a Mack truck. Within seconds of coming around from his sedative-induced sleep, pain screamed at him he was still alive. His eyes focused on the breakfast tray on the wheeled table next to him.

He used the hand control to raise himself into a semi-sitting position. He pulled the tray forward, lifted the lid. Scrambled eggs, bacon, toast with butter and jelly on the side. Not bad for institutional food. He figured he would choke this down now, then get some real food later.

He wolfed it down, not realizing how hungry he was. He was still hungry after he finished the meager portions. Nice appetizer, but not much more.

He pushed the tray table away from him, wondering where everyone was. He had been awake several minutes now and no one had come in. He grabbed the call light clipped to the bedsheet beside his left hand, pressed the button.

A nurse breezed in a few moments later. Short, dark hair, dark eyes. Asian. Emerald green scrubs, white T shirt underneath. She smiled at him.

"You need something?" she asked.

"When can I get out of here?"

"As soon as the doctor signs the discharge orders," she answered.

"When will that be?"

She looked at her watch. "At least another hour," she replied. "He usually doesn't get up here until after nine."

"Well, I feel fine," he lied. "Can I just leave now, and he sign the paperwork later?"

"That's not how it works," came a familiar voice behind the nurse. Reggie looked over her shoulder.

Nick Castle stood in the doorway, leaning against the door jamb. He grinned, moved forward.

"Hey, Lieutenant," Reggie greeted as Nick crossed the room. The nurse smiled and left.

"How you feel, Detective?"

"Like I got blown up yesterday."

"You don't say."

"How's Valerie?"

"Haven't seen her yet," Nick said.

Reggie nodded his head. They both fell silent.

"We nearly got killed yesterday," Reggie whispered after a long time. The words came out as heavy as lead.

"But you didn't."

"He tried to kill us." Reggie's eyes went cold. His jaw set hard. "Now I'm really fucking pissed." He looked his lieutenant straight in the eye. "I'm going to nail this bastard's ass to the wall, mount his head above my fireplace like a fucking trophy."

"You don't have a fireplace."

"I'll move somewhere that does."

Nick understood. He felt the same way. Nearly losing a good friend like Reggie had really rattled his cage. He wanted to see this maniac go down.

Hard.

But he still had a job to do and a second injured officer under his command. He made his excuses to Reggie and disappeared out the door.

The hallway seemed brighter now. Maybe they had turned on some more lights for the Day Shift. He glided past the nurse's station to the other side of the ward. Turned a corner, found Wahl's room. He paused, knocked, then entered.

Valerie Wahl sat in bed, nibbling her toast, reading a book. "Hey, Lieutenant."

"Detective. How do you feel?"

"Like I got blown up yesterday."

Nick grinned. "And what do you feel like doing?"

"Like kicking some ass."

"As soon as you're cleared by the Doc, we'll have you back out there."

"How's Reggie?"

"Ready to leap back into the fray."

"Into the fray," she repeated. "I like that."

"You'll get your chance," he promised. He smiled encouragingly, then turned and walked out.

Nick made his way down the hallway towards the nurse's station. He saw Morris Horn at the desk. He looked up, saw Nick, and waved. Nick waved back as Morris said something clever and grinned at the nurse.

Morris stalked towards Nick looking like a Sherman tank in a suit. They stopped in front of each other. Nick assured him both officers were being sent home today and would be back in action soon. Probably tomorrow.

Morris shook his head. "Times like this remind me why I'm glad I retired."

"Just times like this?" Nick asked.

Nick's phone buzzed in his pocket. He reached in to grab it. Morris gestured he was heading towards the hospital rooms. Nick gave a quick wave, pulled his phone out. He checked the caller's I.D., put the phone to his ear.

"Hello," he said as he strode towards the nursing station.

"Hola, hermano," came Alejandro Dominguez's voice. *"Como estas?"*

"Can't complain," he said in English. He rounded the nurse's station, and the elevator at the end of the hall came into view. "I'm at the hospital. Two of my detectives were injured yesterday."

"The ones from the news last night?"

"That's them."

"Are they going to be okay?"

"They're being released later this morning."

"Good. Hey, listen, the reason I called was to see if you had thought over what we talked about the last time you were here."

Nick remembered the conversation, he told him. And yes, he had thought it over.

"And have you arrived at an answer?"

"I'm starting to think it might be a good idea."

"I was hoping you'd say that."

The elevator arrived. The doors swooshed open. Nick stepped inside, pushed a button for the bottom floor. He promised Alejandro he would call again later in the day. He hit the *CALL END* button, dropped his phone back into his pocket.

Charlie lay on his futon staring at the ceiling. Dressed only in underwear, a blanket pulled up to his chin, he shifted onto his side. He gazed across the cramped studio. His TV was a monster, a 65-inch screen far too large for the space. A few bookcases crammed to overflowing with books, magazines, newspapers. The inadequate kitchenette with its undersized stove and decrepit refrigerator hulked on the other side. From where he lay, he could hear the soft skittering of the cockroaches inside the cabinet under the sink.

He reminded himself to take the pizza box on the coffee table out to the garbage. The smell would attract more bugs. Noticing movement on the carpet, he saw a small insect, some kind of beetle, crawling along. No idea where it came from or where it was going. No conscious thought. It simply acted, just did what it did.

Kind of like me, he thought.

Charlie sat up. He needed to clean the place. A shower and a shave wouldn't hurt, either. He walked stiff legged towards the microscopic bathroom. He did not bother to close the door.

He looked at himself in the grimy mirror. Nondescript features looked back at him. He rubbed his fingers along his jaw. He wished he could grow a full beard. He changed his hair color sometimes, wore wigs and contacts. But he couldn't alter the outline of his face or the angle of his jaw. He could gain weight, maybe lose a little, but that wouldn't be enough.

Charlie again considered San Diego might not be the best place for him anymore. Sad. He liked it here. But the cops were closing in. Finding his diversion apartment was proof of that.

How long before they found the others?

This apartment was rigged, too. After moving in and killing the landlady, he had applied flash paper in a line around the baseboards and into the kitchen, the door, and the window. He ran det cord beneath the flash paper and tied it off to the gas line that connected his stove to the gas main. Everything terminated at a weight-triggered detonator hidden under the doormat directly inside the front door. Anyone stepping on that would be obliterated by a raging inferno.

He wandered back into the main room. He plopped down on the futon again, his shower forgotten. He felt itchy all over. His mind spun like a whirlwind within his skull. Fists opened and closed as frustration built.

There was only one thing to relieve this tension. He looked around, saw things clearer now. He saw the world in high definition. More color. More texture. Then his eyes drifted over a bookcase on the far wall. Over there on the floor leaning against the unit, his suitcase sat, waiting quietly.

It beckoned to him like a siren's call, impossible to ignore.

His path was clear. He had known it all along. He did not know why the decision-making process was always so tortuous. Only one thing would fulfill him, sooth him, make him whole.

Time to hunt.

This would be his last kill in San Diego. Kill tonight, leave tomorrow morning.

Preparations would be a simple affair. Other than his suitcase and whatever clothes he happened to be wearing, he would leave everything behind. All he needed was to transfer money from one account to another, then wipe down the place and Scrub the toilet so they couldn't get DNA or fingerprints.

Charlie had a plan. All he had to do was work it. Scrub the place down, leave and never come back. Pluck one last soul from Splinter, then it was gone, baby, gone.

He leaned forward, picked his laptop off the coffee table. He opened it, went to his banking website. He logged in to move his money. No time like the present.

Nothing to it but to do it.

CHAPTER TWENTY-FOUR

The Vampire's corpse lay sprawled across the hardwood floor. The gap in the curtain remained open. A single golden ray spilled through, illuminated a bright yellow ellipse on the floor. The day wore on. The angle of the intrusive ray moved, inching ever closer towards the Vampire's crumpled remains. An hour later, the shaft of light had crept across the floor further, and eventually touched the Vampire's outstretched arm just above the wrist.

The illuminated remains smoldered in the direct sunlight, then blackened. Wispy tendrils of grey smoke rose as the sunlight sliced through. Minutes passed, the golden ray doing its damage. Eventually, the light burned through brittle bones like a concentrated laser, severing his hand completely.

As the day spun on, the light in the room moved away from the Vampire's hollow husk. It crept upwards, played across the comforter.

Eventually, the room darkened.

Reggie lay in his apartment, arm across his forehead. His headache pounded and the tinnitus was deafening. The doctor had assured him the symptoms would most likely be temporary.

Most likely, huh?

Lieutenant Castle had ordered Reggie to bedrest for an extra day. The work would still be there tomorrow. Reggie knew he was not ready for full duty.

He rolled towards his bedside nightstand, fumbled with the alarm clock, and turned on the radio. He thumbed the dial, found a classic rock station, turned the volume up. The music pierced the high-pitched hum, pushed it into the background. He laid back, staring at the ceiling.

His mind wandered.

The case was going nowhere. The stakeout was a grind. They had to fight tedium as they waited to zero in on their man. They couldn't miss their opportunity.

Then there was his grandmother. He still couldn't believe she was gone. Grandpa Eddie had put the service off a day or two so Reggie could recover. When Reggie had asked how he had accomplished that, the Vampire has smiled and said that there was nothing to worry about except getting well.

Valerie.

The thought of her took center stage. Both the doctors and the lieutenant had assured him that she was fine and would make a full recovery. But her welfare was his responsibility. He himself had not made sure that his junior detective was all right.

He groaned, sat up. He grabbed the sheets with both hands. The entire room slanted at an angle and began spinning. He closed his eyes, breathed deeply. He waited until the world righted itself. Then he stood on wobbly legs. He put his hands out to maintain his balance. Somehow, he managed to get to the bathroom without falling flat on his face.

Miracles never ceased.

He staggered back out on wooden legs and leaden feet. His head swam again, but he had was on a mission. Back at the bed, he half sat, half fell onto the mattress.

He rested a moment, then dressed. Pants, shoes, and socks. Fresh shirt. His pistol and shoulder holster. A jacket to conceal the firearm. His wallet and police I.D., then he was ready to go.

Reggie left and locked the door, made his way to the elevator. He still felt punkish. Tired, oh so tired. But Valerie Wahl was his responsibility. The doors swooshed open. He stepped inside as the doors swooshed closed again behind him.

Down to the parking garage.

He still felt a bit woozy staggering from the elevator into the cool, dim garage. His personal vehicle waiting in its assigned spot. He approached cautiously; an instinct developed over many years as a cop. He knew of colleagues in other parts of the country who had fallen victim to car bombings, and he never allowed himself to become complacent.

All part of the job. When you're a cop, and if you're doing your job correctly, there's usually someone somewhere who wants you dead. Cops manage to piss off all sorts of people with long memories over the course of a career.

Only sometimes, some of them decide to take revenge.

His hand slowly snaked inside his jacket, rested on the butt of his firearm. He paused beside the driver door, scanned the area. Looked all around, hoping he would appear casual to an observer. Once satisfied no one was nearby, he leaned over, glanced at the hood of his car.

Years ago, he had begun putting a small piece of clear tape on the seam of the hood. One half on the hood, the other attached to the side panel. Just about an inch and a half, pressed down so it looked practically invisible. But if the hood was lifted, the tape would tear away, leaving dangling remnants – if you knew where to look.

Reggie knew where to look.

His clear tape was intact. So, unless someone had slithered beneath the car and planted a bomb, chances were he was okay. He opened the car door, slid in behind the wheel, closed the door with a solid thud.

Keys into the ignition, a practiced turn, and the car came to life. Breathing easier, he backed out. He had never been to Valerie's apartment, but he knew where the converted motor court was, tucked away on Park between El Cajon Boulevard and Adams Avenue. White stucco façade, red Spanish tile roofs.

Quaint.

Within minutes he was standing on her doormat, which had flowers and honeybees emblazoned on it. He took a deep breath, knocked on the door.

Waited.

He had his hand curled into a fist, ready to knock a second time. He heard the deadbolt slide back. The door opened, and Valerie stood there in sweats and a t shirt, hair tussled and sleepy, and looking so alluring that Reggie's breath caught in his chest.

"Hey," she whispered.

"Hey," he echoed. Then, "How are you doing?"

She stepped back, silently bidding him to enter. He crossed the threshold while she closed the door behind him and slid the deadbolt back into place.

"The place is a mess," she said.

Reggie looked around the apartment. A studio, about 400 square feet, obviously a converted motel room from the mid-20th century. Probably built sometime after World War Two. Kitchenette at the far wall, bathroom beyond that. Living area up front by the window, her bedroom closed off by a Japanese-inspired four-paneled partition. Tastefully decorated with a minimalist style. Nothing appeared out of place.

Maybe saying the place is a mess was just something people said to unexpected guests.

They both sat down on her sofa which faced her flatscreen TV.

"How are you?" she asked.

"Worried about you."

"I'm fine," she smiled, and it lit up the room. "Thanks for asking."

"Still dizzy?"

"Not too bad," she answered. She touched a cut on her temple that had been closed with a butterfly bandage. The swelling and discoloration around it would take days to resolve. "Mostly it's the headache," she reported. "And this fatigue is killer."

"That's to be expected."

"So, what are you doing here?"

The question caught Reggie off guard. "I just wanted to lay eyes on you," he fumbled.

Her eyes widened. Her head tilted. A strand of curly red hair fell softly from her forehead and across one eye.

She nodded. "Well, I appreciate that."

Silence followed. They simply stared at each other for several seconds. Finally, Reggie stood up, attempting to appear formal and professional.

"Well," he stated matter-of-factly, as if the visit was over, "I'd best be going."

She stood, barred his way. "Is that really why you came here, Reggie? To just turn around and leave?"

Shocked into silence, Reggie's mouth opened and closed. He had no idea to say. In fact, his coming here had been inappropriate, hadn't it? An action he shouldn't have taken, based on feelings he shouldn't be having.

An impish grin slowly spread across her face, and she looked radiant once again. His heart leapt and fluttered. Her eyes, those incredibly green eyes, twinkled in her head. He became completely lost in them.

She grabbed him playfully by his shirt, pulled him to her. Her face turned upwards; her mouth opened. Her eyes closed.

Before he knew it, her lips were on his. She pressed herself against him.

All thoughts of leaving fled his mind.

Charlie Simpkins watched gray skies darken. He considered his options for the one hundredth time. The smartest play was drop everything and flee town. Tonight.

Right now.

His compulsion to kill overrode his intellect. Charlie needed to kill someone so bad he could taste it. He had a pent up need that required satisfaction. Release. If he was a normal guy, he would go out and get laid. But he was not a normal guy – whatever normal was.

Was normal behavior holding a job, paying taxes, obeying the law? Finding someone, having kids? Backyard barbeques, hamburgers, and hotdogs? A beer on the porch? Buying a new car every few years, going on vacations, constantly in debt and scrambling to pay the bills? Robbing Peter to pay Paul?

That was normal behavior?

Well, those other hairless apes could have it, Charlie decided. They were dead already. They just didn't know it yet.

Charlie Simpkins, Serial Killer Extraordinaire, was fully alive. And unlike those other meat sacks slouching around, Charlie had a mission. A purpose. And he had a responsibility to himself to use this his time on Earth to accomplish it.

Because for Charlie Simpkins, hunting people was normal. Killing people was normal. Gearing his entire life to support his mission, his quest, his hunts, his kills was normal to him. He didn't see others as people – at least, not people like him.

He existed above them, beyond them. They weren't even human. They were opportunities for him to discover his elusive Truth.

And sometimes, just sometimes, Charlie would see some jerk walking down the street, smiling, saying hello to people, all with a stupid, shit-eating grin on his ugly mug. And Charlie just wanted to smack him, tackle him to the ground, and bash his head in with a rock until his fucking brains spilled out of his ruined skull.

To Charlie Simpkins, *THAT* was normal.

What Charlie didn't understand, couldn't even begin to fathom, was why that wasn't normal to everyone else.

The sun dropped below the horizon. The Vampire came back to painful life on the hardwood floor. As he became conscious, he howled in agony, held his amputated stump close to him and cradled it in his good hand.

What the hell had happened?

Then he remembered. He threw a poisonous glare at the window. The curtains were still slightly parted. Just enough for a beam of sunlight to fall across him, severing his hand.

He gathered his feet under him, stood up still cradling his injury. He scooped up the hand, which still appeared mummified. He staggered towards the kitchen on joints that creaked like rusty hinges.

He entered the kitchen, tossed the dismembered hand onto the counter. He opened the fridge, and the yellow light spilled out, illuminating a thin slice of the otherwise dark room. He grabbed every bag he had, pitched them from where he was onto the counter near his hand. The door closed on its own as he turned away. He pulled a mixing bowl and a coffee mug out of the dishwasher.

The Vampire knew what to do. He had not done this before, but he had picked things up along the way. Vampiric tricks of the trade. Some vampires could be quite social and were brilliant conversationalists. They enjoyed trading life hacks.

With one hand he squeezed blood into the mug, put it in the microwave. While it warmed and the microwave hummed, the Vampire sliced the bags open with his sharp fingernails, dumped the blood into the bowl. Then he placed his severed hand into the blood.

The microwave went *DING!* He pulled the mug out, drank it down right away. Gulped it down, all of it, every drop. He needed all the healing powers the blood could provide.

He sighed, feeling better already. Now, about his hand…

The Vampire placed the mug on the countertop, looked into the bowl. Sitting in the blood, his hand had reanimated. Muscle and sinew inside, gray flesh outside. He gingerly placed his stump into the blood bowl, approximated the stump with the wrist end of the hand.

As soon as the two edges made contact, healing began. Tendrils of flesh appeared along the severed edges of both the hand and the stump. They filtered outward, reaching for each other, guided by dark forces of nature that even the Vampire did not understand. Skin met, healed. Tendons reattached. Bones fused.

It felt strange. Not painful per se, just unpleasant. Tiny vibrations as the bones mended. The skin grew over completely, leaving no scar.

The Vampire lifted his arm with his newly reattached hand out of the bowl. Dripping blood, the hand would have appeared horrific to anyone else. But to him, it was a welcome sight. He opened and closed his fist. Grip strength seemed to have returned. He wiggled his fingers, testing manual dexterity. Then he ran his hands under water at the sink.

The newly reattached hand proved tender to touch and painful to move. He had the grip and finger dexterity, but range of motion in his wrist was decreased. And rolling his wrist around produced blinding flashes of pain. He stopped doing that, shook his hand loosely, as if that would somehow shake off the pain.

It did not.

The Vampire heard footfalls coming up the steps outside. Two sets. One lighter, softer than the other. He was about to have guests; he was standing naked in his pitch-black kitchen.

He dashed back to his bedroom, threw a thick terrycloth robe on. He walked down the hallway tying the sash at his trim waist. He unlocked his door, swung it open.

Reggie and Valerie stood outside. The Vampire noticed something different about them. Nothing outwardly obvious, but something. He had an inkling as to what it was.

He smiled. "Reginald. Detective Wahl. Please come in."

The Vampire stepped back and to the side, halfway hiding behind the thick wooden door. They entered of their own will, and he closed the door behind them.

"It is delightful to see you two," the Vampire said, rubbing his hands together.

"What's wrong with your hand?" Valerie asked. Nothing got by her, the vampire reminded himself.

The Vampire recounted the story to them both. He left nothing out. And while he recited recent events, he noticed the auras coming off them both. He also caught the scent of recent lovemaking. It lay subtly masked behind the perfumes of soap and shampoo, but it was there.

"Where are my manners?" the Vampire asked. "Please. Be seated. Can I get either one of you anything?"

"We're fine, thanks."

They sat down on the sofa side by side. The Vampire sank into a chair opposite them near the coffee table. The Vampire's laptop lay there, closed, dark, asleep. For the first time, he realized he had no desire to open it up and check the markets. Especially since there were so many other, more interesting things going on!

"Grandma's funeral," Reggie said. "When is it?"

"Nine thirty tonight."

Reggie nodded, looked a bit glum. He missed his Grandma Lottie. The Vampire himself would forever miss his Lot-Lot. Perhaps, if he ever experienced the Final Death, he and his beloved granddaughter could be reunited in whatever plane of existence extends beyond this one.

"It is best to not grieve too much."

"What do you mean?"

"Rather than focusing on her passing, focus on a life well lived," the Vampire said. "Rather than focusing on how much you will miss her, be grateful for the time you had with her. Be grateful for her love, her warmth, her humor."

Valerie placed a hand on Reggie's arm.

"Everything that lives, dies," the Vampire said. "Relationships are temporary. Some last longer than others, but in the end, life is fleeting." He paused, then, "We're all just passing through this world. Make the most of it and take whatever love and comfort you can find."

"You're not just passing through," Valerie pointed out.

"Quite the contrary, my dear." The Vampire clutched the top of his robe, yanked the borders back, revealing his pale chest and torso. Three large-caliber bullet holes shone white in a tight grouping around his heart. "I have experienced death. I just took a second chance."

"What happens if you die for real, though?"

"Then perhaps I will go to heaven."

"What if there's nothing after this?" she asked. "What if we live, we die, and that's the end of it?"

"Is this what you believe?" the Vampire asked.

"I am asking what you believe."

"Without getting into a theological debate, I believe there must be something more out there," he pointed his finger upward, "than just this." He paused, then, "Rather than us being human beings living a spiritual existence, I believe we are spiritual beings living a human existence. I believe – I hope! - that when our bodies die, whatever it is inside us that makes us uniquely human moves to another plane of existence. Another realm, another dimension. Label it what you will."

"Heaven," she concluded. "So, do you believe in God?"

"Yes. Absolutely."

"Why?"

"How else do you explain me?"

"I don't get it."

"Neither do I," the Vampire answered. "I said I believe in Him. I never said I understood His plan." He paused, then, "Personally, I think he has a rather strange sense of humor."

The funeral service started an hour later. Simple and elegant. Just like Lottie. In addition to the Vampire, Reggie, and Valerie, Nick and Morris showed up. The funeral director gave a brief eulogy, blandly said all the right things. Then the service was over, all done in less than an hour. The director breathed a sigh of relief when they had left.

Lottie's cremains would be interred in the New Hope Cemetery the next day, during daylight hours. The Vampire would make sure to drop by tomorrow night for a final farewell. Then he would put his grief aside and deal with this wannabe vampire serial killer, and with Maya.

He could not decide which one of them he hated more.

Across the parking lot, Nick stood at his open car door. He watched the Vampire, huddled with Reggie and Valerie. He had a feeling about those two, and he didn't like it. They seemed more... intimate. The way they sat so close together during the funeral. The furtive glances back and forth.

The answer was obvious.

The question was, how would he handle it?

CHAPTER TWENTY-FIVE

The Vampire lounged in one of LeStat's vintage deep red Victorian wingback chair, one leg crossed casually over the other. He held a newspaper open in front of him. A glass of iced tea sat sweating on the table near his knee. Classic rock a forgotten 70s one-hit wonder played in the background. He still wore his suit from the funeral. He loosened his colorful tie and unbuttoned his top shirt button.

He finished reading an article, tossed the paper aside. He took a sip of tea and found something else to read. Now that the stress with Lottie's funeral had been released, he felt emotionally exhausted.

The night was still young, and he did not relish rambling around his apartment alone. Here he was around people and that helped. He had plenty of time to get home and prep his room properly before sunrise.

The Vampire sighed, sat back into the cushions. He closed his eyes, slowed his breathing.

Centered himself.

Then, he pushed outward with his mind. His consciousness expanded in all directions filling the room, the building. Spilling outside in the early morning chill, searching for Maya. He could not find her. She had not left; she was still in San Diego. This he knew instinctively.

No matter.

He would find her.

He concentrated, eyebrows furrowing. The creases on his forehead became canyons. He pushed out further, searching for this serial killer. His consciousness encountered several people of questionable morals and past evil deeds. In any other time, he would track one of them down for dinner. But he needed to stay focused.

The Vampire blinked and his consciousness retreated, pulling back and contracting into his body. He felt a certain exhilaration.

He smiled, drank his tea.

Across town, Charlie the wannabe vampire with the kewpie doll face, sat disconsolately at a table on Splinter's main floor. Only a smattering of people, and half of them worked there. He nursed a watered-down Manhattan from the bar. Condensation rolled down the outside and soaked through the napkin underneath. When he picked up the glass, the napkin adhered to the bottom, leaving a wet ring left on the table.

Maya sat in The Grotto. She had already zeroed in on the interesting human in the ridiculous clothing and wig. And those eyes! Who were those contacts supposed to fool? She shook her head, almost feeling something akin to pity for the petite young man.

Almost.

His aura radiated off him. Maya knew he was a dangerous man among humans. He enjoyed killing almost as much as she did. He just had different motives.

Maya had seen TV reports about the "Vampire Killer" stalking the streets. She wondered if this runt was who they were all so afraid of. He had the vibe.

Maya got curious.

Charlie sat slumped in his chair. Coming here on a Thursday had been a mistake. Tomorrow the place would be hopping. Same story on Saturday. Sunday not so much because people had jobs to go to Monday morning. And he would be long gone before Monday.

Go home, grab his gear, and skedaddle.

He tossed his head back, drained his glass. He slammed it down, placed his hands flat on the table to push himself up.

That was when he saw her.

Beautiful, ethereal, materializing out of the Grotto. Moving down the steps, black and mysterious, sensual, moving with a preternatural, inhuman grace. Silver hair billowing off her shoulders. Eyes hidden behind sunglasses.

Sunglasses?

She made a bee line towards him, moving only slightly here and there to avoid colliding with a table or chair. Her gait was so smooth she looked like she was gliding across the floor like some supernatural wraith.

He never took his eyes off her. She stopped at the table, looked at him for a beat. Then she sat down.

"Good evening," she said.

Charlie eyed her up and down. She was hot. Gorgeous features, smooth skin. A young Black woman, but her skin looked pale. But not from makeup. He knew the difference. This was different.

She looked bloodless.

He leaned in. "Good evening."

"I am Maya."

"Charles."

"I have seen you in here before."

"Really?" He was certain they had never met. He would have remembered.

"I'm usually in the Grotto."

"Ah," he said, nodding.

"Leaving?"

"I was," he admitted.

"Not much prey tonight, is there?"

"Excuse me?" he stumbled. "What did you say?"

"You heard me correctly," she said. Then she leaned forward like she wanted to tell him a secret. "I know who you are."

"And who am I?"

"The Vampire Killer everyone is looking for," she stated matter-of-factly.

He started to inhale to voice a protest, but she cut him off.

"Don't bother denying it." She paused. "I'm a fan of your work."

"A fan?"

She smiled, allowing her fangs to show. "In the beginning, I was offended."

"Why would you be offended?"

"Two reasons," she responded. "Firstly, you're imitating creatures you know nothing about."

He digested this a moment. Then, "And secondly?"

"You're doing it wrong."

Charlie sat back in his chair, looked around. No one else near them.

"Let's suppose I am who you say I am. Why aren't you frightened of me?"

"I have no reason to be."

She was crazy, Charlie realized. Absolutely insane. Nuttier than a fruitcake. Bats in the belfry.

"You see, Charles," she said as she read his thoughts, "the reason I do not fear you is because unlike all these posers and imitators, I am exactly what I appear to be." She removed her sunglasses, allowing him to see her black, shiny eyes for the first time.

Charlie squinted with surprise, cocked his head a bit. He watched her smile. Pale skin, dead appearance, sunken cheekbones, unblinking eyes, fangs that looked more real than any he had ever seen.

"Ordinarily, I would kill someone like you," she said casually.

"Then why don't you try?" he challenged her. "See how that works out?"

She smiled again, fangs protruding from black lips.

"You and I are kindred spirits," she answered at last. "Both predators. Both wolves in a world overrun with sheep."

"I see." He obviously did not see at all.

"Charles, I find the world more interesting with you in it."

"Why shouldn't I kill you to keep my secret safe?"

"You can't." She smiled at the reaction he tried to keep off his face. "Tour secret is safe with me."

"What the fuck are you?" he asked.

"You know what I am," she answered.

"Well," Charlie said, "I'm happy my work entertains you."

Maya stood. "Make sure it never interferes with mine."

"Or what?" he challenged. But it was too late. She was already gone. Like she had never been there.

Vanished.

Baffled, Charlie looked around, glanced over his shoulders. How the hell had she pulled a disappearing act like that? And was that the street level front door opening and closing just now? Was that her leaving? He never saw her ascending the stairs.

Charlie stood and crossed the floor briskly. He bounded up the stairs and pushed his way out the front door. Outside, he found himself barraged by cold wet air, and enshrouded in fog thicker than when he had arrived. He looked around, both left and right.

"Where did that chick go?"

Kong, standing nearby, frowned in confusion.

"What chick?" he asked in his trademark baritone. The benefits of a large body and an expansive rib cage.

"The black chick. Silver hair. Black corset. Long dress."

Kong knew exactly who he meant. He shrugged. "Sorry, buddy. Haven't seen her tonight."

"She would have just come out," he pressed. "There's no way you didn't see her."

"I'd tell you if I had. I haven't seen anyone come out in the last half hour but you," Kong said truthfully. "The wind blew the door open a couple of minutes ago, but that's it."

Across the street on the roof of the tenement building, Maya chuckled to herself. She watched the interaction below, heard every word. Charlie took two steps backwards, then threw his hands up in defeat.

He never bothered to look up.

Maya turned and walked east. She hopped lightly from building to building, one rooftop to another. When she got to 5th Street, she stopped. The next roof on the other side of the street was over fifty feet away. Ordinarily, she would simply step over the ledge and drop to the sidewalk. But her conversation with Charlie had been exhilarating.

She moved a bit to the right, so she had a clear shot to the other side of 5th. The last thing she needed was to fling herself off the building and collide with one of the trees planted at strategic intervals.

She looked ahead, past the roof she stood on, past the street beyond, and visualized the other rooftop. She visualized her landing. She ran towards the ledge, gaining speed. She flung herself up and out, flying in an upward arc far above the deserted street below. By the time she achieved her apex, she was already more than halfway across the expanse. The ledge hurtled towards her. She pulled her feet up, then the rooftop was beneath and rushing to meet her.

She landed.

Hard.

Something snapped in her right lower leg. She fell forward, skinning the palms of her hands. She sprawled cross the roof and skidded to an awkward stop, her hair and clothes a tangled mess.

Shocked, she lay still for a moment, collecting her thoughts. Then she pushed up and rolled over. Pain shot through her leg and into her torso. She gritted her teeth, fangs gleaming in the low light. She sat up, pulled her dress up, and looked.

Her tibia, the weight-bearing bone in the lower leg, was fractured. It had not broken through the skin, but she saw the unnatural lump on the front of her leg about halfway between her knee and her ankle.

A kneecap where there shouldn't be one.

She needed to set the leg so the bone could mend enough to get home. But such rapid mending required a lot of blood, which she didn't have right now.

She grabbed her leg with both hands, one above the break, the other below. She steeled herself and pulled each hand in the opposite direction. The pain was indescribable. Once she had the bone separated and lined up, she eased the two fractured surfaces together.

A tidal wave of blinding agony crashed over her. She lay there, scarcely able to breath. The initial pain subsided, replaced by what felt like pulsating thunderbolts.

She could feel the bone already fusing. Still, getting home wouldn't be fun. She pushed herself upwards into a standing position. She tried putting weight on the broken leg and was almost blinded again.

She limped over to the south edge of the rooftop. The next building over was about eight feet away. She looked down, saw the alleyway separated the two buildings. Heaps of garbage piled up around overflowing dumpsters. Dirt stained the pavement black. She also noticed a pipe to her right, about four inches in diameter, that ran from the roof down the wall and to the ground.

She flung her good leg over the ledge. She grabbed the pipe with both hands, one atop the other. She dragged her broken leg over and allowed it to swing freely. She squeezed her eyes shut, then opened them as the heat in her tibia subsided. Then she methodically lowered herself hand under hand, using only her upper body strength. When she got to the ground, she rested, supporting her weight on her good leg, her forehead against the cool pipe.

She limped out of the alley onto the sidewalk. She couldn't walk or run all the way to North Park. Not tonight.

A yellow cab crawled up the street towards her. She lifted her arm, waved. The car changed lanes and pulled up in front of her. She fell in and told the driver "University and 30th". The driver nodded, and they pulled away.

Minutes later, the taxi pulled over at their destination. She paid her fare, got out. The driver bade her goodnight, drove off. Maya hobbled towards 29th, the side street that would take her home.

Five minutes later, she stood at her front door. No lights in the nearby homes. No shifting curtains. Everyone asleep with slow, steady heartbeats. She reached inside her corset, extracted the door key. Inserted into the lock, twisted.

Slipped inside as smooth as smoke.

Locked the door behind her.

A young woman, no more than twenty and dressed in tattered clothes, sat duct taped to a straight-backed chair. Legs bound at the ankle, arms at the wrists, torso secured, tape across her mouth. She tried to speak, to plead, to beg. All that came out were muffled, incoherent sounds. But her eyes, bright with fear, told Maya everything.

"You want me to let you go?"

The woman nodded.

"And if I let you go, then of course, you'll never tell anyone about this?"

The woman shook her head, chest heaving.

Maya moved so fast the woman never had time to react. Maya straddled her, wrenched her head to one side, bit deeply. Fangs penetrated soft flesh like knives through butter. Arterial blood fountained into her mouth. She relished that liquid warmth, that sweet/salty/coppery taste. Sure, she could drink from blood bank bags like Eddie did. Or drain animals like some vampires did.

But where was the fun in that? Nothing like imbibing from the source.

Her nameless victim struggled beneath her, of course. As Maya drank, the struggling lessened, weakened, then stopped.

Maya pulled her head back and wiped the bloody drool off her chin. The pain in her leg was almost gone.

"I feel better already," she said.

She pushed herself off, walked away from the husk of what used to be a human being. In the kitchen she wiped her face with a hand towel, tossed the towel onto the counter.

Back into the living room, and she sat down on the sofa. She grabbed the remote, turned on the TV. She had less than an hour before she would have to go downstairs and curl up in her steamer trunk. She found a local replay of the eleven o'clock news. The newscasters droned on about murders here, murders there, a serial killer on the loose.

All this was old news. She was in no danger of being discovered. She would leave Charlie to his work.

Her leg did not hurt anymore. She extended it, turned her foot around, making a circle in the air.

The healing powers of a vampire. Inextricably linked to the amount of blood they consumed.

Maya listened to the weather, sports, the human-interest stories. She turned the TV off. She stood, feeling a familiar stiffness in her limbs that accentuated a growing fatigue.

Dawn was coming.

She would dispose of her kill tomorrow night. She made her way through the kitchen, then she descended the stairs to the bottom.

Every step became more painful as she cut a circuitous course through the cluttered room. Aging, withered hands pressed on boxes and forgotten tables for support. The room spun. Her face was thinner now. Wrinkles on either side of her nose extended downward past her mouth and towards her chin. Crow's feet deepened at the eyes; furrows appeared across her forehead. Her vision dimmed by the second.

She barely made it to the trunk without falling flat on her dusty face. She slumped inside, somehow managed to close the lid.

And then she died, just as she had done for the last one hundred fifty years. One last exhalation. Then the chest shriveled. Maya was a cadaver now, shrunken and mummified.

All was quiet in the house she had murdered so many people to possess.

The Vampire's dried-out corpse lay secure and safe under the heavy comforter pulled over his head. That was after he had checked the Velcro on his backout curtains and had securely fastened all the adhesive surfaces.

Tomorrow night was back to business. He was tired of Maya's threatening presence. Time to kill her. And he was absolutely sick of this puny human who had gained notoriety by mimicking vampirism. He wanted to use this killer's severed head as a soccer ball. Or open him up like he had done the head of that drug cartel.

God have mercy on this pathetic poser if he crossed the Vampire's path before Reggie got to him.

Yes, may God have mercy on him.

Because the Vampire would *not*.

CHAPTER TWENTY-SIX

Valerie's phone blared its loud, irritating alarm at precisely five thirty. Not really awake yet, she rolled over, slapped blindly at the offending tech. She managed to hit the snooze button on her third or fourth attempt.

Too damn early.

She exhaled, buried her face into her pillow. In another minute, her eyes opened again. No way she was drifting back off. She wanted nothing more than to sleep a bit more.

Well, that wasn't necessarily true.

Reggie lay beside her, naked and beautiful beneath the sheets. She reached out, put a hand on his muscular shoulder. He turned over onto his back.

She lay there in the peace and quiet of the early morning watching him sleep. He had never looked more at peace than right now. Gazing at his resting features, she thought she could sense how he must have looked as a child. Her heart overflowed for him. She moved closer, threw her arm across him. He was warm, a human blast furnace in the chill of the apartment.

His eyes fluttered open. He sighed, smiled. Absolute contentment right then. He placed a hand on her arm.

"Good morning," she whispered.

"Good morning," he answered.

"Time to get up."

He pulled her closer. They lay there, arms and legs intertwined, completely at peace with the world. New lovers in that initial stage where they had found each other and were one with the universe. It was an almost spiritual connection.

This was the deep and abiding connection between human beings that most people craved and spent their entire lives looking for, either to experience it once, or to experience it once again.

The alarm went off again, its discordant, earsplitting sound so much irritating noise.

Cursing under her morning breath, Valerie turned over, turned the alarm off. She knew this perfect moment was over.

Moments like this never last forever, which is why they must be savored.

She felt him shift. Suddenly he was against her, muscular arms enveloping her.

Maybe the moment could last a bit longer after all.

"We need to get up," she stated.

"Mmm hmm." He buried his nose in her hair, smelled the faint scent of her shampoo.

"We have bad guys to catch," she said.

She started to pull away. His grip around her tightened. Arms like steel bands. And of course, she didn't really want to get out of bed. Not with this wonderful man next to her.

"Duty calls, I guess," Reggie said. Fully awake, he rolled away from her.

Disappointed, she threw the covers off her, sat up on the edge of the bed. She focused on his broad shoulders, muscled back, trim waist. She smiled appreciatively as Reggie, naked as the day he was born, padded away to the bathroom.

I do love to watch him walk away, she thought to herself.

She put on her panties and bra. She heard the toilet flush. He opened the door and walked towards her, smiling. She gazed and took in his striated chest muscles, washboard abs, and impressive penis.

I also love to watch him walk towards me, she thought.

"All yours," he said as he jerked a thumb over his shoulder.

She went into the bathroom, relieved herself. She took a quick look in the mirror, pushed her tumbling curls off her face, walked out.

Reggie was already half dressed when she came back in. And they would not have time to swing by his apartment before clocking in at the precinct. He was going to wear the same clothes two days in a row.

She threw on something different. They had to keep their relationship – if that's what it was and it sure felt that way – on the downlow. If the brass found out, there would be hell to pay. She would be transferred, no doubt. But worse, it could negatively impact Reggie's career and advancement potential. After all, he was the senior member of the team, and the lion's share of the responsibility rested with him. And walking in at the same time wearing the same clothes, would undoubtedly raise eyebrows.

"I'll take my own car in," she said.

"Good thinking, he replied. "I need to swing by my place. I need an extra box of ammo for my desk at work."

She grunted in acknowledgment, sat down on the side of the unmade bed. She put her shoes and socks on. She stood, put her shoulder holster on, pulled her firearm out, checked the magazine, checked the chamber to make sure there was still a round in the chamber. She flicked the safety on, shoved the handgun back into the holster.

Valerie turned and was surprised to see Reggie making up his side of the bed and fluffing the pillow. Smiling, she joined in. Soon, the bed looked like it hadn't even been slept in.

"Never start the day without making your bed," he said. She looked at him. "My mama taught me that when I was very young. That way, even if the rest of your day is a total goat-fuck, at least you accomplished *something*."

"If you don't mind me asking, what happened to your mom?"

"Cancer."

"God. I am so sorry."

"Thanks," he replied. "It was a while back."

The moment hung there. Seconds ticked by.

"We'd best get going," she whispered.

His eyebrows raised briefly; he sighed. "Right". He stepped away. "I'll see you at the precinct."

They kissed briefly. Nothing more than a peck on the lips, but enough for now.

Valerie picked up her keys, put on a jacket to cover her weapon. Then she stepped outside into the cold gray morning. She locked the door. One could never be too careful in a town this size.

Not even a cop.

Alejandro Domingo sipped his orange juice, stared over his glass at his half-brother. Nicolas had responded to an invitation Alejandro had sent last night. Nicolas ate his bacon, pushed his eggs around on his plate. Then he scooped them up with his fork before putting them into his mouth.

So," Alejandro said, breaking the silence as he returned his glass to the table, "I wanted to know if you've given any further thought to my offer?"

Nick put his fork down, wiped his mouth as he swallowed. "Indeed, I have," he returned. "I have a few concerns."

"Such as?"

"This would be a major lifestyle change for me," Nick stated. "I mean, I wanted to be a cop ever since I was little. But this… this is something else."

"It is a major life decision. No doubt about that."

"What about my pension?"

Alejandro smiled. He told Nick how much money he would be making every month. Nick was dumbfounded.

"You're joking, right?"

"Nope."

"You're sure about that number?"

"Yep."

"You're not doing this out of charity, are you?"

"*Nicolas*," he said, pronouncing the name in Spanish. "I don't do charity cases."

Nick certainly knew that to be true. He thought for a minute.

Alejandro watched him. Cool as a cucumber, he thought. This guy's life is about to change forever in ways he can't even comprehend yet, and he's acting hesitant. Anyone else would be falling all over themselves to say yes before I changed my mind. I'd hate to play poker against him.

"I would need to be brought up to speed," Nick said at last. "I don't know anything about your business model or anything about what you're asking me to do. It will be a steep learning curve."

"I have absolute faith in you, *Nico*. The administrative expertise, organizational and leadership skills you already have will serve you well."

"I need a couple of more days," Nick said. "I need to bring Ramsey's killer to justice."

"You're close?"

"We are."

Alejandro felt like a boat at sea and his sails had just caught the wind. "Excellent."

"Let me finish this case." Nick stood. "Then you'll have my undivided attention."

Alejandro stood, wiped his hands. The two men shook hands over the breakfast table. Then Nick turned and walked towards the front door. Alejandro sat back down. He tore into a warm croissant.

Pepe moved towards the table from the kitchen area. Alejandro knew he was there but kept eating.

"Do you think he will say yes?" Pepe asked.

"He already has."

Valerie arrived at the precinct, entered through the back door. Neither Reggie nor the Lieutenant were in yet. She breathed a sigh of relief as she poured her first mug of lousy police station coffee.

She added stevia, half and half, stirred it in. She saw Reggie push through the revolving front door. Her heart fluttered. That reminded her she was having an office romance, a torrid sexual affair with her boss, her immediate supervisor, something she had promised herself years ago she would never do.

And yet, here she was.

They nodded and greeted each like they would any other day. She realized he was probably as nervous as she. Neither wanted anyone else to find out. They would walk on eggshells for a while, but they would find a way.

She certainly hoped they found a way. She loved her job, and she liked both Reggie and Lieutenant Castle. She had a good first impression of Morris Horn. She had met him before, of course, back when he was a Captain but had never worked directly under his command.

Hell, she was even becoming less uncomfortable being around Reggie's undead ancestor. He had not vamped out and tried to bite her. And despite his protestations to the contrary, he worked well as a team player.

She placed her coffee on her desk, booted up her computer. It was quiet in the precinct right now. She appreciated that tranquility, the calm before the storm.

Things never stayed quiet in a city like San Diego.

Reggie, his own mug filled to the brim, sat at his desk, and booted up. His computer came up. He started opening files right away.

"No results yet on the chemical residue at the Claymore Arms," Valerie said, reading from her screen.

"I didn't think they would," Reggie responded. "Not this fast."

"Are we chasing our tails here?"

"No. ATF is."

"So, what do we do?"

"Keep tracing names and aliases. Talk to Monique again, see if Charlie Simpkins came to work last night."

"Sounds like we're going to spend all day staring at a computer screen."

"A large part of the job gets done sitting on our asses in front of a computer."

Valerie did not relish staring at a computer screen all day. If she had wanted to do that, she would have become a writer. She took another slug of the brownish sulfuric acid that passed for coffee around here, and dove back in.

No way to escape doing the grunt work.

She checked on forensics, called the State Police and ATF. An exercise in futility, she knew. Being a detective meant leaving no stone unturned. Something might pop up and prove you wrong.

Nick came in the rear entrance. He strode straight for his office, something small and oblong tucked under one arm. He went in and closed the door.

Valerie was concentrating on her work so intently she did not notice him enter. Nor did she notice when Reggie got up from his desk about an hour later and silently walked out. She only noticed when he came back about fifteen minutes later carrying two large paper cups of steaming coffee. The aroma filled the room. She looked up just as he sat one of the cups down beside her.

"Thanks," she said.

"Just taking care of my partner." He grinned, winked. Then sat down at his desk.

Taking care of his partner. So handsome. And considerate. And that smile!

Butterflies in her stomach. Again. Pretty much every time she looked at him. This is a mistake, she told herself. A meaningless toss in the hay was one thing. But this! This was something different. Something more. Despite her best efforts, she was falling for this man.

Not smart, girlfriend.

But sometimes we can't help who we love.

Reggie poured over police reports, crime scene photos. He magnified and scoured photos from the blast that had almost killed them. He did not glean anything new.

Reggie was no explosives expert. Basic chemical composition and mechanisms involved with construction and detonation he understood. He had been trained in it just like everybody else. But all that really meant was that he had been "familiarized" with the basics and not much more.

Reggie stood up, pushed his chair underneath the desk. He glanced over at Valerie, who was concentrating on her own work. She was not easily distracted once she got the scent of something. A necessary quality for a good detective.

She had come into a new and uncertain situation and got thrown into the deep end of a deadly pool. Shark infested waters. Sink-or-swim.

Detective Valerie Wahl was swimming.

Reggie quietly made his way across the squad room towards Lieutenant Castle's door. Nick must have noticed motion. He looked at Reggie just as the detective was about to knock. He motioned him in.

Reggie closed the door behind him. He noticed a new nameplate on the desk. Engraved goldplate attached to a polished wooden base.

Lieutenant Nicolas Castillo.

Reggie also noticed a tiny slash angling upwards above the last syllable of *Nicolas*, indicating that syllable was to be emphasized when pronouncing it. And *Castillo*? The Spanish word for castle.

"Embracing your heritage, sir?"

Lieutenant Nicolas Castillo nodded. "If anyone can understand embracing one's heritage, it would be you."

"Absolutely." Reggie meant it. "What triggered it, if I may ask?"

"Ramsey's murder put me back in touch with Alejandro Domingo. He's my half-brother."

Reggie looked stunned.

"Same father."

Reggie's mind ran back over the encounters he had witnessed between the two men. It all made sense now.

"So," Castillo said, rubbing his hands together. "Situation report."

"Same old," Reggie reported. "Sifting through the wreckage. Still waiting on ATF."

"What's Val up to?"

"Running down leads of her own," Reggie replied. "She has resources I don't."

"How is she doing?"

"Doing fine."

Castillo leaned forward on is desk. "So. What's going on between you two?"

"Sir?"

"Don't 'sir' me." He pointed a finger. "Whatever it is, make sure it doesn't get somebody fucking killed. Do you understand me?"

"Yes sir."

"Good. Let's not have this conversation again." He paused. "We on for tonight?"

"Friday night at Splinter," Reggie said seriously. "This shit stain will be there. He needs to hunt."

"Will Eddie be joining us?"

"As far as I know."

"He's got his own problem to solve. Make sure his agenda doesn't run counter to ours," Nicolas warned. "I don't want anyone getting hurt."

"That would never happen with him, sir."

Reggie let himself out. Back at his desk, Valerie turned to him as soon as he sat down.

"Everything all right?" Tension in her voice.

"He knows."

She froze. Blood drained from her face.

"It's on us to keep it under wraps. He's trusting us to keep it strictly professional when we're at work. If we get caught, he goes down with us."

She stayed frozen, scarcely breathing.

"Speaking of work, we're on for tonight."

"Tonight?"

"You know. Catching bad guys. Sort of what we do around here."

An intense look Reggie could not quite read clouded Valerie's eyes. She turned away from Reggie and started typing commands.

Reggie opened a screen window and began typing an email to his contract at ATF, wondering why the chemical breakdown on the blast scene was taking so long?

They both worked separately yet in tandem. Both wondered the same thing. How long would it be before they could fall into bed with each other again?

By four o'clock, dark billowing clouds sat so low and thick they obliterated the sky. They moved inexorably closer as the sun began to set. The marine layer boiled across the coastline, blotting out the spectacular sunset.

The Vampire shuffled through his dark apartment; a warm mug of blood clutched in his fist. He sipped, savored the warmth. The brain fog was lifted with every swig.

Fine by him. All San Diego was threatened if this vampiric rivalry spilled over into the human world. And if other vampires sensed weakness in him, they would descend upon San Diego *en masse*. Then the bloodbath would begin. Bodies would litter the streets. The gutters would run red.

Since when did he care about what happened to the humans?

Perhaps he had been hanging with humans too much. Maybe some of their humanity was rubbing off on him.

Perhaps that was not the worst thing that could happen. He just had to remember that there were bad people out there, despicable people, disgusting people, people who simply needed killing. And he did so enjoy the hunt, ripping murderers, thieves, drug dealers, pedophiles, gangbangers, child molesters, wife beaters and the like apart, limb from limb, bathing in their blood.

After all, humans were *food*. By taking out the worst, he culled the herd. Improved the breed. Cleaned out the gene pool. In a weird way, he performed a public service.

He focused on the night ahead. Splinter would be packed. The chances of collateral damage ran high. If one person panicked, fear would spread like a virus. And they would stampede, having no problem with stomping over each other to escape.

He would simply wade through them. He could not, would not allow their fear to alter his plan of attack. It all came down to a one-on-one fight with Maya. Either he would kill his Vampire Mother and send her to her Final Death, or he would cross that threshold himself.

The thought of dying did not deter him. He did not *want* to die, but he had already died once before, and it really hadn't been so bad. All he had to do was exhale one last time.

And he had.

And here he was, alive again. Well, not really alive. He was a reanimated corpse. An immortal being. An entity people called monster. He scoffed at that. He killed to live, while humans often lived to kill. They killed, murdered, molested, raped, destroyed. Not just other people, but entire communities. Entire ethnicities.

Entire countries.

All too often, they got away with it.

He was small potatoes compared to them.

The Vampire checked his watch. The police would be waiting. He smiled to himself. It was nice to be needed. Respected. It felt good to be trusted. Relied upon.

Perhaps that was why he cared.

Across town, Maya likewise prepared for the evening. Anger and hatred drove her. She felt an overriding urge to kill her progeny and claim his territory for herself. Everything that she had kept bottled up for so long. So many years. Decades.

Centuries!

Establishing her own territory would help ease that anger.

Vengeance was a drug. Becoming a vampire allowed her to wreak vengeance. Every scream of pain, every drop of sweat, every tear her enemies shed, every blathering plea for mercy, every final gasp fed her as much as their blood had. In a world that would never mete out justice on white boys for killing a black girl, her vengeance was the only justice available.

Sure, that had been in the 1800s, but she watched the news. She realized times had changed, but people had not.

Cops knelt on suspects' necks until the suspects died. Six-year-olds shot their first-grade teachers. Teens went on shooting sprees at schools and malls. Protestors became rioters. Broke windows. Burned down buildings. Threw Molotov cocktails. Destroyed businesses. Attacked cops. Looted stores. Powerful nations invaded smaller ones and waged genocidal wars while the world offered "thoughts and prayers" but did nothing to stop it.

Power corrupts. Absolute power corrupts absolutely, so said Lord Acton, a nineteenth century English historian. Give a man enough power, and sooner or later he will not be able to resist playing God.

She looked outside. Full dark. No stars. Thick clouds. Later she would go to Splinter and drop the mental walls. He would come for her. She would draw him in, like a spider patiently waiting for the fly to become ensnared within its web.

Then the feast would begin.

CHAPTER TWENTY-SEVEN

Exhausted, Reggie sat back in his chair. The last thing he wanted was to go undercover. He wanted to go home and sleep. But there were killers out there, one human and one not, and both had to get taken down. Tonight was the night to settle all scores.

Suck it up, buttercup, he told himself. You can sleep when you're dead.

He looked down at himself. Combat boots, black leather pants he had lifted from the evidence room, black silk T shirt, studded black leather jacket. He looked the part of an aging Goth. Some might consider him a bit long in the tooth, but he would still blend in.

Morris Horn shouldered his way in through the revolving door. He sauntered more easily now than back when he ran the place. Reggie guessed that was what happened when you retired and no longer had to shoulder that burden of responsibility.

Morris surged towards Reggie, a grizzly bear in a cheap suit, rumpled shirt, scuffed shoes. His deeply lined face and downturned mouth looked like he wore a perpetual scowl.

Morris Horn looked like a cop and always would.

"Evening, Captain," Reggie greeted.

Morris dropped his bulk into a cheap government-issue chair beside the desk. The tubular steel frame stressed, sagged a bit under his weight.

"You know you can call me Morris, right?" he replied.

"You'll always be 'Captain' to me."

Morris grinned. "Just so long as you know you don't have to." Secretly, he loved being called Captain.

"How's the L. T.?" he asked, motioning towards the office.

"Stressed."

"I'll bet."

"There's something else."

"Oh?"

"I don't think he enjoys the job anymore."

"What makes you say that?"

"Just a feeling," Reggie said after some thought. "He seems distracted. He's speaking Spanish more."

Morris's eyes drifted to Reggie. "Oh."

"He's got a new nameplate with his full Hispanic name."

"That doesn't necessarily mean anything," Morris countered. "Maybe he's just decided to more fully embrace his culture and heritage."

Reggie stifled a laugh. Fully embracing his culture? Okay, Reggie thought, who are you and what have you done with Morris Horn?"

Morris chuckled. "I'm going soft in my old age."

Reggie's eyes focused on something past Morris. His eyes softened. His tongue licked dry lips. Morris noticed. Curious, he turned in his seat to see what had caught Reggie's attention.

His eyes bulged and his mouth dropped open.

Valerie was walking into the precinct. She wore a skintight black catsuit. It hugged her curves and accentuated her physique. Little was left to the imagination. She clunked towards them in spit-shined combat boots. A black leather jacket sat hooked on two fingers thrown casually over the back of her shoulder. Her shoulder holster resided in a leather harness adorned with studs, and extra leather straps that crisscrossed her chest, separating her breasts.

Morris gulped, turned back around. Reggie pursed his lips together, looked down.

Valerie stopped at her desk. "Hey guys."

"Hey," they both chimed back.

She threw her jacket on. Her gun and holster disappeared. She didn't look like a cop now. And those studded straps across her chest became even more alluring.

"What?" she asked.

"Nothing," both men replied, trying to look casual, occupied, professional.

She knew better. Guys had been panting after her since she was fourteen.

"Men," she muttered to herself as she sat down.

"So why the combat boots?" Morris asked.

"Try running in stilettos."

Maya roamed her house, drifting from useless kitchen to unused bedrooms. Photos adorned the walls -- children, grandchildren. Documentation of lives lived. She had murdered two generations of this family, for no other reason than to take what they had for herself.

Not that she felt bad about it.

This was her life now, her Vampire Father had explained. Rid yourself of human trappings like love, compassion, mercy. Predators such as she, he had instructed, could not afford such luxuries. They only weighed one down.

She floated into the living room.

The dead woman she had drained the night before still sat slumped, taped to the chair. Maya's sharp talons sliced through the bindings. She hoisted the stiffened corpse out of the chair, placed it on the floor in front of her. Arms and legs bent upwards at the hip and shoulders, with another ninety-degree bend at the knees and elbows. She considered waiting another day. The rigor would be gone by then. The body would be as pliable as a rag doll.

No, she would stick to her plan. Her first instinct was usually the right one. And she didn't want to come home to a dirty house tonight.

She glanced to the hideous faux mid-century modern clock on the wall. She really needed to do something about redecorating this place. But first. she had a body to get rid of, and then she had a protégé to kill.

She descended the basement stairs, grabbed a large area rug that stood rolled up against the wall. She flung it over her shoulder, stomped back upstairs.

She unfurled the roll beside the body. Then she forced the dead body's limbs straight. She heard ripping and tearing and snapping as she did. She placed one hand on the rug's edge to keep it flat, used her other arm to roll the stiff-as-a-board corpse where she needed. Then she simply let go. The rug rolled back up on its own. The body was almost completely obscured.

She left her bundle, moved to the back door. She opened the door, listened, alert for any sign of danger. She moved through the yard to the gate in the back fence. She opened the latch, peered into the alley.

Darkness both directions.

She dashed back inside, scooped up the rug and its contents, dashed outside so quickly no human eye could have followed her movements. She zipped into the alley, sped to the dumpster, held the lid open, tossed her load inside. She bolted back into her yard, latched the gate, then ran inside the house.

She had not been seen. The body would most likely be discovered. No concern of hers. There was a serial killer on the loose. And this serial killer was draining his victims' blood from two pinprick punctures in the neck JUST LIKE A VAMPIRE.

Who would have thought that some wannabe vampire would make it easy for a real vampire to cover her own kill?

Life was filled with little ironies.

Charlie Simpkins woke up screaming. He had gone to sleep with a barnburner of a headache, which were becoming more frequent. More intense. Lasting longer and not responding to medication.

That progression was never good.

He held his head in both hands. The room spun. Jesus, this was so not good. And tonight, of all nights! Damned inconvenient. He had a hunt to conduct.

Steeling himself for the unpleasantness to come, Charlie forced himself to stand. He took a deep breath, then staggered forward. He caromed about the room, half-stumbling into the bathroom.

Blinding daggers pierced his skull when he flipped the light switch. He leaned on the pedestal sink, waiting for the pain to subside. When it did, he opened his eyes and regarded himself in the mirror.

Deep lines creased his forehead. Vertical furrows drew down each side of his nose and the corners of his unsmiling mouth. Lank hair hung on his head, the color of dead straw. Restless eyes stared back at him. Two days' stubble darkened his cheeks and chin.

Needing a shower, he ran the water, got it warm, stepped in. He pulled the curtain, stood beneath the spray. He was close to the end. The answer of the ages, the truth of the human soul leaving the body. What mysteries, what wonders would be revealed?

The prospect both exhilarated and terrified him.

What if the answers continued to evade? What if the answers were not what he was hoping for? What if Charlie failed in his quest? Then his life, like the lives of those braindead zombies he drained, would be meaningless.

NO!

He would not accept that, would never accept that. His life had meaning! He was better than the cattle he butchered. He was unique in all the world.

He was Charlie Fucking Simpkins, Fucking Serial Killer Extraordinaire!

But he was tired, so very tired. The pain was worse, and he was hallucinating. After all, had he really had a conversation with a real-life vampire last night? Not likely. Either the woman had been the most gifted cosplayer he had ever seen, or he had imagined the entire thing.

He did not know which prospect alarmed him more.

Charlie toweled off, made his way back into the main room. He picked up his briefcase. He knew everything inside was good to go. But he could never be too careful, never too prepared. That's how other killers got caught: they got stupid. Sloppy. Made mistakes. Left clues.

DNA.

But not Charlie. Oh, no. Charlie wasn't like them. They were mumblecore wannabes; brain-addled, slack-jawed, intellectually challenged mouth breathers.

Not Charlie.

Charlie really was the Serial Killer Extraordinaire. The undisputed Big Fish. He was and would always be The One That Got Away.

He sat naked on his futon, settled the briefcase on the cinderblock and plywood that was his coffee table. He turned the tiny dials on the security lock, pushed the buttons. Springs sprung; tabs snapped open. He opened the case, peered at his latest modifications.

Twin needles waited, welded to the rest of the assembly. The huge clear collection bag rested in the bottom, flat and devoid of air. Tubing snaked from the top of the bag and around the impromptu pump he had devised by cannibalizing a couple of plasmapheresis units. The whole thing was powered by a small array of D-cell batteries. He kept hand pump in case the system failed in the middle of draining a selectee.

Satisfied, he closed the case, pushed in the tabs. He spun the tiny dials, locking the unit.

He got up. His clothes waited for him, neatly stacked on the floor along the far wall.

Time to get dressed.

CHAPTER TWENTY-EIGHT

The Vampire shouldered his way into the precinct. Everyone else was already there. He glided towards them.

He noticed their emanations wafting off them, auras only he could see, with meanings only he could understand. The aura coming off Morris Horn said he was lonely, not very happy, still wondering how his life got so upended that he lost his family.

Reggie's face brightened when he saw him.

"Hey, Grandpa."

"Reginald. How are you, my lad?"

"Ready to catch a killer."

"And how are you tonight, Detective Wahl?" he asked.

"Fine," she said tightly.

He leaned in close to her. "Realize that you have nothing to fear from me."

"If I drove a stake through your heart, would it kill you?"

The Vampire, shocked by the bluntness of the question, threw his head back and laughed. Laughed uproariously. Laughter that came from his belly and inhabited the entire squad room. Laughter that threatened to send red tears streaming down his pallid face.

"No, my sweet girl, no," he answered once his laughter subsided. "It would not send me to my Final Death. But it would anger me. Deeply."

"Because someone tried to kill you?"

"Getting a piece of wood hammered through your chest really, really hurts."

She thought about this a moment. "So, then you've…" She let the rest of her question go unexpressed, lingering in the air.

The Vampire cocked his head, shrugged his shoulders, palms upward. Well, of course he had.

"So, all the stuff in the movies and on TV –"

"Balderdash," he interjected. "Poppycock. Hogwash."

"Bullshit?"

"That, too."

Castillo opened the door to his office, motioned them all to join him. They all filed into the office. Valerie, the last one in, closed the door behind her without having to be told.

Lieutenant Nicolas Castillo addressed them all. It was pretty much the same speech he had given every evening. Almost verbatim. But he knew that sometimes there was nothing more comforting to the troops than an old-fashioned safety briefing.

"All right," he said at last. "Everything by the book. No one inside leaves line of sight."

Everyone nodded. Valerie, last one in and closest to the door, exited first. The rest began filing out behind her.

"Eddie," Nicolas said. The Vampire stopped. "A word, please?"

They waited until they were alone.

"Keep an eye on the lovebirds, will you?"

"Of course."

"I know you and Detective Wahl haven't gelled very well."

"Irrelevant to the task at hand."

Castillo started to say something else, then changed his mind.

"Anything else, Lieutenant Castillo?"

Castillo thought for a moment, then shook his head.

"Let us hope tonight concludes all unfinished business."

"Even Maya?" Castillo asked.

"Especially Maya."

The Vampire exited the office. In the squad room, the Vampire glided past Reggie's desk.

"Hey, Grandpa." The Vampire stopped. "Everything all right?"

"Yes."

Reggie struggled to find the words. "There's something going on with Castillo."

"Indeed."

"Yeah, but it's me and Valerie out there in the middle of things."

"I will be there."

"You have your own enemy to face."

The Vampire turned to his descendant, took off his shades. His black unblinking eyes shined brightly under the lights.

"I will die my Final Death before I allow anything to happen to either one of you."

The Vampire spoke his words softly, clearly. No braggadocio, no loud boasts. Just a simple proclamation from an immortal creature who always meant every word he said.

When Reggie said nothing more, the Vampire turned and floated through the precinct and slipped out the revolving door like a ghost.

"He meant that, didn't he?" Valerie asked.

Reggie looked at her, surprised. She had heard every word. "Yes, he did."

Valerie contemplated this, shook her head. "I wish I could bring myself to trust him.".

"He has proven himself over and over," Reggie said, trying to keep his temper. "He just promised to *fucking die* for us," Reggie reminded her. "What the fuck more do you want?"

"I don't know," she replied truthfully. "I'll know it when I see it."

Outside, the Vampire glided to his Lexus, slid in. He took comfort in the solid *thunk* sound of the door closing and latching. He closed his eyes, slowly breathed in and out several times. He needed a clear head tonight. Logical, analytical thinking would best ensure everyone's survival, including his own.

Emotion was the antithesis of intellect.

He expanded his mind, pushed his consciousness outward in all directions. He found the serial killer easily enough. A cluttered, yet remarkably methodical mind. Ordinarily, the Vampire would go to that sparse apartment in Golden Hills and slaughter him. Tonight, he would leave the human villain to the human police.

Tonight, he had a vampire problem.

His consciousness stumbled upon Maya in a dark house in North Park just south of University Avenue. His eyes popped open in surprise as their minds connected. In her home, Maya gasped in astonishment. Then she threw up protective walls.

He smiled with satisfaction. He knew where she lived. He turned the key in the ignition, backed out carefully, pulled into the street.

Maya no longer held the advantage.

Charlie stood in his claustrophobic bathroom, looking into the mirror. He had already applied white makeup foundation. He enhanced his eyes with dark circles, painted his lips black. Then he carefully inserted snake-eye contact lenses. Lastly, he pulled on his wig. The pricey hairpiece boasted deep fuchsia and jet-black spikes of real human hair jutting up and out from his head. He took a step back, checked himself out in the grimy mirror.

Black boots, black leather pants, black T shirt. Black leather studded jacket. Black nail polish reflected the dull light. The overall effect was precisely what he had intended.

One last hunt, then ghost the entire city.

Maya paced from room to room. Normally, she found the night peaceful. No neighbors shouting, none of that. Hell, none of the neighbors had come over to welcome her to the neighborhood or to inquire about what happened to the previous owners.

She remembered a time when neighbors knew each other. They got along, socialized, chewed the fat now and then, provided community. A sense of belonging. A time when neighbors helped each other out whenever one of them fell on hard times.

Those days were long gone.

That wasn't what was bothering her. She had to confront Eddie one last time, and this time she would not talk her way out of it.

Tonight would be a fight to the death.

Maya had never fought another vampire to the death. She had always talked her way out of confrontations. In New Orleans, she had fled rather than stand and fight. She could have never defeated them. Pack hunters. They would have cornered her then attacked her *en masse*.

She was still in the same situation, but with nowhere left to run. Big cities were already populated with her kind. Small towns meant a nomadic existence: stopping off, feeding for a few nights, then moving on.

That could do for a spell, maybe a couple of decades. But Maya didn't want to run, didn't want a nomadic existence. She was tired of feeling like a coward.

This was it tonight, she. Stand or fall. Bare the fangs; flash the claws. Her life and the San Diego territory was at stake.

Winner takes all.

CHAPTER TWENTY-NINE

The Vampire parked in a paid lot. He locked the door, zipped his jacket, shoved hands in his pockets. He felt cold, of course. A walking corpse, he generated no internal body heat. He had grown so accustomed to it over the years, it was just white noise now, something in the background all the time.

Fog swirled beneath the streetlights, buoyed by a chilly breeze. Condensation clung to every exposed surface. Headlights and taillights of passing cars reflected on wet pavement, red and white jewels bouncing along black asphalt.

He moved like a wraith through the misty urban landscape. Buildings and cars materialized out of the shadows, took form, then disappeared behind him as he passed.

Ever the predator, the Vampire's eyes scanned both sides of the street. People were out. They always were on Friday night. Creeps: druggies, alkies. But mostly working folks at the end of a long week. None of them posed any threat to the immortal Creature of Legend that stalked unnoticed amongst them.

As he neared Splinter, his eyes cut through the floating murk. Kong at the plain black metal door. The blue neon sign above, still dark. Oh wait! There it went. It snapped on, letters glowing softly.

He ducked into a narrow alleyway. Enveloped in fog and murk, no human would know he was there. And no human would see what he was about to do.

The Vampire bent at the knee, gathered his strength. He pushed off, exploding upwards. His eyes focused on the ledge of the building as it flew closer. His hands shot upwards. He gripped the ledge and pulled. Momentum pushed him up and over. He landed in a crouch four stories above the ground. He padded across the flat roof, moving to the southwest corner.

The Vampire placed one foot on the ledge, leaned forward. Below him was the T-shaped intersection of F street and 4th. Behind him, 4th stretched northward, crossed over Broadway.

He watched the traffic lights cycle through red to green and back to red. Cars surged and paused, metal blood cells pumping through an asphalt artery. Nothing amiss.

DANGER!

The Vampire dropped to his belly so fast he was down before he realized what had happened. Pure instinct and muscle memory, his body had acted independently.

What had just happened? Why had he hit the deck with such ferocity? He turned his head from side to side. Nothing out of place. He looked past his feet behind him.

He was alone.

He raised his head just enough to peer over the lip of the rooftop. He looked across the street, to the rooftop on the southern border of F street. Then he understood.

Through misty droplets and swirling gloom, Maya had just popped onto the roof and was dusting off the front of her dress. He watched as she strode across the rooftop. She stopped at the northwest corner, peered down through the gauzy haze.

He did not want to relinquish the element of surprise. He lowered his head below the level of the rooftop's lip. Body and head held low to the ground with barely enough room to keep his chest from scraping the rooftop, he scrabbled on his palms and toes towards the opposite corner.

Across the street, Maya scanned the night around her. Her vampire eyes pierced the night like searchlights. She smiled, fangs showing in the semi dark. She already thought of San Diego as her own.

After tonight, it would be.

Movement below brought her out of her reverie. She looked down again. She wistful smile fled from her face, only to be replaced by a snarl. Below her and on the other side of the street, Eddie trotted towards the huge doorman standing beneath that gauche neon sign.

Kong turned as the Vampire materialized out of the fog. His heartbeat picked up as he recognized the creature coming towards him.

"I come in peace," the Vampire said.

Kong wanted to believe him.

"Oh, you can believe me, I assure you," the Vampire said.

Kong reached for the door.

"A moment, please."

Kong stopped, looked quizzically at the monster in front of him.

"There will be trouble here tonight."

"Trouble?" the big man asked warily.

"Another like me," he said. "You will know her when you see her."

"I know the one."

"Stay out of our way," the Vampire whispered darkly.

"And if the fight spills out up here?"

"Run," the Vampire said. "As fast as you can."

Maya stood on the rooftop, livid with rage. How could she have been so fucking stupid? He must have already been here, hiding.

Lying in wait for her.

She stalked across the rooftop and leapt off. She dropped easily into the alleyway forty feet below. She rose from her crouched position, advanced towards the main street's dimly lit sidewalk.

She emerged from the darkness, moved to the curb as she looked across 4th Street. She stepped into the street, casting a wary glance north. Everything was halted at the streetlight at the intersection of 4th and F.

She reached the other side, hopped onto the curb and the sidewalk beyond. She glided closer towards Splinter. The big man had his back to her, facing north. Most of the club patrons would be coming either from the north off Broadway, or from the east down F Street. She calmed her mind and silenced her movements.

Kong was scared, scared enough he had put in his two-week notice to the owners earlier today. Astonished, they felt this came at the worst possible time. They reminded him of the ongoing police investigation and that there was a serial killer stalking the patrons. They offered him more money. He turned it down. The way he saw things, after spending every weekend for the last seven years standing outside while everyone else had fun, and never getting a pay raise in all that time, he was simply done with it.

Finish strong, he told himself, then walk away from this forever. New pursuits. New chapter. He smiled, warmed as hope for the future swelled within him.

Never underestimate the benefits of reinventing yourself.

Kong did not hear Maya's approach. Her stealth was absolute. She paused a few feet behind him. She heard his steady heartbeat, read his thoughts. Sensed his true desires.

A poet, huh?

Well, the world needed poets. The world needed artists of all kinds, especially with all the craziness going on nowadays. Art could dispel fear and anger. It could cool hot hatred. It could foster understanding.

Art could speak to the human soul.

Art filled the world with beauty and wonder.

Art was humanity at its best.

She would not kill this mountain of a man, this human the size of Bigfoot, who also possessed the heart of a poet. Better to let him live.

"Good evening, Kong," she said.

Kong spun around, studied her a moment. Short, barely over five feet. Slender, dainty. African American, dark skin that somehow looked bloodless. Eyes hidden behind fashionable sunglasses. Corset cinched at the waist. Flowing dress. Boots underneath.

"Go ahead."

She stepped around him, glided towards the heavy metal door.

"Let me," he offered.

She pulled on the handle with one arm, opened the door like it was weightless.

"I got it."

They stared at each other for a moment.

"You're real, aren't you?" Dread in his voice.

"A real what?"

"Vampire."

She smiled, showing her fangs. Real ones.

"The other one told me to stay out of your way."

"Sage advice." She paused, then, "I doubt if we shall see each other after tonight," she added. "Farewell, Ernest. And best of luck to you."

Maya turned and disappeared inside. The door clanged shut behind her. It reminded Kong of all those old prison movies he had seen where the convicted felon gets locked up in his cell for the first time, knowing he would never breathe free air again.

But really, fucking *vampires*?

"I'm done," Kong grumbled under his breath. He turned and walked off into the night.

Inside, huge speakers blared the discordant noise that passed for music. Not Maya's personal tastes, but it complemented the themes of darkness, danger, gloom, despair. She failed to understand what people found attractive about this so-called Vampire lifestyle. Yet just as the current crop aged out, got jobs, got married, had kids, took on more traditional responsibilities, a fresh batch of disenfranchised youngsters appeared. A never-ending supply of misfits and outcasts shunned by society, left alone, cut adrift.

Not that Maya felt sorry for them.

To each their own, right?

People were free to live on the fringes, far removed from the mainstream. The fringes often attracted new pilgrims.

Mainstream life was not what their parents had promised.

Some blamed their parents. Others blamed a discriminatory and exclusionary society. The truth, Maya suspected, was more nuanced than oversimplified talking points. Perhaps the truth lay somewhere in the middle, that gray area no one talked about. Most parents did their best for their children, to raise functioning adults.

The great paradox of being a parent was, if you did it right, you worked yourself out of the job. Effective parenting meant raising a child that could survive and thrive on their own.

And therein lurked a darker, more problematic paradox. By the time a child became an adult, the society that the parent had raised that child to function within no longer existed. Parents could not raise a child for the society of the future. The future was a moving target. No one knew where society was going, when it would get there, or what it would look like.

That was why Maya preferred the present.

Live for today, for there may be no tomorrow.

For her, there might truly be no tomorrow.

She grabbed the iron handrail and descended the concrete staircase one step at a time. Black eyes moved constantly behind the dark glasses. Silvery hair billowed away from her face. The front of her dress danced from the rhythmic movement of her legs underneath.

She spotted him almost immediately.

Eddie Marx, human son of German immigrants, born in Hoboken, New Jersey in 1898. Maya's vampiric first born. He sat alone at a table near the dance floor. Having spotted her, he glared at her from behind his sunglasses. Violent emotions coming off him. She smelled his hatred and lethal intent.

No apprehension. No nervousness.

No heartbeat.

A truly magnificent beast. One of the deadliest creatures to ever stalk the Earth, Eddie Marx feared *no one.*

The door at the top of the stairs opened behind her. Three women and one man entered. They didn't know where Kong was tonight, but they guessed that meant no cover charge. Talk about luck!

Maya cruised directly across the floor towards Eddie. He surveilled her approach, ready to explode into deadly motion. She pulled a chair out, sat down. She folded her hands, placed them in front of her. The Vampire leaned forward, clasped his hands as well.

"So," she said.

The Vampire said nothing.

"I hate this music."

The Vampire said nothing.

"We can still avoid bloodshed."

"Leave my territory," the Vampire said.

He turned his thin hands palms upwards, a short of shrug without moving the shoulders. The lower half of his face remained impassive.

She sat back in a huff. "You are one of the most stubborn creatures I have ever met," she exclaimed. "How about I wipe that smug grin right off your face?"

The Vampire shrugged, said, "Bring it on."

She stood. "Before the night's out, I will."

The Vampire grinned. "Ooooooooh," he cooed. "Now we're talking."

Maya stood up, backed away.

The surveillance van crept down 4th Street, carrying Valerie, Reggie, Morris, and Nicolas. They passed Splinter's unattended door.

The van parallel parked in a faded handicap parking spot. Nicolas demonstrated admirable big city parallel parking skills, then crawled through the blue curtains separating the front cabin from the back.

Morris sat at his surveillance station in front of a monitor. Headphones sat perched on his skull, not yet down over his ears. Reggie and Valerie waited silently.

They opened the door, got out, closed the door back without a word. Nicolas sat down in front of his monitor. He and Morris powered up their equipment.

Outside the van, Valerie and Reggie walked side by side. They stopped near where Kong should have been.

"Where's Kong?" Valerie asked.

"Don't know."

"Do you think he's running late?"

"He's never late."

They both knew something was wrong.

He grabbed the metal handle, pulled the door open. Valerie crossed the threshold onto the top landing. He followed her inside. They descended the staircase with a sense of purpose.

Music assaulted them as they scanned the crowd. They saw the Vampire sitting quietly near the dance floor. An untouched adult beverage slowly warmed in front of him. He saw them but made no overt acknowledgement.

"You think that other vampire is here?" Valerie asked.

"Probably."

"What if she wins?"

"We track her down and destroy her in the sunlight."

She shuddered. His simple, matter-of-fact tone held no illusion that Reggie would do precisely what he said. She understood the other vampire was evil, but to be so casual about destroying her seemed... *callous*.

Then she remembered the shootout and the carnage she saw in her rookie year when the Department responded to the firefight at Reggie's old apartment. Reggie was accustomed to dealing with vampires. He a five-year head start on her.

They reached the bottom of the stairs. Reggie leaned close.

"Grab a table. I'll get drinks."

Reggie went to the bar, shouted an order to the bartender. Valerie sashayed across the floor. She chose a table at the far end from the bar. She could see the entire main floor, the hallway to the bathrooms, the staircase. She could even see the stairs leading to The Grotto.

A good vantage point.

She sat down, stole a glance at the Vampire. He ignored her completely, his attention focused elsewhere. She followed his gaze across the floor, up the stairs, and into The Grotto.

Was somebody already up there slinking in the shadows, waiting for the right time to pounce?

Not my circus; not my monkeys, she decided. Let him handle vampire shit.

Don't overload your plate, Val.

The Vampire heard Valerie's thoughts. She was correct. He did not acknowledge her for fear of blowing her cover. He would not be why some pathetic loser serial killer called it a night and slipped away.

He noticed Reginald slip by him carrying a drink in each hand, but never broke gaze from The Grotto. Maya sat there alone in the dark, aloof, and far removed from the rest of the club.

An apt metaphor, he thought.

Reggie placed a drink in front of Valerie. She thanked him. He flashed his dazzling smile, sat down next to her. Now they could both scan the entire club from the street level door and staircase, across the entire bar and seating area, band riser, dance floor, even to the hallways, bathrooms, and rear emergency exit.

Reggie adjusted the earwig in his ear.

"Can you hear me?"

"Loud and clear," came the response.

"How about me?" Valerie asked.

"Same, same," Nicolas said.

They sipped their drinks, put them down. They would nurse these drinks for the next several hours, drinking just enough to stay in character, but not enough to get sloppy with the work. That could get people killed.

Maya watched the entire play unfold before her. The two cops were there with Eddie. Well, more accurately, Eddie was there to watch their backs as they stalked their serial killer.

While she liked him, she did not care whether Charlie Simpkins lived or died. Sure, she thought the world was more colorful with him in it. But if he got caught or killed, it would not alter her life. It was just fun watching a wolf amongst the sheep.

The wolves were interchangeable. True predators in a world of sheeple were rare. That's what made it fun to observe. But each were easily replaced. If Charlie got caught or killed, there was someone else out there somewhere, slicing and dicing their way to take his place.

Such was the hypocritical nature of man.

Men loved to speak of humanity: peace and love, tolerance and inclusion. Convenient words easily spoken when times were good. But when the chips were down and someone had been wronged, humans became vile, vicious, vengeful creatures. Peace, love, tolerance went out the window. And they committed acts of barbaric cruelty, then justified it by saying some atrocity had been previously done to them.

No creature on the planet could surpass *homo sapiens* when it came to heaping violence, cruelty, depravity, sadism, and inhumanity upon their fellow human beings.

CHAPTER THIRTY

The night moved on. Valerie had taken up at a separate table. She knew the killer picked loners close to closing time. She suspected he came in early to scout, pick a victim, then toy with the entire process as it suited him.

The band showed up. They brought in their instruments, amplifiers, microphones. The drummer started assembling his kit. The others plugged everything in, slung their guitars and basses over their shoulders. Then they started tuning up.

The crowd inside increased. Everyone seemed in a good mood. Some of them wondered where Kong was. Others were happy they didn't have to pay to get in. That meant more money for drinks.

Charlie Simpkins, soon to be a previous resident of San Diego, parked his van facing south on the east side of 4th, near the intersection with G Street. He noticed the windowless van parked in the gloom across the street when he pulled up but paid no mind. An older van with the name and phone number of an electrical repairman was not an uncommon sight.

Charlie looked over his shoulder. His briefcase lay in the back, waiting. He smiled to himself.

He shouldered the rusty driver's door open. He got out, wrestled the protesting door closed again. When he got to wherever he was going next, he was going to ditch this heap and get something else.

Swirling fog greeted Charlie. The night had grown colder, and the fog had rolled in thicker. Real pea soup. Hard to see anything.

He walked north, looking once again at the dark, seemingly unoccupied van parked across the street. He had seen that van before somewhere. But where? He couldn't place it. That disturbed him.

He paused at the crosswalk, pushed the button for the pedestrian light. He stood there, looked across the street. Even through the gloom, he could make out blue signage glowing pale and weak. The heavy door was closed.

Something was wrong with this picture. What was it? Seconds later, he knew. A group of four goth types shambled down the opposite sidewalk. When they reached the door, they paused, looked around. They seemed confused. Then one of them flung the door open and motioned to her friends. The rest of them went inside, began descending the stairs. The door banged shut behind them.

Where the hell was Kong?

The light changed. Charlie stepped off the curb. He walked inside the crosswalk, just feet away from the cars that occupied each of the lanes. As he crossed, one car revved its engine, trying to startle him. Determined to not react in any anticipated fashion, he stopped, turned, and looked directly at the car.

Inside the car, the driver said, "Check out this fuckin' guy."

The driver let his foot off the brake. The car lurched forward, came to stop with the bumper about two inches from Charlie's knees. Charlie balled up a fist and swung an overarching swing and brought his fist down hard on the car's hood. The front end dipped a bit from the impact.

The driver opened his door, got about halfway out of the car.

"Hey, motherfucker! What the fuck's your problem?"

"What the fuck is yours?" Charlie replied.

A handgun appeared in the driver's hand like magic. He pointed at Charlie.

"Motherfucker, I'll shoot your ass."

Charlie did not waver. He stood still, like a stone statue. His eyes burned directly into the body and soul of the driver, whose gun hand started to waver ever so slightly.

The driver now seemed unsure. None of this had gone according to plan. People usually cowered whenever he pulled a gun.

Not this guy.

"Either shoot me or get back in that metal roadkill you call a car," Charlie growled. "But don't waste my fucking time."

The light changed. Car horns blared. The driver seemed frozen in place, unable to act. Charlie smiled, turned, and finished walking to the curb.

The driver looked back at the cars waiting for him to move. Finally, he got back in and took off. The driver flipped Charlie the bird as the they disappeared into the night.

Charlie stood on the sidewalk seething. Miscreants like that were what made the world such a fucked-up place. Uneducated morons who thought carrying a gun made them tough. Made them hard. Those mindless asshats had no clue, no understanding what being hard really was.

The kid with the gun had never killed anyone. Charlie had seen it in his eyes: the uncertainty, a hint of fear. Charlie had looked into the eyes of hard men. Hardened criminals, murderers, serial killers, veteran cops, guys coming back from Iraq or Afghanistan. Men who came from different backgrounds, different parts of the country. The one thing they all had in common was, they had killed other human beings. They had all been forced to find that line within themselves, the line that most humans never cross, that line some people even deny exists, and they had stepped across it.

A line that once crossed, could never be uncrossed.

It scarred people for life and followed them for the rest of their days.

No one got a do-over.

He breathed in and out, centered himself. Time to get back on his game. After all, he was Charlie Simpkins, the Serial Killer Extraordinaire, the guy who had an entire city of edge and the police baffled. He had a reputation to uphold.

He would show these zombies one last time who and what he was, and why people were right to fear him.

As he stood there watching the traffic ebb and flow, his mind engaged once more. Something wasn't right tonight. The mood, the atmosphere, the whole vibe this evening. It floated in the air itself.

Something just felt... wrong.

The voice in his head urged him to abort. Walk away. Get back in his van and leave San Diego. Right fucking now. The voice kept warning him, over and over.

All the signs were there.

The parked van. Dark. Unmoving. Vaguely familiar. Yet so innocuous. He might have seen it anywhere. But where? And where was Kong? That guy never missed work.

Bad omens.

The voice in his head kept pleading with him. It was the voice of caution. The voice of reason. The voice that had kept him from getting caught or killed.

Ordinarily, He would have listened. He trusted its sage advice. But that voice was drowned out by another voice. Another impulse, another imperative. A stronger compulsion.

The itch that must be scratched.

Charlie Simpkins was in a mood tonight, frustrated, ready to explode. The darkness within that propelled him could not be denied. Any attempt to contain it now would be as ineffective as standing on a beach and waiting for the waves to stop crashing onto the shoreline.

Charlie couldn't deny what he was. Didn't want to. There problem wasn't him. The problem was all the other people out there, living brief, miserable, pointless lives. Human sheep, content to be herded, told where to go, told what to do from the cradle to the grave. Passive, submissive, anonymous and stupid, easily led, easily ensnared.

Not Charlie Simpkins. He looked like them, acted like them. But he was nothing like them.

He was a predator in a world teeming with prey.

"Excuse me?" came a female voice from behind him.

He turned. A young woman and her friend, both decked out in Goth attire, black and white makeup, and a dribble of fake blood at the corners of their mouths, stood a few feet away.

"Where's Kong?" she asked.

Charlie had to fight the impulse to smash her face in, knock her to the ground, and bash her head to a bloody pulp against the concrete sidewalk. He said nothing. But in his mind, he bashed her head again and again, hearing the skull fracture like the shell of a boiled egg, seeing bright red blood flash across gray pavement.

Both women stepped back. They saw something truly dark and dangerous slithering behind this stranger's eyes. On a visceral level, they knew they had made a mistake by speaking to him. They moved quickly towards the door and slipped inside.

He watched them go, flicked his tongue across his teeth. He forgot about them immediately. They were not worth another second of his valuable time.

He gazed out into the hazy night. Fog swirled, spun by wind eddies. His eyes drifted to the parked electrical van once more. It disquieted him. But he had to see this through no matter what.

Charlie yanked the handle back, stepped inside. He took the stairs one at a time, descending slowly, one hand lightly wrapped around the iron banister.

Good crowd tonight. The bar was busy, the customers crowded four deep. Quite a few tables were occupied. The house band was still tuning up -- if you could call it that. The music would be as jagged as glass shards. It usually gave him a headache, but the regulars here seemed to revel in it.

No matter. Charlie was here on business.

He queued in line for the bar. He placed and paid for his order, a simple bottle of beer. He turned away, eyes scanning the room again behind serpentine contact lenses. He focused on a lone male sitting quietly at a table.

Pale. Thin. Waxy sallow skin.

Curious, Charlie ambled through the crowd, sashaying this way and that, avoiding people and tables. He moved towards this Pale Hunter, who had spotted him, but appeared outwardly uninterested. He knew he and this hunter were kindred spirits, worthy of mutual respect. Professional courtesy.

He walked up to the table, pulled out a chair without asking, and sat down uninvited across from the person he now called the Pale Hunter.

The Vampire had been aware of Charlie's presence. His mood had soured the moment he laid eyes on this arrogant little pissant. He noticed the evil wafting off this sorry excuse of a sentient being right away. Evil so virulent and putrid, he could smell its foul stench.

It disgusted him.

It took every ounce of the Vampire's self-discipline to keep from killing this impudent jackal for sitting down uninvited across from him. One movement of his arm, one flick of his wrist, his hand flat, long thin fingers extended. Fingernails like talons. Slicing the throat.

Blood gushing between fingers, pouring from beneath clutched hands. Eyes bulging. Unable to speak, blood spreading down the front of his clothes, pooling like red water on the concrete floor.

The thought pleased him.

"What are you smiling at?"

The question, asked innocuously enough, brought the Vampire back to reality. Charlie sat across from him, very much alive. No torn flesh, no gaping wound, no geysering blood.

Reality was overrated, the Vampire thought.

"Something that brought me momentary pleasure."

"I'm Charlie."

"Yes, you are."

"What's your name?"

"Unimportant."

Charlie paused. This guy was different, all right. But also, familiar. His overall appearance, his restrained aura, his slow and deliberate mannerisms reminded him of someone. Then it hit him.

"You're one of them, aren't you?" Charlie asked.

The Vampire's eyebrows wrinkled together behind his sunglasses.

"Them?"

"I met another one recently. A Black woman. Maya." He paused, then, "I think she liked me."

"She would."

"Do you like me?"

"No."

"Why not?"

"You are an amateur," the Vampire hissed. "I am a professional."

"I'm a killer just like you. And her."

"You are nothing like us."

On the stage, the drummer counted off a four-beat on his drumsticks. Then the band charged into their first number. It was as bad and as patina as the Vampire had feared.

"Is your friend here?"

"Maya is not my friend."

"You're kind of standoffish, aren't you?" Charlie sipped his beer.

"Why are you here?"

"The same reason you're here," Charlie replied. "To hunt prey."

"Perhaps I have found mine," the Vampire growled.

"No need to be rude," Charlie countered. "I'm trying to show you professional courtesy."

"It would be wiser to leave me alone and give me a wide berth," the Vampire stated. "If you were a professional, you would know that."

A few tables over, Reggie leaned back in his chair, appearing casual. But he was watching the conversation out of the corner of his eye. He could not hear what they were saying, but Reggie recognized the look on Grandpa's face, the disgust, the contempt.

Was the pipsqueak who they were after?

"You could at least try to be polite," Charlie grumbled.

"I am being honest."

"How about I reach across this table and rearrange your dental work?"

The Vampire unclasped his hands, laid them flat on the bistro table. He leaned slowly forward.

"Go ahead," he said.

"Excuse me?"

"I shall not."

Charlie considered his options. He had challenged the Pale Hunter, and the Pale Hunter had called his bluff. This monster before him, this walking corpse that fed on human blood, was not in the least bit afraid of Charlie. That much was clear.

Charlie said, "Fuck you, you bloodless corpse," and stood up.

"Now you reveal your true self," the Vampire replied.

Charlie glared down at the Vampire. He grabbed his sweating bottle and stalked off. He lumbered right past Reggie and never even looked at him.

Reggie saw the Vampire glance in his direction, then slightly tic his head in the direction of the retreating Charlie. Reggie understood. He put his hand over his mouth, trying to appear casual, natural.

"Target acquired," he spoke lowly.

"Acknowledged," he heard Castillo say.

"Who?" Valerie whispered into his ear.

"Short guy with the red streaked hair. Snake eye contacts."

"Got him."

From her darkened vantage point within the Grotto, Maya watched events unfold. She heard the conversation. She was not surprised when Charlie had gotten up and stormed off.

Eddie had that effect on people.

She picked out the two undercover cops. She also picked up on the pheromones wafting between them. Even though they were trying to remain detached and professional, she could smell their mutual desire.

They were in love.

That's nice, she thought.

But if they got in her way, she would butcher them both.

In the van, time plodded on. Both Morris and Nicolas kept their headphones on while staring at the live feed. Empty coffee cups sat beside their feet on the floor. Wadded food wrappers littered the floor.

"I hate stakeouts," Morris blurted. "About as exciting as watching paint dry."

Morris looked at the LED clock above his monitor. Red digits relayed to him the time in hours, minutes, advancing seconds. A new minute clicked into place.

"You certain he's gonna take the bait?"

"Did you see what she's wearing?" Nicolas pointed. "Hell, I'm gay and I'd do her."

Morris chuckled. "TMI, Nico."

"Seriously," Nicolas continued, "he'll take the bait."

"The trial will take for-fucking-ever," Morris said. "It'll be years before he's convicted."

"Maybe he'll resist, pull a weapon; give us an excuse to kill him. Save the taxpayers a shit-ton of money."

Morris had known Nicolas for years now. Decades. He never heard such darkness come out of him. He pried his eyes away from the screen at looked at his former protégé.

"I'd be good with that."

Detective Valerie Wahl had her target in her sights. Everyone kept waiting for him to make the first move. He might be the killer, but then again, maybe he was just another socially awkward, disenfranchised creep.

Time to find out.

She downed the last of her drink, stood up.

"Umm, Valerie," she heard Reggie say guardedly, "what are you doing?"

"Detective Wahl?" Lieutenant Castillo chimed in.

She ignored them, ran her hands down her torso, adjusted her boobs. If she was going to do this, she had to sell it. She strode across the space, stood in front of Charlie where he sat. He looked up at her.

"Hey there," she said. "You wanna dance?"

"How about if I buy you a drink instead?"

She flashed a smile that she hoped was seductive. She sat down across from him. A waitress wandered by. Charlie ordered drinks for them both. The waitress took the order, adjusted her corset, disappeared into the crowd.

"So," she opened, "come here often?"

"Does that line actually work?"

She grinned, shrugged.

"The answer is, yes. Whenever I can." He waved around in several directions. "A great place to indulge one's fantasies."

"And what fantasies do you indulge?" she cooed.

"Depends on who else is here on any given night."

"And what do you do once you find the right partner?"

"I scratch my itch."

He smiled. A darkness there that chilled Valerie to her core.

"And does it take two in order to scratch your particular itch?"

"Absolutely."

Reggie sat up a little straighter. Outside in the van, Nicolas and Morris leaned in, worked the controls to zoom in on this mystery man's face. But the cameras were low-resolution, and the lighting was bad. His features were indistinct. Hopefully they could enhance the images later.

"So, what's your name?" Valerie asked.

"Charlie," he said. "And yours?"

"Janet."

He knew she was lying. "Well, Janet, what should we do next?"

She had him on the hook. She needed to reel him in.

"What do you think we should do?"

Charlie thought about the syringe in his pocket filled with Ketamine.

"Whatever you desire," he parried.

The Vampire sat without moving as Charlie led Valerie onto the dance floor. The band was in the middle of a song, but that didn't seem to matter here. Charlie and Valerie found a spot between other gyrating couples and began their own dance. Charlie turned out to be surprisingly good. The Vampire had assumed Charlie's dancing would be more like someone getting shocked by an electrical outlet.

He had assumed wrong.

But Valerie was operating on a whole different level, that of God-given talent. She swished and swayed, ground her hips, moved her hands across her body. She was good, and it became clear to the Vampire that she knew it. He smiled to himself, shifted his eyes off the dance floor and towards the Grotto. Up in the dark distance, with the ceiling so close a grown man couldn't stand up straight, sat Maya.

Waiting to make her move.

He understood. She wanted him off balance, on pins and needles wondering when she might strike. The fatal flaw with that was, he did not care when she made her move. He could make a move of his own and end this.

Attack or defend; live or die. One fate or the other, this thing ended tonight. Before the next dawn.

The Vampire had lived far too long anyway. He did not want to die, but he was not afraid of it. The Final Death would not be the worst thing to endure. No, the worst was going on and on, night after night, year after year (and now, century after century), fumbling through this terminal Forever Night, ruminating on all that he had lost. Sure, he was wealthy. Money in the bank, real estate holdings in several states and a couple of foreign countries, an investment portfolio that earned over ten per cent in a bear market that was threatening to slip into full-blown recession.

None of that mattered.

What mattered was what he had lost. The people, loved ones lost over the ages.

The people one loves, he mused. Family. Friends. Descendants. Those are only things that hold lasting value. The people one holds in love and who love him back are a man's legacy.

What, then, would be the Vampire's legacy?

Time was his fiercest enemy. Time was everyone's enemy. He had just been given more time than most. But time eventually ran out for everyone, even vampires.

His father, his mother, his lover Danae, his own son. More relatives down through the years, and most recently, his beloved Lot-Lot.

Without her, his melancholy knew no bounds.

His legacy, his way of leaving the world a better place, would be seeing his sole surviving descendant succeed, both on this case, and in life. He would ensure Maya did not threaten, harass, or murder his great, great grandson. She would do something that simply out of spite.

But time was her enemy, too. He could use that against her. That was the key to striking at Maya where she was as vulnerable as he. One, or perhaps both, would die with the coming dawn.

The Vampire would be at peace with either outcome.

CHAPTER THIRTY-ONE

Condensation collected on the outside of Reggie's glass, ran down the bottle, puddled around the bottom. He had been hit on by a half dozen girls and a couple of men. He had declined them all. He felt a slight twinge of jealousy watching Valerie dance with several partners over the course of the night. She had finished with their suspect, and he had gone back to his table while she remained on the floor.

Reggie looked around. Valerie was dancing a slow dance with a young Hispanic woman who was as thin as a rail and wore platform stilettos. He caught sight of their suspect, Charlie, who sulked alone at his table. He had refreshed his drink a couple of times over the course of the evening. Reggie hoped that if Charlie was sloshed, he might be easier to subdue.

He shifted his gaze to Grandpa Eddie sitting still, an undead statue. No movement to his face. No discernable rise and fall to the chest. And of course, no heart beating within it. No circulating blood. No pulse, no blood pressure. For about the thousandth time, Reggie wondered at the dark magic that allowed his great, great Grandfather to walk undetected amongst the living. But his ancestor himself did not know, did not understand why or how this was possible.

Grandpa Eddie referred to anything about vampirism he did not understand as magic. When asked why, he had replied, "What is magic if not science or technology we do not understand?"

Reggie had never forgotten that.

The Vampire sat, his face impassive behind his sunglasses. He gazed upwards. Maya had not moved. No one had attempted to join her. It was like she had silently forbidden anyone to enter her realm.

Alone and aloof. That told the Vampire everything he needed to know. Not that it told him anything new, but it confirmed that she had not altered her established pattern of behavior.

Vampires were creatures of habit. They were chained to certain behaviors, certain routines and rituals to ensure their protection against any who would harm then during daylight hours. It was a matter of survival. Like all other creatures on Earth, vampires shared that same universal instinct for survival.

The Vampire grew impatient.

Valerie came off the dance floor, her face flushed almost as red as her hair. She plunked down into her chair. A fresh, ice-cold drink awaited her. Surprised, she glanced up and smiled at Reggie.

She curled her fingers around the stem, hoisted the glass to her lips. A fruity burn slid like sweet molten lava down her throat. Warmth in her chest. She licked her lips, placed the glass in front of her. She wiped her face and forehead with an extra cocktail napkin.

The young Hispanic woman she had been dancing with ambled up. Upswept hair with a sprinkle of dark glitter across her cheeks and forehead, she was a pretty woman beneath all the layers. She invited Valerie to join her. She pointed at a booth already stuffed with vampire Goth women.

No men.

When Valerie pointed out that the booth looked full already, the young woman said they could pull up an extra chair. Valerie thanked her but declined. The woman walked away disappointed.

Valerie looked to Reggie, who had a smirk plastered across his face.

"Popular girl," he said.

"Shut up," she replied.

He grinned good naturedly at her.

Across the room, Charlie watched everything play out. There was something "off" about the luscious redhead. Her name was definitely not Janet. Even as a kid, he could always tell when people were lying, even people who were good at it.

Something aroused his interest anew. Non-Janet had looked towards the black guy. They had interacted briefly, subtly, then they had both whispered something. But they were too far apart for lip reading.

They were speaking into some kind of sophisticated communication system. But why communicate in such a way? Made no sense to him. What kind of sick, twisted, voyeuristic, vicarious game were these two playing?

And more importantly, could he join in?

Then a cold jolt hit him like an icy lightning bolt to the brain. They weren't playing a game. They were hunting.

Hunting him.

Cops. Trying to find him. Arrest him. Bring him in. Stop him from completing his life's work.

His first impulse was to kill them both. Chances of escape were slim. The Pale Hunter would not let him go. Hell, what if Vampy was working with them? He was not worried about the cops. But tangling with a vampire was a different matter entirely.

He thought about leaving then hesitated. Cops downstairs meant cops upstairs as well. Another piece of the puzzle fell into place.

That van outside was their command post. It looked like a junker, but it was no doubt a state-of-the-art electronic surveillance center.

He had stupidly ignored the warning signs he had sensed. Now he was trapped.

He needed to stay calm and think this through.

Valerie covered her hand over her mouth then spoke into the mic hidden in the wrist band of her catsuit.

"The suspect seems agitated."

Reggie resisted the temptation to turn around and scour the room.

That is your killer, the Vampire spoke telepathically to Reggie.

"God, I hate it when you do that, Grandpa," he said as he rubbed his temple.

"What?" Valerie asked.

"Nothing." Reggie had spoken out loud without intending to. "He's our guy."

"So, what's the move?"

Reggie checked his watch. It was after one now. The club closed at two. State law and all.

"I'm working on it," he said.

"Keep it by the book," Castillo whispered into their ears.

"Roger that," both cops answered back.

"What's the move?" Valerie asked again.

"Still working on it."

Valerie stood up.

"Val. What are you doing?" Reggie asked.

"Making a move."

She strolled towards Charlie's table. He watched her approach, his defenses up. He would kill her the first chance he got. He had to abort, no way around it. Others would stop to render aid, and he could flee in the confusion.

She pulled a chair out and sat down without waiting for an invitation.

"I saw you sitting over here all sad and lonely," she cooed. "Thought I'd come over and keep you company."

"What makes you think I want your company?"

"You need somebody's company."

"But why yours?"

She grinned. "I bring a lot to the table," she answered. "And to the bedroom."

Charlie noted her pretty face, charming smile, and smokin' hot body. His eyes focused past her, beyond her. He saw the Black guy who now looked so incredibly out of place he might as well have had a neon sign flashing around his neck, watching them and pretending he was not. Charlie likewise noticed the

Pale Hunter. That creature seemed quite intent on what Charlie and Valerie were discussing.

Could the Pale Hunter hear them? From all the way across the room with all this ungodly noise? Perhaps he could ask Maya about this. In fact, perhaps he could convince Maya to make him a vampire, too. Then his Life's Work could stretch out across centuries, across eons, into eternity.

A Mission, everlasting.

Charlie liked that idea.

"You have no idea what I'm looking for tonight… *cop*."

He noticed both the Black man and the Pale Hunter stiffened in their seats. Charlie dropped all pretenses. He slipped into fight or flight mode.

"What makes you think I'm a cop?" she asked.

"Well, you are, aren't you?"

"Do I look like a cop to you?"

Charlie almost killed her right then.

"It's rude to answer a question with a question," he snarled. "Look me in the eye and tell me you're not a fucking pig."

She hesitated, and that was all Charlie needed to see. His suspicions confirmed, he remembered the Ketamine syringe.

"You can't deny you're a cop and then arrest me," he said. "That's entrapment."

"Look, I thought we might have some fun," she said. "I guess I was wrong."

"Everything about you is wrong." His hand snaked into his pocket under the table. His fingers curled around the spring-loaded pocketknife he carried. The same knife he had used to kill his apartment manager. Four-inch blade, incredibly sharp.

"I'm leaving," he stated. "Don't follow me," he added, knowing that she would.

"Is that a threat?"

He pulled the knife out of his pocket, held it in his cupped hand. His thumb rested on the spring button.

"Take it any way you like."

He stood up, began turning away from her. She leaned across the table, made a grab for his arm.

And left herself open.

A rookie mistake.

Charlie pushed the button on the knife. The blade opened in the blink of an eye and locked into place as Charlie brought his arm back in a reverse arch. Quick, efficient. The knife went across the front of her throat and sliced through skin and muscle.

At first, Valerie felt no pain. She was simply astounded. The world seemed to stop. Everyone frozen in place. Her hand drifted up to her throat and clutched just as blood gushed out, spilling between her fingers, over her hand, and down her front.

Charlie took a step back. Reggie surged forward, as did the Vampire. People around him shrank back. Charlie held the knife up, brandished it as he moved towards the staircase. No heroes here. Everyone gave him a wide berth.

Reggie gripped Valerie by the shoulders just as her knees buckled. He saw the blood pooling around her feet like red water.

"Val!"

The Vampire knelt beside her, quickly assessed the damage. She was terminal.

Valerie's panicked eyes pleaded with Reggie. She tried to speak, but he shushed her. She clutched his arm with red wet hands.

Reggie looked at the Vampire, tears blurring his vision.

"Do something."

"Like what?"

"I can't lose her, Grandpa."

Charlie had gotten to the stairs by now.

"You do not understand what you're asking."

"I don't care."

"There would be… ramifications."

"Grandpa. Please!"

Valerie reached out towards the Vampire. He looked at her. She nodded with the last of her fading strength.

The Vampire removed his sunglasses. His shiny black eyes reflected in the low light.

Charlie was climbing the stairs.

"Very well then," he said. "Leave this to me." He paused, then, "And Reginald?"

"Yes, Grandpa?"

"Do not let him escape."

Reggie pulled his gun, stood up. Then he bolted towards the staircase.

Valerie clutched at the Vampire's arm. He looked down, saw her bloodless face, pale lips. He read her mind.

Please don't let me die.

"There are consequences," he warned. "Long-term consequences."

I don't care. I love Reggie.

The Vampire empathized.

"Very well."

He lunged forward quickly and bit deeply. He supped, feeling her warmth, her lifeforce draining out of her. Then he nicked his own lip with a fang and placed his mouth over hers. Blood and saliva dribbled into her slack mouth. He heard her final thought.

Thank you.

The Vampire stood up, towering over Detective Valerie Wahl's lifeless corpse.

"Do not thank me just yet, Young One," he whispered. "I have done you no favors here tonight."

Charlie burst through the metal door at the top of the stairs. He had barely taken two steps when he found himself face to face with two cops. One was Hispanic, thin, well dressed. The other a Black man who resembled a brick wall in a crumpled suit.

Both had guns already trained on him.

"Freeze, asshole," the Hispanic snarled.

"Drop the weapon," the Black guy ordered.

"No," Charlie replied.

"I said drop the weapon."

"No."

"He said drop the weapon," the Hispanic said.

"Or what?" Charlie challenged. "You'll shoot me? Do I look like I give a fuck?"

"How about I just fucking kill you?" Reggie said as he stepped into the fray.

Charlie smirked. "You can't, and you know it."

"No?"

"Look around!" Charlie gestured expansively. "Security cameras, CCTV, all hooked into Government servers. You're on candid camera. The cloud is forever, Loverboy. And the cameras see all.

Charlie noticed the Pale Hunter had silently emerged from inside Splinter. No one else seemed to notice.

"You can't just kill me. You have rules. Laws. And the law says that even people like me have rights."

Silence fell upon them. The three cops glanced at each other.

Charlie grinned, evil menace behind it.

"You know I'm right. You have to play by your own fucking rules."

The Vampire stepped forward, stood beside Reggie.

"Gentlemen," the Vampire addressed them. He looked to Reggie.

"May I?"

Reggie paused, looking down the barrel of his pistol. His rage and hatred knew no bounds. He was tapdancing on the edge of the abyss.

Charlie stared back at Reggie, completely unafraid.

A darkness black and deep filled Reggie's mind. It obliterated his intellect, obscured his logic. Reggie was pure animal now, a primal man, wanting to kill the person who had just killed his woman.

Reggie placed his finger inside the trigger guard, began to exert pressure. To squeeze the trigger, not to jerk it.

Never jerk it.

Somewhere, deep in Reggie's soul, a voice in the boiling darkness of his hatred, faint, indistinct, screamed something. It screamed it again, the voice becoming louder. Decipherable.

Don't do this, it said. Because then, he wins. Don't make him right about you.

His finger eased off the trigger.

"You are a good and moral man, Reginald Downing," the Vampire said. "A far better man than I."

The Vampire stalked forward. His prey grinned at him, thinking he was ready for what the Vampire would bring. His prey crouched, knife steady and held out in front of him.

"Gonna give me something to work with?" Charlie taunted. "Or are you just a bit... too long in the tooth?"

The three detectives dropped their weapons to their sides, stepped back. They knew what was coming. They just didn't want any of it on their clothes.

The Vampire advanced not at all concerned about Charlie's pathetic weapon. He ducked and weaved, then his hand flashed out. He grabbed Charlie's knife hand by the wrist and squeezed, compressing tendon and bone. The hand went numb immediately. The knife clattered harmlessly on the pavement. The Vampire shifted, grabbed the back of Charlie's elbow, and *pushed.* He heard satisfying snaps as tendons ruptured and bones fractured.

Charlie grunted and twisted with the angle, trying to minimize the damage. He swung a fist with his free hand but could not get any real power behind it. He couldn't land a punch.

The Vampire grabbed Charlie by the throat with his free hand, crushed his esophagus beneath an iron grip. He lifted Charlie off the ground.

"No matter how tough you think you are, no matter how strong, or how fast, there is always someone tougher, stronger, faster, and more ruthless," the Vampire said. "Most people never meet that person." His eyes narrowed. "You have just met yours."

Charlie dangled in the air, his feet a foot and a half off the ground. For the first time, fear began to creep into his eyes. The Vampire saw it, smiled sadistically.

"Now you know what it is to be a victim, Charlie Simpkins."

The Vampire lowered Charlie to the ground. He still held him by the throat. Charlie's face was turning purple. His lips were cyanotic.

Morris, Nicolas, and Reggie all stood by silently. Occasionally, one of them looked around, making sure no civilians saw this, or worse, recorded it on their phones and upload it to social media.

The Vampire yanked Charlie towards him.

"You think you are dangerous?" the Vampire taunted.

With his one good hand, Charlie pulled the Ketamine syringe out of his pocket, jabbed it into the Vampire's neck. He grunted as he pushed the plunger all the way down.

The Vampire stiffened, went stock still. Then he trembled, like every muscle in his body locked down. A look of shock spread across his undead face. His breaths came in shallow rapid pants.

"Dangerous enough," Charlie snapped.

The Vampire's grip never weakened. His panting gave way to mocking laughter. Charlie's face fell.

"You think a syringe can effect one who has been dead for over one hundred years?" the Vampire asked. "You know nothing."

Charlie thought about pulling the needle out of the Vampire's neck. Maybe stab him again, this time in the eye.

"Because you *are* nothing," the Vampire said, completing his thought.

Before Charlie could react, the Vampire bared his fangs and shoved his claw like fingernails deep into Charlie's neck on both sides of the esophagus. He closed his grip until his fingers touch somewhere near Charlie's cervical spine.

Charlie's eyes bulged in shock. His mouth opened. No sound came out.

The Vampire pushed down, forcing Charlie to his knees. He placed his free hand on Charlie's shoulder over the collarbone, extended his arm until his elbow locked. He pushed with that hand while simultaneously pulling on Charlie's throat. The Vampire snarled, then yanked back hard, ripping a huge chunk of Charlie's throat and underlying tissue clean out.

Blood gushed everywhere. Charlie's hands immediately tried to clutch at the gaping hole to staunch the bleeding. Reggie saw directly into Charlie's anatomy. Light glinted inside, illuminating the back of his throat as his life force spilled over his hands, drenched the pavement at his feet.

Merciless, the Vampire kicked Charlie in the chest, savagely sending him backwards onto the pavement. Bright red fountained up as the dying serial killer fell back.

"Fucking amateur," the Vampire rumbled.

Charlie reached out to clutch at the Vampire's leg. The Vampire took a step backwards.

This can't be how it ends, Charlie thought. My mission. My life's work! No answers. No truth. Now I will never know. People would have known my name forever*! It's not fair!*

The Vampire squatted beside him.

"There is nothing special about you, Charles. A year from now, no one will remember your name," he said. "You have been squashed like the insignificant, annoying little insect you are."

His strength gone, Charlie rolled onto his back. Eyes looking upward, pleading.

Just like all his victims.

In those final seconds, Charlie's face drained of all emotion. The inner light faded; his eyes glazed over, became lusterless. He died with nothing more than a feeble sigh that escaped from the terrible rent in his throat.

Everyone looked on, awash with mixed thoughts and feelings.

Still lost in the Bloodlust, the Vampire looked at the gory chunk still grasped in his dripping hand. He tossed the chunk through the air. It landed wetly at Reggie's feet.

"A pound of flesh," the Vampire snarled.

By the time they got back downstairs, everyone had fled. By the looks of things, they left in a hurry. Bottles spilled on tables, glasses at the bar. Overturned chairs. Musical instruments left onstage.

Valerie lay still in a pool of her own coagulating blood. It felt like a dagger in Reggie's heart to see her like that. Panic and grief gripped him.

"Did you do it?" Reggie asked.

"Yes," the Vampire said, licking his fingers clean of Charlie's blood.

"Will it work?"

"We will know by tomorrow night."

Morris stood by the body. Nicolas descended the staircase, a white sheet folded and tucked under one arm. When he got to her, he and Morris covered her up.

The Vampire noticed none of this. Burning hatred blazed anew as he glared up into the Grotto. His enemy. His challenger. His nemesis.

Maya.

The Vampire stepped away from the police and the corpse. He stalked towards the Grotto and the darkness that consumed it. Towards the darkness that had long ago consumed Maya and now threatened to consume him.

He climbed the concrete steps. She did not move. She waited, an undead Jack in the Box with fangs, held down by a locked coiled spring.

Tight, waiting to be sprung.

The Vampire stopped in front of her.

"Charlie is dead?"

"Very."

"Did you Turn him?"

"No."

"But you Turned her."

"I made the attempt."

"The attempt?"

"I have never Turned anyone before," he stated. "I am unsure of the correct procedure."

"It will be interesting to see if it succeeds."

"You will not see it," he replied. He snarled, his upper lip lifting one side, exposing a single fang.

"Prepare for the Final Death... *Mother.*"

CHAPTER THIRTY-TWO

Maya exploded into motion. She grabbed the heavy table, heaved it up and over, tossing it in the Vampire's direction. One edge clipped him across the face, knocking him back. He tumbled backwards down the stairs onto the main floor.

Reggie, Morris, and Nicolas all jumped, drew their weapons. When they saw Maya descending the stairs, they opened fire. Bullets impacted her chest. Professionals that they were, they all fired at center of mass. She staggered back, screaming and spitting.

They stopped firing, knowing they could not kill her. Conserve ammo. Their goal was to give the Vampire a few seconds to recover.

They succeeded.

The Vampire leapt to his feet, hissing, hands slashing, thin fingers tipped with razor-sharp fingernails. Claws like a jungle cat.

"San Diego is mine," she spoke. "Leave. Begone. Flee as I fled my last feeding grounds."

"I will kill you to defend what is mine," the Vampire responded. "Are willing to die to take it?"

She stole a quick glance towards the humans. "How about I kill them first?"

The Vampire moved laterally, putting himself between Maya and them.

"Go ahead."

He crouched slightly, bending at the knees. Hands by his sides, fingers extended, elbows bent.

Claws out.

Maya smiled, a predator anticipating the meal to come.

They moved simultaneously, charging at each other. Fangs bared, claws extended. Muscles tense.

Souls hating.

They slammed into each other with a force that made the humans wince. Maya slashed at him; he grabbed both her wrists and pushed back, holding her at bay for a moment.

"Should we shoot her?" Morris asked.

"This is between them," Reggie answered.

"Harsh."

"Their world. Their rules. Not our place to interfere."

Maya swung her foot, kicked the Vampire squarely in the groin. He faltered, the pain blinding him. She wrenched one hand free and slashed at him, gouging four deep furrows across his face, from his ear to his nose beneath one eye. His face snapped around from the impact, then he looked at her, his hatred so deep his black eyes began to change, still black but now with hints of a deep crimson red.

His face wounds did not bleed.

The Vampire lashed out instinctively. He scored an impact, dragged his fingers across her chest, lacerating clothes, rending flesh beneath. The force staggered Maya, pushed her back two steps. He pressed the attack, baring his fangs and going for her throat.

She managed to get an arm up and deflect his thrusting head.

Nicolas turned and headed for the stairs.

"Where you going, lieutenant?" Reggie asked.

"Someone needs to stay with the body upstairs," he responded. "And someone needs to call this in."

Both Morris and Reggie knew he was right. There was nothing they could do here. And even though the thought of leaving Valerie here unattended broke his heart, Reggie turned to follow Nicolas upstairs.

The vampires would settle this as only they could.

The humans scampered up the staircase as the unearthly combatants continued waging their private war. Clutching at each other, they spilled over a table. They went crashing to the unforgiving concrete floor. The table overturned. Chairs got upended. Glasses shattered.

The Vampire kept his mind blank. He knew that if he took time to think, he would be Finally Dead. He was not going to give up his city, his territory, his home, and his feeding grounds to a vampiric parasite like Maya.

Sometimes, family had nothing to do with those who made you. Sometimes, family was the people you loved and who loved you back. The ones who accepted you as you were, loved you unconditionally, and demanded nothing in return.

Using his speed, the Vampire slashed again. Nails created a gruesome gulley along Maya's left jaw. She kicked him hard in the belly, then landed another kick to his chest. The Vampire flew backwards, crashing over another table and tumbling to the floor.

Maya did not press her attack. Instantly on his feet, he read her mind. This was not going the way she had hoped. He had proven himself more capable than she had predicted. The confidence she showed outwardly was a façade.

She was scared.

He realized that she had been scared all her life. Her ever-present fear and the lingering bitterness she had about her own assault and murder fueled an undying hatred.

"Don't you dare pity me!" she growled through gritted teeth.

"I don't," he answered her. "I understand what made you the monster you are."

"A barbarism so horrific I came back from Death itself to exact justice."

"You exacted revenge."

Maya shrugged. "Sometimes, they are one in the same. As you well know."

Somewhere, a church bell rang in the new hour. No human could have heard it in the subterranean club, but both vampires did. Four bells. Four a.m.

Dawn was approaching.

To the Vampire's astonishment, Maya bolted and charged up the stairs. He went after her with everything he had.

Outside, Lieutenant Castillo took charge of the scene. Other units had arrived. Cruisers parked at different angles, sat across the intersection. Engines silent, doors open, lights flashing. CSU was just now pulling up.

Charlie Simpkins' ravaged corpse lay on the pavement. Throat ripped out, bloody chunk on the sidewalk nearby. Rheumy eyes open, pupils dilated, staring upwards into nothingness. There was little question as to cause of death. The body lay in a pool of coagulated blood that reflected darkly off the sidewalk.

A fitting end, Nicolas thought. Good riddance. The world was a better place with Charlie Simpkins no longer in it.

The CSU techs stood at the rear of their van, donning white coveralls over their street clothes. They zipped up, adjusted medical masks and gloves, grabbed clipboards and black pens.

Reggie stood near the body, careful to not get too close.

Morris had retreated to the shadows. He leaned against a wall, quite relaxed. Why not? He was no longer a cop, no longer in charge of anything but himself. As long as he got paid, he was cool. Tomorrow morning, none of this would be his headache.

The heavy metal door to Splinter burst open from some tremendous force from inside. It did not simply swing open. The door exploded outward, ripping off its hinges with a loud screech of twisting, tearing metal.

Everyone spun around, gasped as the door broke clear and flew forward. The heavy door landed on the concrete with a bang, slid close to a yard before coming to a stop near Nicolas' feet.

Maya erupted out of the darkness, moving so quickly she could hardly be seen. She pushed past one uniformed cop, knocking him to the ground and breaking three of his ribs. She leapt from the sidewalk to the top of the Coroner's van, then leapt again, this time upwards and across the intersection. She landed on a rooftop and disappeared.

The Vampire flew out of the black hole that was Slinter's doorway. He skidded to a stop, looked around.

"Where?" he asked.

Reggie pointed. "Up there."

"Thank you."

"Hey, Eddie," Nicolas called.

"Yes?"

Nicolas tossed something to him. Something small and compact. The Vampire caught it in midair, glanced down at it, then looked to the lieutenant, an unspoken question in his eyes.

"GPS tracker."

The Vampire slipped it into his pocket. He then bounded to the top of the Coroner's van. From there he crouched and leapt, following Maya's scent. He landed atop the same building, then sped away.

The CSU techs and the uniformed cops all stood aghast, speechless. Finally, one of them looked at Nicolas.

"What the hell was that?" the female cop asked.

"What?"

"That!" she pointed. "Those two... people? How the hell did they do that?"

"What two people?" he asked innocently.

She could not believe what she was hearing. "Uh, the two people who just jumped onto a fucking rooftop!"

The lieutenant looked confused. "Leaping onto a rooftop?" He shook his head. "I didn't see anyone leap onto a rooftop." He looked to Reggie. "Detective. Did you see anything?"

"No, Lieutenant Castillo," Reggie chimed in. "I didn't see anything like that."

"See?" He now glared at the young cop. "We didn't see anything," he grumbled. "And neither did you. Do you understand?"

The young cop gulped, not wanting to derail her own career, but still... "What about that door?"

"What door?"

"The one that got torn off its hinges and thrown at you."

"Oh. That," Castillo smiled. "Why, that door was like that when we got here. Wasn't it, Detective?"

"Yes, Lieutenant."

"I know what I saw, sir."

The easy smile left Nicolas' face. A menacing look spread across his face, chilling the young cop to her core.

"You saw exactly what I say you saw," he snarled. "And you never saw two people jump up to the rooftop. And that door was on the ground when you got here." He paused, then, "Do you understand?"

"Yes sir," she sighed in defeat.

And in that moment, Lieutenant Nicolas Castillo truly hated his job.

The Vampire moved quickly, vaulting from roof to roof, building to building. The jumps across multiple lanes should have caused him trepidation, but he was so focused on Maya, he simply kept going.

He had considered his car, but he was afraid she might escape. She already had a head start. He could not see her. He relied on his sense of smell. Like a dog following his nose.

Suddenly, the scent was gone. He skidded to a stop. He saw nothing. He heard nothing. Frustration rising, he tilted his head back, sniffed the air. Turned, sniffed in another direction.

Nothing.

He was about to scream in rage when, as if sensing his distress, the wind shifted. Her scent, faint as it was, now filled his nostrils. Like a bloodhound tracking its quarry, he bolted forward and kept moving. He ran at incredible speed, savoring the kill to come.

Up ahead, Maya moved quickly, running, jumping. She wished she had taken the time to get another car. Her Vampire Son would pursue her regardless.

If she could not outrun him, outfight him, or outsmart him, then at least she could lead him to where she wanted to make her stand. A place where she felt comfortable. Where she felt safe.

Where she felt strong.

As she rocketed east across the rooftops, she allowed her mind to think of her house. She thought of the interior layout, mentally recited the street address.

Now he knew where to go, where to meet her. Where they would fight.

Where one of them would die forever.

Back at Splinter, Nicolas and Morris stood near the wrecked door. Fog still thick like an old 40s noir movie. Condensation clung to every exposed surface. Moisture beaded on the enormous black door inert on the sidewalk. Morris half expected Humphrey Bogart to appear out of the fog wearing his trademark fedora and trench coat.

They both overheard a CSU tech marvel aloud at the force it must have taken to rip a door off its hinges and hurl it across the sidewalk. When asked directly, both Nicolas and Morris claimed it was like that when they got there.

Downstairs, Reggie stood near the bar, watching investigators scurry about, taking photos, shooting video, collecting evidence. Valerie had been placed into a body bag. Her face and neck were still visible. He watched her disappear as they zipped the bag closed.

His heart was in his throat. Adrenaline coursed through him. His pulse and blood pressure were off the charts. He feared that Valerie might not wake up. What if Grandpa Eddie had failed? Or worse still, what if she woke up and felt differently about Reggie?

They hoisted her remains onto a waiting gurney and secured her in place with long Velcro straps at the knees and the chest. Then one of them pushed the laden gurney towards the emergency exit.

As they pushed her away, Reggie feared that he had lost Valerie forever. His grief knew no bounds.

Upstairs, Nicolas' thumbs typed furiously as he sent a text. Morris noted the furrowed brow and serious expression on his former protégée's face.

"Everything all right?" he asked.

Nicolas hit SEND. "Fine."

"Someone texting you this time of night?"

"I sent a text to my brother."

"Your what?"

"Alejandro Domingo." Nicolas noted Morris' expression. "Same father, different mothers."

"Good to know," Morris said. "I guess the question now is, what's next?"

"I'm glad you asked," Nicolas answered. He did something on his phone, then held it up for Morris to see. The screen displayed a street map of the city. A pulsating red dot moved in one direction, then turned, then turned again.

"The GPS tracker you gave Eddie." Morris looked at the location. "He's headed into North Park."

"He's after that undead bitch that threatened all of us."

"Shouldn't we go help?"

"Not sure what we can do," Nicolas said. "This is a vampire thing."

"Point taken."

Movement at the open entrance garnered their attention. Reggie had climbed the stairs and was now emerging from the club. He walked over to his colleagues. His shoulders sagged with fatigue.

"Here's the plan," Nicolas said. "We stay here and follow protocol and procedures. We have two crime scenes to work."

"What about Grandpa Edie?"

"He's gotta do this on his own."

Maya sped along the empty streets of North Park. No sound. She rushed eastward on University Avenue, knew that Eddie trailed behind her. If the roles had been reversed, she would do the same.

The final conflict had been set in motion. Events had to run their course. No turning back. No do-overs, no negotiations.

No peace.

She would fight him one on one and would prevail. Her very life depended on it. She had avoided conflict before, making the grievous error of civility with those New Orleans vampires.

Look how that turned out.

She should have stayed and fought. She probably would have died the Final Death, but perhaps it would have been worth it. A death protecting what you hold dear has dignity.

Running from your problems doesn't solve them, she realized. Problems have a nasty habit of following a person and then pop up like herpes, at a different place, at the worst possible time.

Maya slowed, came to a stop directly beneath a streetlight. She stood on the corner of 29th and University, in front of a shuttered building front. The cavernous space inside had once housed a coffee house called Claire de Lune, which had been a creative and cultural hub for artists of all kinds on the local North Park scene. Creatives from all over San Diego had flocked to it for years.

Now it sat empty. Dark, foreboding. Slightly creepy. FOR LEASE signs plastered on the inside of the enormous front windows.

Maya turned, looked westward. In the distance, she caught sight of her protégée. He dashed forward, following her scent. She saw him skid to a stop himself about a block away. The intense, vicious look on his face told her everything she needed to know.

Killing Eddie was the right thing to do. The only thing to do. Sending him to Final Death was preferable to fleeing again. She was cornered. Nowhere left to run.

There is nothing more dangerous than a person with nothing left to lose.

She took off her sunglasses, glared directly at him. He took his off, stared straight back at her.
Time is short, she mentally pushed. *The dawn approaches.*
You shall never endure another, he pushed back.
After I kill you, she thought, *I will drain that beautiful great, great grandson of yours. I will Turn him, make him mine. Just like you.*
The Vampire understood Maya's ploy. By threatening his family, she was saying he was already defeated. Trying to get a rise out of him.
Good luck with that, he responded.
She cleared her mind of conscious thought. He did the same. She tilted her head, motioned towards a side street. The Vampire barely had time to register her meaning before she took off again, moving just as swiftly as before. She disappeared in a dark blur and was gone.
He moved forward, but more slowly. Caution seemed prudent at this point. Still moving faster than a human, he moved at what for him was a relaxed pace, one he could maintain all night. Her scent was unmistakable; every footstep left an olfactory signpost.
All he had to do was follow.
He moved away from the lit street. Houses on both sides. Dark. Quiet. Everyone asleep. No streetlights. Dark shadows and swirling fog.
He slowed to a walk. He heard the heartbeats of sleeping humans inside their houses. Behind locked windows and doors where they felt safe. Safe from the world, safe from the environment, safe from criminals.
Oh, if they only knew.
No one was ever truly safe in today's world.
And no one was ever truly safe from the likes of him.

If he fell tonight, no one in all of San Diego would be safe from Maya. She would feed indiscriminately on innocents. The mother coming home from her third part time job to put food on the table. The working man shuffling home from a twelve-hour shift because he wanted to buy those new sneakers for his kid. The bus driver up early to shuttle the public to their morning shifts. The baker. The barista.

The paramedic. The firefighter. The cop.

Their wives.

Their children.

The Vampire was not fighting for his own life; he was fighting for theirs.

Criminals deserved the justice he meted out. They chose their lives. So, they had to face the fatal consequences. But honest, hardworking people just trying to get by and raise a family was a different thing entirely. They did not deserve to be slaughtered on a whim. They did not deserve to live in fear. They did not deserve to be stalked by a cold-blooded, amoral, merciless monster.

Honest people deserved better than that.

They deserved *better* than Maya.

He closed off his mind as he glided deeper into the shadows. His silent movement kicked up swirling eddies of fog that reached out for him after he had passed.

Grass wet from dew. Car windows fogged up. Water droplets beaded up on car hoods. The Vampire flitted past them silently; a supernatural specter moving on a breeze; hinted at, glimpsed at the periphery of one's vision, but when turning to look directly, it was already gone.

With his mental defenses up, Maya would not know when and from which direction he would attack. Homefield advantage, indeed! She had only been here for a few weeks. He had called San Diego home for decades. And if he ever gave it up, he would never leave its fate to the likes of Maya.

As he strolled along, he found one house from which no indications of life emanated. He stopped, stared at the house.

Dark inside. Sitting silently, squatting in the dank night. No car in the driveway. No light on the porch. No movement inside.

The stench of death emanated from it. He smelled it from across the street. People had died here. Violently.

People. Plural.

Maya's kind of place.

He moved closer, approaching diagonally. She was inside watching the front, cognizant of the back. But there was more than two ways in. And really, going through a front door? That was too blasé for him.

He would search for a more dramatic entrance; to engage Maya in what would be the Final Act for this unfolding drama.

Every drama had to end sometime.

CHAPTER THIRTY-THREE

Maya waited inside. She had entered the house through the back, had placed silver-bladed knives in various rooms throughout the house. She had staged them so they would not be obvious, but within easy reach.

Vampires were deathly allergic to silver. She had no idea why. Touching silver caused something akin to anaphylactic shock. Lips and tongue swelled, red rash and hives appeared diffuse across the pale skin. Pain radiated throughout the body. And if the blade was plunged in deep, like into the heart, well, that could certainly incapacitate a vampire long enough to lop off a head or set him on fire, sending him (or her) to the Final Death.

Maya had no intention of setting Eddie on fire. She liked her home, wanted to stay here a while. Decapitation sounded good. No vampire survived a disconnected central nervous system.

She stalked over to the front window, peeked through a gap in the curtains. Nothing but shadows and gloom. Slate gray fog roiled on the breeze. Cars sat unused in driveways. Houses hunched against the elements.

Almost five a.m. Dawn was coming. He had to be close.

Outside, the Vampire had already crept up her driveway, disappeared beneath the carport roof. He saw the side door at the top of three steps. That door would probably put him in the kitchen. This was a common design to houses of the period. But Maya might anticipate that. The Vampire decided to leave the side entrance alone.

He made his way through the side yard. Another house, quiet and still, rested beside him. He came to the fence, saw the gate. He reached out to open the gate, then paused. He took a step back.

The Vampire surged forward two steps and leapt up and over. He pulled his knees to his chest at the top of his arc, cleared the gate easily. He landed soundlessly. Short brown grass in the dehydrated back yard. He plastered himself against the outside wall.

He closed his eyes, breathed out. Calmed himself.

Maya deserved to die. She had invaded his territory; had violated the sanctity of his family. She had invaded his Lot-Lot's home, then threatened his Reginald. And she had murdered Father Ng.

No way she lived after tonight.

He turned and looked down the length of the single-story house. A couple of windows, a back door. She would anticipate his entry through one of these portals. He knew that he would.

What to do?

Something caught his eye. Immediately intrigued, he found himself looking at the dark, squat, and wide window and the basement beyond.

A basement?

Rare in San Diego.

The window was designed to open only part way, creating a vent. The window was locked. While prudent, a simple window lock would prove no match for him.

He felt along the edge of the window, found the locking mechanism that rested sturdy and strong on the other side of the glass. He placed one hand at the corner of the glass where it sat within its metal frame and pushed.

The lock held. Impressed, he pushed harder. He heard a soft click as the mechanism buckled beneath his power. The window opened outward, stopped at about a thirty-degree angle.

Enough room for a child or perhaps, but not enough room for a man, even a slender man such as himself.

The Vampire grasped the upper frame with both hands. He pulled and pushed downward, applying a steady, increasing pressure. The bolts holding the frame open broke. The window fell open and lay on the ground. The Vampire slipped through.

He dropped to the floor with the grace of a jungle cat. He stayed still for a moment, crouched down, hands on the cool concrete. He heard movement upstairs. Not urgent or running.

He heard soft footfalls towards the front of the house. She was trying to see him coming from outside.

She did not know he was here.

A sadistic grin slowly spread across his pasty face. A fang gleamed silver in the night. He rose to his feet, hands at his side.

This might be fun.

Things were wrapping up at the Splinter. Both bodies had been photographed from every angle imaginable. The entire property, both street level and below, had been carefully videotaped. At several points, the police videographer had stopped, squatted, panned, tilted, zoomed in, zoomed out. Everything to document the evidence. Both corpses had been hoisted into the Coroner's van, which was pulling away right now.

Reggie looked worried and exhausted. Both Morris and Nicolas understood. The woman he had been hoping would be his girlfriend (and maybe more!) was dead. But in the world of vampires, death was not always permanent.

Sometimes, it was just damned inconvenient.

Castillo signed a control form, handed it back to a technician. The tech moved away, fulfilling her duties. Morris drifted over to him. They both looked at Reggie, leaning against the building, forlorn and alone.

"Damn," Morris breathed. "It's gotta be hard on the guy, you know?"

"I'm glad it's not me."

Morris nodded in agreement. Then he frowned, serious.

"People were asking a lot of awkward questions."

"The questions aren't awkward," Nicolas replied, "it's the answers."

"How do you write this up?"

"I don't know, he answered. "It sure as hell can't be the truth."

"The secrets that weigh upon us down are the ones we never share."

Surprised by this profundity, Nicolas looked at Morris, his eyebrows raised. Morris shrugged.

"Been reading philosophy books lately," he explained. "A lot of spare time these days."

Nicolas smiled. "It will make future conversations more interesting."

Reggie staggered towards them, shuffling on zombie legs, like his knees wouldn't bend anymore.

"Get out of here," Nicolas said. "I got this."

"I don't know where to go."

Lieutenant Castillo reached into his pants pocket, extracted the handheld GPS tracker. He held it out in front of him.

"Go help kill that bloodsucking bitch."

Reggie turned the unit on, pushed a couple of buttons hidden around the edges. The thing zoned in on the Vampire's location. His eyes focused. His face filled with purpose. He walked away without a word.

"Was that a good idea?" Morris inquired.

Castillo looked east. The first hints of dawn, a lighter blue sky that promised the sunrise to come, hung there beyond the city skyline, beyond the mountains further out.

"He'll call us if he needs us," he answered.

The Vampire sensed the coming dawn. It started as a tension headache and an insidious sense of dread. It would metastasize like a free-growing cancer soon enough. He had little time left.

Assuming he survived tonight, he would have the responsibility of raising his Vampire Daughter. She would need to learn how to use her newfound powers, when and where to feed, and precautions to take to survive the daylight hours. Of course, "survive" was a misnomer. Valerie would in fact be dead as a doornail. Just like every other vampire on Earth.

Just like him.

The Vampire pushed these thoughts out of his head. He put his game face on, slipped into combat mode.

Even in the gloom, he picked out details of the stairs leading upward. Bare wood, knotted pine. Color dulled with age; the wood sagged a bit in the middle from decades of use. The stairs would likely creak under his weight. Even in life, the Vampire had only weighed about one hundred forty-five pounds. But it would still be enough to trumpet his approach.

He placed his feet at the side of the steps, where they were nailed into the joist. Moving one foot and one step at a time, the Vampire silently made his way towards the top. He took care to make no sound and to not drop his mental walls.

He reached the top of the steps. No landing. Legs spread wide, feet at the far end of the final step. A closed wooden door stood, inches from his nose.

The Vampire reached out, grabbed the doorknob. Turned slowly. The door was not locked. Stupid of her. Had she not anticipated he could make his way up from beneath? Like a great white shark surging from the depths to snatch a seal swimming near the surface of the ocean? He had seen such events on TV. The shark would shoot up from the inky depths, breech the surface and snatch the hapless seal, its powerful jaws clamping shut around it.

Surprise attack.

Swift. Vicious.

No quarter, no mercy.

The prey never stood a chance.

The door swung open. He took his foot off the top step and padded into the kitchen.

Reggie went back to the precinct, took a long drink of water. So many emotions swirled through his head, making his mind a whirlwind, twisting in all directions. What would he do if Grandpa Eddie died? What would he do if Valerie did not wake up?

Something forgotten shifted in his pants pocket. He pulled the GPS tracker out. The red dot that indicated Grandpa Eddie appeared to be stationary. Either he had met the Final Death, or he had reached Maya's lair.

Reggie placed the tracker on his desk and pulled out his firearm. He had not fired it, but there was no such thing as being too careful with firearms.

He leaned forward in his chair, knees apart. He pointed the weapon downward, pointing towards the floor. He pushed a button on the side of the handle with his thumb. The magazine dropped out of the butt and into his other hand. He inspected the magazine, counted the bullets.

Full magazine.

He slapped the magazine upwards and securely into place. He manually opened the beech partway, just enough for him to see the amber gleam of the fully jacketed round resting inside the chamber. He allowed the breech to inch closed.

He stood, holstered his weapon. He patted the sides of his pockets, reassuring himself he had three other magazines full and waiting on his person. Then he grabbed the tracker, strode to the pegboard that held all the precinct's car keys.

He snatched the key for an unmarked car, headed for the back door.

Peeking out the window, Maya gulped. The eastern sky continued to brighten. Low humidity meant no cloud cover. In minutes, the sun would peer over the horizon, turning the mountains purple, bathing the land in golden light. She fought that same familiar headache, a mental cloudiness that returned every morning. Her body ached it began aging.

Joints stiffened.

Maya did not see or hear the Vampire creep out of the kitchen and pad silently to the edge of the living room. He stood framed in the arched doorway.

"Maya."

He whispered it so softly the single word was a hint, something sensed but neither seen nor truly heard. Too subtle for regular auditory senses. Human ears would not have picked it up.

Maya heard it. Gripped instantly by a primal fear, she froze in place, feet rooted to the ground. The walking corpse momentarily became a statue.

How could she have been so stupid?

Maya straightened her back, squared her slender shoulders. She plastered a confident smile on her face, turned around to face him, even though confidence was the last thing she felt.

"Eddie," she breathed. "At last."

The Vampire did not reply. He stood there, seething with hatred, black unblinking eyes boring into her, into her heart.

Into her soul.

The time for talk had passed; like a freeway exit sign glimpsed through a cloud of dust in a rearview mirror.

His continued silence unnerved her. She gulped. He saw.

A tiny victory for him.

She moved laterally to her right. The Vampire mirrored her movements by moving left. He never took his eyes off her. And he kept himself in front of her, an immovable barrier blocking the doorway between her and the kitchen.

Between her and the basement.

The vampire bolted forward, a black blur in the gloom. Maya tried to turn but was too late. He crunched into her like a savage freight train. She grunted from the impact. He slammed her into the wall so hard drywall cracked from floor to ceiling.

Mouth open, fangs bared, she clawed at his eyes and face. He squinted his eyes shut and turned his head to protect them. He ignored the pain as her talon nails opened four deeply furrowed gashes on each side of his face.

The Vampire hoisted her up in the air and wrenched around, starting momentum. He threw her overhead. She sailed across the living room and thudded against the far wall. She hit headfirst, her neck snapping like a twig. She fell in a heap onto the floor.

The Vampire held his ground.

This was not over.

After a moment, the twisted mass of bone and flesh started moving. Her arms first, turning to place open palms on the hardwood floor. She doggedly pushed herself up, got a knee under her.

He could not yet see her face, but there was something wrong with her head. He watched as she used the wall for support. She got one foot under her, then the other. Then, she turned towards him.

Maya's head hung to one side at a ninety-degree angle. With the vertebrae in her neck broken, it now rested on one shoulder. She glared at him, a mother furious with her child. She grabbed her head on each side. Grunting with effort, she forced her head atop her shoulders, aligning it above her neck. Bones cracked; tendons snapped as she lowered it back into proper position.

"That hurt."

The Vampire stalked towards her. She sprung at him, hands open, talons out. He slapped her hands away and slashed with claws of his own. Sharp nails sliced through her clothes like they weren't even there. His hand raked upwards, starting just above her pubis and slashing upwards through her abdominal cavity and continued upwards to the fleshy area between her breasts.

Maya staggered back, hit again the very wall on which she had broken her neck. This time she stayed on her feet.

Her intestines spilled out of the rents in her abdomen. Black eyes bulged; her mouth fell open. No sound escaped her for a moment as she held the slimy, serpentine insides that hung to the floor and lay in a jellylike mass between her feet.

"Now look at what you've done!" she shouted. "My dress is ruined, you ungrateful little shit!"

He looked at her, a small shrunken woman, shriveling before his blurring eyes. That damned dawn approaching.

"You are an existential threat to my family."

"Family," she spat. "You don't know the meaning of the word." He said nothing. "I should have let you bleed out that night. Danae was right to reject you."

Maya obviously did not know about his and Danae's reconciliation in the final hours of Dane's life. His mouth spread into a lopsided grin.

The Vampire had only moments left. Too late to get home, too late to seek shelter.

Too late even for the basement.

Final Death was upon him. How quickly it had come! He had always thought he would have more time.

At the end of all things, no one ever has more time.

Final Death was inevitable for every plant, every animal; inevitable for all of God's creatures, even dark ones such as himself. He regretted not having been better prepared. But that was a fool's folly, too, wasn't it?

At the end of all things, no one is ever truly prepared.

Maya's legs trembled. Blood red tears spilled at the corners of her eyes. She sunk to her knees, looking incredibly aged.

His body failing him, his strength waning, the Vampire had one last thing to do. Maya could not survive the dawn. That meant protecting his family, protecting his bloodline, even though it meant Final Death for himself.

So be it.

The Vampire surged forward, his body screaming in agony as he forced the undead husk he inhabited to move by sheer force of will. He grabbed a handful of Maya's silver hair, kept moving towards the back door, dragging her behind him. Her intestines dragged behind her, leaving a gruesome slime trail across the wood.

Maya screamed, but it came out as yelps. She was in no shape to fight back. She was being dragged to her Final Death. Her Vampire Son was determined to take her there, even though it meant dying himself.

That was when she realized her fatal error.

No one ever defeats an enemy that determined.

The Vampire lifted one leg and kicked hard at the back door, destroying the doorknob, twisting the hinges beyond their breaking point. The door ripped free and cartwheeled into the sunlit back yard.

He stepped out into the inferno that was the backyard. Light everywhere, fire burning his eyes. He grunted as he yanked Maya outside, pulled her closer. Bringing her to heel. She had stopped screaming now. Her head lolled from side to side, her arms and legs limp noodles.

Steam rose off them both. Their hair. Their boiling skin. From beneath their clothes.

The Vampire took two more steps, stopped. He could not go any further. He lurched around towards Maya. Keeping her hair in a death grip, he fell backwards, taking both himself and her farther from the back doorway and the safety of the darkness within.

His skin mottled, turned red. Blisters bubbled up, filled with putrid fluid, then popped. Viscous green and yellow pus oozed. The pain was excruciating, like nothing he had ever felt. Worse than being shot in that alley so many years ago.

Worse than anything.

Steam gave way to black smoke as the sun's rays hit them full force. In his final seconds, he watched Maya's corpse shrink, crumple within her clothes. Then the clothes caught fire.

She was no more. Truly gone. He hoped that hordes of demons escorted her to whatever Hell awaited.

The Vampire's head thunked onto the ground. In those final moments, all he could think of was family. Danae. Reginald. His Lot-Lot. His heart exploded with a love that knew no bounds. His only regret was that he could no longer keep watch and protect them.

Because that's what a man does for his family.

A quiet smile etched across his mouth. That final motion peeled his lips away from his charred teeth and off his bones. Black flecks, thin as burned paper, carried on the morning air like embers from a fire.

And then the Vampire, that undead creature, that immortal being, the impossible Beast of Legend that had once been sired by man and born of woman and given the name Edwin Thaddeus Marx, left this mortal realm and met his Final Death with courage and grace. An undead creature who died like a man.

Mission accomplished.

CHAPTER THIRTY-FOUR

Reggie sped through the early morning streets, dreading what he might find. The GPS guided him down University, past what used to be Claire de Lune's.

He hung a hard right just after 30th, drove south into the residential neighborhood. He saw one elderly man, dressed in worn slippers and a faded bathrobe, standing on his front porch. Coffee cup in one hand and cigarette in the other, the old codger craned his neck like he was expecting someone.

Reggie stopped, grabbed his two-way radio, got out.

"You the police?" the old man asked. "I called about the racket next door." He pointed to the house on his left.

Reggie flashed his badge.

"Some kind of commotion over there," the old guy said. He rubbed one hand over the top of his bald head. "Sounds like they're killin' each other."

Reggie listened. "I don't hear anything."

"They're quiet now," the old man said.

"Is it usually loud over there?"

"Nope. Quiet couple, keep to themselves." His expression changed as he thought of something. "You know, I haven't seen them outside in weeks now. Their car's gone, too. I thought they were on vacation."

Reggie keyed his radio.

"Lieutenant Castillo, this is Detective Downing. Come back."

"This is Castillo," came the response almost immediately. "State your current location."

Reggie recited the address. Then he added, "Officer needs assistance."

"On our way."

Reggie looked at the neighbor. "You'd best go inside, sir."

"Do you think it's bad?"

"I don't know yet," Reggie lied. "But I want you safe in case there's trouble."

The old man's face softened. He nodded, raised one hand in farewell. He tottered back inside.

Dread hung around Reggie's neck as he hopped onto the front porch. He peered through the front window. Curtains drawn, but through a slight parting, he saw stillness and darkness beyond.

He grabbed the doorknob. Locked. No warrant, but he could plead reasonable suspicion or exigent circumstances later. Right now, he was just worried sick about Grandpa Eddie.

He retraced his steps away from the door, off the porch. He rounded the car port and headed towards the back yard.

Reggie lifted the latch, pushed the gate. It swung wide on quiet hinges. He took a breath, sighed. He attached the radio to his belt, unholstered his firearm. Safety on, he extended his arms outwards and down at a forty-five-degree angle.

He crept forward quietly, knees bent, ready to spring forward, back, or sideways at any moment. He rounded the corner and advanced into the back yard proper. He looked across the yard, came to a stop.

What the hell was he looking at?

Charred human remains lay scattered across the yard. One appeared to have been wearing a dress at some point. They lay close, one hand of each touching. The back door lay splintered on the ground. Twisted hinges indicated violent force.

Grandpa Eddie!

His hand dropped to his side. His knees buckled. He sank to the dry ground. Tears welled up in his eyes.

He was still kneeling, curled forward, when Morris and Nicolas got there. They had both stopped the minute they entered the back yard. They read the scene, understood what had transpired. They approached Reggie slowly, one on each side.

"Reggie," Nicolas said.

Reggie's head lifted. His eyes focused. He wiped the tears away, took a deep breath.

"Yeah."

Reggie pushed himself to his feet. Both Nicolas and Morris made sure to not help. Reggie would not want it, would resent it. He was grieving, but he was still a cop, still a man. Still had to show strength, even if strong was the last thing he felt.

"Grandpa Eddie," Reggie pointed.

"What can we do?"

Reggie frowned in thought. Then he stepped past them to stand over Maya's corpse. He raised one leg and with a grunt, brought his foot down hard, shattering the fragile burned-out skull. Then he did the same thing to her rib cage. The other two caught on, joined in. After about three minutes, they stepped back, looked down at the fruits of their labors.

Maya's remains laid in utter ruins. Bones crunched into black powder; clothes compressed into ash, layered as thin as burnt tissue paper.

"Fuck you, bitch," Reggie muttered under his breath. He spat onto her ashes.

Nicolas and Morris glanced at each other. They said nothing. They both understood Reggie's anger. They were amazed at how well he was holding up considering the circumstances.

"Now what?" Morris asked.

Reggie's eyes squinted as his brain went into overdrive. He could not accept that his Grandpa Eddie, who had lived, died, had been resurrected a vampire was now simply... *gone.*

No. There had to be a way.

Wait a minute...

"Lieutenant, do you remember when we went over to Grandpa's house that night and he was growing his hand back?"

Nicolas nodded. "Yeah. Why?"

"I've got an idea."

Two unmarked squad cars pulled up beside the Vampire's apartment building. Nicolas and Morris got out of one, Reggie out of the other. They met between the two cars.

"Are sure you this will work?" Castillo asked.

"No," Reggie replied. "But I can't live the rest of my days wondering if there wasn't something more I could've done."

They opened the trunk on Castillo's car. The body bag containing the Vampire's charred bones rested inside. Reggie grabbed the bag by the handles. Morris closed the trunk. They climbed the tiled stairs with the iron railing in silence.

Reggie handed the bag to the lieutenant, pulled out his keys. The door opened like nothing terrible had happened. They filed inside, closed the door behind them.

Reggie took the bag, headed into the bathroom. He laid the bag flat on the floor, unzipped the bag. Smoke wafted out, thin tendrils. The bones were still hot. Nicolas and Morris stood near the doorway.

"Help me put him in the bathtub."

Reggie placed the Vampire's skull in the huge clawfoot bathtub. They wordlessly worked together, reassembling the bones, approximating where they would connect inside a living (or unliving!) body. A grotesque jigsaw puzzle where proper completion could mean the difference between life and death.

Once completed, they stood up. Morris stretched his back.

"Okay, kid," Morris said. "Now what?"

"We need to sleep."

"When do we need to be back?"

"Before sunset."

"What happens then?"

Reggie shrugged helplessly.

Morris and Nicolas left.

Reggie staggered into the living room, set his phone's alarm. He had arrangements to make. People to bribe. People to threaten.

But now, sleep.

Reggie's alarm went off. He hit a button to silence it. He swung his legs off the sofa. He listened, heard nothing. Not just nothing out of the ordinary, but truly nothing.

He could see why Grandpa had chosen this place.

He held his phone, stabbed in a number.

Someone picked up. Reggie spoke; they listened. He was very clear about what he wanted, and when and where he wanted it. When the other person protested, Reggie reminded them they were guilty of several felony crimes, many of them Federal. It was in their best interests to comply.

He ended the call, hung his head. God, he hoped this worked. It probably wouldn't, but at this point, Reggie had nothing left to lose.

Later, Nicolas and Morris showed up. Reggie thanked them for coming, then told them who he had called. Nicolas and Morris understood perfectly. Reggie asked them to stay here. He had to pick someone up.

"Who?" Morris asked.

"Valerie," Reggie answered. "I don't want her to wake up and not see a friendly face on her first night as a vampire."

"If she wakes up at all," Nicolas said.

"And what if she wakes up and peels your face like string cheese?" Morris added.

"It's has be done," Reggie said, standing fast.

This was going to be one unusual night.

Around five thirty, a knock came. Nicolas opened the door. Monique the Blood Bank manager stood in the doorway, yellow light spilling down above across her dark face. She did not look happy.

"Monique," Nicolas said. "Come in."

Monique entered without a word, hauling a medium-sized suitcase. Nickolas closed the door.

She pointed to the case. "What the hell do you want with all this?"

"You don't want to know."

About twenty minutes later, footfalls sounded outside. A key hit the lock; the deadbolt slid back. The door opened. Reggie strode in, relief plastered all over his face. He was so happy he could barely contain himself.

A beat later, Valerie walked in. Dressed for work, wearing a pair of large, very dark sunglasses. Monique thought it odd. She remembered the other guy she had seen, also pale, also wearing sunglasses at night. Wraparounds.

Valerie looked and moved much like before. Alabaster pale skin, slightly translucent. Wide mouth, voluptuous lips, firm breasts, flat tummy, strong powerful legs. That same untamable red hair. But if one looked harder, watched her for a while, subtle differences in movement and appearance became noticeable.

"Detective Wahl," Nicolas said, trying to sound professional in front of Monique. "Nice to see you."

"Nice to see you, too," she responded. "She turned her head slightly. "Hello, Morris."

"Detective."

"I take it you've been briefed?" Nicolas queried.

"Reggie explained on the way over."

"Well, then would someone please explain it to me?" Monique demanded. "I've been blackmailed to bring close to a hundred units of blood under the threat of going to prison."

"The word 'blackmail' has such negative connotations," Reggie said. "Think of it as enhanced persuasion."

Everyone followed Reggie out of the living room. Instead of heading into the kitchen, he turned left into the hallway, then made an immediate right. He flicked on the bathroom light.

Valerie was fascinated. She looked at the bones of her creator, her Vampire Father. She had so much to learn, so many questions to ask. She hoped this crazy idea worked. But then again, she had just awakened on a morgue slab after dying the night before. So, who was to say what was crazy and what was not?

Monique stared into the tub with wide, unbelieving eyes. She knew real human bones when she saw them. But what the hell had happened? They looked... burned.

Someone had been set on fire?

And what was up with those oversized canines in the upper arch?

Oh my God.

"She backed away, waving her hands in front of her.

"Uh-uh," she said. "No way. I ain't part of this."

"You're already part of it," Valerie said softly, blocking Monique's exit.

Monique hesitated. Valerie's calm, confident demeanor unnerved her. There was something about this redheaded stranger. But right now, she had to leave, and damn the consequences.

Monique moved forward. "Out of my way." She started to push past Valerie.

Big mistake.

Valerie exploded into motion. She unceremoniously slapped Monique's hands away, grabbed her by the front of her clothes. Then Valerie Wahl, newborn vampire, plucked the rotund woman up off the floor and held her above everyone else.

"What was that you were saying?" Valerie asked casually.

Terrified, Monique could not find her voice.

"Listen very carefully," Valerie instructed. "You will do exactly what they say. To the letter. You will never utter a word of this to anyone."

Monique did not respond.

Valerie shifted, holding Monique up with one arm. She pulled off her sunglasses, revealing her shiny obsidian eyes. She bared sharp fangs.

"Do you understand?"

Monique's bladder contracted. She peed herself, yellow urine staining her clothes.

"I'll take that as a yes." Valerie lowered Monique to the floor. "You screw this up, and you answer to *me*."

Monique's voice still eluded her. She nodded as the newly minted vampire replaced her sunglasses.

"The suitcase," Reggie said. "Go get it."

Monique stumbled out of the bathroom. Valerie followed into the living room and watched her snatch up the luggage. Then she headed back into the bathroom.

Reggie had ducked into the kitchen and returned with a couple of kitchen knives and two pairs of scissors. He passed them out, pulled his own knife from his pocket and flicked it open.

"Get to work."

"I love it when he's forceful," Valerie cooed seductively. She flicked her tongue around her top lip sexually towards Monique, who recoiled, horrified.

Valerie chuckled.

Then they got to work. Everyone grabbed blood bags and sliced them open over the tub. The blood stained the black bones crimson red. They kept at it, working silently. A small pile of empty plastic began forming a heap on the floor.

Morris looked into the tub. The bones were now partially submerged.

"How many do we need to open?" he asked.

"Let's cover the bones and go from there."

"How long do you think this will take?"

"I don't even know if it will work."

"This blood smells funny," Valerie observed. "Something chemical."

"It's the anticoagulant," Monique said to her. "The inside of each bag is coated with a chemical to keep the blood from clotting."

The group kept at their task. Minutes later, all the bags lay empty. Some remnants from the bags stained the floor. Inside the tub, the Vampire's skeletal remains lay submerged beneath a small red lake.

Lieutenant Castillo, Morris, and Monique staggered into the living room, plopped down on the furniture. Morris grabbed the remote, turned the TV on. The TV tuned in on a classic movie channel. A black-and-white Humphrey Bogart movie played.

"What are you doing?" Monique asked.

"Passing the time," Morris answered.

Monique stood. "I have to leave."

Castillo rose, stood in her way.

"You can't keep me prisoner."

"How about I arrest you? You knew what your techs were doing, and as long as you got your cut, you looked the other way."

Her shoulders slumped.

Castillo shook his head. "Everybody wants to be gangster until it's time to do gangster shit." He paused, then, "Sit the fuck down."

Eyes bulging, mouth agape, Monique sat down. Morris took his eyes off the movie to look at his former protégé. He saw a steely glare in the eyes, a tightness to Nicolas' clenched jaw, a slightly forward-leaning, aggressive posture.

Morris grinned approvingly, turned his attention back to the TV.

Reggie led Valerie into the kitchen. "You hungry?" he asked.

"Starving."

"You know what you are, right?"

"A hot, sexy vampire."

Reggie grinned. "Let's get you fed."

Reggie pulled a coffee mug out of the cabinet, extracted a full blood bag out of the refrigerator. He squeezed the frigid blood into the mug until it was nearly full.

"He nukes it in the microwave," Reggie said. "He says it tastes better warmed up."

Valerie grabbed the mug, sniffed it. "He'd know."

She placed it in the microwave, entered numbers, pushed the button. The motor hummed; the mug inside turned slowly around atop a glass plate for even heating.

The microwave shut off with a *DING!* Valerie opened the door, held the mug in front of her, sniffed again.

"Smells good," she said. She put the mug to her lips, took a tentative sip. Then she drank deeply, tilting her head back and chugging it down.

"How is it?" Reggie asked.

Detective Valerie Wahl, San Diego Police Department, and newborn vampire had just participated in her first feeding. She put the mug on the counter, wiped her mouth with her arm.

"Tastes good."

In the bathroom, all remained quiet. Still. Bones in the tub, submerged in blood. No movement, no sound. A casual observer would have noticed no change.

But a casual observer would have been wrong.

The blood level in the tub had receded significantly, even with the rubber plug in place at the bottom of the tub. Red rivulets stained the white sides. The bones were barely covered now.

But they weren't just bones in there anymore.

Ligaments had appeared, ligaments that attached to bones and contracted, pulling together, and forming joints. Deep red muscle fiber appeared as sinewy red worms venturing out, folding in upon themselves, getting bigger, forming tendons, attaching to the bones.

Bubbles formed on the surface of the red bath, popped as more bubbles appeared from underneath. Like soup coming to a slow boil. Steam formed, floated lazily like fog on a lake.

The level kept dropping over the next several minutes. Now, the ragged corpse appeared, red, rail thin, no skin or hair. Just bone and sinew and muscle. Eyes black like stones welled up, filled the eye sockets. The rib cage connected around deflated lungs and a dead, unbeating heart. The fibrous abdominal wall completed forming, held the intestines inside.

A soft sound now, almost a hint of a whisper and nothing more. Movement swirled just beneath the surface.

A pause.

There it was again!

Then...

A thin red hand, all muscle and tendon and ligament and bone, long fingers ending in sharp, pointed nails broke the surface, slowly lifted out of the blood bath, quivered a moment, then clutched the rim of the ancient clawfoot tub.

Journal entry, 08 April

How delighted I am to make this entry. I never thought I would ever again. Not after what happened. I had always been told that sunlight would invariably bring about the Final Death. But I must have unfinished business in this world. Otherwise, why am I still here?

While I am pleased to be back from the netherworld, I am also a bit disappointed. I had anticipated my soul, my consciousness, winding through the cosmos, landing at a destination of peace and harmony in another realm, another dimension, another plane of existence.

What people refer to as Heaven.

I had hoped to have all my questions answered. Instead, I was trapped in endless darkness, floating on a black ocean without water. I remember getting the impression that I was waiting for something, like being placed in a holding cell.

Purgatory, perhaps?

I remember a meme I saw online. It goes something like this: Life and Death were talking one day, and Life asked Death, "Why is it that with all the pain people go through they love me and hate you?" And Death looked at hm and said, "Because you are a beautiful lie whereas I am the terrible truth."

I shall continue in this realm and try to do as little harm as possible. Just as water rushes in behind a ship sailing on the ocean, I will try to leave life as unbroken as possible in my wake.

My hatred for criminals continues unabated. If they cross my path, then they get what they get. They chose their path, just as I chose mine all those years ago. Cause and effect.

We all reap what we sow.

In the weeks since my unexpected resurrection, I have grown back to full strength. It took another blood bath to finish growing back my skin and hair. My eyelids were the last thing to return, and the most painful. I have never understood how the tiniest of body parts can cause such enormous amounts of pain.

By the third night, I was strong enough to venture outside my apartment.

I have relished my time with my Vampire Daughter. Valerie has taken to the Vampire Way with gusto. She is lovely, vivacious. And to her credit, she has a wicked sense of humor about her. Her gifts are similar to mine, with one or two minor variations. All in all, her gifts may help in her work. She is still a detective, permanently assigned to the night shift due to her newly diagnosed allergy to sunlight.

She has a new Lieutenant. My own Reginald!

Nicolas Castillo has resigned from the Police Department, took an early retirement. He has embraced his Latino heritage. He has been fully accepted and embraced by none of other than Alejandro Domingo. Nicolas has taken his rightful place as brother and business partner. They now co-manage their family's business empire.

I wish them well.

Morris remains the same as always. After our case, he returned to his office in the strip mall. Still the P.I., and still living in that grimy one-room apartment.

I addition to work, Valerie and Reginald have continued their romance – discretely and away from the job. Reginald purchased the very house that Maya had commandeered. It tics off a lot of boxes. A quiet neighborhood, a quick commute and the basement is a great fallback whenever Valerie needs it. As far as the more intimate details of their relationship, I leave that to them. They seem happy and in love, and that is enough for me. The rest of it is no business of mine.

Speaking of business, I have retired from my stockbroker career. My proteges must fend for themselves now. I have taught them all they need to succeed. Whether they succeed or fail is now solely up to them.

Valerie has proven herself an apt pupil. She has asked numerous questions, most of which I was able to answer. Some of the more esoteric subjects, though, remain as much a mystery to me as they do her. As they do for everyone.

We all need to believe in something. I believe it is time for a change.

As I trained Valerie these past several weeks in the ways of Vampire survival, a deep discontent began welling up within me. A restlessness I have never felt before. I understood it was my predatory instinct telling me that one of us would need to leave and establish a new territory.

So, either Valerie or I need to leave from San Diego.

Valerie has a life here with Reginald, whom I am convinced she loves. And he loves her. Far be it from me to interfere with that. Relationships are difficult even under the best of circumstances. And with both being cops and one of them a vampire, they have so much stacked against them the only way to face it is together.

Taking this into consideration, and since I have long embraced my solitude and my penchant for holding the affairs of man at an arm's length, I have decided that after defending San Diego against Maya, I shall now willingly bequeath it to Valerie. I shall be the one to leave.

Permanently.

This is why I always rented instead of owned. It is much easier for me to pull up stakes. Time for me to seek life elsewhere.

Where shall I go?

Perhaps the Pacific Northwest. I have not been there in decades, but I do have a friend, Caleb, who resides in Northwest Washington. We have not spoken in years, but we parted on amical terms.

He is not Vampyr like me, but he is of the supernatural world. He is strong and noble and follows an unwavering moral compass. He is one of the good ones. And he is not without his own fearsome powers upon which he can call at will.

I look forward to new adventures.

Onward!

AUTHOR BIO

Mark Allen was born and raised in Jacksonville, Texas in the 60s and 70s. He wrote his first short story for a 4th grade English assignment. He got an A+ on the assignment, and he's been writing ever since. In 1980, he graduated High School and joined the U.S. Navy. He served as a Navy Hospital Corpsman and earned the designation of Fleet Marine Force (FMF) Warfare Specialist. He retired in May 2001.

As his Naval career was winding down, Mark returned to his first love, writing, only this time writing screenplays for feature films. He wrote and directed DELIRIUM (York Entertainment 2007) and wrote and co-produced EARLY GRAVE (Fenix Pictures 2013).

In 2014, Mark was diagnosed with Stage 4 throat cancer. During radiation and chemo, he began writing what would become his debut novel, NOCTURNAL. Mark is now 9 years in recovery and suffers long-term disabilities and chronic pain conditions related to the cancer and the treatments that killed his cancer. Grateful to be alive, Mark pushes on.

In addition to JUST BEFORE DAWN, Mark is the author of NOCTURNAL and BLOOD RED MOON. He is a proud member of the Horror Writers Association and lives quietly in the Pacific Northwest.

He writes every day.

465

Printed in Great Britain
by Amazon